Also by Piper CJ

The Night and Its Moon

The Night and Its Moon
The Sun and Its Shade
The Gloom Between Stars
The Dawn and Its Light

No Other Gods

The Deer and the Dragon

THE DEER AND THE DRAGON

PIPER CJ

Bloom *books*

Sourcebooks, Bloom Books, and the colophon are registered trademarks of Sourcebooks.

Published by Bloom Books, an imprint of Sourcebooks
P.O. Box 4410, Naperville, Illinois 60567-410
(630) 961-3900
sourcebooks.com

Cataloging-in-Publication data is on file with the Library of Congress.

Printed and bound in the United States of America.
WOZ 10 9 8 7 6 5 4 3 2 1

To queer women everywhere who ended up in relationships with men as ongoing proof that who we love is not a choice.

Before we start, a word from Piper

Disclaimers on Religion and Mental Health:
You hold in your hand a work of fiction, comedy, commentary, and irreverence. While it has been thoroughly researched and informed by my lived experience in the church, it is in no way representative of the religious majority or meant to be a how-to handbook on interacting with the supernatural of any realm or pantheon, or a reflection on the personalities of the beings within them.

Regarding mental health, we find ourselves in the shoes of Marlow, our protagonist, who does not look upon her mental health journey with kind eyes. While this is authentic to my experience with mental health and the experience of many, it in no way endorses a world that regards mental health issues as shameful or flippant, merely as one character's walk through those waters. For help or more information on mental health matters, please visit mentalhealthfirstaid.org and other resources.

Notes on Sex Work:
There is no trigger warning for sex work, just as there are no trigger warnings for loan officers, real estate agents,

veterinarians, or authors. Sex worker empowerment and destigmatization is an issue that is important to me and is prevalent in many of my works. If something about sex work causes you discomfort, my goal is not to make the environment more comfortable for you, but to encourage you to confront thoughts and feelings of whorephobia. For more information, please read the lived experiences, articles, and input from sex workers themselves as they contribute to tryst. link/blog/tag/articles and other resources.

Content Warnings:
This novel is intended for an adult audience and may contain themes and elements troubling or unsuitable for some readers. A thorough list of content warnings for this and all Piper CJ works can be found at pipercj.com/gallery/content-and-trigger-warnings

CHARACTER PLAYLIST

MARLOW

HONEY
WICKED GAME
GET OUT ALIVE

CUTTS
JESSIE VILLA
ANDREA RUSSETT

CALIBAN

THE DEATH OF PEACE OF MIND
DON'T FEAR THE REAPER
SAVE TONIGHT

BAD OMENS
BLUE ÖYSTER CULT
ZAYDE WØLF

FAUNA

B.O.M.B.
GUMDROP MENACE
STRUT

EMLYN
ESKELITE
EMELINE

AZRAMES

POLTERGEIST!
WHERE ARE YOU?
SUGAR

CORPSE, OMENXIII
ELVIS DREW, AVIVIAN
SLEEP TOKEN

SILAS

GLITTER & GOLD
WAR BRINGER
COME WITH ME NOW

BARNS COURTNEY
THEFATRAT, LINDSEY STIRLING
KONGOS

Pronunciation Guide

Azrames	az-RAY-mus
bunad	boonad
Caliban	CAL-ih-ban
Canaanite	KAY-nuh-nite
Fauna	FsAW-nuh
Silas	SIGH-liss
sølje	sole-yeh
Xuân	soowan

Chapter One

I STARED DOWN THE BARREL OF THE LESSER OF TWO EVILS: THE flesh-and-blood disappointment of a human man, or a life trapped in my imagination with a fictional lover.

I remembered reading that the brain stops forming at twenty-six. I watched the man across from me chew his food with his mouth slightly ajar, not bothering to swallow before he went on to name-drop yet another notch in society's belt. He was holding his chopsticks wrong. He had mixed wasabi directly into his soy sauce. He'd spoken at a cringe-worthy volume throughout the meal, drawing curious, if disgruntled, stares. There wasn't a single etiquette he followed, and it wasn't even close to the worst thing about him.

I wasn't sure if I hoped the bit about the brain was true. I was halfway through my twenty-sixth year and not so sure that this was the finished product I wanted for my mind. I was doing my best to be normal. This was what normal people did, right? They went on terrible dates with ordinary humans. They didn't see things that weren't there. They didn't cling to ghosts and maladaptive fantasies they'd conjured in the dark. They took their medications they went to therapy, and they learned how to distinguish what was real.

If my brain had stopped forming, however, it might come with perks. On the one hand, it meant that this bovine-mannered date wouldn't be a core memory. The man in the suit across from me—Jared? Joshua? I'm pretty sure it was Josh—would be a forgettable date after a long string of mediocre sex and dating apps. On the other hand, maybe it meant my courtship habits and hidden, wish-fulfilling coping mechanisms were cemented in stone and there was no hope for me. Perhaps I was doomed to repeat a cycle of Joshes. This was my curse.

"Marlow?"

Oh, fuck. He was staring at me. Had he asked me a question? I squinted my eyes slightly, peering through the din of the too-expensive restaurant and the polite chatter of upscale patrons for a clue.

"Come again?" I attempted an apologetic smile.

His perplexed look was one I understood. Of course he would be confused that I hadn't been listening. This was our second date, and he expected more from me. After all, I'd been utterly delightful last time. Painted, waxed, and squeezed into the most stunning dress, sporting the glossiest hair and the most charming smiles, I was a living superlative. I'd spent my life learning how to make the perfect first impression.

My profile had been curated to snag any curious suitor. First was a high-resolution picture that a friend had taken four years prior on a boat in Rio de Janeiro, where the greens and grays of the coast matched my eyes. "Where was that picture taken?" gave prospective dates an easy conversation opener. The next two had been selected to attract the outdoorsy types, from the HD pic of me flexing on a mountain in yoga pants and a sports bra to me on the beach laughing with friends— which also created the perfect excuse to show off a bikini body and gave me an easy way to screen out anyone who didn't like curves. I rounded out the profile with a picture of me alone with my coffee cup and computer, looking very serious and business-like, immediately followed by a photo of me jumping on the bed holding a bottle of wine, dress flying up, muddy blond curls a cloud around my face, smiling as if I were having the time of my life. Whatever dream you wanted to project onto me, I gave you the option right there in my intricately tailored series of images.

"Who are you?" the app had asked.

"Whoever you need me to be," my profile replied.

Every date was spent in a song and dance of asking the right questions, laughing at the right pitch, tossing my hair over my shoulder, arching my neck, lowering my lashes, and, as always, keeping them talking. They'd leave thinking they'd met their soulmate. I'd leave wondering if I could catch the newest episode of *Fire and Swords* or if I'd have to wait until it was on a streaming service.

"I asked if you've been to the Galápagos," he repeated.

"No." I kept my tone as light as possible. I glanced down at the elaborately plated omakase sushi that had doubtlessly cost more than half of the country made in a month. This was why I'd agreed to go on the second date. I loved good sushi, and free just so happened to be my favorite price. The salmon belly was the most well marbled in the hemisphere. I'd come back with terrible company just to eat my weight in the stuff even if it meant thinking about what sort of life these ocean animals had before they ended up on my plate.

He grabbed the sake kettle and tilted the alcohol into his glass first, then mine.

I kept the disarming smile on my face as I said, "I've wandered my way through a lot of South America, but I was teaching English as a second language and I—"

"Oh, you have to go back and do it the right way. I have a friend who works at the most incredible resort you've ever seen. The fish swim right underneath..." His mouth kept moving as my thoughts drifted into the restaurant's ambience while I started to think of marine life. I liked aquariums. I wondered how long it had been since I'd been to one. Maybe I'd go to the city's aquatic zoo, bring a bag of magic mushrooms, pop in my headphones, and listen to music while counting sharks over the weekend.

Josh required little encouragement to continue the conversation. It only took a pleading look to the waitress and a firm "*No,*" when asked if we wanted desserts for her to bring the check without waiting for his argument on digestifs. She knew from the very intentional way I'd selected designer pieces, from the delicate chain around my neck to the bag that dangled over the back of my chair, that I could afford the bill if I'd requested it. My deadpan stare challenged him to give it to me. In my early twenties, I would have rushed to cover the check so that Josh wouldn't expect anything from me. Now I expected him to procure his Amex as penance for making me watch him chew with his mouth open. It was the least he could do.

I idly wondered if Josh had ever asked me what I did for a living. Perhaps that was my own fault. I'd gotten so good at getting others to talk about themselves that I'd become excellent at living in the shadows. I wonder how many of my dates knew more about me than my name and how spectacular I was in bed.

We'd scarcely stepped into the cold, cloudless night before he asked, "So, should we go back to my place?"

"Oh." I pouted slightly to underscore my feigned regrets while shrugging into my coat, saying, "I'm so sorry. I called a rideshare while I was in the bathroom. It's only two minutes out."

Josh looked like he'd been slapped. I wondered how many times a man with a forty-thousand-dollar Rolex was turned down. Then again, it had been a running pleasure of mine to play catch and release. The bigger the fish, the more satisfying it was to throw them back into the water. Everything about this evening had me wishing I'd stayed in to watch the documentary about whales rather than wasting the perfume by stepping out into the world.

"What about the concert?"

I frowned, scarcely looking up from my phone. "Concert?"

Confusion faded into agitation as he studied my face. "Next week, the one I—"

Fish. Everything about this man was a fish. When they tell you that there are plenty of fish in the sea, they forget to mention that half of marine life is boring, scaly and a part of an identical school of thousands just like him. I would rather be alone, high, and looking at tropical fish next weekend. "Oh, I'm so sorry, Josh—this is my car!"

"It's Jacob."

I grimaced. I really was sorry about that one. I should have checked his name from the dating profile when I'd escaped to the restroom.

He knew the evening had soured but still had the balls to go in for a kiss. I intercepted with a side hug before launching into the street to stop my car. I closed the door and took off into the night before my date had time to recover from his wounded ego. The driver asked precisely the right number of questions, which was zero. He left me alone to the buzzing phone that illuminated the back seat of the vehicle.

(Kirby) How was the banker?

(Nia) CFO, right? Big money

(Kirby) Not like tech guy. Mar, could you call him up again? We used to go to much nicer places when you were sleazing it with the tech guy.

(Marlow) I'd like to sleaze it up with a loose bag of cheese and my sweatpants

(Nia) You were supposed to get laid. How am I supposed to live vicariously through you if you're pulling a celibacy act

(Kirby) No, that's fair. She's always been a slut for cheese. No one made you get married, Nia.

(Nia) And so what? I'm supposed to live with the consequences of my actions?

(Marlow) I'm just going to call it an early night

(Nia) And waste a great hair and makeup day? Damn, there must be some fantastic cheese back at your place

I clicked the button on the side of my phone, turning the screen into an obsidian mirror and leaned my head against the window, watching the black and auburn blur of homes, shadows, lawns, and fences as we crossed through a neighborhood. I used to look at houses and wonder about the lives of the people who lived inside. What did the family do to afford a home so close to downtown? What did a three-story house with fantastic landscaping cost in one of the world's flashiest cities? It had been a long time since I'd cared.

I saw the driver frown as the GPS turned into the northern part of the metropolis. It wasn't an unusual reaction. No one lived in the warehouse district. There was no reason for a girl of any repute to take a car to the warehouses in high heels and red lipstick. He pulled up along the sidewalk and eyed what had once been a bread factory. His expression deepened into worry at the smattering of lights and darkened entryway.

"Is this right, miss?"

"Home sweet home." I smiled. I flashed him my screen to show the glowing rating I'd sent his way as I slid out of the car. His eyebrows remained knit, but he shrugged as I closed the door. He wasn't paid enough to care.

A blanket-like quiet pressed in as the car pulled away—a sound challenging to achieve anywhere in the city. There was no traffic, no pedestrians, no indication that anyone but the phantoms of long-dead industry tycoons haunted these corridors. The April night clung to the last of spring's chill, sending goose bumps up and down my bare legs. I fished a metallic rose-gold card from my purse and pressed it against the panel, satisfied when it buzzed.

I rounded the brick corridor for the atrium, where an ever-attentive receptionist waited to respectfully greet me. She was one of four and arguably my favorite. No matter how short my skirt, how high my heels, or how late the hour, she remained polite without speaking. I knew her boyfriend's name, I gave her chocolates every holiday, and we never failed to gush about the new episodes of *Fires and*

Swords if I loitered in the hallway, but she had an innate gift for knowing when I was overwhelmed and needed silence. Perhaps intuition was a prerequisite for anyone who took a job in luxury apartments.

Though she'd never say it outright, her expressions conveyed the same long-standing concern that I'd stumbled through the door after too many dates to count. She'd helped me get into the building when I was a bit too drunk to see my phone and buzzed me up to my room whenever I'd lost too much brain function to recall how my card worked. It seemed like a safe bet that she was not the sort of person who got high at aquariums.

The small bank of polished elevators waited quietly, all in disuse given the lateness of the hour. One opened for me the moment I pressed the button.

I didn't wait for the elevator doors to close before slipping out of my heels, dangling the sharpened ends from one hand. I caught the brief, disapproving narrowing of eyes through the rapidly closing doors and flashed my most dazzling smile. Part of me respected her bravery. It was bold to be judgmental of the residents when they knew precisely how much these apartments cost.

I pressed the glittery, metallic card onto the pad to gain access to my floor—second from the top. The penthouse hadn't been available, and I'd been okay with it. Everyone who lived here had their reasons for wanting to stay off the world's radar, and there wasn't a better establishment in the city for those with deep enough pockets to erase themselves from the map. The building's discretion had been worth the downgrade, and as someone who lived alone, I couldn't have justified the extra space unless I was looking to install a private bowling alley.

The elevator door opened noiselessly onto my floor. There were thirteen units in the entire building—two per floor, save for the lucky bastard who'd snagged the thirteenth. I walked barefoot down the sparkling black marble to my room and pressed my thumb into the pad, allowing it to scan my fingerprint until a subtle click told me the mechanisms had unlocked.

It was dark in my apartment and stayed that way. I'd had the features for automatic lights disabled the day I'd moved in.

I tossed my purse onto the floor, leaving it in a jumble with my shoes. I walked to the window and stared out over the twinkling lights of the city and the sliver of river I could spot from my unit. I was a sucker for a good view.

The hairs on the back of my neck prickled in the way they did when one knew they were being watched. The rush of gin, moss, and mist filled the room the moment before I heard it. I breathed it in like a prayer.

"Leave it open" came a male voice from the shadows.

I fought the deep, conflicting bloom that emanated from somewhere near my center. My toes curled, heart thundering at the purr of his voice. "Don't do this to me," I grumbled half-heartedly, but I was certain he heard the ghost of a smile in my voice.

"Didn't go well?" he asked.

I continued facing the window but reached over my head for the zipper. Years had gone by, and I was still breathless every time he spoke. It was so easy to lose my resolve whenever those silken words tumbled over his lips. I managed to give the thin metal a tug but lost my grip on it as I said, "He was utterly forgettable."

"They all will be," he said, brushing my hair away from my neck. Goose bumps started at the nape of my neck and slithered down my spine. He held the top of my dress in one strong hand, using the other to gently tug the zipper. He stopped before releasing it more than a quarter of an inch. I waited for the next sensation, but nothing came. Tension swelled as I swallowed another deep breath of earth and perfume.

"What?" I breathed.

The electric current of his touch coursed through me.

"Holy fuck," I murmured, falling to pieces.

His fingers began to work their way up the hem of my dress, nudging it up over my hips. My stomach clenched. My lips parted in a stifled gasp, eyes closing as he came up behind me. His mouth sucked gently on the tender place where my throat met my shoulder. Every sense in my body homed in on the delicious sensation. His mouth moved to the back of my neck, hands dropping from my hips to urge me forward. I leaned into the floor-to-ceiling glass, letting the cold seep into me as his hand slid from my inner thigh, higher, *higher*.

"Oh god," I gasped when he grazed the soaked evidence of my black-lace panties.

"You know better than that," he chided softly at my choice in words, a teasing warmth in his voice. He relaxed his body into mine until I was pressed wholly against the window. "Now, are you going to let me in?"

My face betrayed the battle going on in my head and heart. My body ached for him. My breasts peaked against the thin dress. The pulsing in my chest extended into every piece of me, and I felt my heartbeat in my greediest places. My fingers clenched against the glass. He chuckled lightly.

"Nothing without your permission," he said, fingers still grazing me with tantalizing slowness. The tingle of the water between my legs trickling onto my inner thighs elicited a low groan of approval. His fingers continued to move over the thin fabric.

I gasped against the sensation, and he leaned into my throat once more, smiling through my pleasure.

"You know I'm..." Words felt useless.

"You're what?" he pressed me into the window with more force.

"I'm trying to stop."

His fingers quickened as he said, "As if I don't know you, Love. We both know it'll never make you happy. But if you'd prefer mundane restaurants and forgettable men over what I can offer you..." His hand stilled.

9

My lust, my greed, my denial came out in a single, short sound. My eyes opened as I turned back to the shadows, but I knew what I'd see before I turned.

Despite the bandage-tight dress around my hips and the puddle of evidence on my legs, I knew he wasn't there. He hadn't been there in a long, long time.

Chapter Two

THANK GOD I ALWAYS SLEPT WITH MY PHONE ON SILENT.
Josh had been busy after he'd left the restaurant. I'd
missed seventeen drunken texts and had two voicemails all
anchored around the theme of how we had something really
special, and we could go the distance, before pivoting into
how I was an ugly slut. I skimmed the first few before delet-
ing the voice messages without listening to them. I blocked
his number but didn't bother to hide my social media from
him. Allowing old dates to see how much better I was doing
without them was a favorite pastime of mine, and I would
hate to rob him of that opportunity.

One of the best features in the apartment was its heated
floors. The moment my toes touched the twinkling black
marble, they were greeted with the warm kiss of walking on
obsidian sunshine. I turned on the tea kettle and scooped
the ground coffee into the French press, just as I did every
morning. My eyes drifted to the smudges on the window
and I frowned. The morning light reflected beautiful shades
of yellow and orange off the warehouse's floor-to-ceiling
glass and snaking river, illuminating the imprint of my face,
forearms, and hands. Pale yellow light caught the streaks
where I'd clenched my fingers into fists. My toes curled at the
memory, thoughts longing for the scent of moss. Normally

I'd wait for the maid, but I wasn't sure if I wanted her seeing my near-perfect outline.

But cleaning was a post-coffee task.

I pressed a few buttons on my phone, and it connected to the apartment's sound system. In the mornings, I kept the music happy and easy. I toggled over to a beachy playlist that I'd loved while lying poolside in the tropics. My therapist had agreed that veering away from the lyrical tragedies of soulful ballads had done wonders for my mental health.

The happy beats pulsed through my apartment, loud enough for me to twirl while quiet enough not to disrupt my slowly waking soul. The apartments had been blissfully soundproofed, so even if the owner of the penthouse had owned a buffalo, the reinforced floors never would have let on. I didn't worry about the volume as I let the music carry me to distant memories of ninety-degree weather, to sand between my toes, to sunny days, to smiling faces, and to a life far, far from this one.

I grabbed the oat milk from the fridge and stared back at the small pieces of sentimentality I'd allowed myself. I had a magnet with the cover of my first book that had sent me into hysterics the first time I'd seen the trinket in a bookstore. A second magnet of the Columbian flag secured a picture of Nia and me grinning in the autumn sun while Kirby held a bucket of apples over their head like it was a UFC belt. It was one of the few bits of evidence that I had friends. Beside it, a small, grainy, black-and-white photo of my great-grandma holding my infant grandmother on the shores of the Norwegian fjords was one of my only tokens of sentimentality.

The kettle clicked and the spell of ruminations broke— both of sensual hands on my hips and of joyful, tropical days. Memories and fictions wouldn't serve me, at least, not unless I was writing.

I let the coffee steep in its French press while I did the laziest form of my morning routine: skin care, messy bun, and a slouchy T-shirt. Having my own place meant no one could force me into the tyranny of pants. I grabbed my laptop, my coffee, a spoon, and a jar of farmer's market honey before settling onto the couch. I liked my coffee dark and sweet and had once read that local honey had healing properties. It wasn't the sort of thing I wanted to fact-check, as I didn't want anything interfering with what may or may not have been the placebo effect that lent itself to my clean bill of health. Plus, living alone also meant no one could judge me for spooning in honey every few gulps.

He'd made fun of my questionable combination once, though he'd amended that he certainly didn't mind. My caffeine abuse made sleep harder for me, and if I was awake in the dead of night...well, one thing often led to another.

I combed through thirty new emails and idly wondered if the staff at Inkhouse ever rested. There were always new edits, rewrites, legal documents, proposals, marketing needs, or strings of panicked messages over bootlegged copies of my books circulating. I scanned to see if anything sounded important but only clicked on the messages from Allison. She'd been my beta reader since my first *Pantheon* novel and exclusively sent love letters. My mouth quirked up at the soliloquy regarding my brilliance and attention to detail and describing how she'd nearly killed her dog by chucking her tablet across the room after the plot twist. I bit my lip at the dose of serotonin that coursed through me.

I closed my email tab to see what the group chat had sent in the overnight hours. They'd shared a handful of short, thirst-trap videos of hot girls, screenshots of various memes, and Nia had waxed poetic about her husband bringing her breakfast in bed. I clicked out of the chat without responding. They knew I was behind on my deadlines. I had work to do, people to please, asses to kiss, and changes to make. The *Pantheon* series wasn't going to write itself.

I'd focused on a different world region for each of the novels. My debut had followed a valkyrie as the protagonist. It had revolved around the Nordic gods, Valhalla, and the Viking wars of the first century. It had taken the world by storm, debuting at number five on the *New York Times* bestseller list. Inkhouse signed the series for five books in total, giving me a king's ransom for an advance. The second book was a conflation of Greek and Roman gods and deities—a sequel that had outsold the debut novel ten to one.

When asked what had led to *Pantheon's* juggernaut success, I told them that my mythology novels had something that glittery vampires of yesteryear lacked: kinky, gratuitous sex.

I was now struggling through the third installment. My main character was a Brazilian wilderness guardian on the cusp of the colonization of the late 1500s, and my only editorial note was that I was coming on a little heavy-handed on my stance on deforestation. As much as I loved elementals and their lore, I struggled to connect to the lush jungles, sheer mountain ridges, and flooded lands near the Amazon. Perhaps I could convince my publisher to fund a trip to the rainforest and write amid the toucans and jaguars. I was relatively confident that anything that could be written from my apartment in the city could be written in a hammock amid tropical greenery with a cocktail in hand.

Instead of focusing on my edits, I clicked through a couple pages on animal adoption. Every few weeks I talked myself out of getting a chinchilla, a rabbit, or a cat. I knew it wasn't wise to own an animal, given my propensity for transience. But knowing didn't stop one from wanting, and I was admittedly lonely. My memories wandered to the exotic pet I'd invented for myself as a child. A white fox had played with me in the woods, had kept me company when I was sad, and had been my only friend in the world when I'd had none. My strict parents would never have allowed an animal in the house, but my imagination had always been vivid, and I'd needed something to stay sane. I missed that fox from time to time, though my imagination had taken on a more mature theme over the last few years. No amount of sushi with Joshes or disappointing hookups had staved off the ache for something real, though I did try.

I'd told Nia that I wanted what she had, and she informed me that no, I didn't. I was suffering from a textbook case of Grass Is Greener syndrome. As much as her happy life with a supportive husband called to me, so did my siren's song of hopping on planes, living in solitude, and sleeping with strangers. She was right, of course. She knew that her marriage to Darius was the exception that proved the rule. I'd never met anyone else who was glad they'd tied the knot.

Then again, I didn't know many people.

Well, that wasn't quite accurate. I knew everyone. Some I knew through social media, others through dates, and many from my previous life as a lady of the evening. I just didn't like, speak with, or care about many. People were tiresome and rarely seemed solution-oriented. Why would they bother complaining about where they lived if they weren't willing to pack a suitcase and move? What was the point of telling me how much they hated their spouse if divorce wasn't an option? Their problems were exhausting, and I didn't have the emotional capacity to feign empathy for half of them. Particularly as my lifestyle grew more controversial and obscure, it hadn't taken long to prune my friend group further and further until I'd whittled it down to three—all of whom I saw almost exclusively through the accessible magic of the internet.

It would be nice to love and be loved. It would be really goddamn pleasant to have someone else make the coffee while I slept in. I wanted to wake up with someone beside me, to watch *Fire and Swords* while cuddled on the couch and to have a built-in guardian to babysit a chinchilla if I needed to be away for a few days. But though I continued to put myself out there, my heart wasn't open to falling in love.

I tilted my head up from the couch to look at the still-present smudges on the window, then looked away. I'd do what I always did. I'd explain away the psychosis that felt so, so real, with a familiar mantra: It had been wishful thinking.

I'd willed myself into believing I wasn't alone. I'd leaned into the glass, hoping, wanting, craving, dreaming. There was no one there, nor had there ever been.

My phone buzzed.

(Nia) Please tell me you're leaving the house today? I'll
    never know what happens in Brazil if you lose your mind
    to isolation
(Marlow) It isn't just Brazil. I'm doing a blender of South
    American lore. Thus the name.
(Nia) Pantheon, yeah, yeah, very clever, I'm obsessed, I get
    it, now answer the question
(Marlow) I'll get curry from the Indian place down the street
(Kirby) You know that means she's ordering in. You think we
    don't get your sneaky wording by now. Leave the house,
    you bastard. Go on another date. Bone a stranger in a
    club bathroom. Just leave your goddamn apartment.
(Marlow) Make me.
(Kirby) Don't tempt me. I'll come over there.

Kirby would if I gave them the opening. Both they and Nia would. Despite living within an hour of me, my friends knew better than to show up at my place. I was reclusive enough to ignore the buzzer even if they stood outside my apartment and pressed the button for an hour. They understood, and they didn't push. Even when Nia had dropped off soup during my bout with bronchitis, she'd left it with the receptionist, knowing me well enough to get that I considered showing up unplanned an act of aggression.

I appreciated my friends more for it.

Allison, the only other person I counted as a friend, lived on the West Coast. We kept our conversations limited to the worlds I created and the characters within them. It was the way I wanted it. As long as I could stay disconnected from the dullness around me, I'd be satisfied. At least as satisfied as one could be while forced to live in reality.

We both know it'll never make you happy, he'd said. *But if you'd prefer mundane restaurants and forgettable men over what I can offer...*

He knew as well as I that mundanity wasn't what I wanted. The only pieces of this life that brought me joy were escaping it. Sometimes through food, sex, drugs, or rambling through the markets in a country where I didn't know the language. For a few minutes, sometimes even for a few days, I could pretend that I was someone different. I could let go of the chains that shackled me to the earth and disappear into a marvelous *something*.

It may have been too early in the day for drugs, but I walked to the bar cart and flicked the top off a bottle of amaretto. I spiked my honey-sweet coffee until the almond liquor refilled the mug nearly to the brim. It was a drink strong enough to purify one's innards and kill the common cold. But the alcohol helped. Each tingling buzz aided me in closing one of the many open tabs in my brain, which would allow me to focus on just what I was writing, just what I was watching on TV, just what I was eating. The noise was too much to handle without a little containment.

A text came in from my editor. She announced in no uncertain terms that she knew I'd seen her emails and was ignoring her. She told me that she loved me, that I was very pretty, and very talented, but that she'd paint the streets with my blood if I didn't get her five new chapters by the end of the week.

I chuckled at the message.

The company had paired me with EG, the perfect hostile, irreverent counterpart.

I sent her an emoji with a wink and a kiss. EG responded with a middle finger, an eggplant, a fist, and three droplets of water.

Her threats were an effective rallying cry.

I put on the shittiest audiobook I could find while I brushed my hair, tidied my apartment, and waited for the initial buzz from the alcohol to kick in. I refused to read anything worthwhile these days. Not only did I not want to compare myself to the greats, but nor did I want to risk being accused of idea theft, but I found that spite was my favorite motivator. Every terrible idiom, every clumsy sentence, every ill-conceived plot and obnoxious main character highlighted ways in which I'd like to do things differently.

Gandhi told us to be the change we want to see in the world. He was probably talking about kindness or charity or something, but I preferred to apply it to becoming the author I wished everyone else was.

I returned to the living room a few times, swigging deeply from the coffee until the alcohol tingled in my fingers and toes. By the time the liquor's effects hummed gently in my ears, I clicked off the audiobook and settled in to write one, then three, then seven pages. It wasn't exactly five chapters, but EG would get what she'd get. I'd looked up only twice, each time to fill my coffee cup with pure liquor. When I finished, I sent them to my editor without proofreading. I glanced at the clock to see that it was already five in the afternoon. I'd eaten nothing. And I was gloriously shitfaced.

Ignoring the day's worth of notifications on my phone, I went directly for the food app and made good on my promise to get dinner. I ordered three dishes, planning to freeze a few of them so I'd have lunches and dinners for the next few days like the responsible meal prepper I was. I flipped on a mindless show about the hunt for Atlantis so I didn't have to be alone with my thoughts while I waited for my butter chicken and rice. By the time the delivery person buzzed for entry, my tingle had worn off.

My huff sent the loose pieces of hair around my face into a cloud as I sighed at the liquor bottle.

I'd sworn to myself that I wouldn't drink when sad, or bored, or angry. I'd allocated my love for controlled substances to writing, dating, and going of social outings. It was a rule I'd made in my era of sex work. From the shame-based public narrative, I'd expected escorting to be drug-addled and woeful, doing lines to get through a session or to numb myself from an encounter. Instead, I made more money each working night than I could possibly spend in months, ate at the best restaurants on the planet, was flown to gorgeous locations, met a number of the world's high-and-mighties, and was able to save up enough money to live exclusively off of what I'd set aside while I launched my creative career.

Still, I kept to my rule. I only drank to create, or in the company of friends. No matter how good it might feel to remain toasted around the clock.

(Kirby) Haven't heard from you all day. You alive?
(Marlow) Ate, sent off pages, and I'm going to the aquarium this weekend.
(Kirby) Did you drink water?
(Marlow) What are you, my mom?
(Kirby) We both know I care way more about you than your mom does.

I closed the chat again without answering. My contentious relationship with my mother was no secret. I huffed loudly to the empty air as I grabbed a can of sparkling water from the fridge and curled into a ball on the couch.

Kirby hadn't pushed the point any further. They didn't dare repeat what they'd implied far too many times, but I could feel their pain. I was alone. I didn't speak to my parents given the enormity of our religious fallout. After I'd grown too old for a fictional fox, the only creatures with whom I interacted were lukewarm romantic distractions that lasted anywhere from one night to six weeks. My friends insisted that an empire of nice apartments, designer shoes, bestselling novels, and complicated gadgets was worthless if I had no one to share them with.

My most promising shot at love had ended two months prior, on February 13.

For nearly three months, I'd come so close to falling for a girl with a bright Irish accent and a sparkling personality. Her name was Eve. She had hair so red that I would have sworn on a Bible it was fake, but she'd merely laughed and pulled up pictures of her as a toothless toddler with crimson curls. She was interesting, educated, grounded. She never asked anything from me, only offered encouragement and support. She loved my books, but not so much that it made me uncomfortable. She was never demanding of my time, energy, or attention. She was in STEM and easily one of the most intelligent people I'd ever met. Despite her laboratory work, she played the fiddle, spent most weekends singing folk songs at an Irish tavern, and had a ravishing gallery of photos in medieval cosplay. She was funny and kind and had Nia and Kirby enthusiastically planning our wedding after the second date. Our sex had been spectacular. She was everything I'd been looking for.

Almost.

After a tearful breakup over the phone where Eve had demanded to know what she'd done wrong, I'd uselessly repeated that she was perfect. She'd called me a coward for breaking up the day before Valentine's Day, and she was probably right. But the holiday hadn't been the only motivator. I knew exactly who and what was sabotaging my love life. My heart was spoken for as uselessly as if I'd fallen in love with a book character. If I couldn't step out of my own hyper-fantasia, I'd never move on. I just needed to learn to channel the cup of imagination, containing it to its glass within my novels, not allowing it to spill out and get on my dress, drip down my inner thighs, ruin my panties, crumple my clothes to the floor, or create my outline against the wall-to-wall window overlooking the river.

And that's why I huddled on my sofa, hugging my knees to my chest, and vowed that tonight would be the night. I had to tell him to stop visiting me.

I waited as the sky turned from blue to pink to black.

I crawled under the covers and stared at the silhouetted bottle of sleeping pills I'd forgone.

The bedside clock clicked from midnight to one to two in the morning.

It was 2:40 a.m. when I felt his presence. His weight pressed into the bed. The sheets shifted with his movements just as they might with a flesh-and-blood partner. My heart skipped painfully.

He pushed up against me, hands stroking, lips brushing, mouth sending chills up and down my spine as every inch of my skin rippled into gooseflesh. My body responded, wanting things that my heart and mind had forbidden. My hips arched with need, but they were traitors acting on their own volition. I'd rolled away, tucking my face against the pillow.

"Bad day, Love?"

"I'm not your love, Caliban." I whispered the name I'd given him long ago. My choice had amused him, but he seemed to like it.

After a long pause in the darkness, he merely said, "You are."

I stayed on my side, staring out the bedroom window at the naked, winter trees. There was a crescent moon that night, a sharp, bright sliver too thin to cast any light onto the evidence of madness between my four walls. I normally secured the curtains, but tonight I'd been trying to stay awake. I'd been waiting for him.

"You're not real," I whispered, speaking to the hallucination that held and broke my heart in the same hand. Loving him was my most foolish mistake. I didn't want to be in love anymore.

Caliban's cool breath moved a tuft of hair over the bare skin of my throat. His fingers glided along my jaw, cupping my chin. The scent of a green, misty forest consumed me. "If there's anything I could do to change your mind, I'd do it. Ask it of me."

"Caliban—"

He made a patient sound. "But you won't. We've been through this," he said. "I know you remember."

My throat worked through my nerves, swallowing the lump of emotion, but I said nothing.

I couldn't forget the last night I'd seen him, though I'd tried.

I'd been twenty-one for six months. Red and green and blue lasers of a sleazy club thumped through the memory. It was the night I'd graduated from college. I'd smelled like cigarette smoke and had done too many bumps in the bathroom. Despite the drunken fog that blurred the memory and the empty spaces where liquor had expunged details, I couldn't let it go.

It was the night I'd ended my ability to see him.

I had stumbled home from a night of partying. I'd been living in a basement apartment in a seedy neighborhood that Caliban, my parents, my friends, and anyone with a mouth had told me to run from. Still, it was all I could afford unless I was willing to live with roommates, and I was not. I'd fallen down the outdoor staircase that reeked of piss, twisting an ankle and limping into the apartment. I'd slammed the door and secured the deadbolt, gritting my teeth against pain and regret in equal waves.

I'd been served shot after shot at a bar of something blue that tasted like cotton candy. I'd danced to the worst pop songs on the top forty station, been tongue-fucked by the starting pitcher on the college team in the single-stall, all-gender bathroom, and gotten in the car with someone too drunk to be driving. I was exhausted but, like many other naive idiots in their early twenties who had no concept of sugar and its role in hangovers, had been deeply committed to mixing my vodka with cherry-flavored energy drinks. The uppers and downers vibrated through me as the world wobbled. I slammed my palm into the textured apartment wall, searching for an outlet that gremlins must have snatched

22

while I was clubbing. I sank to the floor, succumbing to the linoleum.

"Do you want me to turn on the light?" Caliban had asked, setting a bottle of water beside me.

I'd been having a good night. A great night, even, save for the twisted ankle. This was exactly how one was meant to celebrate major milestones. I was living the dream.

At least, I'd convinced myself I was having was fun until I heard his voice. The moment his silken words washed over me, the carefree facade cracked. What followed were not pretty, lady-like tears but the heartbroken sobs of the lost. I pulled my knees to my chest.

"Help me get to the shower," I'd slurred.

And he had. I didn't remember when a candle had been lit in the bathroom, or when he'd gotten me out of my dress. His ghost-white shape was an anchor in my swimming vision, rooting me to the present as I slow-blinked at him. He'd left the curtain open, soaking my bathroom floor in water so that the small orange flame might cast friendlier shadows than the ones that haunted me. I scarcely remembered the soothing touch of his fingers raking back my hair as I puked or the steadying presence that had held me as I'd cried on the bathtub floor. I'd been too wasted to appreciate how my cheek had felt against his bare chest. The spinning walls hadn't permitted me to savor the moments as he'd washed my regrets away with soap and hot water.

"You're not having fun" was all he'd said. I didn't want to see the solemn expression that accompanied his words. He was so beautiful when he smiled. His crooked grins over white teeth, his snowy shock of hair, the winks he'd throw my way with bright, gray eyes that scalded me like a brand, electrifying every part of me. Tonight, I knew that looking at him would mean seeing resolute strength in the set of his jaw, that disappointment would pinch his brows, that there would be no smirk, no cavalier joking, no playful moments that would plant seeds within me, growing into a garden that blossomed only for him.

23

I'd cried into his arms so hard I'd nearly thrown my back out.

"It's your fault," I'd sobbed through the whirlpool of coke and alcohol.

His fingers had moved against my hair as he listened. I'd coughed on the shower water, choking on the pounding droplets as I continued, "I drink to forget the fucked-up shit I imagine at home. I don't have friends because I just want to be here. I cancel on plans, bail on dates, rush out because there's something better for me in the dark. I refuse to live with anyone in case you visit. I hook up with strangers to try to pound out the memory of how it feels when you…" My voice had broken. "You're not real. I can't keep playing this game. I need to get help. I can't be like my mom…like my grandma… I can't do this. I'm never going to be able to move forward with my life if I keep living in this fantasy."

His arms tightened around me. His low voice was gentle but firm. "Love…"

"I don't want to be in love with you," I'd cried, squeezing my eyes tightly shut as I buried my face against him. I meant it. This pathetic, maladaptive daydream was destroying me. My wet hair plastered to my face and stuck to his chest. My tears, the shower water, the churning, twirling room had smothered me as I fought to get out everything I'd needed to say.

He'd kissed the crown of my head as he continued to run his fingers along it, stroking it with calm, steadying shushes. He'd brushed his lips against my hair that night under the running water just as he kissed it now.

My heart cracked as I looked down on the events of that night as if little more than a phantom floating above an ethereally beautiful man chipped from the stars themselves, arms around the wasted slivers of a twenty-one-year-old, candlelight flickering in the bathroom, steam filling the space, hot, angry bullets of shower water soaking them both as that version of me sobbed.

The kiss pulled me out of the memory, dragging me into the present. I was halfway through my twenty-sixth year again, between silken sheets, overlooking the river. My exhale contained the weight of the world.

"You'd said I wasn't real and that you didn't want to see me again," he recalled. It wasn't an accusation. Just a calm, quiet fact.

"I was drunk," I said.

"*In vino veritas.*"

"And I haven't seen you since," I responded to the black nothingness. "That was the night that made me move, you know. To try to change my life. A week later—"

"I know," he said, and he did.

Nearly six years had passed, and it was still one of the worst nights of my life. My eyes spiked with tears as I shoved the visions aside. Regret had coiled in me like a sleeping snake. It had slithered throughout me whenever he'd visited for five and a half fucking years. I'd hated myself for those words.

"You should know by now, Love" came his soothing voice as his lips brushed against my ear. "Our word is bond. We're very literal."

I twisted my sheets between my fingers, remembering the perfect mouth, the sharp teeth, the twitch of a smile that used to accompany his words. I wondered why he'd used *we*, but I supposed he meant the two of us. And he was right. "Five goddamn years without your face...but you didn't stay away."

He ran a thumb from my ear along my jaw, cupping my chin from behind as he said, "You told me you weren't going to see me anymore. You said nothing about staying away. And with everything going on, you're as much my escape as I am yours, Love. Neither of us wants this to end."

I remained curled on my side, back to him. This was part of why he only came at night these days. He knew that it was easier for me to deal with the empty space in the dark—to cling to whatever semblance of hope or deniability—when shadows cloaked the room than it was to speak to an empty room in the light of day. My vision unfocused, lost to the budding trees that lined the river. If I'd still lived in the countryside, it would have been too dark to see the way the branches quivered in the overcast night. Instead, low-lying clouds captured the muted, honey-colored city lights, holding the night in an auburn glow.

"I do," I said quietly. My declaration spread between us like smoke filling a room.

Caliban went deathly still behind me.

I closed my eyes against the silhouetted cottonwoods and oaks as I said, "I won't have a shot at a normal life unless you're gone."

He tightened his hands around me, fingers pressing into me as he pulled my back against the hard wall of his chest, enveloping me. "You don't mean it."

"I do."

His voice dropped an octave as he said, "Don't make a rash decision, Love. Think about this. If you say—"

"The visits, the sex, whatever it is we have...it has to stop. It's ruining my life. I'm losing my mind, Caliban—what's left of it, anyway. My heart can't belong to..." My voice splintered.

A sharp stab of pain shot through me as I opened my eyes and looked at the neat row of orange prescription bottles that rested on my bedside table. Store-bought serotonin helped make the world a little more bearable, but only a little. I looked so put together on the outside. I paid my bills, I went to therapy, I brushed my hair, I didn't scream at strangers on the sidewalk. The world would never guess that my vivid imagination—one that had proved grossly profitable as an author—had slowly eroded me from the inside out as fantasy splashed over the cup, soaking my life.

He exhaled, and a feeling akin to lying on the misty forest floor encompassed me once more, his breath the cool chill of a fern leaf dragged along my skin. The silence rattled between us. He allowed the pause to stretch, late spring wind whipping from the north as it howled against my window. Its music nearly lulled me into sleep before he responded.

"May I make you a counteroffer?"

I held my breath, waiting for him to continue. He could be very persuasive. When I said nothing, he went on.

"Nothing you don't explicitly ask for."

A memory scratched the back of my mind as I thought of deals with the devil.

I chewed on my thumb and considered his proposal. I wondered how many times we'd negotiated. He was quite good at it, after all. His tongue, like his eyes, was silver. I wondered how many times I'd been locked in a heated debate with my burgeoning psychosis, speaking to the empty shadows. I contemplated the wisdom of refusing to tell friends or therapists about him. Maybe I just didn't want to add a new set of pills to the tiny orange army that kept a vigilant watch over me. Maybe I didn't want to risk alienating my already-dwindling friend group. Maybe, irrespective of my feeble attempts, we both knew that I didn't want to let him go.

"You mean, unless I say the words…with everything? Sleeping in my bed? The kisses? The…" I couldn't bring myself to mention our sex again. If I pictured it, if I spoke of it, I'd crave it. I'd want his fingers moving against me. I'd want him to suck an earlobe into his mouth, to drag his teeth along my throat, to use his cool fingers to explore my body. He'd sense the shift the second my mind switched to memories of him teasing my entrance, murmuring approval at how I opened up for him. His cock made everything else feel like eating ashes after experiencing caviar. Nothing filled me, nothing overpowered me, nothing worked its way into my limbs, blood, my soul the way that he did. He consumed me like cold fire, and he knew it.

"Nothing you don't ask for," he repeated.

I rolled toward him and regretted it. There was nothing there, save for the reminder of my insanity. I closed my eyes, preferring the blindness of shut lids as I felt every part of him. His hair, his smooth skin, the cut of his jaw, the strong shoulders that had held me, the arm that relaxed around me. He already had me at his mercy. The only thing I hated more than having him here were the nights he stayed away.

I felt so real. It always did.

"I'm crazy," I said, voice broken.

It took him a while to respond. We'd gone back and forth on my sanity over the years, and I'd said on no uncertain terms that arguing with a figment of my imagination only made things worse and further proved my point. I'd conceded that, yes, I'd always had a terribly lifelike imaginary friend, but I rationalized that it was normal and healthy for children to have inventive imaginations. I'd told myself it was an asset, that the same love for fantasy that had given itself to fiction and novels and gods and powers had simply been poured too strong, splashing over the edge and drenching my waking mind.

But I was no longer sure if that was true.

His fingers moved in slow, tempting patterns along my back, then slipped around my arm once more, holding me like a vice. "Then be crazy in my arms. What do you say, Love? Do we have a deal?"

Chapter Three

(EG) The marketing team needs your permission to run this blurb about sex work. We want to weave it into your narrative.

(Marlow) Did they decriminalize it between now and the last time we had this conversation?

(EG) It's empowering, Marlow. It's best if you take control of the story before anyone tries anything.

(Marlow) You mean, before anyone tries to dox me. But this is part of why I used a pen name for the books and had a stage name for my clients. I should be layers removed from this, don't you think?

(EG) You're smart, Mar. You know it's going to come out. You told the company about your former line of work when you signed for a reason.

THE PHONE BECAME A BLANK SHEET OF BLACK GLASS ONCE more as I locked the screen without replying. I tugged the duvet up higher, groaning against the worst way to start the day.

EG was right.

I'd told her on our second meeting, long before the ink dried on our contract. I'd insisted that the meeting be over video chat. I needed to see her expression when I told her with a proud, cheery face that I'd been able to write the first *Pantheon* novel because I'd saved up from years of sex work. I'd planned to decide whether to give Inkhouse my partnership based on any flicker of judgment, any twitch, any hesitancy. EG's face had lit with the only brand of validation that could have won my business.

It wasn't the sort of conversation I liked to have before caffeine, but my editor's work hours were eternal. Before shutting off my phone I reemphasized that my decision was final. I'd enjoyed escorting—it was talking about it that I didn't like. At least, I enjoyed eating like royalty, the connections to society's upper echelon, and abusing the metallic, limitless cards of any man foolish enough to think he could impress me by taking me to an upscale shopping mall. I made them all pay, literally. Financial domination was my favorite flavor of the girlfriend experience. It meant charging exorbitant prices for my companionship, expecting only Michelin Star restaurants, Birkin bags, and jewelry worth more than what either of my parents made in a decade.

I hadn't told EG all of the details, nor was I convinced I wanted to. I wasn't sure where I'd start if I were to make it a part of my publicly available backstory. I didn't exactly want to create a how-to handbook for young women. It had been empowering for me—life-changing, even—but the dangers of being groomed into a life beyond your control weren't something I wished on anyone.

I guess if I chose to tell her, I'd need to begin with day one. As with most tales, this domino effect had tipped into my life quite by accident. Unlike most stories, this one started on the sweaty streets of Buenos Aires.

I met my first escort on a failed attempt at escaping to the far side of the globe. One week out of college, crawling out of my skin with anxiety, and with no direction for my life, I'd clicked on a sponsored ad to teach English as a second language in Medellín, Colombia. I hadn't given myself the chance to change my mind. I'd thrown everything I owned into a suitcase, found a subletter for my shitty basement unit on Craigslist, and gotten on a plane.

That was when I let hyper-independence take the wheel. I thought I could get a fresh start and get away from Caliban—but any reputable psychiatrist would have told me that psychosis isn't something you can outrun.

I closed my eyes once more, wishing a cup of coffee would materialize in my hands. In the meantime, I'd enjoy the succulent warmth of the duvet cover, letting my cozy, trapped body heat transport me to dream-like memories of my year just above the equator.

I could still feel the baking sun on my skin when I thought of that day.

Except, unlike the cocoon of a comfortable bed, misery was all I felt.

✦

DECEMBER 23, AGE 22

Sweat beaded along my upper lip. My feet were covered in blisters from the plastic rub of cheap shoes. I was desperate for a bottle of water and a cold shower. I'd been waiting for the bus in ninety-degree heat when a curious, pretty girl in Louis Vuitton heels paused at my side. They were chunky, tall boots that she'd paired with high-waisted black shorts, a black bralette as a top, and a cross-body bag with yet another designer logo, though I hadn't been well versed enough in name brands at the time to know a Chanel bag when I saw one. She'd managed to make her wealth look sporty rather than stuffy, which was quite an accomplishment. Ten seconds of mental math estimated that I could sell the clothes off her back and buy three roundtrip tickets from Los Angeles to Bogotá.

She grinned at the sunburst tattoo on my right ring

finger, breaking the silence. "I've been wanting to get a tattoo on my hand," she said, "but I hear they hurt like a bitch! And people say the ink falls out really easily. I rarely see hand tats in Buenos Aires. Most ink has kind of a thuggish reputation, I guess. It's cool as hell, though."

I returned the smile and lifted both hands. I had its counterpart on the opposite finger.

"Live by the sun, love by the moon," I said, referring to the tiny, matching moon on my left ring finger. "It seemed so profound when I was eighteen." I left out the part where the tiny finger tats had been too painful for me to dare return to a tattoo shop. My two celestial pieces of inky rebellion would have to suffice.

"And how old are you now?" she asked.

"I just turned twenty-two."

"Sag or Capricorn?" She smiled. "I'm an Aquarius."

Astrology wasn't something I cared about, but I'd memorized enough about the signs to know where my dates fell. "Sagittarius. My birthday was the twenty-first."

"Aw, we missed your golden birthday by a year. But you bagged a great astrological sign. Independent, adventurous, straight shooters. Our signs are super compatible for friendship."

I nodded along, because that was all I could do.

Her accent was North American, but between her black-and-auburn hair, her golden skin, and an ambiguous almond to her eyes, she could have been from any side of the pond. If it weren't for the heels, she would have been a full head and shoulders shorter than me, though I was average height by the most generous of North American estimations.

"You're right. About the ink, that is," I said, trying to steer the conversation into my more knowledgeable territories. "My tattoos stand out. And I don't know how adventurous I am. I'm six months into this yearlong contract and I'm struggling. I wish I could say it was homesickness, but it's more just…being a person. What about you? Do you live here? Visiting family?"

Her laugh was warm and easy. She tucked a lock of hair behind her ear. "No, I've been staying in Montevideo. There's a lot of money there. I was just here to meet a client for a few days. My friends and I rented a villa outside of Rio de Janeiro for Christmas, so I'll head there next."

"You travel for work, then? What do you do?"

She giggled. "My life's a party. Back to Rio—have you been there yet?"

I looked around the sidewalk, glancing between the palm trees, the shiny buildings, the bustling pedestrians in their tailored suits, their flashy bags, their sunglasses that cost more than my rent. I couldn't think of any reason she was talking to me. I shook my head. "No. I work a lot, and I haven't had anyone to go with."

"Well, it doesn't look like you're working right now. And if you wait for someone else to define your life, you'll never go anywhere or do anything," she said matter-of-factly.

"You might be on to something," I mused. I'd used my PTO to take the holiday off and gotten on the plane to visit Argentina with no plan in mind, but I certainly wasn't making the most of it. Unhappiness had boarded the plane with me.

She frowned, fully soaking in how alone I was. I'm not sure if she was looking at the dishwater-blond hair, the evidence of ink, or the clear signs of economic disparity between me and the others on the sidewalk, but it was obvious that I didn't fit in. If she hadn't been so friendly, I would have been embarrassed standing next to someone in designer heels, and yet, nothing about her made me feel judged.

"What brings you to Buenos Aires?" she asked.

My lips twisted into the corner of my mouth. I looked between the pristine streets and the skyscrapers that lined the downtown. "Those travel accounts made it look so colorful and European. It just seemed like the kind of place I should visit while I'm in the area."

She tilted her head, curtain of silky hair cascading over a sun-kissed shoulder. "What do you consider the area?"

33

Teachers had developed something of an unsavory reputation among the expatriate communities, or so I'd learned in my six months overseas. We were the backpacking barrel scum of the international community. I didn't have to tell her. She was a stranger at the bus stop. I could lie. I could tell her that I was a factory manager, a digital nomad, or that I worked at an embassy. But I had a feeling she wouldn't believe me.

I hedged before opting for honesty. "I've been teaching English to preschoolers in Colombia. I just thought I'd pop over here see what all the fuss was about. Plus, it's only, like, two and a half hours in the air. It turns out it's equally hot, and fifty times more expensive. And I'll deny it if you ever tell an Argentinian I said this, but the food is nowhere near as good."

Her lower lip lifted as she considered. "You like kids, then?"

I stared at her for a moment before giving the first honest answer about my job in six months. "Not at all. Don't get me wrong, I care about my students. They're a delight. And working with them has made my Spanish excellent. But I don't like being around children. Definitely pounded the final nail in the 'motherhood is not for me' coffin. But college was wrapping up and I had no plan for my life, so, might as well go make memories, right?"

I chewed my lip uncertainly. I wasn't good at knowing when I'd overshared.

She frowned. She looked me up and down a final time before saying, "I like your vibe. Give me your cell." She stretched out her hand, wiggling her fingers expectantly.

I didn't know why I complied, but I did. I handed the beautiful stranger my phone. She punched in her contact information just as a glossy black town car pulled up. With a hand on the door, she said, "A preschool teacher doesn't need to spend Christmas alone in a big city; she needs a beach day and a drink. Come to Rio. Hang out at my villa. Sing

34

Christmas carols with a pitcher of sangria in your hand. You'll only be responsible for the airfare to get yourself there. Just text me when you land. I'll give you directions."

"What's your name?" I shouted at her, but she was already gone.

Taylor. That's what she had typed in my phone. And for all I knew, Taylor was a smooth-talking kidnapper and I was being set up to have my organs harvested. But that didn't feel like the case. I'm not sure why I did it, but I took her up on her offer.

I'd taken ten days from teaching, intent on using the entirety of my time off on exploring Buenos Aires, but it had taken me roughly three days to learn that I couldn't afford to breathe the city's air, let alone do anything fun. I went back to my hotel, showered, and popped four sleeping pills to avoid Caliban confronting me to talk me out of going. A budget airline had me on a flight the next morning, leaving one of the most expensive cities on the continent and heading toward what would either be paradise or a story that ended with me waking up in a bathtub full of ice and missing a kidney.

It was just shy of a three-hour flight, followed by forty-five minutes in the customs line, thirty minutes waiting for my bag, and a two-hour cab ride to the small beach town south of the capital. I was sweaty, disoriented, and nervous and questioned the wisdom of my impulsivity every twenty seconds.

I remained glued to the window in the back seat of the cab, fixed on the dreamy landscape as I fretted. The buildings reminded me a lot of my home in Colombia, as did the scooters, the heat, the narrow alleys, and the markets. The cityscape slowly gave way to greenery. Tall clusters of trees and thick, tropical grasses populated one side of the car. Through the other window, the ocean broke in large, tube-like waves as it washed up on long, sandy beaches. Before long, I was in a six-bedroom villa on the beach. Taylor was the friendliest, perkiest, most generous person I'd ever met. Two of the

35

bedrooms were occupied by unnaturally beautiful friends, Ivy and Quinn, both of whom oozed similar compassion and support. They were so kind that, at first, I was convinced they were insincere. My hackles went up, terrified that my naivety had lured me into a trap. I wondered how long it would be before the organ harvesters showed.

But no. Instead, it was something far rarer.

They were just really good people.

Taylor, Ivy, and Quinn were escorts.

Taylor was exceedingly open about her life. She dangled her feet in the pool, holding a sangria in one hand and snapping pictures of her friends with the phone in her other. She told her stories with a happy face, whether discussing backpacking down the Chilean coast or being the arm candy at a red-carpet event. She told the tale of how she'd started escorting, her pitfalls, her mistakes, and how she'd gotten to where she was now. She and her friends were exclusively word-of-mouth, she said. They only worked with elite, prescreened clientele.

And I didn't want to teach preschoolers. I didn't particularly want to talk to men, either, but I did want to pay my bills. I wanted to be able to move out of the basement apartment. I wanted to pay off my student loans, to take vacations on the Yucatán Peninsula, and to escape the cycle of intergenerational poverty that had kept me under its thumb.

By the end of the day, she'd help me pick a new name, set up a covert profile, and book my first client—a weekend in Montevideo scheduled for the end of the month. Taylor connected me with a few of her old patrons whose schedules conflicted with her own, saying she didn't mind passing them off on me. Community over competition and all that.

Quinn made a comment about how I was fortunate that I had only two tattoos—both of which could be covered with chunky rings—as it would make it easier for me to fly under the radar. Ivy and I were similarly gifted—or cursed—with ample chests, and she gave me several pairs of strappy lingerie with the tags still on. She made a comment about her shopping problem and how she was happy they'd be getting some use. Taylor was thrilled that I could speak Spanish, as there'd been a few clients who had passed the screening but needed a bilingual provider, which only Quinn was.

The ones she'd selected for me were good starter clients, Taylor said, as they'd already been vetted and gone through the appropriate background checks. She promised she'd walk me through it before I started booking on my own and told me never to meet someone without exercising my due diligence.

"That said," she amended, "the world is not a scary place. In the hundreds of cities I've traveled and the thousands of people I've met, I've only had two bad experiences. And both of those happened in my hometown. People like to comfort themselves by believing the scary things are out in the world. It keeps them from living. It's often the danger out your front door that blinds you."

"Are you…" I looked between the drink in my hand and my toes as they dangled in the water. "I don't know how to ask this. Do you…get something out of this?"

She giggled. "Are you asking if I'm a pimp? No. We all work exclusively for ourselves. And if anyone ever approaches you with offers to hook you up with clients for a fee, run for the hills. Pick a cover industry, pay your taxes, and start living large."

"A cover industry?"

Ivy smiled. "If anyone asks, I'm a model."

Quinn raised a finger. "Translator."

Taylor explained, "And I'm a tour guide. The cover helps with explaining your life to your family, but it's more about the law. As long as your income is taxable, the government doesn't care what you do."

The first day in Brazil was a beautiful, confusing, colorful, dazzling dream. We'd eaten fruit, drank innumerable pitchers of sangria, relaxed, and genuinely laughed. Taylor was right. Her life was a party. But it wasn't the drugs and rave music and bandage-tight dresses that I'd pictured when envisioning a party. It was the relaxation of a life spent without worry.

I left the windows wide open that first night, listening to the tropical birds and watching the shadows of curious macaques jump from branch to branch. I'd been warned that the cute little monkeys might steal your things, but I'd never been so close to one, and it was a lesson I wanted to learn for myself. I hated being sweaty and typically despised sleeping without the air conditioner, but the wind off the water was deliciously cooling. I soaked in the wind, the waves, and the tropics as I let both the stress of my job and the financial nightmare of this trip wash away.

"Starting a new career, are we?" came a voice from an unseen speaker in the shadows.

I looked into the gloom where I knew he'd be leaning against a wall. A spike of defensiveness worked through me as I feigned nonchalance. I'd hoped he might show up, though I never knew for sure if he'd come. Of course, I'd gotten on the plane to get away from him. I'd hoped to be set free from my hallucinations. My hopes had been lies that I'd been unwilling to admit until the red-eye flight to South America and the relief that had flooded me when the rush of gin and moss had filled the space beside me. I wanted him here. I wanted him in my life. I just hated myself for it.

My legs twisted beneath the thin sheet. "Teaching English was always temporary. I've just shortened it by half a year. Why? Are you showing up as my conscience?"

"Never," he said. "Whatever makes you happy. I know that struggling to pay the bills does not make you happy. But I've said it before: if you'd let me help with that…"

"Yes. You can help by making sure I only book the richest clients and make the most money so that my boat sets sail on an endless sea of cash by this time next year," I said. I plopped the pillows behind my back and sat up in bed, looking expectantly into the gloom. The ocean crashed in lulling waves on the beach beyond the open villa window. I listened to it break time and time again, peering into the darkness while I waited for his reply.

After a long period of silence, I began to worry.

He said nothing.

"Caliban?"

But no answer came.

✦

DECEMBER 29, AGE 22

"How was your first night?"

I spun toward the darkness, doing little to fight the inner glow tugging up the corners of my lips. My heart squeezed, his voice both excitement and balm all at once. It was exactly what I needed to end my out-of-body experience. I wished I could see his face. His question held the edges of a smile. And god, how I missed that smile.

The night had been spectacular, and he was the only one I wanted to share it with.

Taylor had made sure I was compensated for the exhaustion of travel in addition to my time on the clock, helping me set firm boundaries and holding my hand over text as she insisted that time was my only nonrenewable resource. It wasn't enough for clients to buy my tickets, but to show their gratitude at my willingness to get on a plane and stay in a hotel while away from my home.

The five-star Wagyu steak house in Montevideo, Uruguay, had been a haze of flavors and colors and nerves. The client, to my surprise, had been an attractive, well-dressed, polite, and friendly man, though woefully short for society's unreasonable norms. He'd greeted me with a kiss on the cheek and a bulging envelope filled with USD, as something Taylor had drilled into me was that I always needed to get paid before the date began. He'd opened my doors, pulled out my chair, and asked me about myself. I'd played my role as upscale girlfriend perfectly, straddling the line between sexy and conservative in a long-sleeve dress with a plunging neckline. The dress belonged to Ivy. Where she'd let me keep the lingerie, she expected this particular piece of clothing back when I was done. My aim was for everyone at the restaurant to think I was a trophy wife, while he remained the only one excited for what might come next. He'd paid for the most expensive multi-course meal, which was delicious and added an extra three hours on the clock for my eventual paycheck.

The best part of the sex was that he'd left the television on. He'd flipped me to my back, and I'd looked over his shoulder to watch a rerun of an old comedy with the subtitles, making encouraging sounds and digging my fingernails into his back with theatrical pleasure at the right moments. I knew this episode. It was the one where the main characters locked themselves out of their apartment on Thanksgiving. I stifled a laugh when a character stumbled out of his apartment with a turkey on his head, which was my favorite brand of poorly written comedy. The man had felt my body clench and assumed I was close to climax.

Good.

The show had made me loosely aware that, though I'd eaten more than six hundred dollars in tiny foods, I was still hungry. Afterward, we lay in bed for another hour, playing the pillow-talking role of lovers. And then it was time to go. I'd been given an additional stipend to book myself a luxury room under my own name—somewhere safe where the client didn't have access to me.

His hotel had been lovely. His suite was three times larger than the place I'd been renting in Colombia, with towels more expensive than any shirt I owned. Still, all I had to do was enjoy my dinner and watch TV.

Taylor had been right. This was the best.

I checked in with her afterward to let her know I was safe, and she scolded me for not turning on the GPS on my phone during my date. We were a network, she said, and the world wouldn't understand us, so we had to have each

40

other's backs. If she was unavailable, then I should share my location with Ivy, Quinn, or one of the others in our line of work who she promised to introduce me to once I returned to the States.

This was so much better than disappointing lays with broke one-night stands. My overcorrection from an upbringing in purity culture meant that virtue had never meant much to me. If I wasn't going to raise my standards, I should at least be getting something out of it.

I had one more comped night in Montevideo before I'd go back to Colombia, collect my meager earthly possessions, and quit my teaching job. They'd asked for thirty days' notice, but I was ready to make good on what everyone already believed to be true about English teachers and live up to my transience, vanishing in the night. Once I stepped into the high-end life, I was unwilling to go back.

I'd left his hotel with more money in my purse than I'd seen in my entire life. I leaned my head against the window in the taxi and grinned at the night sky, buzzing with a euphoria that felt strangely like a cocktail of alcohol and MDMA, despite being stone-cold sober. I recognized the feeling while watching the buildings and trees bleed into a colorful swirl of paint behind the window. This was how it felt to not worry about money.

I'd propped my pillows up and sat in the dark but left my hair, my makeup, my dress exactly as they'd been. For the first time in my life, I wouldn't live paycheck to paycheck. I'd never imagined what it might feel like to eliminate credit card debt, cover my rent, and still have money left over for food. Not only that, but I'd made a powerful connection with an elite new contact, had an extravagant meal, and gotten to watch one of my favorite comedies.

Answering his question, I reached to the bedside table and felt around until my fingers wrapped around the paper wad held together with a small rubber band. I procured four thousand dollars in cash.

"You're welcome," he said, that same smile playing on his voice. "You look beautiful, Love."

"I'm sure you do, too," I sighed.

I set the money down and slid backward, beckoning him to me. I closed my eyes and tilted up my chin, waiting for the hands I knew would come as he approached the bed. They started at my shoulders, running gently over my collarbones, up my neck, and into my hair. He planted a slow kiss on my throat, lingering on my jugular long enough that I could have sworn he was feeling the way he made my heart race.

I ran my hands over him, breathed him in, and was utterly overcome by his presence.

This had been why nothing else felt real.

The client, his suite, his money, it was as if it had happened outside of reality—like an unimportant dream quickly shaken from the mind. Because this touch, this kiss, the taste of his tongue on mine, this enveloping scent of gin, mist, and moss...this was real.

"Are you happy?" came the low rumble of his lips against mine as he cupped my face.

"Now I am."

Chapter Four

I T WAS THE STRICT UPBRINGING OF MY DEEPLY RELIGIOUS
parents. It was the stress of college. It was the toils and failures
of my first job out of school. It was the mental and emotional
taxation of living dollar to dollar. It was the struggle of adjust-
ing between this medicine, that therapist, this schedule, that
routine. It was the transience of living abroad. It was the sex
work as it coincided with indifference to romance. It was the
deadlines and ceaseless texts from my editor to turn in new
pages. It was the fantasy novels and the impossible standards
they set for love. It was my newfound passion for writing that
made the very thought of leaving the house lose its sparkle.

Those were the reasons my heart was unavailable.

It had nothing to do with my vibrant imagination, the
lifelong presence that filled me in the shadows, or the tantric,
unparalleled orgasms that shattered my very cells until I was
one with the universe. It wasn't that my only friend, the one
who made me laugh, the one I trusted, who I shared every
secret, every hope, every dream with, waited in the night. It
had nothing to do with my only reprieve, my only salvation
living in the shadows, visiting me in the dark, caressing me,
holding me, refusing to let me go.

It couldn't be that.

That would be crazy.

Chapter Five

I DRUMMED MY FINGERS AGAINST MY TABLE WITH MANIC excitement. I'd passed the time to go to sleep and caught a second wind fueled by giddy adrenaline. Three days of empty takeout boxes surrounded my laptop like tiny tombstones, sentinels overwatching my slipping sanity. I polished off the remnants of a coconut rum and water, then grabbed one bottle after the other and refilled my glass with the lazy drink.

"You need to sleep," Caliban said, heavy hands resting on my shoulders as his fingers began to knead my tightly woven muscles. Under different circumstances, he may have succeeded in relaxing me.

"You love when I stay up late!" I said, glancing at the clock. It was nearly three in the morning. The bright white glow of the computer burned into my retinas in the otherwise-dark apartment. "Besides, I'm celebrating."

"I love when you stay up late so that we can spend time together," he countered. "Not so you can drive yourself mad."

"That ship has sailed, my friend." I sipped at my rum drink as I spoke.

He chuckled, brushing his lips against my temple. I closed my eyes to appreciate it only briefly before enthusiasm over my project consumed me once more. "I'm proud of you," he said, "but not surprised. You've been working on this for a long time, and you're immensely talented. It was time someone else saw that, too."

"There had just been so many years of rejections…"

"They weren't the right fit," he said, voice matter-of-fact. "It took a while to get you in front of the proper eyes. And I've been more distracted than I like. Things have been…" He made a dismissive sound and then pressed a kiss into my temple. "I'm sorry, Love."

I waved away his words and stared at the email anchoring me to the planet.

I'd been writing since I could hold a pen.

My first exercise in creative fiction had been my journal. I'd known from the day I asked my mom to buy me a diary that she'd be reading it. So with poetic imagination, I began to spill my life's fabricated details onto the speckled black-and-white notebook. I wrote for the church newsletter. I rewrote biblical parables in a modern setting. I wrote for class. And then when I started college, I'd begun working on a novel. I was a junior when I sent out my first query letter, and a junior when I received my first rejection. I knew my odds of getting struck by lightning were higher than my chances of being published, but I continued writing anyway, launching into the second novel in a series that would never see the light of day.

My first six months in Colombia were peppered with rejection letters, but Caliban had encouraged me to keep trying. He'd said the agents, editors, and publishers who passed on it weren't a good enough fit, which felt like a painful mockery from my own ego. He told me he was certain something great was right around the corner. That if I just held on…

Now here I was, rum-drunk in the dead of winter, staring at the same email that had sent me into a tailspin hours earlier. An agent wanted to represent me. Not just any agent. Julian Asher. The woman with a list of blockbuster authors and number one bestsellers longer than my phone number. She'd

45

loved the first book so much that she immediately asked if there was more and was thrilled to learn that I was already sitting on an unpolished draft of the second book.

"We need to do something," I said. "We need music. I'll make cocktails. I'll get us dinner. Or whatever meal happens after midnight."

I may have continued rambling, talking a mile a minute before he said, "You know precisely what I like to eat."

My face heated.

We used to make each other laugh. He'd been terribly funny, wise, patient, and clever. But every time I cracked up at a joke alone in my home, it would take only a second for the mood to turn, my face to fall, my heart to cool. He'd said time and time again that it made him sad to make me sad, so our bouts of laughter became fewer and further between as we walked a tight rope of conversation that wouldn't set me off.

I closed my laptop and turned toward the thick shadow, always regretting when I did. It was easier to stay pointed away from the empty space. I closed my eyes, resting my elbow on the counter and propping up my chin. I allowed the silence to stretch between us, and he didn't prod.

He knew when my mind was working.

What a sensation to know someone well enough to hear the cadence of their silence. I knew his mouth turned down in a gentle frown simply from the shift in energy. Though he didn't rush me to speak, I sensed he knew he wouldn't like what I was about to say.

"I think I started writing this book because I was so sure using my imagination would stop this," I said at last. "That I could channel all of this excess creativity and get it out of my system. But you didn't go away. And then I thought maybe I was still holding on to you because I needed the rock while escorting, or the reassurance while querying. That you'd go away if this day ever came."

The smile returned. I sensed it from his inhalation before I felt him. I stopped speaking the moment cool hands slid up my thighs. The contact was as much for me as it was for him, I supposed. If I couldn't see him, at least I could feel him. "Do you want to talk about your books?"

I gave a short, dry laugh. "Is there anything you don't already know?"

His voice contained a playful lilt as he said, "You don't know the half of what I know."

"So, tell me," I said.

His lips drew a chilled, electric line from my ear down my jaw. His mouth ended on my throat as he murmured, "I thought I was just your imagination? If that's the case, shouldn't you know everything I know?" His hands stilled as he said, "I want you for so much more than sex, Love."

Though my eyes remained closed, I tilted my face away from him.

"I want it all," he said. "You've corralled me into the smallest corner of yourself. I need you to hear it from me when I say: I'd give you the world. Instead, I'm giving you everything you're allowing me to offer."

I smiled, though it wasn't entirely joyous. Appreciating the support of my subconscious genie, I asked, "While you're granting wishes, can you make sure this book sells? If Asher's representing me, then I have a shot with one of the Big Five publishers. It's a pipe dream. But then again, so is getting an agent in the first place. Even making this much money...well... it's been a dream for a while. I may as well continue dreaming."

The vibration of his low chuckle tingled against my throat as he said, "I think I can pull a few strings."

✦

SEPTEMBER 8, AGE 24

"Caliban?" I asked into the gloom. I thought I'd heard a noise. A pop somewhere. A shift of weight. The squeak of a shoe. A breath, maybe.

I hated the silence that answered, even though I insisted it

47

was what I wanted. Maybe my inability to make up my mind was why I couldn't get him to leave. Because he was right. I didn't want him gone. And yet...

Maybe my cocktail of drugs was finally working. Maybe my therapist had a breakthrough. Maybe paying off my debts, my student loans, my car, and taking up permanent residence for months as the number one *New York Times* bestseller had satiated the long-needed urge for success. Maybe the new apartment, the nice clothes, the relaxed schedule, the validation from the only two friends in my life, and the fully remote lifestyle of a writer had chipped away at whatever had remained of the trauma that had forced me into manifesting a walking fiction. Maybe sending the polished version of the second novel to EG only to have her send me a four-minute voice message crying about the heartbreaking plot twist and the gorgeous lore had filled my long-empty cup that craved validation. Maybe seeing my face, my pen name, the *Pantheon* novels on pop-up ads and social media posts and banners on every web page had fixed the part of me that had needed him.

Maybe I'd healed from whatever had cracked within me when I was so young that I'd needed to create an imaginary friend in order to survive.

Maybe the neglected part of me that had wandered away from my family toward the woods, that was scooped up by strong arms and urged back into the sanctuary of inattentive parents, no longer needed to conjure an unseen presence. Maybe my first memory of a smiling face and comforting friend had covered a darker, harder memory that I was unwilling to face, no matter how hard I dug for what might have really happened that day.

Maybe the white fox that had accompanied me for years was the product of a lonely child in a trailer park, a heartbroken failure in a religious home, the coping mechanism of a girl who had been denied a pet and had to invent one. Maybe the one I saw as I took silent trips into the woods in my teens, the lithe fox made of little more than starlight and dreams that would walk beside me, was a product of wishing I hadn't been so deeply and profoundly abandoned.

Maybe I'd fabricated a face when I'd needed a friend and used the only vocabulary that my deeply evangelical parents had understood when I described my guardian angel.

Maybe I'd imagined the way my mother's face had flicked from joy to concern to panic as I went on to describe my interaction with my guardian throughout the years, explaining his omnipresence, describing the sideways tilt of his smile, the strength of his hugs, the joy of his friendship, his beautiful animal form, and the way I'd prayed for God to protect and bless him, just as I prayed for myself or my parents. Maybe I'd been reading too much into her response when she'd called our pastor in tears and begged him to pray over me, to bring the church elders to cleanse our home.

Maybe I'd stopped talking about him the day I'd been dragged to therapy because I knew nothing good could come from speaking his name. Maybe I'd worked through my issues regarding the church, my family, my life, my studies, and had felt complete, healed, and fine. Maybe I'd moved overseas the week of graduation to use my literary degree for English and to seek a new start, leaving behind my very specific, consistent brand of psychosis as if it had geographical ties. Maybe my breath had caught in the ten-hour flight between North America and Colombia when a hand had slipped over mine in the darkened cabin, filling the empty seat that had remained vacant between me and a sleeping passenger, when lips pressed against my temple, and I knew my problems would follow me wherever I went.

Maybe after returning to the U.S., after the escorting, after the novels, after the luxury apartments and bank accounts filling to the brim and the golden designer ring that glimmered on my finger as if I were a married woman, I'd stop thinking about who I was or why I was here.

Maybe if his visits stopped altogether, I could let him go. Maybe if they continued every night, I could believe in them. Maybe if I didn't wait on bated breath to see if a day, or a week, or a month would go by before I'd feel his presence again. Maybe I wouldn't close my mouth, breathing through my nose, praying for the distant, mossy scents of cypress and gin.

Maybe.

Chapter Six

A LOUD VOICE CALLED OVER THE CROWD. T-SHIRTS, JEANS, cosplay, and the permeating smell of popcorn filled the air. Harsh, unflattering fluorescents hung forty feet overhead, washing out the throngs of attendees. There had been so much noise, so much commotion from the time the doors opened that I was shocked I'd been able to hear him. The single word pierced the air like an arrow to the heart, slicing through the cluster of people.

I flinched at the name, head whipping up. He repeated it, shouting the false identity over the heads of those around him. "Maribelle?"

God, I already hated these fucking conventions. This was my second May wasted on the tour circuit. A necessary evil, perhaps, but an evil nonetheless. I hated leaving my house long enough to get groceries, let alone to be swarmed by thousands of strangers, assaulted by their conversations and the smells of the deep-fried foods, repeating the same answers, forcing the same smile for hours. I did my best to be polite, but I was so overstimulated by the end of each convention that it took me five days of silence to recover. EG accompanied after I'd failed spectacularly at my first convention, growing so anxious that I'd made a woman cry and left three hours early.

They'd offered me attendants and security and handlers, but my bubble of trust was miniscule, and EG was the only person I wanted around me amid the hordes. She probably didn't get paid enough to put up with my bullshit. Then again, I'd made Inkhouse a lot of money. I suspected she was doing fine.

I didn't need another reason to hate events, and yet, I hadn't even considered the worst-case scenario. The doors to the convention had been on their hinges for less than an hour before my nightmare personified descended.

If I hadn't already been miserable, this new, fresh hell tore through me.

Hundreds of people pushed in around him, but he'd set his focus on my table. The warehouse was not big enough to contain the swell of my anxiety as fight or flight overcame me, little more than a mouse with her leg caught in a trap. The lusterless lights were suddenly too bright. The world was the wrong color. He seemed taller, somehow, more powerful than I'd remembered him being. Nothing looked right as I soaked in the too-wide grin of a man I distinctly remembered as the only date I'd walked out on.

Richard.

I pinked at the long-dead name, eyes shooting to EG, who was already searching my face for answers. My lips pursed into a tight line. My look communicated two simple words: *Help me.*

He bypassed the snaking queue of expectant readers who clutched their installments of *Pantheon.*

EG was a sharp woman, and she knew me well. Her eyes widened, darting between the rapidly approaching stranger and me as she asked, "Is Maribelle your—"

"Yes," I hissed, and that was enough.

This man was shouting my escorting alias for the world to hear. I barely had time to answer her before the long-abandoned client was at my table. I hadn't seen him in more than two years. We'd gone on half of a date, and it was one I'd

52

hoped to leave in the past. He'd been a referral from one of my favorite clients—one who'd bought me my black strappy bag with the triangular platinum logo. The bag alone had cost him just shy of five thousand dollars. I'd considered bringing that exact bag today but had settled on a seven-dollar tote bag from my local bookstore.

I lived my life in extremes.

I'd been braced to see former clients at any number of restaurants, bars, or events. I'd kept my eyes peeled, relying on mutually assured destruction as my lone comfort, that even if I spotted a man from my past, he would be just as reluctant to admit where he knew me from as I would.

I'd never thought I'd see one at a convention for bookworms.

EG was on her feet in a flash. She moved around the table in the time it took to blink, attempting to intercept him. She put a hand on the man's arm, and despite being half his size, she took control of the situation fully. She used her most authoritative customer service voice to usher him away, allowing me to stammer through my meeting with the next fan in line. If the heat pulsing through my face was any indication, I had to be a worrying shade of reddish purple. The girl in line fidgeted nervously at my obvious discomfort, and I winced as I misspelled her name in the signing. I doodled a butterfly and apologized profusely for my blunder.

Over the fan's shoulder, EG and my assailant disappeared behind the shuffle of bodies, and I did my best to return to my job.

EG reappeared at my side. She offered the next in line a friendly smile while she leaned into my ear. "He left quietly and apologized. I think he understood his blunder. Would you like me to put security on him?"

Richard. His name was Richard.

I thought of my date with the man and suppressed a shudder.

"You said he left?" I asked. I smiled at the next in line,

asked her name, and signed her book. I added a few doodles of hearts and stars for embellishment while she gushed about the second book in the series, particularly loving how I'd portrayed Artemis's character. I nodded along with the friendly fan. She thanked me and hugged her book to her chest. I wanted to give her my whole attention, but I kept one eye on my editor.

EG waited for a break between attendees before saying, "He was very polite. Do you think he'll give you any trouble?"

I didn't know how to answer her. Telling her that he'd technically done nothing wrong would require explaining why I was afraid of him in the first place.

I offered a smile to the next reader, but the joy didn't reach my eyes. I saw it as she looked back at me with a mild disappointment. Of course, I wasn't giving her my best self. I rallied my joy as I looked down, conjuring a grin from the depths of my belly before I looked up once more. I beamed at the fan, thanking her sincerely for reading the *Pantheon* novels. She recovered from her disappointment and asked if I could tell her anything about the third installment. I winked and repeated the only tidbit I was legally allowed to share: it would take place in South America.

"Mar—Merit?" EG corrected, calling me by my pen name. Her voice was low, but we were still in public. "Do you feel safe? Is there anything I can do?"

I appreciated her. She was my rottweiler.

"I'm fine," I promised.

"I know you're strong, so I'm not just asking about you. Is *he* going to be a problem?"

I shrugged, as much for myself as for her. "He wasn't a problem two years ago. I don't see why he should be one now."

I finished out the sixteen-hour day, allowing the staff to collect the books, collapse the table, and do whatever house-keeping was necessary. EG offered to walk me to my car, but I was parked in a well-lit garage and walked with my keys on a swinging lanyard, ready to bludgeon anyone from a distance.

I poured myself into my Mercedes, checking the back seat for goblins before I started the engine. The luxury vehicle was a flex I'd been able to purchase in cash after a monthlong booking with an inventor known for his fleet of yachts. He'd talked my ear off for thirty days straight and had been the lone reason I stopped doing vacation bookings. This vehicle was my swan song to sex work. After that, the advance for *Pantheon* came in, followed by the royalties, and the money I'd stashed in stocks and savings continued to grow.

Life with a full wallet wasn't so bad.

I melted into the chair as punishingly upbeat music blasted on the radio. I'd been playing it at an unbearable volume to psyche myself up for the event. Now that the conference was over, it was the last thing in the world I wanted to hear.

I hit the volume button as if it were personally responsible for my inner turmoil and rolled out of the garage in silence. The quiet soothed me as I eased onto the interstate, falling into something of highway hypnosis as an internal GPS pulled me home while my mind remained elsewhere. The city lights disappeared, fading into something else entirely as I approached the warehouse district. The engine's hushed purr and the consistent sound of rubber on the pavement occupied my mind, allowing everything else to drip from me like condensation from a tailpipe. It took roughly forty minutes to get from the convention until I could put my car in park in the safety of my parking garage. I'd left most of the toxicity on the freeway, and in its place, the drained husk of a human remained. I pressed the button to kill the car, closing my eyes and relaxing against the headrest as a headache bloomed between my temples.

Normally I was all too enthusiastic to escape back into my apartment, but instead of opening the door, I leaned forward until my head bumped against the steering wheel and let the stillness calm me. The sensory overload of conventions was an essential poison, and their necessity didn't keep me from hating them. I allowed the silent moments to act like leeches, sucking the discomfort and suffering and misery of having to exist as a human in this world from my body. It took a while before I could take in a full, relaxing breath.

The day was over. I'd survived the crowd, the noise, the lights, the brush with fear and the brush with my past. It was time to kick off my shoes, unhook my bra, and eat ice cream directly from the tub while watching the unhinged professor on the History Channel tell the world about how aliens had built the pyramids.

I locked my car, flinching at the horn's chirp of confirmation, regretting shattering my newfound silence. Even the click of my heels was too loud. I craved nothingness, and every noise infringed on my need for reprieve. As the door to the garage closed, I held my breath and hoped my favorite receptionist was working so that I could avoid idle chitchat while crossing the lobby. My eyes stayed down as I replaced my building card and fished through my tote for my phone. In case someone else was on shift, I wanted to have a faux conversation at the ready to hold up an apologetic finger and halt any further small talk in its place. It was a selfish thing to hope, but then again, I was allowed to be greedy about my desire for peace.

A tingle started somewhere between my shoulder blades, spreading out like wings as it filled me. I abandoned my search for my phone, hand lowering from my purse. Something felt different even before I turned the corner. My steps slowed, ears straining for a noise, a smell, anything unusual.

I turned the corner to see…nothing.

In three years, the desk had never been left unattended. Even if the on-duty receptionist needed something, they would grab someone from security to wait by the door. My steps slowed as I stretched out my intuition, allowing its instinctual fingers to prod the space around me. I stopped, a sliver of adrenaline piercing me like a needle. I scanned the atrium but saw nothing out of the ordinary. A few careful steps toward the desk showed a perfectly normal, tidy station.

A half-eaten cup of noodles sat by the computer—evidence that the receptionist had been there only moments prior. I stared at the vacant chair for a while, allowing the quiet classical music that was always piped through the building to cover my uncertainty. I peered at the sleek computer to see half of its screen dedicated to live footage of the building.

Nothing moved.

I dismissed the chill as paranoia. It had been a stressful day, and I'd arguably been watching too many horror movies. I couldn't help it if fear was better than boredom and I enjoyed the schadenfreude of watching stupid people die. After all, if they expected to survive, why did they always run *up* the stairs when a killer entered their house?

The gratuitous violence slipped from my mind as I let go of the irrational nagging sensation. I blew out a breath, expelling lingering anxiety as I abandoned the room and headed for the elevator bank. I hit the button and frowned as the red digits lit up to display its quiet descent from somewhere up above. I'd been so spoiled to have an elevator waiting on ground level each night that even the smallest inconvenience made me feel disenfranchised. It was the first-worldiest of problems, but I was tired, and tired people are grouchy no matter how spoiled they are.

I stepped into the elevator but couldn't keep my forehead from creasing as my eyebrows met in the middle. I couldn't justify the frown that plagued me.

Generally, the toils of the day bled from me with the gravitational pull of the earth, each ascending floor shedding new layers of exhaustion as I drew closer and closer to home. Tonight, my nerves thickened as the numbers ticked upward. When the metallic doors opened, I stayed in the elevator. I couldn't explain my reluctance to leave the safety of the rectangle.

Nothing had happened. There was nothing wrong. Nothing.

I stuck my palm out just as the doors began to close. They

bounced harmlessly off my hand before I stepped into the hall. Six steps to my door. Two long breaths. Three seconds of allowing my rose-gold card to hover above the pad before I pressed it into the door. The mechanisms released and the door eased open. I gave it a gentle shove and allowed the light from the hall to pour into the dark room.

In my hand, my phone buzzed.

(Kirby) Hey, when you get home can you send me that
   song? The really sad one that gave me like three new
   reasons to be depressed?

I hit the dial button, and Kirby picked up on the first ring.

I could hear the sounds of cooking and party chatter in the background as they came on the line. "Listen," they said through a short, annoyed sigh, "I don't know the name of it if that's why you're calling. If I knew it, I would have searched for it myself."

"No," I said, "I just had a weird feeling and thought it would be better to be on the phone."

On the other end, Kirby quieted. "Where are you?"

"Home," I said.

Their relief was palpable. "Jesus H. Christ, don't worry me like that. Did you hear a ghost?"

I wished it were anything that logical. I was still shaking my head before realizing I hadn't answered. "No, I just have an uncanny feeling. I'm standing in my hallway."

"Do you want me to come over?"

My face fell. This was the question I'd needed to get me to stop being a pussy and enter my apartment. Kirby was a good friend, and I knew their offer was sincere. Even if I'd wanted them to come over, would I just stand in the hallway for thirty minutes until they arrived? Besides, they were clearly entertaining guests. I exhaled dramatically and crossed the threshold, closing the door behind me. I kicked off my shoes and tossed my purse onto the island that separated my living room from my kitchen. I rallied my energy as I grinned mischievously into the phone, asking, "Wait, is today Outlook calendar night?"

The one night per week that their synced calendars matched up with everyone else's in their polycule.

"You know it," they practically sang from the other end. "Just making pasta before…"

"Don't tell me." I laughed, not needing to hear the detail of how they'd synced their schedules to make their unicorn life work. "Also, don't get too full. Go have fun, you freak."

"Group sex is not freaky. You're just boring."

"Go to bed, vet. You have to get back to the horse-pital in the morning. I wouldn't want a hungover party surgeon digging in my livestock's guts."

"I'm a veterinary surgeon. Fuck you."

I grinned. "Whatever, horse girl."

"Horse *person*," they corrected, a smile in their voice.

"Bye, Kirby."

"Wait!" they urged. "Jokes aside: are you sure you're okay? You feel safe?"

I rolled my eyes. They were nearly a year younger than me yet somehow always the parent. "I'm fine. I was just being paranoid. Try to talk me out of getting drunk and binging another slasher marathon. Go have enough fun for the both of us."

"Love you," they said cheerily as the line disconnected.

I went directly to the refrigerator and grabbed a twist-off bottle of beer and took a swig, savoring the gratifying pop of bubbles after a taxing day. I'd trade horror films for alien conspiracy theories. I hummed to myself as I looked for the remote. I swore I'd left it on the counter. Maybe the island? Or the coffee table?

A small light went on in the corner of the living room.

I jolted so hard that beer splashed from my bottle onto my forearm. Eyes wide, I stared at the figure waiting in the

59

corner. Lurking near the television, just on the dark side of the curtains, was one face I'd hoped to never see again. Nausea roiled through me. The coppery tang of fear filled my mouth.

"Richard," I breathed on an exhale.

Black pants. Black shirt. Gloves. Oh god, *gloves*.

"Maribelle," he replied coldly. "Or, should I call you Merit? Or Marlow?"

Ice pumped through my veins as I remembered the first—and last—time I'd seen him. He'd passed the background check. He'd put a thousand down on the evening. He'd booked for three hours: dinner, drinks, and date. The three-hour minimum kept the client list short, wealthy, and worth my while. I'd even liked some of my patrons...

Except with him. He'd made one seemingly innocent comment within the first hour that I'd been unable to shake. Even two years after the date, the minor exchange sent a shudder down my spine.

The dinner flashed through me.

We'd finished drinks when he'd said, "So, shall we go up to the room?"

No. I informed him politely that the second hour was on me, so there was no need for reimbursement, but that I wasn't feeling well. He'd been visibly disappointed but hadn't seemed angry.

Prior to that, the meal had gone well enough. We'd chatted about our favorite movies, his life as a neurosurgeon, his very strong feelings on the *Star Explorer* franchise, and his upbringing in a tiny town. I usually didn't mind dates with doctors, as they often had interesting stories that made fantastic party anecdotes. I hadn't been thrilled at the way he kept referring to his job as *cutting into people*, but then again, my clients were often odd. It came with the territory.

The date had been utterly standard until he mentioned in passing that his childhood home had burned down. I'd frowned and reached across the table to touch his hand,

60

apologizing for his loss. I had perfected the empathetic pout and loved the opportunity to use it. Endearing exchanges like this generally earned me several hundred in tips.

"I'm so sorry you went through that," I'd said.

"I'm not," he'd responded, a distant twinkle in his eye.

That had been it. Nothing more. The food from our dinner had turned to ice chips in my stomach. My gut had forced three words to the forefront of my mind in a way I couldn't ignore.

The Macdonald Triad was what all the true-crime podcasts I listened to while cleaning my house or wasting time on a plane had called it. The triad was composed of three ingredients: cruelty to animals, bed-wetting, and arson. Of course, he'd never come to dinner and tell me that he'd beat a neighborhood cat with a hammer or mention chronic childhood incontinence, but something about the sparkle in his eye communicated all I needed to know. I wasn't ready to justify it, nor did I need to. The triad was of one the only warning signs one had when looking into the eyes of a serial killer.

I could, of course, never know if I'd been insane or paranoid, but I was lucky to have Taylor in my life. She'd hammered it into me before my first date: I held all of the cards. I could end a date for any reason; whether he made an off-color joke or wore pungent cologne, dates were at my discretion. For all I knew, he was just a well-paid brain surgeon who liked movies about space a little too much. But it didn't matter. I'd offered my most convincing condolences and gathered my purse. The abrupt end of our date was public enough that those sitting at the bar around us had turned to watch the poor man's failed attempt at romance.

He'd furrowed his brow as if trying to decide whether or not he should walk me to the door. He looked up over our empty glasses and asked, "Can we reschedule when you feel better, Maribelle?"

"Of course," I'd agreed, blocking his number before I'd even walked out of the restaurant.

I'd rushed home from the restaurant, crashing into strong, unseen arms. Caliban hadn't believed me when I told him nothing was wrong, which was fair, as I was lying. I didn't want to worry him. Or perhaps I was the one who didn't want to face that I'd either put myself in danger or that I'd been acting paranoid.

But my gut had been right.

"Richard," I said again, eyes darting from his dark shape to my phone. I'd left it on the island near the fridge. I calculated the time it would take me to lunge for it, to dial the police, to call for help. My mind flitted to my options. Knife? Possibly. Running for the elevator? He'd get to me before I hit the front door. My fingers tightened around the beer bottle, grateful for any blunt object as I stared twenty-six years of horror movies in the face. My eyes watered, heart thundering. Finally, I asked, "Where is the receptionist?"

"Out" was all he said, mouth pulling wide in a slow, evil smile. There was something not quite human about the way his lips turned upward, almost as if he were borrowing the smile from the wide jaws of a panther.

My stomach rolled. I had to do something. I couldn't stand here numbly until he moved. In the flash of a few pulsing seconds, my memory paged through hundreds of hours of slashers, thriller novels, and murder podcasts searching for a solution.

Placate. The surviving victims had mollified their attackers.

"You look good." I smiled, keeping the tremor from my voice. I put on Maribelle's confidence like a mask, shifting into her skin. "How have things been in the surgical wards?" I asked, slowly shifting my weight to the balls of my feet. It wasn't yet wise to bolt, but I needed to be ready to run.

"Oh, you know," he said, rising from my corner chair with glacial slowness, "cutting and dicing, slashing and hacking, this and that."

An unfaltering smile remained on my face as I took a step

backward into the kitchen. I knew I was corning myself, but if I put the island between us, I might be able to create the space I needed to get to the door. I'd still have to make it to the stairwell and sprint from the building. And then down the empty streets of the warehouse district. And if there was no receptionist or security guard…

Richard was fit. I wasn't ready to stake my life on outrunning him.

Another backward step. Perhaps I could distract him. I fought to keep my voice level as I did my best to offer a charming, apologetic half-smile. "I'm sorry we didn't get to reschedule our date. Would you like to catch up now?"

His eyes shone black as if his pupils had swallowed his irises. His smile widened further, almost as if small strings were responsible for tugging it into the most sinister grin as he said, "You know how I found you?"

I swallowed as high, loud fear rang in my ears. My clammy palms nearly forced me to drop my beer bottle. I didn't know what kept me from trembling, aside from shock. He took another step forward. I mirrored it with a backstep.

"Do you know that little bookstore on Main Street? The one that always hangs those pride flags in the window? Guess whose smile I saw. Merit Finnegan, bestselling author of the *Pantheon* series, followed by the grinning face of the prostitute who stood me up. I just had to see it for myself."

It should have been the least of my worries, but a small part of me died at the word. No one shouted your alias for the world to hear with camaraderie on the brain. No one broke into your apartment in the middle of the night with good intentions. No one referred to sex workers as prostitutes unless they swung to hurt. I'd been doomed from the start, but now I knew: there was no way this night ended well.

I trained my face to remain calm. *Keep him talking,* the voice in my head screamed, clawing at the scraps of information that had been drilled into my brain. *Survivors humor their captors.* "I'm so sorry, Richard. I haven't been taking dates since I began writing. I've been busier than I could have imagined. I'm so blessed that my dating life was able to set me up—"

"I would have stopped then, you know."

I calculated the distance between myself and the knife block, only half listening as I tried to form a plan. My eyes drifted casually over it to see...

"Are you looking for these?" He made a sweeping gesture to the knives he'd set on the small table beside the corner chair. Renewed fear pulsed through me, filling me with deeper dread as each second passed. He'd preemptively collected anything I might use against him. He wasn't open to bonding. There would be no placating.

I marked each utensil as he continued. "Maribelle, Merit Finnegan, they were both lies. You're not real. Nothing about you is real. That's when it occurred to me that it didn't matter whether you're a whore. You were still a liar, Marlow Thorson."

My full name. The final, chilling nail in the coffin.

Our game had come to an end. My eyes darted. His teeth glistened.

He lunged in the same fraction of a beat it took for me to make a move. Rather than turn my back on him, I jumped forward and to the side toward the table of knives. Richard snarled and spun on me as I wielded my only weapon. I swung the beer bottle as hard as I could. It made contact, but he barely registered the blow. I lost my grip on the glass, and it shattered to the floor.

Each tooth in his grin remained manically feline as he glistened with feral delight. He dipped and picked up the shattered bottle. I dove for the knives. My knees smacked the marble with bruising impact, stealing my breath. I didn't have time to be consumed by the pain-fueled stars that filled my vision. I knocked the table to the side, its glassy surface shattering into ten thousand pieces as I wrapped my hand around the steak knife that clattered to the ground, gripping

64

it by the blade. I scarcely felt the spike of pain as it bit into my skin, struggling through the free-flowing blood to adjust my hold and find the hilt. I tightened my grip, distantly aware of a sharp, high crunch that sounded like blade on bone.

A guttural, animal scream tore through me.

The sound didn't come from pain but the sudden, horrible fear that erupted from my belly as hands wrapped around my calves and yanked me backward. The high squeak of flesh on marble rang through the apartment as he reeled me in like a fish. He grabbed my forearm and squeezed until the tendons became too useless to hold the blade. The knife clanged against the marble floor as fresh blood rained down around it. I whimpered against the hold and thrashed, desperate to remember something, *anything* helpful.

Richard wrapped his hands around my neck. He grunted, eyes bulging as he sank his gloved hands into me. His face turned red, forehead vein popping as vitriol and power coursed from him into the hands crushing my windpipe.

Rather than tear at his hands for release, my fingers flew for his ears. I tugged as hard and fast as I could on his sensitive extremities until he yelped in surprise. It scarcely bought me the time to draw a fresh breath before he recovered from my swipe. He raised a hand and hit me so hard my jaw nearly popped out of place. My ears rang. Pain and panic devoured me as my vision vignetted. Richard's malevolent shape towered over me. I rallied to claw for his eyes when he struck me again. I clung to the outer edges of consciousness like it was a metal bar lathered in oil. A vein in his forehead throbbed as he went in for the kill. This time when he wrapped his fingers around my neck, I scarcely had the ability to scratch at his arms.

My last thought before unconsciousness began to pull me under rang through my mind as clear as a bell:

Be sure to get skin under your fingernails so they can avenge your death.

Chapter Seven

S CRATCH. EVIDENCE. JUSTICE.

Rot in prison, motherfucker. Let my pretty, smiling face grace the news beside your disgusting mugshot as they announce your place on death row.

If I was going down, I'd drag him to Hell with me.

They were the last thoughts as the darkness closed in before...

Richard froze. His hands slackened slightly on my throat. I gasped for air as his eyes bulged like a guppy snatched from water. I was free the second his fingers flew to his own neck, clutching uselessly as he began to turn a violent shade of purple. I scrambled to get out from underneath him as fast as I could, hands gnawed and shredded by the shards of glass that littered the floor as my legs kicked out. Under any other circumstance, I would have watched him flop to his side and die on my living room floor. I would have stared at the violent criminal in a limp fetal position between the television and coffee table. If it had been anything else, I would have grabbed the steak knife and plunged it into him over and over and over until I knew he was gone.

But what I saw instead stole my every thought.

Shock replaced fear or victory or vengeance.

A strange glitter populated the space where Richard had

towered. The sparkle had to be stars from oxygen deprivation as I gaped. A bloodied hand flew to my neck to ensure
I was still getting air, as I'd surely lost my mind. The rippling
shape of a man stood just behind where Richard had been
only moments prior. The man's hand remained outstretched,
frozen as if he'd left it where Richard's head was meant to be.

Hard, golden eyes scanned the room. His gaze lifted to me
and snagged. Surprise punched through him like an electric
bolt as he held my eyes.

"Who are you?" I tried to ask, voice coming out hoarse
and raw as each word squeaked past the bruising on my
larynx. I was loosely aware of the hot blood on my neck as
my shredded hands continued to gush.

The man tilted his head, parting his lips to answer. He
knelt to bring himself closer. As he moved, I was hit by a
scent like the thieves' oil my mother used to smudge on my
temples when I was sick—frankincense and myrrh, bright
and overpowering spices. I tried to move farther away, but
he lifted a large hand. "How can you..." He blinked several
times before changing his tactic. "This is just a dream," he
said unconvincingly. The skin near his eyes went taut, face
strained with an array of emotions.

I shook my head as I fully examined him. Hercules may
as well have been in my apartment, except the air around
him shimmered, his eyes smoldered, and he was visibly pissed
at being here. Gold-brown hair, vibrantly gilded eyes, and
dressed for battle, with the burly, well-muscled frame to fit.
He'd stepped straight from literature in pale beige-and-white
leather into my living room. The shimmer behind him hadn't
dissipated—the pulsation of something my brain refused to
understand.

"Tell me who you are," I insisted.

His frown intensified. "You can't see me," he said.

The fuck I can't.

Metaphorical fingers tightened around my throat. My
eyes shot down to Richard, then up to the stranger. Looking

into his eyes was like looking at the sun, honey-bright retinas burning into mine as I demanded, "What did you do to him?"

"He was marked," the stranger said, voice thick with confusion. "I had him choke on his tongue...I...how can you...I shouldn't be telling you this. You shouldn't be asking. You shouldn't..." He looked around my room, eyes catching above my doorframe. "Shit."

"Who the hell are you!" I tried to yell past the barbed-wire scrape of my throat.

"Are those your sigils?"

My heart continued thundering with painful intensity. Adrenaline overpowered me, numbing me as it became too much for my body to handle. Though hazy vision, I followed his line of sight, but I saw nothing. "What sigils?"

"Did you do them, human? Did you put them up?"

"I..."

His face twisted into a snarl. "Listen, human, forget about tonight. Call the police. The man died while attacking you. It isn't even self-defense. Not really. You won't get in any trouble. I don't know who's visiting you, but..."

"Silas" came a smooth, familiar voice.

The stranger—the man he'd called Silas—went statue still. For the second time that evening, his lips pulled back into a growl. "Shit."

Caliban stepped out from the shadows. Tall, rippling, sterling, and breathtaking as I hadn't seen him in years. It had been so long since I'd looked into his face. He strode the line between gravity and indifference while looking between the stranger and Richard. I caught the quickly controlled flash of concern as his gaze went from Richard's still-purple face to me. His gaze returned to Silas before he said, "Thank you for taking care of my mark."

"*Your* mark?"

"Caliban," I rasped.

"Caliban?" Silas repeatedly uncertainly as he looked between me and my guardian. He took several steps backward.

"If these are your sigils, I didn't mean to interfere. I was just telling the human—"

Caliban ignored Silas the moment I spoke his name. He was at my side in three swift steps. He knelt and wrapped a strong arm around my back. Moss and rain and cypress washed over me like a low, cool cloud settling on the forest floor. I relaxed into it as if disappearing into a fairy tale, choosing fantasy over the pain, the blood, the nightmare in my living room. He rested a hand against my throat, sending a gentle tingle along the injury. The stranger's eyes widened.

"This is *your* human?"

Their exchange was little more than noise. Tears rimmed my eyes as I looked at Caliban's perfect, compassionate face. "Help me."

He waved the unwelcome man away. He didn't take his diamond eyes off me as he said with a clear, dismissive voice, "I owe you, Silas."

I didn't see the stranger leave. He didn't use the door. But the next thing I knew, he was gone. I was too disoriented to make sense of any of it.

I looked up into Caliban's face—the face of my guardian angel. I'd nearly forgotten how perfect he was; from the cut of his jaw to the sensuous curve of his mouth, he'd always looked like the prince from a fairy story. For years, I'd convinced myself that's all he was—a fairy tale.

I grit my teeth through the throbbing pain that still coursed through my hand as my blood gushed freely. I would need stitches, and I'd need them soon if I wanted to remain conscious. Still, I couldn't think of my cuts over my more pressing question. I let my eyes do the pleading as I spoke through sandpaper, saying, "But you... He..."

"Shh" came his gentle reply.

He scooped me up from where I rested on the floor and carried me to the island at the center of my kitchen. First, his fingertips pressed into my throat. A minty, soothing balm rushed through my raw passages before the throbbing ceased.

He kissed my sliced, bleeding palm, leaving a smear of blood across his lips before meeting my eyes once more. I looked from the crimson stain on his mouth to my hand only to see that the gash was gone. The world fell to staticky noise. I heard the sink running and idly felt the tug of a rag on skin as he cleaned the blood off me, but I was quite certain I'd died.

There was no other explanation.

My eyes drifted from Caliban's quiet attention and fixed on Richard's purple corpse. After several minutes, I had the sensation of floating and rested my head against Caliban's chest. If I'd died and gone to heaven, then I might as well enjoy it. Strong arms carried me from the kitchen to the bedroom. He lifted my bloodied shirt off over my head, and I raised my arms to let him. He tugged on my pants, waiting for me to lift my hips off the bed as he helped me out of the ruby-red remnants of the nightmare.

"I'll be back in a minute," he said quietly.

"Don't leave," I begged.

"I'm not going anywhere," he promised.

My eyes remained screwed, unblinking, on the open doorway as I struggled to discern where fact ended and fiction began. A hard, black pulse, like obsidian twinkling in an unheard shock wave, throbbed from the room beyond. The entire apartment moved against the shudder, iridescent stars gleaming against dark smoke as its tendrils drifted down the hall and into my room. After several moments, Caliban returned to my room. I realized I hadn't fully breathed until he entered. A headache took its cue upon my exhale.

I wanted to speak but had nothing to say.

"It will be like it never happened," he said. "He's gone."

I looked up at him, cursing myself for the helpless, kicked-puppy need that overtook me as I asked, "Where have you been?"

"You almost died," he said, voice pained.

I'd been attacked. I'd barely escaped death. A stranger had murdered my assailant and disappeared into thin air. A bomb made of dark, glistening shadow had erupted in my living room. But the only thing I wanted to know was why Caliban had left.

My head spun through glass and adrenaline and golden glitter as I sputtered, "What happened? Who was that man... Silas...?"

"Not who. What."

My expression rearranged to tell him I understood nothing.

"I've marked all those who've wronged you," he said. "Consider me protective. I can't control who answers the marks."

I stared into his star-bright face, begging this to be real. He was even more beautiful than I remembered him. From his strong chest to his gentle smile, he looked like he'd been chipped from the moon itself. I struggled to puzzle together the night's pieces. "Why did he come—Silas?"

Caliban looked away, lips in a tight line. "I did what I had to," he said.

"Couldn't you have helped me?" I wasn't sure why I asked, except that I'd missed him. Every night I'd come home and hoped he'd be there. Every night I...

"No" came his soft reply. "By the gods I wish I could have. I would have done so much more than make that slug suffocate on his tongue. I would have needed him to suffer, to beg your forgiveness before I gave him the execution he deserved. But you and I made a binding deal that I'm forced to honor until your last breath, Love. I can't do anything in your home without your consent."

My mind whirred. "But I..."

His fingers continued to move against me, calming me, grounding me. "You wouldn't have been able to ask me to kill him. Not when you couldn't speak. And even if you could have, you wouldn't have called on something you refuse to believe exists."

My shoulders rolled forward. I collapsed like a dying star as I shrank away from his statement. "But clearly I..."

"Clearly nothing. There are no technicalities with contracts like this." My hair was already behind my ears, but he tucked it again, an unconscious gesture in soothing, perhaps as much for him as it was for me. "Though I do wish it hadn't been Silas," he added with what might have been quiet regret.

I could have fought. I could have argued. But all I wanted was to touch him. I reached for him, asking, "Will you stay with me tonight?"

He continued the tender motion of brushing hair away from my face. "Of course I will. And in the morning, you can forget any of this ever happened."

How could I forget? There was a corpse in my living room. I'd spend the day in a police station. I'd have to call lawyers. Oh god, I'd have to call EG and explain that the projects were on hold. I'd need to tell my friends. "But Richard—"

It was as if he'd heard my thoughts. "All evidence of him is gone."

"How did you…" I decided the answer didn't matter. Part of me wanted to get up and see the wreckage of the living room for myself, but a stronger part of me needed to stay in bed. Whatever I saw would be something I either wouldn't understand or wouldn't trust. Even now, with Caliban holding me, it was easier to believe I was dreaming. The injuries were a hallucination, as no scratch remained. The attack was a nightmare. I was injury-free, which had to mean none of it had happened. Richard had been the worst sort of delusion.

I rolled toward Caliban in the dark, resting my head against his chest once more. He pressed another kiss to the crown of my head. The confusion, the panic, the chaos had died into the distant thrum of numbness. I lifted my hand to feel where the blood had dried in my hair.

"Why now?" I asked.

He frowned down at me.

"Why can I see you now after all these years? You said I couldn't see you again..."

"No," he corrected with gentle solemnity. "You said you didn't *want* to see me again. It's a gray area, and one I'm taking advantage of right now. There is an absence of wants in the moment of death. Rules are every bit as important as their loopholes."

My thoughts tipped and tilted. I was already numb from the trauma, disoriented from the insanity, and still flooded with survival endorphins. I struggled to make sense of heads or tails, fixating on one word alone.

Death.

"Do you want me to get you in the shower?" he asked, frowning down at the quickly drying blood on my hands.

I didn't move.

"Marlow..." His patient sound was pained. He cupped my cheek, waiting for me to look up at him. "You're in shock."

His words stole my breath like a punch to the gut. I screwed my eyes against the shadows to stare into the face that looked back. "Were you there?"

The rush of earth and amber and the freshness at the core of creation brushed against my hair as he breathed out. Chills rose over my cheek, my back, my chest. He held me closer as he said, "How could I stay away?"

"You were there the whole time, and you didn't help?"

He tightened his hold. "I know you can't understand the forging absolution of agreements, but—"

"You were going to let me die," I said, clinging to the finality of the word like a lightning rod. I didn't care what storm struck in its aftermath.

I heard the patience tinge with the barest color of frustration as he said, "I know you don't understand when I talk about verbal contracts. And right now, you're in shock. But Marlow, I've never let you down. Believe me when I tell you that even though it couldn't be my hands, I moved mountains to keep you safe. I've—"

"You would have stood there and watched me die."

He pulled away from me as he tried to put a hand beneath my chin, saying, "Humans have nothing like the sovereignty of binding contracts in your realm. They're oaths, Marlow, and that transcends time and place. There's no—"

I jerked away from his touch.

"Silas saved me. That *stranger* saved me. Not you."

He grimaced at the name. There was an authority to his voice, a demand as he spoke. "Then give me free rein in your home, Love. Let me into your life. If it's what you want, open it up to me."

"Get out."

His eyes flashed, patience becoming anger as his fingers tightened around me. "If you want me, then you're going to have to say so."

I sat up. "Fuck that. Get out, Caliban. Get out, and don't come back. How could I—"

His mouth worked against words left unspoken. A muscle in his jaw feathered. He kept his hand gentle, though his fingers were clenched with emotion as he said, "Don't give commands out of anger. For the love of the gods, I wish I could explain to you—"

Tears began to spill as I said, "There's nothing to explain. You would have let me die. Leave. Leave, and don't come back."

"You don't—"

"I do!" I cried, words trembling as all the fear and desperation and horror from the night coursed through me along with the shuddering anger. "I've wanted freedom from this for twenty years. I mean it, Caliban. Don't come back."

The moment hung between us, suspended in time.

I saw his face, felt his final intake of air, watched every unspoken word flicker.

It was the surface of a lake fracturing in early winter. I could almost see ten thousand cracks as they broke between his silver eyes. He closed them, blowing out the last, slow

74

breath of air. After a heartbreaking eternity, he slid off the bed and pressed another kiss to my forehead. It was with cool finality that he said, "You've told me before, and I know I need to listen, even if you're one hell of a habit to break. A life with me isn't what you want. I'm sorry I couldn't be there for you in the way that you needed me."

"Caliban!" I shouted half in hate, half in desperation.

He stepped into the shadows before giving me the opportunity to fight. When the scent of cypress left the room, the shock left with it. The spell that had been holding me together shattered and I rolled into the pillow, screaming into the feathers as I sobbed until there was neither salt nor water left in my being. For what could have been an hour or what might have been years, I repeated his name over and over again. I wanted to yell at him. To fight with him. To throw things. I wanted to be angry, to be held, to be talked down from the cliff like he'd done so many times. My pleas were incomprehensible as I begged him to return.

And somewhere between the heaving, the crying, and the shuddering, my body gave out, and I fell into a deep, exhausted sleep.

Chapter Eight

WERE COPS ONLY HOT IN MOVIES? I WAS CERTAIN I'D NEVER met a policeman who hadn't looked like an NPC. Perhaps it was more comforting this way. Bland, unremarkable faces. Forgettable, business-casual slacks and shirts. One even had a mustache so cliché that it felt like it had to be a joke. They were kinder qualities than being forced to speak with a runway model when being asked to give a statement.

Two detectives interviewed me on my couch while investigators bustled about my unit as if it were an active crime scene. I was told it was standard, but I knew it wasn't. Perhaps if I hadn't drowned myself in crime shows during my depressive episodes, I would have believed their easy lies. Still, I gave them free rein of my apartment without a warrant.

What could I possibly tell them? What could they possibly find?

Oh, yes, the man you're looking for? The one who murdered our receptionist? It's a man named Richard. He tried to kill me. How do I know him? Please put it on the records that he was a former client from when I was an escort in a country where sex work remains criminalized. Oh, yes, my blood pooled everywhere near the demolished table. There was a bloodied knife, injuries, a corpse... Who took his body? Well, a black pulse of shadow did. How did I beat him? I didn't. I'm meant to believe he choked on his own tongue thanks to a sparkly stranger who came from nowhere. How am I not injured? I was. Never fear, it's gone. Something about sigils. Don't worry about it.

Aside from my shattered coffee table—a clumsy accident—my apartment was spotless. They'd frowned at the crystalline shards, but after I'd allowed them a sweep of the unit, they were satisfied that the only victim in Apartment 12 had been my furniture. I promised to clean it up but had little to offer them by way of statement.

Someone had put the security cameras on a harmless loop, repeating hours of mundane nothingness everywhere save for the parking garage. If it hadn't been for the footage of me pulling into the lot, I might have lacked an alibi for the window when the receptionist had gone missing. Given the horror on my face and genuine sorrow that I would never again see the wide-eyed girl who loved *Fire and Swords,* the police left me alone to process. They told me that security detail would be put on the building while they continued to investigate the case and left a card on my island, should I think of any other details.

The detectives did not contact me again.

But as the police left, I knew one thing for certain.

I had not imagined this. No fabrication of my daydreams or nightmares would have brought the boys in blue to my doorstep. No detective would have taken my statement if I had just been crazy. They were investigating a murder. My coffee table was shattered. I may not have a wound on my hand or a dead man in my living room, but this was real.

And if this was real...

I had to speak to Caliban. Urgency flooded me every bit as intensely as the fight-or-flight that had kept me clawing to life the night prior. A murder had happened in my building. A golden stranger had come from nowhere to make the man choke on his tongue. My bruised larynx was fine. My body was whole. But my head was full of memories that cast a new light entirely, and only one person had the answers I needed.

I did little more than gnaw on baby carrots, shuffle listlessly from bed to the living room, and stare at the empty space above my door for three days, day and night. I bought a tacky black light from a gift shop to examine the frame as if I were a forensic scientist looking for fingerprints. With a flair for the dramatic, I waited until midnight, held a candle to the outline, and searched for any sign of a sigil. An intrusive thought tempted me to cut open my veins and smear the evidence of my life over the threshold just to try *something*.

He would return. He had to. And when he came back this time, I would know he was real. I'd have so much to ask. So much to say. So much to apologize for.

Days bled into weeks.

Tiny green buds revealed themselves on the trees as the coldest season abandoned the city.

The clouds broke apart; blue and warmth leeched into the city as spring turned into the first hints of summer.

I wrote no new pages. I rarely answered emails. I'd ghosted Nia and Kirby, save for double tapping the videos they sent, giving the message a little heart so they knew I'd seen it. To avoid being alone with my thoughts, I let my laptop roll from episode to episode until I'd finished all eight seasons of a medical drama. When I wasn't mindlessly watching television, I was googling "imaginary friends," from the zanna of Romanian folklore and the hidden people of Icelandic lore to the tulpa created through one's concentrated belief. My search engine was inundated with fairy tales and folklore.

With each day that passed, my anxiety grew thicker until it felt as real as any living thing. It was a flowering vine as physical and tangible as the summer gardens that lined the riverbanks. The supernatural vine's tendrils spread out, filling my apartment, releasing its poisonous mist from its blossoms into every nook and crevice of my home. I inhaled the wounds, the confusion, the loss the moment I awoke and suckled on it like I was nursing a wound until I fell asleep. I couldn't keep living like this. Insanity or not, I had to do something. If I couldn't get any work done, then I could at least put my skills to work and do some research.

I'd gone weeks without seeing Caliban before. I could do it again, even though my skin itched, my legs bounced, and my toes tapped against every surface. I'd figure out how to bring him back before too much time passed. I'd fix this. Soon it would be a horrible memory.

The conviction of my wishful thinking did not sway reality.

After a month, I was so irritable I couldn't write a single word. Spring waxed into summer. The notifications on my inbox surpassed ninety-nine, then added a little plus sign to let me know that they would no longer be informing me of my negligence.

On the second month, I buried myself in library books, first from the public library, then from the university's archives. I shouldn't have had access, but I was connected. I'd brushed in, unannounced, to visit a very flustered dean of admissions, who'd ushered me to the librarian who oversaw the delicate texts covered in plastic and kept in air-tight rooms with low lighting so as not to damage ancient acquisitions. The librarian was excited for a chance to dissect lore for a bestselling author on fictional mythology. She chatted my ear off while I paged through text after text, then offered me her private number so I could come back day in and day out.

Figuring out where to begin was a true stab in the dark.

I began my needle-in-the-haystack research with shadow people, which yielded no results. The term was a descriptor for another phenomenon altogether and could be psychological, malevolent, friendly, or benign. I scrunched my face against what I knew of mythology and launched into North American lore, opting for geographical anchors. Combing through online ledgers and digitized texts in my evenings yielded little results, particularly as I didn't know what I was looking for.

The librarian confessed that she'd read my novels and was

very hopeful that my localized research on North America meant that the subsequent installment might be on indigenous lore. I'd given a canned nonanswer, ever the politician. I hadn't decided what the fourth book would entail. I'd been given a sizable advance on the promise that there would be several more in the series. But as it stood, I could barely get through book three.

Her guesses on my reason for invading the archives ceased after I'd shown up a fourth, then a fifth, then a sixth day.

I'd frowned up at her after she'd spent an hour quietly overseeing my studies of her sacred texts. They'd made me wear gloves before delicately handling the loose parchments, but I continued to find nothing of interest. I tried to make the most of having someone breathe down my neck. Looking up over the aged, fragile piece of paper in the basement archives, I asked, "If I say *sigil*, what's the first thing that comes to your mind?"

The librarian mirrored my curious expression. She sank into her chair, eyes moving up and to the side as she scanned her memories. "You're looking for resources on sigils? Have you spoken to any practitioners?"

I gave her a quizzical look.

"Sigils could be about anything. Wards, deities, angels, demons."

I shuddered at a few of the words in her list. My religious upbringing triggered an unintentional flinch at the thought of fire-and-brimstone sermons on angels and demons. I wondered if she could count the creases in my forehead as my confusion intensified.

Unbothered, she said, "You should be looking within the witch community. They might have more resources than our library."

"Witches?" I repeated, struggling not to make a smartass comment about Halloween. At least she hadn't suggested I speak to a priest.

The librarian nodded. She pulled out her phone and sent

me the contact information of her friend who performed guided psychic meditations, as well as the usernames of three of her favorite witches on social media. She implied that, given my reputation in the mythological community, I might be able to swing for the fences and speak with someone high in the echelon.

I looked at her skeptically. Images of pointed hats and cauldrons and crows peeled my mouth into an apologetic half-smile. "I generally prefer to keep my research...academic."

Disappointment flickered through her. She weighed me before saying, "You can't study something while looking down your nose at it."

She had a point, and I was desperate. That said, I'd done so much to distance myself from religion and belief that the idea of dipping my toes into spirituality made me cringe. Still, if imaginary friends were real, maybe witches were, too. So, off I set.

The librarian's initial contact proved useless, which did little to earn my confidence in the witch-identifying community. The woman gave me a tarot reading over a video chat, assessed my aura, and informed me that I was destined for greatness. I offered a deadpan thanks and sent payment via the site she'd listed on the bottom of the screen.

A second self-proclaimed practitioner consulted the Prime Creator, rang a few bells for a sound cleansing, then cleared my chakras before asking for fifty dollars. I wasn't religious, per se, but I also wasn't entirely convinced that a white woman from Nebraska was qualified to be the authority on chakras.

They were making it hard to keep an open mind.

I stared at my phone for a long while before calling the third contact on my list. I looked at my reflection in the dark, blank screen, sighing before I set off on what would surely be another fifty bucks wasted. I hadn't been given a number for the final contact, only a Skype username. The mindlessly upbeat chimes rang for five seconds, then ten, then fifteen. A rather frazzled woman with the outgrown roots of blue-green hair in a hooded sweatshirt and with a toddler on her hip bloomed into view as she answered the phone.

"Hi, yes, what is it?"

I was caught entirely off guard. It wasn't the metaphysical stars, curtains, and incense I'd been expecting. She made no attempt at a calm, soothing voice. I blinked through my disorientation, rallying as I got down to business.

"I'm sorry," I said. "Before we get started, I'm not sure how to pronounce your name. I got your information from—"

"It's Xuân, more or less pronounced like the bird: swan. I used to go by an Americanized name but then thought: Fuck it. If they can learn to say Joaquin Phoenix, then they can figure it out. And you? Are you calling from Pearl's school? I left a message with the secretary that she wasn't feeling well."

"Does your kid's school video-call you?" I asked. It was a symptom of rarely thinking before I spoke. I kicked myself for sounding snarky.

"Yes," she said to my surprise. "I didn't like people being able to get a hold of me all hours of the day, so I got rid of my phone. If someone wants me, they can send an email, or look me in the eye when they talk to me. Welcome to my computer. Now, what do you want?"

I struggled to remember why I'd thought calling her had seemed like a good idea. "I'm reaching out because I need advice on…how to see something. I was told to ask a practitioner. Your information was—"

Without waiting for me to finish, she asked, "Have you meditated yet?"

I nodded. "I did a guided meditation—"

"Pearl! Stop it!" she scolded the off-screen child. Xuân continued to bounce the baby on her hip as she said, "No, not a guided session. Use your clairs. Try to look through the veil."

When I looked startled, she gave me a tired expression and approached the screen. My phone pinged as she forwarded a guided meditation called *Piercing the Veil for Beginners*.

"Here's what you're going to do." Xuân cleared her throat. I was quite certain that she was keeping her child off-screen by holding out her foot while the baby continued to vie for her attention. "Light a candle and picture a dial. Like, a radio dial. You're going to watch that volume knob turn all the way up in your mind's eye as if you're making music blast, okay?"

"What does that do?"

"It should help in turning up your clairabilities. Give it a shot, and call me back if you fuck it up." Xuân disconnected before I could ask further questions.

The religion-resistant parts of me revolted as I lit candles, played relaxing music, and sat cross-legged in front of my door, looking directly at the spot Silas had glanced at so many nights ago. I told myself that this was nothing like praying. This was different. This was meditation.

But it didn't feel different.

I did my best to relax. I closed my eyes and pictured a dial.

Nothing happened. The sigil became another god to pray to, something that neither existed nor answered when I called, no matter how badly I needed it. It was childhood all over again. And just like when I was a kid, no matter how ignored I felt, I didn't give up.

May became June, July, then August. Time faded into the final days of summer.

"Come on, fucking come *on*," I'd pleaded, frustration obliterating any hope I had at peaceful meditation. If I had conjured him from my imagination, then I would have been able to poof him into existence now. The longer he stayed away, the more convinced of his reality I became and the more desperately I needed to speak with him.

A man had vanished. There were multiple invisible things out there. I'd spent years with him. And the answers were at my fingertips—or, they should have been, had I not commanded him to stay away. But if I could get him back, I could fix this. And then together we could cast everything— every odd comment, every coincidental bout of good luck, every curious childhood memory, every odd piece of my life—under a new lens.

I cleared my mind. I stared. I meditated. I read. I researched. I reached out. I texted. I scanned. I watched documentaries. I cannibalized books on ghosts and fae and curses and witches. I pored over texts. I video-chatted. I scoured forums. I filled notebooks with deranged excerpts and sketches and theories. I developed deep, purple smudges from sleeplessness. I lost four pounds in my reluctance to eat. I sobbed.

But no matter how hard I cried, Caliban did not return.

Chapter Nine

A MAN CALLED RICHARD MONTAGUE…"
"Oh my god!" I waved a hand at the dinner party of three. The smell of fresh-cut onion, hot peppers, and the spice of stir-fried meat filled the home and accompanied the static hum of the television. My head snapped up at the mention of the familiar name. Nia squeezed Darius's arm to silence him while the tacos sat on the table, untouched. It had taken invitations, then coercion, then threats before I finally agreed to abandon my cave of solitude for a get-together. They'd been kind to invite me to their house in the suburbs, and I'd given them every reason to regret it. I sprinted to the counter to fetch the remote and cranked the evening news while the reporter showed the face of my attacker.

"Who is it?" Nia whispered behind me.

I motioned for her to wait, and I knew she would.

I stood in front of the TV as if the anchor were speaking to me alone. As soon as they flashed to footage outside of Richard's now-abandoned residence, I whipped around to Nia.

"Write down the address! Oh my god, write down the address!" My hand moved on instinct to the piece of paper I'd kept tucked in my back pocket in the months following the attempt on my life, but I would not mar it with his information.

She fetched her phone from her back pocket in hasty compliance while her husband grumbled something about the tacos getting cold. I remained glued to each word as if my life depended on it. The story ended, and I released the breath I'd been holding. I punched the downward-facing arrow repeatedly once the anchor transitioned into a fluff piece about the high gas prices.

"What is it?" Nia asked.

"I knew him," I said.

"From..." she prompted.

She knew of my previous line of work and knew I wouldn't be comfortable talking about it in front of her husband. If Darius couldn't be patient enough to wait for tacos, then I didn't have the energy to explain my years of escorting to him. To be fair, he was a good man—one of the few I tolerated, particularly now that I considered him my brother-in-law. He'd probably be fine with my covert career, but the fact remained, it was my story to share. He loved his wife deeply, and for that alone, he received a free pass for any and all minor faux pas. I nodded, and she understood.

Nia Foster had forced her way into my life like a bulldozer, and I'd let her.

She'd seen my rather public fallout with my family in the wake of the first *Pantheon* book. My mother's novel-length rejection of my blasphemous lifestyle and romanticization of heathen gods on her publicly available social account had made the news. It was a little less dramatic than a six o'clock anchor reading about my attempted murder, but a few online magazines had taken screenshots of my mother's social media posts about the destination of my immortal soul and the tearful videos I'd made in the heat of my emotional state as I'd reacted to my abandonment.

But as P.T. Barnum once said, "There's no such thing as bad publicity."

My fuckups had captured an audience, whether

prospective book-buyers, opinionated pundits, or the online community who I'd come to know and love as friends.

Nia had sent me a direct message informing me that she was my sister now.

I'd left her messages on read as days turned into weeks, watching the updates roll in as she spoke to me as if we were family. She told me things like how my new brother-in-law was fixing the sink, how my new mother loved my book and spent their entire barbecue telling the neighbors about it, how my new uncle was also pansexual and was very proud of me, and sent me a few funny pictures of cute animals with the hopes that I might see them and smile. She told me that we shared a city. She sent her messages into the void, never expecting an answer. Day after day she checked in on me until one vulnerable day, six months after the release of the first *Pantheon* novel, tears free-flowing and in the fetal position on the kitchen floor, I opened the thread and messaged her back.

She'd won the battle against my reluctance to let anyone in, and one chip at the stone of my heart at a time, she'd become my family.

I looked at my sister now and the phone glowing in her hand. "Can you text it to me?"

Nia's mouth twisted into a corner as she looked at her phone, then up to me. Her face shadowed under the kitchen lighting as she tilted her head, no longer interested in food as a much darker question consumed her. She was too smart to believe that I had innocent intent. "Why do you need his address?"

"I just do," I said.

The Fosters and I had made plans to make the most of summer while it lasted. I'd planned for us to sit outside, sipping beers and playing card games. But though I remained physically present through what remained of the meal, my mind was elsewhere. I ate Darius's take on Mexican food with polite enthusiasm, but Nia knew the instant the story came on the news that she'd lost me.

Her husband relaxed once he'd eaten, carrying on happy conversation about a sports team that I didn't care about. His pleasant voice accompanied us through dinner, allowing me to retreat into silence as my mind raced, ignoring him completely. No matter how much I loved Nia and liked the man she'd married, I couldn't bring myself to care about football even in the best of times. These were not the best of times.

He asked about dessert, but she went in for a hug instead, saying, "I know you have to get going."

"Thanks, Nia," I murmured.

"Don't be stupid" was all she said.

✦

I considered myself intelligent most of the time.

I'd been a good student. I'd developed the social intelligence necessary to navigate complex situations, whether playing chameleon when on a client's arm or trying to be cool at a hipster coffee shop. I was something of a wordsmith. But no amount of education or savvy had prevented me from barreling toward what would undoubtedly be a very poor choice.

Perhaps I should have gone home and collected myself.

No, I *definitely* should have waited and formulated a plan before launching into action. Still, when the cab driver asked for an address, I repeated the one glowing from my phone screen. He'd happily complied, pointing the taxi south. It was a farther drive than I'd anticipated, and a far heftier cab fee than I was used to seeing. He eyed me as if I might bolt, but I handed him my card with a confident smile, perhaps hoping to convince us both. I compensated him well in a tip for the drive he'd have to make back to the city. He thanked me heartily as he let me out onto the cold street with nothing but yellow police tape to stop me.

I pulled out the folded piece of paper that had become a staple of my back pocket and examined the complex shape within the circle. It might have been an oversized arrow with acute angles folding in on one side, save for the proportions. If the circle had been a clock, its tips would have hit the three o'clock, six o'clock, and ten o'clock. A pointed eye at its center drew the attention, somewhat like the evil-eye ward I'd seen on many a necklace and bracelet. The final piece, puncturing the arrow and plunging into the eye, was a flame where the fletching should be at precisely the twelve o'clock position.

The sigil.

The third witch had been right. She hadn't needed fancy bells or whistles or payment. She hadn't made a theatrical show of hums or chants. She'd bounced the toddler on her hip, sent me a link, and hung up. Truth needed no frivolity. It had been all I'd needed.

In the absence of crystals and tarot readings and the Prime Creator, I'd meditated and failed spectacularly. I couldn't clear my thoughts. I couldn't focus. I couldn't relax. And so I continued on my fruitless endeavors. I tried and failed, and tried, and failed and tried. With an inexplicable tenacity, tinged with desperation for something to work, I attempted every day for nearly an hour until one day I opened my eyes and...there it was on my wall.

It had stolen my breath.

It was beautiful and terrifying and filled me with a roil of complex emotions, all questions with dissatisfying answers. The shapes, the lines, the arrow's feather-like fletching.

Was I supposed to be happy? I guessed so. I was pleased that I'd found it, of course.

Should I be scared? Maybe. The sigil certainly didn't look friendly.

Did I have a right to be angry? Perhaps. It had been painted above my door without my knowledge or consent, after all.

I looked up from the elaborate shape scrawled on lined paper to the house.

I possessed only two clues. The sigil and the knowledge that the man who'd tried to kill me had been marked. The psycho killer's home was my best hope at finding answers.

I'd expected a police presence at the long-dead Richard's home, but the neighborhood was void of any sights or sounds of life. I folded the sigil and tucked it back into my pocket, then snuck around the house only to find the doors locked.

I didn't really have a contingency plan for locked doors. The man was dead, after all.

The ground-floor windows were also, unsurprisingly, locked. Unfortunately for those who wished to deter breaking and entering, I was both acrobatically inclined and clinically insane. The second was perhaps more pertinent as I clutched the rainspout with my hands and knees, shimmying toward the gutter on the back of the late, great Richard's house. I'd come this far, after all. I wasn't about to leave without exhausting all of my options.

Fortunately, given his surgical career, the man was loaded. This meant the man had not cut corners on his home. His rainspout was secured down at every possible joint and made of the sort of reinforced metal that would matter only if the sky were raining bullets. I hadn't climbed rock walls since college. Despite my muscle memory, I had little to no grip strength.

"Don't be a chicken," I grunted to myself, forcing resilience where none existed.

I was seconds away from plummeting to a broken ankle at best and broken back at worst before I flailed for the second-story balcony. It was so close. I tightened my knees on the gutter, fixing my sneakers on the tiny grip afforded by the joints, and grabbed the balcony's rods with both hands at once, trust-falling into the second floor.

Shit.

I'd fucked up.

Climbing was easy compared to pulling myself up. I had no muscle mass in my chest or arms. I groaned as I hooked my elbow around a bar and swung my knee up onto the barest sliver of ledge. I would have taken my sweet time grumbling, complaining, and bitching, if a neighbor's light hadn't flown on. The adrenaline gave me the boost I needed. I scurried over the railing and flattened myself on the porch until the light went off, the neighbor's curiosity presumably satiated when they saw nothing.

And now, the moment of truth. I wrapped my fingers around the handle to the sliding glass door. Much to my relief, the second-floor balcony was unlocked.

The moment I crossed the threshold into Richard's house, I was hit with an inexplicable sensation. It was as thick as stepping into a cloud of pea soup. I blinked against it as if I'd submerged myself through a physical wall.

But my eyes adjusted to see…nothing.

I couldn't explain the heaviness in my chest. My muscles tensed. My body went into primal survival as all my senses urged me to flee. But the house was quiet. The room was vacant. Nothing was wrong.

Stop it, I chastised myself. *Of course, you're afraid of the man's house. He tried to kill you. But he's dead. He can't hurt you. Now grow a pair and calm the hell down.*

But I couldn't calm down. My hands shook as I tiptoed through the home.

There was an eerie sterility to his house, even in the shadows. Everything was reminiscent of a showroom, as if no one had ever lived here. If it hadn't been for the evidence tags in yellow that intermittently dotted the residence, there would have been no reason for me to believe that a human had ever stepped foot in this house. The furniture was too perfect. The floors were too clean. The pictures on the wall were too perfectly spaced. Everything was in monochromatic shades of black, white, and gray. If I hadn't known he was a psychopath before entering his home, this would have confirmed it. I paused at a single picture to stare at the stock photo of a happy family of models smiling back at me.

Oh, yeah. This guy was definitely nuts.

My guts twisted, muscles tensing as my heart raced uncomfortably. It continued to pick up speed as if the erratic organ knew something I didn't. I should be relaxing now that I'd confirmed beyond a shadow of a doubt that the space was vacant. I was being stupid. I was being irrational. I should be brave.

But bravery was rarely in the cards for me. Stupidity, however...

I debated turning on the lights, but wisdom won out. I was sure someone would call the cops if a curious neighbor spied evidence of someone snooping through an active crime scene. Instead, I turned on the flashlight on my phone and began to pick my way through the house's blue-black shadows, every forward step filling me with thicker dread. I followed the feeling like a thick mist as I wandered down the stairs and through the late surgeon's home. I paused at a closed door. I couldn't explain why, but a sinking gravity told me this was the entry to his basement.

The man is dead, I repeated to myself. *Don't be afraid of a dead man's basement and squiggles on the wall, you coward.*

The antagonistic pit in my stomach urged me once more to run. It told me to get out of the house. It begged me to grab for the front door, to tear into the yard, to sprint down the street until I could flag down a car.

If the fear was growing closer, then so were the answers.

I opened the door and peered into a solid black rectangle.

I swallowed and checked for a light switch. Yes, if I shut the door behind me, I could flick on the lights so the neighbors wouldn't see. I lifted my phone to the wall, heart thundering so hard that it caused my hand to shake. I forgot to breathe as I took a single step into the basement.

He's dead, I reminded myself. *There's no one here. He's dead.*

I eased the door closed as the light switch flickered with an audible buzz. The fluorescent light blinked once, then twice as it flooded the space below me. A large cement floor with a single drain in the middle was the only thing I could see.

I took one step down.

Run! Run, run, run! whined the voice within me.

I shoved the voice down with two invisible hands, then took another step.

A sturdy workbench dotted with yellow evidence markers populated my view as I got lower and lower. The thrumming in my ears was so loud that I wasn't sure if I could hear someone even if they were in the room screaming my name. My head spun, stars dancing in the center of my vision before I realized I'd been holding my breath. I took a steady breath in as I finished the descent and made my way to the center of the room.

What did I plan to do here? Meditate?

It had taken me weeks to comfortably settle in, relax, clear my mind, and see through the veil, as Xuân had called it, even in the comfort of my own home.

This room was wrong. The walls were flat and glistened with the strange high-gloss enamel of waterproofing. Deep below the antiseptic scents of bleach and paint ran an undercurrent of iron and rust. It was too bright for such a small space. And with each new observation, the balloon of dread swelled until it reached carrying capacity.

A sensation like ten thousand centipedes crawled from the floor up my spine and urged me up the stairs. I gave myself over wholly to the fear, bathing in the tingling dread as I conceded to its pleas. I'd had enough. I turned on my heel and sprinted to the top step, hand flying for the handle. I turned it and met instant resistance.

My eyes flared wider than they'd ever been before as I sucked in a breath. I looked down at the keyhole where a smooth surface should have been.

"Fuck!" I shouted at the locked door. I rattled the knob several times, then banged my palm against the barrier in quick, helpless succession. I twisted it time and time again until my hand pinked against the metal. My jaw nearly popped as I ground my teeth, panic and fury striking like lightning.

"No!" I cried out. I rested my forehead against the door for the barest of moments while I shoved every feeling, every fear, into an airtight box within myself. I couldn't panic. I couldn't cry. I needed to find a way out.

But I was allowed to be angry.

Of course, this psychopath would have installed a door set to lock upon closure.

"It's okay," I said to the empty room as I slowly rotated from the door, facing the staircase, the workbench, the single drain at the room's center. I forced myself to voice every thought as I soothed the caged animal that clawed within me. "It's fine. No one is here. I have time. Richard is gone. No one is coming for me. I can figure this out."

I immediately looked to my phone but knew before my eyes hit the corner of the screen that there would be a flat line where service was meant to show perfect bars. I'd expected it, but it didn't make it any easier. The thick cement walls canceled out even the strongest of city signals.

I forced myself to descend the stairs. The police had already been here. They'd found every earthly horror. There couldn't be anything bad…which also meant if there were any tools or keys, they would have bagged them for evidence.

"Marlow." I tried speaking to myself as if I were my own friend. "You can do this. You've been through the worst things that can happen to a person, and you've survived. Everything has an answer, and you'll find it."

But my parental voice lacked believability. Bile rose in me as I moved away from the door, stepping deeper into the basement. Maybe there'd be a small glass window I could break and scramble out of. I crossed to the vacated workbench, searching for a tool, a clue, for something. Maybe…

My breath caught. My heart stopped. I froze as I caught movement from the corner of my eye.

I spun on my heels and gaped at what I saw.

94

I tilted my chin down, staring into the messy hair, the pale face, the too-wide, Cheshire-cat smile of an inhumane child.

I choked on the chaotic nightmare, the hallucination, the impossibility.

The cup of my insanity had tipped over, violently splashing into every aspect of my life. I was alone. I'd been trapped in frantic solitude between four walls, a drain, and a single bench. There had been nowhere for a kid to hide.

I shook my head against the horrendous apparition as something clicked within me. Hallucination or not, I recognized the toothy, feline grin. Several months prior it had been burned into my mind by the now-dead man who'd grinned in my living room. I gaped in horror at the figment. I summoned courage, therapy, psychiatry appointments, and wasted hours of grounding exercises as I addressed the child.

"Please don't be real" was all I could say. I'd spent months convincing myself everything was true. Now, I needed to be wrong.

Four feet tall, waifish thin, and in little more than a potato stack stood a beautiful, terrible ghoul. He positively sparkled as he said, "My, don't humans say the funniest things."

I locked onto the enormous, sky-blue eyes and stumbled backward. There was nowhere to go.

I lifted my hands as if to fight him off, demanding, "Who are you?"

"You smell delicious," the little boy said, eyes twinkling. "What is that smell? So good, so good… What a flavor, what a flavor…"

He was real.

I was in my apartment all over again, helpless, looking for knives that weren't there, wishing for a phone even if it didn't work, knowing I couldn't make it to the door in time to escape. The tornado of déjà vu whipped me in its violent winds until I was so dizzy, so nauseous I could scarcely breathe. Except, at least in my apartment, I'd known my enemy.

I had no frame of reference for the kindergarten night-mare that faced me now.

"Oh!" He gasped with boyish wonder, smile widening until it was bigger than his face. His teeth seemed to sharpen to a point as he looked at me. "Here I thought I wouldn't be fed any longer after ten years of meals…and now my food can see me. What a delightful dessert. So delightful."

I skidded backward until I slammed against cold cement. A sickly-sweet smell rolled off him, like the sugar and flesh of an infected wound. I searched for something familiar, something that made sense. The Cheshire boy looked no older than six and no younger than six thousand. There was a terrible ancientness to his bright, childish voice. The corners of his mouth reddened as if scabbed from cracking, breaking, and bleeding as his lips pulled far beyond his ears. The fluorescent light overhead flickered as if the very wiring in the home knew I was doomed. Though he stood a head and shoulders shorter than me, I knew that I would not survive him.

"Tell me who you are," I gasped again.

He clasped his arms behind his back and took a step to the side, then another. He eyed me all the while as he said, "I think you know."

"Who?" I asked again, though the question was useless. The answer didn't matter. I was going to die.

"Call us legion, for we are many." He winked and giggled with the high, bright twinkle of a death bell. "You're just our type. How kind that my host sent a treat, even in death."

"Stay back," I said, voice quivering. I raised my hands uselessly as the little boy advanced.

The world screeched to a halt on its axis at his reply.

"No," said the child, aquamarine eyes glinting with preda-tory glee, "I don't think I will."

Three things happened at once. I crossed my forearms over my face to brace for impact, squeezing my eyes shut. The boy lunged. And a sound—a loud, resonant clanging—cut through the basement.

He had taken less than a half-step toward me before a flash of blinding, glittering light flooded the basement. The brilliant sheen was scarcely recognizable between my tightly shut lids. The child cried out as the high, metallic ring of a sword pierced the air. My arms folded, hands shielding my eyes from the white light as a sizzle and pop bounced off the walls of the room.

Then it stopped. The only noise was the explosive sound of my heart in my ears.

I lowered my hands the moment the blinding passed and saw a tall, muscled figure standing just above the drain in the center of the basement. My eyes widened with recognition. We locked eyes for a horrified moment.

"Silas?" I gasped.

"You can't be fucking serious."

Chapter Ten

"WHY ARE YOU HERE?" CAME THE BOOM OF HIS STINGING demand.

A sharp wave of thieves' oil and spice flooded the space where the infection had festered moments before. The pulp from where the cat-like child had stood only seconds ago oozed slowly toward the drain at the center of the room. Aquamarine dripped where crimson blood should have been.

I shook my head, mind tumbling, heart thumping in the cage of my chest. All I could do was beg. I looked at Silas, eyes pleading as I asked, "Can you help me get out?"

A muscle in his jaw flexed. Through clenched teeth, he said, "You shouldn't be here!"

"What was that?" I panted. My eyes darted between the turquoise liquid and the man responsible for its demise.

His jaw ticked once more in thinly controlled temper.

"Silas!" I demanded. "You have to help me."

"Stop saying my name," he hissed.

The skin around his eyes went taut. For the first time, I noticed the sword clenched in his fist. It was how he'd taken out the cat-like boy, and I'd been too horrified to look. I tried to remember if he'd been holding or wearing a weapon on our first encounter, but too much of that night mixed like swirling paint. I only remembered Silas reaching his hand in a way that seemed to go *into* Richard's skull, as if he'd pulled the man's tongue backward through his mouth and into his throat. It had all been so impossible. And yet...

"It's better for us both if you pretend you never saw me," he said.

"I beg to differ," I said breathlessly.

"I shouldn't be talking to you. You're not my human," he said.

Rage rocked through me. "I'm no one's human! I'm alone and locked in a basement. And whether you like it or not, I *can* see you. For the love of god, you have to help me."

His brow creased. "Answer my question first, human."

"Marlow," I corrected breathlessly, hands still flat against the cool wall.

Surprise shone through the glittering crown of each iris. His eyes were every bit as metallic in their golden glow as Caliban's were silver, as if one wore the sun and the other the moon.

"What?" he asked, the word coming out in a baffled staccato.

"My name is Marlow."

His russet brows lifted further as he said, "Oh, so you're stupid."

The assertion was enough to stabilize me. I shook my head as if he'd splashed a bucket of cold water on my face. I wanted to be angry but could only manage confusion.

"Excuse me?"

Silas wiped a bluish stain from the child-like monster from his sword before re-sheathing it. It was with tired patronization that he said, "You let yourself into parasite-infested basements and give out your name. It explains why you allowed a sigil to be painted above your door without even realizing it was there."

"I—" I choked on my indignation. My defense fell to the ground. I only understood half of his insults. "I know *your* name!"

He dusted off his hands on his pants, cleaning his palms from any specks of bluish goo. He didn't bother to look at me as he said, "No, you don't. You know what I'm called as of late. You may also use the name Silas, though I'd prefer that you not call me anything at all. Spare us both the headache and pretend you didn't—"

"Wait." I lunged for him, digging my nails into the exposed flesh of his bicep.

He looked at my hands as if the fangs of a venomous snake had punctured his skin. The bright, striking smell of spices intensified as his eyes burned with surprise that I had touched him. His gaze shot from my fingers to my face as he demanded, "What the hell are you?"

I didn't release my hands. I searched his face for help, for sympathy, for *something*.

"You can't let me die," I said on a hurried exhale.

He breathed in slowly, looking at me as if seeing me for the first time. His appraising scan of my face, my eyes, my body was enough for me to loosen my grip, if only slightly. He plucked my hand from his arm with a powerful motion and dropped it to my side. I took a step back, feeling utterly self-conscious. I didn't know what he was looking for, but after what the cat-child had craved, I wasn't sure I wanted to find out.

Finally, I said, "I came looking for Caliban. Or for you, to be honest. For something. For *anything*."

He made a face as he looked to the blue pulp on the ground, saying, "Well, you found something. Good for you."

"Silas, *please*," I begged. "Caliban hasn't visited me in months. Summer is almost over and I don't know what to do. I've tried everything. I don't even know where to start. I've read everything. I've talked with countless witches—"

He scoffed at the word.

I knew men. I knew how they worked, how to assuage them, how to get what I wanted. But as I studied the beautiful face before me, I found no familiar purchase. His reactions

100

weren't clicking. It was like grappling against an oily surface, desperate for a point of contact. Struggling to reason with him, I plowed forward with honesty.

"I came looking for a way to find him. I had no leads, except that Caliban said he'd marked Richard…the man you killed in my apartment. This is his house," I clarified at his quizzical expression. "You said Richard was marked. Is that why you're here for this…*child*? Some mark?"

Silas's face gathered in disapproval. "The parasite had nothing to do while people stopped coming to the basement. When I killed the host, it released the…wait. It's so easy to forget you shouldn't be talking to me. It's your fault the parasite showed up. Anyway, use your cell phone, human—"

"Marlow."

He tilted his head back as if to laugh. He bit his lip, forcing the sound back into his belly before he relaxed. He looked at me and said, "You will be dead within a month if you keep throwing that around. Good luck with your life."

"I don't have reception!" I lurched toward him again, gripping at the broad stretch of muscle once more.

Silas wrapped a thumb and forefinger around my wrists and removed my fingers from his arm once more, plucking me from him as if dislodging a leech. "Clearly you can see through the veil…sometimes. Maybe it's because of—what did you call him? Caliban?—the sigil he had over your home."

My nod was too eager considering I couldn't entirely confirm what he was saying.

Silas went on. "The parasite's markings are an extension of his host's. You shouldn't be able to…I don't have time to figure out why you can see us, let alone touch us. Maybe this host and his attachment had sigils up as well. But when it comes to *him*…" He grimaced ruefully at the memory of the one who'd spent more than two decades by my side before his face softened. "Actually…he—*Caliban*—already owes me one. Marlow, you said?"

I nodded.

Silas made a contemplative sound as he relaxed into his shrugging posture. He scanned me once. "Next time he visits, ask him to lift your veil."

My mouth dropped open. I decided against explaining to this stranger that I'd been abandoned. I'd sent Caliban away, and he'd obeyed. Finally, I asked, "Can you do it?"

"Of course I can."

My face lit. "Will you?"

A dark chuckle. "Absolutely not."

Maybe it was his displeasure, or maybe it was my own fear seeping back into my bones, but the spiced scent of anointing oil fought for my attention against the sickly-sweet odor of festering wounds that still dripped on the floor. The basement shrank, closing in on me as it became entirely too small. The bald rods of fluorescent lights were too bright. It was as if I heard the sirens in the distance telling me the tornado would approach once more.

I couldn't let him leave me.

"Please!" I calmed my voice before repeating, "Please, Silas. Do this for me. I really, really need it."

"You'll go mad," he said with certainty. From his level chin to the set of his shoulders, I knew the conversation was over. Yet the voice within me told me that if he'd needed to go, he could have. Instead, he said, "And even if I wanted to..." He saw the light in my face and clarified, "Which I *don't*—there's a bond that happens when one of us takes in a human. It's a permanent decision on both ends. I don't want to be responsible for you in this lifetime or the next. If you get into trouble, it would be my fault. And *clearly*, Marlow—human woman who's gotten herself into two near-death situations in a single season—you would get into trouble."

"Three," I said.

He arched a half-curious brow before turning his back on me.

"The man in my apartment, the boy tonight, and this basement now. If you don't get me out of this room, I'll die down here. It's locked and no one is coming for me. I can't call for help. If you leave me, you can add my blood to your hands."

He took a step away, but I felt his hesitation. He rotated toward me. I watched the debate in his eyes and hated him for his indifference. I wasn't sure what he was weighing. What incentive could there possibly be to allow me to starve to death until my bloated corpse was found by a forensics team in the subsequent weeks? I didn't know this man—this thing—from Adam, but he was my only hope, and he was genuinely considering murdering me through inaction. My eyes narrowed incredulously as I watched him.

"Silas!" I yelled.

"I'm thinking."

"About *what?*"

I knew I didn't have room to argue. I couldn't push him. I couldn't force him. He was...nonhuman. Even in the cold, unflattering light of the basement, there was a beauty, a handsomeness to him that I rarely, if ever, saw in *anyone*, even art. His broad shoulders, square jaw, and rippling muscles were astounding on their own, but there was something else about him. An unmistakable glitter fluttered around him whenever he moved, almost as if he were glowing. It was a second light, a cleaner, better light than the one that hummed and flickered ominously overhead. He was in the same white-and-beige leathers I'd seen him in when he'd snatched me from certain death. Even then, he hadn't done it to save me. He'd been irritated that I'd seen him. I supposed some things didn't change.

Richard had been marked. Even if I didn't know what the words meant, I clung to the fact. This mark had brought Silas to my apartment then, and though I had no concept of the specifics, I knew a similar incentive had to have pulled him here now.

"I suppose it wouldn't hurt for Caliban to owe me two favors," he said finally, voice thick with reluctance. He sighed, "I guess that means we're taking the stairs."

It was unceremonious, but I didn't care. I bathed in relief, practically dancing as Silas led the way. He rested a hand on the doorknob until it melted into a shimmering constellation of copper and gold. When he moved his hand away, the knob retained its earthly shape, but the door opened noiselessly on its hinges. He stepped onto the top floor of the house and ushered for me to follow.

I'd barely released the anxious breath after cresting the stairs before I dared ask, "And the veil?"

"Not a chance. And please, Marlow." He paused, resting his weight on my name.

I looked at him expectantly, waiting for him to tell me to stay safe.

"Do us both a favor, and never see me again."

✦

I shivered on the corner outside of the taped-up house like a wet kitten, rain-drenched and trembling. The night was dry, but every part of me felt dirty, soaked, and terrified. I sat directly beneath the puddle of a streetlamp as if the light might keep away the terrors that lurked in the shadows, and I stared at the sleeping houses, wondering if any of them knew who and what had existed just a few homes away. I couldn't get warm no matter how tightly I tucked my arms against my chest, hugging myself against the curb and waiting the twenty minutes it took for a driver in the remote neighborhood to find me. I triple-checked the license plate to ensure I was getting into the right vehicle and not crawling in the car with yet another Cheshire cat.

I'd lost the remaining scraps of my mind.

I was in desperate need of the pudding cups and numbing pills of a grippy-sock vacation. It had been nearly a decade since my dad had come home to find me in a snowbank outside of the house next to an empty orange bottle and driven me to the ER. They'd put me on a seventy-two-hour hold, which had leeched into the three-week in-patient stay before they determined that I was no longer a harm to myself or others. I'd wanted to drift off while looking at the bright, silver burn of the moon and diamond-soaked night sky. It was a memory I'd done my best to bury. While I no longer wanted to end my trips around the sun, I was an inch away from having the driver take me directly to the psychiatric facility to check myself in voluntarily.

The last time I'd been unable to deal with the world, it had been because of my imagination. This time, it was because of my reality.

It had been years since I'd given a rideshare driver a poor rating, but if this loud-mouthed son of a bitch didn't shut the hell up, he was getting one star. The man with one knee on the wheel and an arm loosely draped over the passenger's seat couldn't smell the trauma pouring from me despite my raised hackles, my crunched position, my wild eyes, and my unwillingness to speak. I reeked of confusion and terror, yet he didn't stop prattling.

The driver's voice and the deafening dubstep thumbing through his speakers competed for my attention against flashing visions of the night. My nerves were so frayed from my brush with the nightmarish, cat-like child with the vibrantly blue blood. I'd been trapped in a locked basement. I'd walked into the killing room of a man who'd wanted me dead. Agony wrapped its icy talons around my heart and squeezed, forcing the remnants of dread through my veins. Then there had been Silas. Sword. Golden eyes. Shimmer and indifference and power. He'd said so much, and I'd understood none of it, save for one.

He'd told me to ask Caliban to lift the veil.

The veil.

I knew enough from literature, mythology, and fantasy to understand its meaning.

I could see through the human realm into the one filled with Cheshire-cat children and tall, muscular men with short tempers and, hopefully, Caliban.

It was all I wanted to think about, but the rideshare driver remained on his boisterous soapbox voicing his opinions on politics and religion. I was officially resigned to giving him zero stars and refusing to tip when he started referring to women as *females*. I did my best to tune him out while I focused on Silas's words.

A bond. If he lifted my veil, we'd be bonded.

"And that's why, I told her, listen: men are hunters. We're not made for monogamy, we—"

"I'm sorry," I said curtly. "I'm really tired. I need to sleep. Would you mind turning down the music so I can nap for the rest of the drive?"

Despite seeing little more than the back of his head, I caught his profile as he suppressed a sneer. He turned down the music and allowed me to remain with my thoughts.

My eyebrows bunched as I returned to Silas's implication. On the one hand, it didn't seem horrible to make someone who'd already saved me twice responsible for my ongoing wellbeing. On the other hand, I had no idea what sort of implications might come with such an agreement. And if I were Shiva and had third and fourth hands, they would force me to consider both that Silas had unequivocally said no and that Caliban had left me.

The driver pulled up in front of the warehouse, and I exited without saying goodbye. My card let me into the building, and it was with sinking disappointment that a new, unfamiliar face greeted me from the receptionist desk. She was chipper and talkative. I instantly disliked her, though my dislike for friendliness was hardly her problem.

My mind opened like internet tabs, one after the other, new thought after new thought running simultaneously until the computer of my brain slowed, each new page sluggishly sorting through thoughts and possibilities.

The house.

The basement.

The child.

His smile.

Oh god, that scabbed, toothy, horrible *smile*.

The six-year-old had unhinged his jaw like a snake. If he had been given five more seconds, his sharpened teeth would have sunken into my flesh. He was going to eat me. I couldn't explain how I knew, but I felt it in my bones. Perhaps my dread had been sensing him all along. I'd detected the predator slinking in the basement wearing the humanoid skin of a boy.

The elevator doors opened, and I forced my feet forward. Another card, another pad, another beeping door before my apartment swung open. I switched on the light closest to the door to reveal...

My heart dropped.

I was not alone.

"What..."

Silas turned to me from where he'd been eyeing the photos on my wall. His arms remained folded across his chest. His eyes darkened, nothing particularly friendly greeting me as he surveyed me.

"How did you get here?" I'd meant for the question to come out with force, but every piece of myself that had broken and scattered at the sight of the childish entity cracked once more. Renewed fear coursed through me. The ground wobbled as I realized how little control I had over my own life, my own autonomy, my own safety. A locked door meant nothing when beings like Silas, Caliban, or the Cheshire cat could slither in. "How did you get in? How did you get here so much faster than me?"

"Come in so you don't look like a lunatic shouting at an empty apartment," he said.

"No."

I remained planted in the doorway, watching the man who stood in beige and white in the middle of my living room, knowing he'd stood in the exact spot only weeks before.

"How did you get in?" I insisted.

His lips remained pressed in a tight line. He huffed an impatient puff of air before saying, "Anything can get in. For all you know, there are beings in your closet and under your bed at this very moment."

"That's not funny." I swallowed.

"Good, because I'm not joking."

I tried to breathe. Tried to remember that he hadn't hurt me. Tried to convince myself that he wasn't my enemy…but then again, he'd very nearly let me die in a locked basement less than two hours prior. Apparently, two hours had been long enough for him to vanish into whatever hole he came from and reappear with a conscience. Perhaps he'd come to apologize for valuing my life so little.

His eyes softened. He looked at me for a long time. Finally, with resignation, he said, "I'll do it."

I blinked.

The veil.

I lurched into my apartment on autopilot, closing the door behind me. I didn't trust him enough to move any closer. I eyed him for any sign of deception. I'd barely been able to convince him that my life was worth saving, and a moment later he wanted to offer me the gift of sight?

I shook my head. "But…the bond. You said…"

"I've had time to think, and I changed my mind."

"How much time?"

His chest moved with his deep inhale and exhale. He extended a hand, asking, "Do you want it or not?"

I looked at his outstretched palm uncertainly, then back up at him. I scanned the clean, modern lines of the apartment as if hoping Caliban might be waiting, but I knew better. I'd told him to leave. I'd told him not to come back. If I wanted to see him again, I'd have to find him. And in order to find him… If I took Silas's hand, if I bonded myself to the shimmering stranger…

From the shadows came the coo of an airy female voice. I made out the subtle hourglass edges of hips and legs as she stepped into view. Her musical words were laden with an unmistakable smile as she said, "I wouldn't do that if I were you."

Silas dropped his hand. A renewed string of curses bubbled from him with an angry, male snarl as he said, "Ah, for fuck's sake."

Chapter Eleven

S HE'S ONE OF OURS," SAID THE LITHE FEMALE SHAPE STEPPING
from the shadows. The living room flooded with the
cloud of fresh-cut pine, a splash of the sea, and the tingling
feeling one only encounters near ice. The loose fit of her
burnt-red bohemian pants swished around her, clinging to
the wide curve of her hips as she came forward. "I know you
can smell it on her."

Silas took a defensive step forward as if squaring up for
battle. "Barely! It has to be, what, an eighth? If that?"

"It's enough," the woman said. She was too beautiful
to be real, as if she'd emerged from a painting. She turned
to me with both grin and apology as she said, "I'm sorry
we had to meet this way. Cute place, by the way. I'm
Fauna."

She extended her hand as if I was meant to shake it, and
my eyes bulged at the gesture. I struggled to keep from raking
my hands through my hair, convinced the mad-scientist fluff
wouldn't make me look any saner.

"Who the fuck are you people!"

I could barely even look at the ethereal woman who stood
in my room with supernatural grace and beauty. She was little
more than curved lines and incomprehensible splashes of brass
and diamond. None of it made sense. Part of me longed to

slip into ignorance once more. It would be so much nicer to resume believing they were fictional.

Silas muttered to me, "Told you there might be something in your closet."

The woman shot him the middle finger before offering me a sympathetic pout.

I must have looked as shell-shocked as I felt.

Fauna's icy white hair was divided by a block of copper. Her pale skin was smattered with freckles of both ginger and pearl. She did indeed look every bit her namesake, like a baby deer had shifted into beautiful human skin with an attitude. She folded her arms over her chest and sank her weight into a hip. I was caught between the desire to throw on all the lights to soak in every detail and the gratitude that only the hall light and orange glow from the city illuminated the parties before me.

"This isn't how I wanted to see you again," he said to the woman called Fauna.

"And I'm not convinced I wanted to see you at all." She blew on her nails as if banishing dust, then extended her five fingers, examining her handiwork.

"I like what you've done to your hair," he said. And I couldn't tell if his tone was mocking or sincere.

She winked as she said, "Of course you do. Change is fabulous. I'll take it from here, Silas."

He planted his feet. "She said she wanted—"

"Let me tell the story, sweetheart," Fauna said to Silas, waving for him to stop talking. Rotating to me, she explained, "Silas here went back to his overlord after your little encounter." She looked back at the man and narrowed her eyes into predatory slits. "Oh, you don't think we know already? Don't be thick." She returned her gaze to me as she said, "Anyway, his power-hungry divine was *thrilled* to hear that such a curious human wanted to bond to his *special angel*." Her fingers tapped against her bare arms impatiently as she continued. "It would have been so convenient to have the

Prince's favorite plaything bound to you. Your master would have loved that. Take the time you need to lick your wounds. We applaud the effort, but she's ours."

"We have a claim to her." His retort was like metal sharpened over iron.

Fauna guffawed, gesturing for him to reconsider his words. "What claim! That she asked you first out of desperation? Listen, sweetie, blood is thicker than empty wishes."

A muscle ticked in his jaw. His bright, golden eyes darkened into a flat shade of cold amber as he said, "We have a claim from infancy. She was dedicated."

I could have sworn Fauna rolled her eyes so hard that it made a popping sound. "Your master makes such a fuss about free will but sends out his little slaves to make more little slaves and have newborns undergo ceremonies, or splash some water or sign life-debt contracts for him long before they know their own name. She's made no such dedication."

Through clenched teeth, he pressed, "She didn't have to. As a baby—"

"Give it a rest."

I couldn't decide who to look at. My vision swung between them like the clacking, pendulous silver balls of Newton's cradle, unable to fix on either. They were discussing *me*? And what did it have to do with my childhood? I looked between the couch, the blank TV, the island. I wondered how long it would take me to run to my bedside table and what cocktail of meds would bring me back to reality.

"This isn't your fight, Fauna," he said, doubling down.

"I disagree."

Silas hedged, trying a new tactic altogether. "Tread lightly. I don't think the Nordes want to get involved. It's not your war."

She scoffed, though even her sarcasm kept a light, airy tone. With a voice like starlight, she said, "How about you let us decide what we do and do not want to involve ourselves in, mmkay?"

In the time I'd known him, Silas had worn a few masks.

He had been baffled when I'd first connected with his gaze many months ago. He'd bristled with agitation when standing between me and the pulpy remnants of the Cheshire cat. The self-assured look he'd worn into my apartment had vanished as a new frustration painted his features.

He locked onto me, burrowing through my glaze of confusion with eyes, which burned like matching halos. "Marlow, you wanted to see beyond the veil? I can do that. You want powerful angelic allies? I can offer that. You want—"

The word didn't just trigger me. Fauna reacted as my stomach churned.

"'Angelic'! Okay, we've had enough of you. Your would-be pawn and I have some catching up to do." Fauna laughed at the heavenly moniker as she set to work. She planted her hands against his chest and shoulder, shoving him through the door. "Out you go! I have a long-lost citizen to talk to."

Thieves' oil and sea spray, masculine and feminine, frankincense and pine, angel and other, they were glitter and glow sandwiched between the kitchen appliances and the electronics of my very human living room. I tried to swallow, only to realize all the moisture had evaporated from my mouth.

I wondered if they'd notice if I reached around to pinch the bare flesh of my arm. Once. Twice. I had to have fallen asleep in the back of a cab after I left Nia's, tumbling from one bizarre nightmare into another. I bit down on the inside of my cheek, hoping for a similarly rousing effect, wishing this were a dream.

Nothing changed, save for the painful rush of iron as blood filled my mouth.

Fauna gave Silas a hard push while I remained statue still, mere steps from my front door.

Silas was her physical superior in every way. He was nearly three times her size and knit entirely of battle-ready muscles. It certainly wasn't force that urged him from the door. He planted his feet as he made his final plea. "Citizen is right," he said, latching on to the last thing she'd said as he petitioned me for my attention. "Fauna is barely more than a civilian."

"You're one to talk," she bit, teeth clenched as she pushed.

He had eyes only for me as his tone switched to pleading. "Let me take you into this, Marlow. You'll enter the veil with a substantially higher ranking, access you can't even imagine. You don't know what you're giving up if—"

"Hush" was all Fauna said as she gave him a hard, final shove. Even in her exertion, there was something intangibly mesmerizing about every move. When Silas's feet crossed the threshold, he did not stand in the hall. The man vanished altogether.

I stared after the empty particles where he'd been as the door swung shut.

She slumped against the closed door and breathed in relief. "Useful sigils—true sight, that is. I haven't seen that particular bit of art in the better part of a thousand years. The Prince's idea, I'd guess?"

I stared at the gorgeous, chaotic creature.

"The Prince?" I repeated, devoid of comprehension.

Fauna cocked her head curiously. I struggled to look back, too overwhelmed by her celestial beauty. She took a few appraising steps toward me. When my face betrayed no connection, hers lit. "Are you to tell me you don't...no, no, of course. That makes a lot of sense. We'd wondered why you hadn't taken his offer. Sure, sure, he's not one to brag. Though it would be easier for everyone if he had."

She stepped away from the wall and slid onto the cream couch with ghostly grace. She patted the seat beside her, offering my own sofa to me. Every tap of her hands reminded me of the tinkling of silver bells.

Despite her effortless elegance, she remained utterly nonchalant.

"I don't think I want you to be real," I said to the embodied dream.

She rested an elbow on the back of the couch, relaxing her head onto her fist. Her lips quirked into a tilted smile as she asked, "Would you prefer this to be in your imagination?"

I squeezed my eyes shut and I said, "What I prefer doesn't matter. I've been desperate to get back to Caliban, to access this world, but you...you can't be real." I opened my eyes, and yet she remained.

"I have evidence to the contrary, sweet pea. Come sit by me."

"Who are you?" I asked. And because I didn't know what else I could possibly do, I complied, quietly taking a seat several cushions away.

Despite her loveliness, a threatening undercurrent told me that if she wanted, she could rip my esophagus from my throat with a single snatch. The only thing I could do was ask my questions and hope for the best.

"I'm Fauna," she repeated. "I'm...hmm. I'm trying to decide which words might strike a chord with you. What did you study again?"

Was she asking me about my college major? I'd forgotten entirely. I wasn't even sure I remembered my own name. Between the shock in the basement and the baffling events that had unfolded in my living room, I wasn't positive I could identify tits from toes.

Finally, a semi-intelligent thought came to me.

"Double major," I responded reflexively. The normalcy of the question caught me off guard as I recited an answer I'd given a million times, from panels to interviews to first dates that went nowhere. "Literature and linguistics. With concentrations in Spanish and Nordic studies." Would she ask for my résumé next?

She flashed a starlit smile at that and asked me in Norwegian, then Swedish, then Icelandic which of the Scandinavian languages I spoke. She lost me when she switched to Old Norse, though I caught most of her words, even if I couldn't respond.

"How many more could we do? Faroese? Finnish? Danish?"

"I can read Danish," I said. "I didn't touch any of the others."

She tilted her head to the side, silver and copper tumbling over her shoulder, the shortest layers pooling near her collarbone as the rest tumbled below her breast. "Isn't it lovely, how the blood calls to you? Here you are in the godforsaken American Midwest, and—forgive me if I'm wrong, but—your mother gave up her language, right?"

I dipped my chin numbly. It was true. My mother had wanted only English spoken in the house. The more she rejected our heritage, the deeper I'd dug in my heels. My grandmother had been delighted when I'd been able to hold a conversation with her at long last. My mother's chagrin was an emotion I'd never truly understood, but I also hadn't tried. Everything I did was disappointing to her.

I opened my mouth to ask Fauna how she knew about my mother but closed it again wordlessly. I wasn't about to win a Pulitzer for my journalism anytime soon, as I couldn't form a coherent thought beyond reverting to denial. If she truly was a product of my imagination—which I still wasn't sure whether or not I hoped she was—then she'd know anything I knew.

"I can't blame her," Fauna said. "I'm sure the things she thought and felt were very scary for her. Generally, we like to leave humans with distant fae blood to their own devices. Unless, of course, some angelic asshole is trying to bond with a Norde just to fuck with the Prince."

Her sentence was a word salad, so I took a stab at the piece I understood.

"Are you saying you're fae?" I asked.

She offered a half-shrug. "Me, Silas, the Prince—what's fae besides a word you've used to help understand facets of the preternatural?"

"Preternatural?" I repeated.

116

She made a sound of controlled patience. "Preternatural is for something beyond what is expected, which, for humans, *we are*. Supernatural is what humans prefer to use when talking about us, but it's simply inaccurate. It's a word for things beyond the natural, which the realms find rather egotistical of humanity. As if you're the determining factor on what is and isn't natural."

"And…what exactly *are* you?"

Curls cascaded over her shoulder as she tilted her head. She chewed her lip for a moment. "Fae is fine as a catchall. I'm closer to what you'd consider an elf, I guess. Skogsrå is the technical term in our pantheon, but no one seems to know it. Basically, I'm a god you don't care very much about. Maybe a nymph, if you're using Greek…which, given your literary career, I suspect you might. Humans have created all sorts of nifty little words to help compartmentalize their understanding of our kingdoms. Like *angels*." She said the word again and giggled. She surveyed the apartment as if seeing it for the first time. "I know I said your place was cute, but damn! What the hell do you do with a literature degree that affords a place like this?"

"I…I write books," I said. "The *Pantheon* series…and before that…well…"

"Gods, we know you write; we just didn't know it paid this well. I read the first one, mostly to see if you mentioned me. I was gravely disappointed with how you described Álfheimr and equally disappointed that I was not your main character. But, all is forgiven. Wait, why the face?"

She studied me for a minute before recognition clicked.

"Oh! Money! Jobs! The sex work? We know about that, peanut. Congratulations, by the way. There isn't a deity alive who doesn't use sex as a form of worship—oh, no, I'm wrong. Silas's owner has very particular ideas about sex. I wonder if that's why all of his angels have sticks up their asses. They need to get laid." She got to her feet and wandered to the neat line of books that had my name emblazoned on the spine. She plucked one from the row and smiled. "I suspect you have the Prince to thank for this, too."

I didn't have to ask what she meant, as it was a reflection of my own insecurity. I'd never believed I'd deserved success. There was no such thing as luck, after all.

"Well, shall we?"

I frowned. "Shall we what?"

She plopped my book to the table and gave me a tired look. "You nearly bound yourself to an angel so that you could see beyond the veil." Fauna wiggled her fingers, hand extended toward me. "Are we bonding, or what?"

There it was again. That miserable lightning bolt through my core at her use of the word. *Angel*. Years of fists on pulpits, of fear of eternal damnation, of verses and pews and water and communion made me recoil. I realized it wasn't that I wanted her to be fake. I'd been willing to accept hidden people and folk tales. I was ready for witches. But the church-heavy language had triggered something within me. I *needed* it to be fake. If angels were real, did that mean my mother had been right about everything? The stitches I'd sewn up around my childhood began to burst, every memory threatening to spill out as I stared at Fauna, quite certain I was going to be sick.

"Now?"

Her face twitched into wry amusement. "Do you have something better to do? From my understanding, you were so desperate to step into the veil that you tracked down a murderer, and from the smell of it, you encountered his attachment. Unpleasant little fuckers, aren't they? But this tells me either that you're dumb or that you've already let go of whatever expectations you had for this life. Knowing the company you've kept, I sure as hell hope it isn't the former."

My throat worked, struggling to swallow as if I'd taken a large pill without water. My heart stuttered arrhythmically as I examined her awaiting palm.

"My friends? My life? My job?"

"It's not going anywhere. Come and go...if you want."

I got to my feet uncertainly and looked at her patient hand, as still as a marble statue. I had seen hundreds of deer in my lifetime, even those yearlings with the red and white spots that I spied across her now. They'd frozen with the same unnatural stillness available only to something that had survived a lifetime of being hunted. Yet she had not treated the angel as if she were a creature of prey.

I looked beyond her into the pockets of shadow within the apartment, wishing Caliban would step out. But he wouldn't be saving me from this decision. I was on my own.

"What will it be like?" I whispered.

She looked up into her memories, eyes wide and doe-like as she searched for an appropriate response. "Have you ever woken up from a dream and struggled to remember what was real? Sometimes it takes you a few moments to gather your bearings, to collect yourself, to come back into the present?"

I nodded.

"That moment upon waking, but forever."

"That sounds awful."

Fauna tsked. "And I assume you knew there would be drawbacks. Why else would you have spent nearly three decades of this life saying no? Though I guess, given your apartment and your success, your human life must be pretty satisfying. Live deliciously and all that." Her hand fell to her side.

"No," I replied. "It's not."

Her sparkle returned. She winked. "Most humans spend their lives asleep to reality. What do you say, Marlow? Are you ready to wake up?"

Chapter Twelve

I NEEDED A MOMENT TO GATHER MY THOUGHTS, AND IT CAME in the form of a scalding shower. It had been surprisingly easy to convince Fauna to wait.

I'd told her that I needed to scrub myself clean after all I'd been through, and she agreed that I reeked of pus and trauma and that I could use a good soaping. I'd practically collapsed with exhaustion the moment the boiling-hot water hit me. It burned my skin, which I welcomed. Each scalding droplet reminded me that this was real. *I* was real. I was alive. I sank to the shower floor, struggling to shampoo my own hair. A distant, painful memory of Caliban holding me in the shower years ago while I'd cried tugged at my heart.

You're not happy.

I missed him so intensely whenever I ran the hot water— each droplet like a rain of memories, drowning me in him. He'd never tried to get me to change. He hadn't scolded me or told me to clean up my act or been disappointed when I came home wasted or with a stranger on my arm. He'd only cared whether my choices were bringing me joy or stealing it from me. And he knew that half of what I did was a bandage to patch the bleeding wound of the one thing I'd believed at my core to be true: none of it existed. An imaginary friend can't take corporal form. I needed to drink, get laid, date, medicate, fly across the globe, to run as fast and far as I could to get away from him, and none of it had worked.

Nothing, except telling him not to come back.

I squeezed my eyes closed, forcing the images from my mind.

When I finally opened the shower curtain, I gasped at Fauna leaning against the sink, eyeing a piece of paper. I could scarcely make out her shape through the dense steam that filled the room. I scrambled for a towel, but she didn't bother to look at me.

"This was in your pocket?" she asked, flashing the hastily scrawled sigil with fold creases down the middle. My crumpled pants, shirt, and underwear remained balled on the floor. I couldn't imagine what had possessed her to let herself into the bathroom and dig through my pockets, but then again, I was the crazy one.

I yanked the towel from the hook and tucked it against my still-dripping body. Hair drenched against my neck and shoulders as I gaped at her. "Don't you know about privacy?"

"No," she said dismissively, then waved the paper again. "You had this in your pocket when you were out of the house, and you saw both Silas and the parasite?"

Water plastered my hair to my forehead, dribbling into my open mouth as I stared at her.

"Fascinating," she whispered. She brought the sigil close to her face, turning it over as she examined it from different angles. "I can't believe that worked. But then again, if anyone could make something so powerful, it would be the Prince. Come on, sweetie. I have questions. And I'm hungry."

I'd barely stepped onto the bath mat, soaked hair dripping loudly onto the floor as she flung open the bathroom door. The cold shock of the hall beyond hit me as the steam rushed from the room. She left it open as she stalked to the kitchen with purpose.

"It's after midnight," I called after her.

She gave me the time I needed to towel off my hair and

change into an old T-shirt and sweatpants. At her very specific request, I ordered a number of doughnuts, pastries, and deep-fried sweets from a twenty-four-hour dessert shop. She wasted time with cartoons, not questioning the way I gaped at her like she was a dog walking on its hind legs who'd learned to talk. It took forty-five minutes of colorful children's shows before the food arrived. I turned off the TV the moment the delivery man showed up at our doorstep. She was elbow-deep in sweets before she was ready to hold a conversation.

"So, let's talk about your true sight," Fauna said, mouth smacking through bites of sticky pastry.

I wondered how she managed to make tearing into a glazed doughnut look dainty.

"True sight?"

She shook crumbs from her fingertips. "It's in your blood, of course, but when combined with this sigil…I'm just fascinated it worked on you even while out of the house. And a piece of paper, no less! I have theories."

When I'd left the church, I'd rejected all facets of the spiritual. Anchoring myself in reality had been a cornerstone of my psychiatry. Hundreds of hours in therapy began to unravel. I parroted what I'd trained myself to say. "Fauna, none of this is real. I—"

"Babe, all of this is real. For the love of the gods and goddesses, how did he remain patient with a nonbeliever for so long? I've been around you for all of three hours and I'm already tired of your repetition. Be less boring."

"I'm batshit," I said quietly. "Mental illness runs in my family, on my mom's side. We're all nuts. We—"

Fauna finished off the last of a glazed croissant, using her fingertip to clean the plate. My stomach grumbled. I hadn't wanted to eat, but it hadn't made it any easier to watch an entire box of chocolate, maple, and vanilla baked goods disappear between her perfect, pearly teeth. She sucked her finger clean as she nodded. "Yes, Lisbeth was one of us—is one of us. Well, technically, it's your great-grandmother, Aloisa. She's the best. So much cooler than you. Way more open-minded. She would have believed anything. Speaking of anything…"

Fauna got to her feet and wandered into my kitchen. She began loudly opening and closing drawers. My eyes stung against the lateness of the hour as I watched her invade my privacy as she continued riffling through my things.

"What are you doing?" I asked, but she didn't answer. I allowed her the chaos while I grimaced at the mention of my mother.

John and Lisbeth Thorson, the model Christian couple, pillars of the church. A woman as rigid as the ruler of judgement by which she measured the world around her, and a man as absent and forgettable as the John Does who shared his name. My mother wasn't quite Margaret White, but she had several qualities that would have made *Carrie* fans proud. I spoke up to be heard over the sound of Fauna's snooping. "My mom was—is—obsessed with angels and demons. She's schizophrenic, Fauna. She saw and heard things that weren't there. Eventually, she stopped talking about it. She had to. Do you know how many jobs are taken off the table when you're diagnosed? Do you know how stigmatized it is? I couldn't risk getting slapped with that label. I didn't want the world to close down for me like it did for her, or for my grandma."

She planted both palms on the kitchen island and leveled her stare before saying, "Did these voices in your mom's head ever tell her to hurt herself?"

I frowned. I was ready to answer when the sound of papers and loose cords from my junk drawer stirred my attention. I stood at long last and crossed to the kitchen. "Can I help you find something?"

She continued her hunt as she said, "A marker. A Sharpie, preferably. Now, about these voices, did they ever tell her to do things? To hurt others? To wreak havoc? What did they say to her?"

I waved her aside and closed the kitchen drawers and cabinets as I crossed to the stand beside the couch. It housed remotes, a surround-sound manual, and a variety of writing utensils. I procured a black marker and she snatched it from my hand.

"Why do you need it?"

She bit the cap and kept it in her mouth as she crossed to my floor-to-ceiling window. Through the plastic cap, she said, "Because angels and demons aren't the only things out there, and your warding sucks. Now, answer my question."

I shook my head, still-damp tendrils pooling against my shirt. "No, they didn't really talk to her. I knew she kept seeing them long after she stopped bringing them up. She saw them and heard them…but they were just there. Around. And…hey!"

The high-pitched squeak of felt on glass cut my reverie short.

"You'll thank me later," she said through her mouthful as she continued to draw lines, circles, curves, and curls.

"I doubt it!" I recoiled at her final product, which might as well have been slapped from a grimoire onto my living room window.

"I shouldn't have been able to get in here. Any god or the creatures from their pantheons could stroll on in."

I trailed after her, lips parted in horror as she headed toward my front door to continue her vandalism. I was too stunned to speak, but she continued talking as if she weren't breaking every rule of socially acceptable behavior. Back to me, intent on her art, she said, "Schizophrenia is real, just as clairvoyance is real. Seeing through the veil can be wonderful, or it can ruin your life. The best way to tell whether you're clairsentient is the message coming from the other side. Unless she had a parasite…well, a parasite would tell her to do terrible things. You would know. You met one of those creepy little fuckers. But it sounds like you're all suffering from a terrible case of great-grandma Aloisa getting knocked up by the fae."

She nodded at her handiwork and set off down the hall.

"That's permanent marker. You can't just—"

"I'm pretty sure you have the funds to take the hit on the deposit." She rolled her eyes as she stepped into my guest bedroom and headed for yet another window.

I trailed her graffiti helplessly. Unsure how to intervene with her property destruction, I pressed my fingertips into my temple and asked a question instead. "My mom... You're saying she was just seeing through the veil?" My question was underscored by the orange prescription bottles as we left the guest room and stepped into my bedroom.

"Poor clairsentient humans," Fauna murmured, voice quick to correct my train of thought. She popped the cap onto the back of the marker, clearing her mouth as she multitasked drawing and responding. I watched, a passenger in my own apartment as she defaced my bedroom window. She looked at the medications, then answered the unspoken question. "No, the pills did not dull her, or *your*, ability to see through the veil. They simply make life more bearable. Psychic abilities can be...a lot. Even if you can't turn them off, you don't deserve to suffer. Give yourself a tiny pinch of relief. Survive it."

"Psychic?"

"There," she said, satisfied. "Are there any other doors? Windows?"

I winced at the symbols she may as well have ripped from the occult. "You've destroyed everything in my apartment. It looks like we're trying to summon the devil. My place now looks as crazy as I feel, so thanks for that."

Fauna made a face that I had made countless times to my students in Colombia. She was a teacher doing her best not to throw shoes at her student. She rallied for self-restraint, leaning into the comfort of my couch against the lateness of the hour. "People have paid unspeakable prices for the kind of warding I just gave you. No one from beyond the veil can pop in without an invitation. Between these walls, you're safe from everyone from the boogeyman to Zeus himself. Be grateful."

"When you say Zeus…"

"The guy has trouble keeping it in his pants. You don't need him in your bedroom. As for your abilities, it doesn't matter what you call them," Fauna said. She recapped the pen and handed it to me. "None of the words matter. Everything you say has been made up by humans and filtered through time and culture. Use language however you want. Whatever helps you understand that you can see and feel and experience more than is limited to your realm."

"Then what is it really called?"

Her nose twitched, patience evaporating. I experienced a moment of true fear in the ten seconds it took from her face to go from agitated to contemplative. Fauna leaned away from me as she rolled a question around on her tongue. Her eyes danced with curiosity for a long, long time. "Why did you choose to call the Prince *Caliban*?"

I blinked. "What does this—"

"Just tell me."

My lips parted. I probably looked like a salmon in the jaws of a bear as my mouth opened and closed uselessly against a series of nonanswers. Finally, I said, "It's from *The Tempest*. The character was the son of a witch, and Caliban always seemed so magical…"

Her mouth quirked into a half-smile. "Shakespeare tracks for someone with a degree in literature. You did well."

My bunched brows asked the question I couldn't articulate.

"It's not his name, of course. Fauna isn't mine. Silas isn't the angel's real name. We don't give out our real names, though if people are astute, they can sometimes guess the outer edges of our names. Like you, choosing *Caliban*. Important, magical… the character was half-monster, in human shape, right? It's a good name. It shows your insight. In fact, I suspect it's why you've lived by your many aliases. Because at the end of the day, it isn't just for safety or anonymity. It's because some part of you knows that names have power."

"What does that…"

126

"Oh my *gods,* I'm trying to remember you have redeeming qualities." She leaned forward as if to tell a secret. "What does that have to do with language? With fae and elf and demon and psychic and realm? Come on, Marlow-Merit-Maribelle. Put the pieces together."

And so, I did.

She offered a satisfied nod as she saw it click behind my eyes. The realm words weren't just old or lost or strange. They were too powerful, too important to be shared. Instead, we were left with the outer edges, as she'd called them. Whatever we did to communicate those thoughts would suffice.

Fauna led the way back to the living room as if it were her home and I were the guest. Still in the hall, she asked over her shoulder, "Can I ask what your grandmother was named?"

"Dagny."

She released a heavy sigh. "That tracks."

"Why?"

"*New day.*" She settled onto the couch. "It's a pretty name for a someone who wants their end to look like a beginning. Aloisa wanted a fresh start. And? Did she get it? I mean, her name would have taken her to a new place, a fresh start, regardless. But, did Aloisa and her daughter live happily here?"

"No," I said quietly.

My thoughts flitted briefly to the small, square home that smelled of sourdough bread and brown-orange shag carpet. Her green, plastic-covered couch and amicable smile had served as a constant in my youth. She was always available to babysit, as my grandmother had suffered from terrible agoraphobia, and had nowhere better to be. If Grandma Dagny could see through the veil and had no guidance for who or what she saw, perhaps leaving her house was a fear worse than death. Flavors of her insanity had trickled down my maternal line, passing from her, to my mother, to me. At least my grandma had been the friendly brand of nuts. My mother, on the other hand...

"Are any of us actually crazy?" I asked.

Her rich, musical laugh caught me off guard. "All of you, probably! I can't imagine what it does to the human brain to have fae blood pumping through your veins! And to be…oh, what's the word…come on, it's a really good one that you humans recently started using. What is it when you know something is true but you're told over and over that you've lost your mind?"

"Gaslit?"

"Gaslit!" Fauna echoed enthusiastically, clapping her hands together. "Such a good word. It's overused, though. At this pace, it'll be devoid of meaning within the year. But yes, Dagny's wires are crossed, her chemicals are wrong, and I hope she received all the treatment to make her life easier. I even hope you…" She frowned, then said, "I'm sorry we don't intervene more often. It's better this way. The days of roaming freely in your realm did…not end well, for man or fae." Rather abruptly, she turned to the large, black rectangle against the wall. "Wanna turn the TV back on?"

I looked at the ethereal being made of starlight and speckled like a baby deer and practically snorted. "The cartoons…I don't get it. You really want to watch TV? Why?"

"Life is long! Come on, Miss Mythology. You know what fucked-up shit the gods used to do for entertainment? Now we get to watch producer godlings torture actors. If we're lucky, they're very, very sexy actors."

"How could you care," I asked, "when you look the way you do?"

Fauna made an arrogant face, biting her lip and leaning in across the table as she said, "Why, do you find me very, very sexy?"

I blinked. Wordlessly, I handed her the remote.

She giggled and clicked it on, flipping through the channels as she said, "We do, sometimes. A few of us get bored and appreciate the adulation of eight billion humans through film or TV. Maybe I could audition for *Fire and Swords*. I look like a princess, don't you think? My acting is quite good. Wait until you see me play the role of helpless forest maiden looking for a big, strong man."

I dared to ask, "What do you do with the big, strong man when you find him?"

Her eyes darkened and her voice lowered as she said, "Well, that depends what kind of mood I'm in."

I wasn't sure that I'd be able to speak if I stayed. I abandoned her to watch TV as I walked numbly to my bedroom. I could hear her giggling at the cheesy dialogue and gasps over the dragons even as I closed the door behind me. I lay down, hair still wet from the shower, and let the pillow absorb what remained of the water and, with it, everything I thought I knew of the world.

Chapter Thirteen

ESUS CHRIST!" I JOLTED AWAKE, HEART LEAPING INTO MY
throat until I practically choked on it. I scrambled backward
so quickly that I nearly tumbled from the bed.

Fauna winked from where she'd been staring at me,
waiting for me to open my eyes. "Not quite, but you're
getting closer. Cool guy. He put his clairsentience to way
better use than your dumb ass. Hate his fan club, though."

"What are you doing in here?" I sputtered. The sun wasn't
even up. The gentle gradient of dawn set my room into a
lavender glow. The purples reflected off her hair, showcasing
her outline as she leaned forward enthusiastically.

"I'm hungry. Let's get coffee."

"I have a French press…" I stammered.

"No, I want doughnuts. Or muffins. Let's go out."

I stared at her for several long moments. "How can you
go out?"

"Quite easily," she said. "Wanna see?" She procured a
baseball cap and a pair of sunglasses as if she'd been clutching them to preempt this question. "I'll just be a very pretty
human."

"But why would you want to?" Coursing with adrenaline, I crawled out of bed and sidestepped toward my dresser,
as I wasn't confident it would be wise to turn my back on

her. "Aren't you people—things—normally...invisible? And why muffins?"

She looked at me as if everything I said gave her further confirmation that I was born yesterday. "Because muffins are delicious. Come on, mythologist. Your second *Pantheon* book was all about your Greeks and Romans, right? Tell me: how often did nymphs interact with the humans?"

"Often, I guess. But..."

She pushed past me and helped herself to my drawers, rummaging around until she wrapped her fingers around a thong and an athletic bra. She shoved them into my hand and headed for my closet.

"I can dress myself," I said.

"Yes, but you're not being very quick about it, and I want to see the city. I never get to go out with a friend. Plus, I have so many theories to share with you. Your sigil? The Prince? You being a dipshit with a death wish? Let's go be gals on the town."

"Gals on the town?" I copied each word woodenly, certain I'd misheard her. My inability to articulate a single thought probably wasn't doing me any favors. "Fauna, I know you're trying to get my brain on board with all this, but—"

"Yeah, that's part of it, Crazy Pants. I'm going to talk to the barista and place our orders while you wait off to the side so you can see me interacting. And we're going now before the world is awake because it's a Saturday, and no one gets out of bed this early, so it'll be dead inside. We'll be able to talk." She'd selected a pair of black leggings and a slim-cut athletic top. Her eyes crinkled with her smile. "Unlike you, I'm very clever."

"You're dressing me like we're coming from yoga," I said.

She beamed. "Now your outfit matches my pants. Bohemian suits me. And lots of city ladies get up early to go to exercise classes. No one will bat an eyelash. Now, we're wasting daylight and it's going to be a beautiful, summer day."

"We're not wasting daylight. The sun isn't even—"

"Can't hear you!" she sang as she danced from the room, voice trailing down the hall.

I grabbed my phone and saw sixteen notifications. I grimaced as I unlocked the screen.

(Nia) Let me know when you get home

(Nia) You did go home, right?

(Nia) Don't make me regret giving you that address

(Nia) Jesus, Mary and Joseph, if you went to a murderer's house, so help me god, I will be the next face on the news next for being the one who ENDS YOU MYSELF

Two missed calls

(Nia) Please pick up your phone. I gave you an address from a serial killer report and now you're not answering.

(Nia) Pick up your goddamn phone

Missed call

(Nia) I'm telling Kirby. We're going to kick your ass.

(Nia) You'd better not be dead or I'm going to regret my last text being mean to you

Missed call

(Nia) At what point do I call the police? Is it now? Do I call them now?

Two missed calls

(Nia) Three things. One, your doorman should be fired because they never should have confirmed that you're home. That's dangerous. I could be anyone, I shouldn't be privy to that information. Two, I'm glad they did, because now I know you made it back. Three, get ready for an ass whooping.

My thumbs moved quickly as I messaged her back that I'd run into an old friend and she'd stayed over. I apologized, gave a half-assed promise to never make her worry again, and closed the thread. Fauna and I had just parked after a twenty-minute drive—one where she'd pressed every button, flipped through twenty radio stations, rolled down the window, and been a conduit for chaos for every waking second—when my phone went off again.

I put the car in park.

(Nia) Liar. We both know you don't have friends.

My grumble was somewhere between a huff and a sigh. I turned to Fauna. "Take a photo with me?"

She glowed at the request, lit from some secret, inner sun as she said, "The great artists of yore used to paint and sculpt me, but sure, I guess I can snap a picture."

I held the phone out for a selfie, then immediately frowned down at the resulting image. She looked like a celebrity smiling next to a gremlin.

(Nia) Oh, it's a *hot* friend. Okay, I take back everything I said.
    Go be happy.
(Nia) I take back *half* of what I said. You're not forgiven for
    making Kirbs and me worry.
(Nia) Still, I hope your night was fun. And I want explicit
    details later

"Give me your card," Fauna said, holding out her hand as we stopped outside of the hippest coffee shop I could find in the city. I was such a shut-in that I'd had to search *cool cafés near me* before guiding my Mercedes into the sunrise as if I knew what I was doing. The morning light made her glitter with fairy-like qualities. The separate blocks of her copper-and-silver hair caught against the gold of the early morning light that bathed the sidewalk. A light, summery breeze ruffled her strands and brushed me with the same gentle fingers of sea spray, salt, and freshly cut pine I'd noticed on her before.

I frowned at the card. "Do you know how to use it?"

She sank her weight into one hip. "I watch the people-monkeys dance for me on your human television. That makes me an expert. Now, give it. Go in and take a seat."

I had to admit she was right. If I had stood beside her, I would have been able to convince myself that I'd been communicating on her behalf while in yet another in a long string of episodes. That said, I was very curious as to how the next few minutes would go. I was utterly ready to sit in despondent, caffeine-free quiet in the corner of the room until I realized no hot drinks were arriving.

Instead, I watched the barista fumble with the tongs, stumble over their words, and ogle like they'd seen a ghost when Fauna flashed them her brightest smile. She thanked the barista with a wave and sauntered as if she were walking the catwalk from the counter to the table before sliding into the seat across from me. She planted a blueberry scone in front of me and dug into a small mountain of honey-sweet treats in front of her.

Living in a converted warehouse hadn't stopped me from appreciating exposed brick, the shiny metal of ceiling duct work, or the industrial piping that could so easily be flipped into an artistic space. Enormous, arched windows made me wonder if this had once been a church before the era of gentrification. Now, canvases from local artists covered the cream bricks. Perky peonies dotted every table. The air was rich with freshly brewed coffee, warm bread, and the glow of early morning light.

It would have been aesthetic as hell even if I hadn't been eating with a goddess.

"Um, your majesties?" the barista called from behind the counter. The few patrons on the mostly vacant shop dared curious glances. All eyes lingered on Fauna.

From behind the sunglasses, Fauna winked. She clicked her tongue and shot a finger gun as she popped up to fetch the drinks.

"Never give out your real name," she said moments later as she returned to the space across from me. "Speaking of which, have I told you that you're a dumbass?"

I wrapped my fingers around the deliciously warm cup.

I'd begun to thank her before remembering that I'd technically paid for it. "You may have mentioned," I said. I took a sip and made a face. My tongue barely made it back into my mouth for me to demand, "What is this?"

"Six pumps of sugar. And caramel. And vanilla. Other nice things too. All the goodies. You're welcome."

I popped off the lid to ensure the liquid was still dark. I could barely spot the brownish hints of coffee amid the pale swirl of liquid toothaches. I looked up at Fauna, intent on scowling, but struggled to muster the expression against her frustrating beauty.

Fauna's ball cap and sunglasses only added an air of mystery. Instead of camouflaging her, they seemed to confirm the suspicions of workers and patrons alike that she was, in fact, someone worth hiding. I chewed on my lip as I considered the implications. Perhaps that was part of its charm. Her poor attempt at a disguise acknowledged their deeply rooted intuition that she was something *other* while giving them the excuse of believing she was a famous actress or singer who happened to be getting coffee with a tired hag.

She was clever. I'd give her that.

I slid the sugary drink toward her.

"More sweets for me." She positively twinkled as she accepted the offering. "Okay, you pick the topic. What should we cover first? Your sigil, or—"

"I want to know how you know me. I want to know what you have to do with any of this. Why would you intervene? Why—"

"Yikes, I got it." Her eyes flared dramatically. She wiped her hands on her pants, then drained the last sugary dredges of her coffee before switching to my still-full cup. "Go get yourself a new drink first. You're unpleasant. I hope it's just morning grumpies and caffeine deprivation. I'm going to be really bummed if I swooped in to save a wet blanket."

I bottled the irritated quips as I stood, extending my hand for the return of my credit card. If I hadn't already felt the blooming headache of sleeplessness and caffeine withdrawal, I would have fought her on the issue. When I ordered a black coffee with a side of honey, the barista quietly asked me who my friend was, and I told her that I was on a breakfast date. She blinked in disbelief, which offended me. I was half-tempted to give her my pen name when she asked for a name for the order, if only to give myself a sprinkle of credibility. Instead, I offered her something in a moment of bitterness. I waited impatiently by the counter until she slid a coffee over, saying, "Divine One?"

"That's me." I lifted a finger.

I slid across from Fauna just as she finished the last of her goodies.

"Spit it out, nymph," I said.

She snorted. "Maybe you do have some of your great-grandmother in you. Honestly, it would be better for all of us. Let that inner warrior shine. I saw the picture of her. The one on your fridge?"

I scalded the roof of my mouth with the far-more-acceptable coffee while my mind flashed to a black-and-white photo in a small magnet frame on my refrigerator. It was one of the few images of my grandmother before she'd left Norway. It was grainy, but I loved that they'd been in the traditional woolen dresses worn only on special occasions. The heirloom had been passed down my maternal line, though I hadn't seen it in years. The red-and-blue bunad was probably still in a cedar chest somewhere in my mother's storage.

I expected I wouldn't see the heirlooms again unless my mother died or stopped being a bitch long enough to apologize.

The former was more likely.

In the image, my great-grandmother Aloisa held the tiny bundle that would grow up to be Grandma Dagny, the sweet, agoraphobic, first-generation immigrant on North American soil. The fjords behind her had always been my favorite part of the image. It looked like it had been taken from something written by Hans Christian Andersen.

My memories faded into the present as the black-and-white picture dissolved into the bricks, the coffee shop, and the nonhuman in front of me. "You met both of them?"

She glowed, apple-round cheeks alit as she said, "Aloisa's a spitfire. We all understood why Geir fell for her. He loved her and his kid—your grandmother, that is."

"Geir?" I repeated the name quietly. Was that supposed to be my great-grandfather?

"Do you want to meet him?"

My heart dropped, then bobbed somewhere in my entrails. I looked over my shoulder as if she were surprising me with a setup on this coffee date. The lost organ continued anxiously beating somewhere between my intestines, keeping me alive while sending me into surefire sickness. Suddenly the coffee smell was overpowering. The morning light hurt my eyes. Was it just me, or was there less oxygen than there'd been a minute ago?

Fighting anxiety-induced nausea, I asked, "Why did they leave?"

Fauna leaned back in her chair. Mouth downturned, she said, "Salem wasn't the only place that had witch hunts, you know. Aloisa may have been human, but a lot of Europe was going through some religious shit pretty much side by side in the timeline. Ask Silas and his asshole of a master if you want more details. Aloisa thought it would be best to keep Dagny safe by leaving the country. This is supposed to be the land of religious freedom, right?" She gave a dark, humorless chuckle. "The angels fucking love it here."

I drank deeply from my cup, then asked, "Why are you here?"

"Oh." Fauna blinked. "In this country? I am and I'm not. We can go anywhere. We just generally...don't. Most of us spend our time in our respective realms because they're objectively better. You have some fun things here, don't get me wrong. I really like your croissants, and your ridiculous shows are worth the visit alone. The Nordes don't make sour gummy worms. Plus, mortal sensations are extra tingly. I'll explain that later. But, thrill seekers love coming to the human realm."

"So you're a thrill-seeking fae."

She swirled her cup. "Listen, I have no incentive to be on dead land. Your so-called angels and demons just use the mortal realm as a neutral battleground so they don't fuck up their own kingdoms. It's kind of brilliant, in an evil-genius sort of way."

I stared at her in horror.

"Come on," she pushed. "You write fantasy and have spent years fucking a demon, right? Shouldn't this be an easy pill for you to swallow?"

Fauna was just a smudge as my vision blurred. I tried to repeat the word, but my mouth had dried. It came out as little more than wind over dust. "Caliban...you said...*demon*..."

"Oh," she mumbled into the second cup of molasses she'd attempted to pass off as coffee. "Let's tackle that later."

The ground opened up beneath me. My body felt weightless as my soul plunged into the pits of hell. The church I'd spent my life running from, the world I'd denied tooth and nail, was at my door. A high-pitched ringing forced me into a memory. My mother's panicked words hung heavy in the house as she insisted that my imaginary friend was not of the Lord. It had been so cruel, so heartless, to take my only friend from me, and had planted within me the first seeds of doubt in my mother's wisdom. She'd accused something so good, something so kind and gentle and beautiful, of being evil. It was the seed of distrust that grew roots over the years so I could see her fanaticism for what it was.

Except she'd been right.

"Are you okay?" Fauna said the words, but they were muffled as the ringing continued.

Sweat prickled over my forehead. My mother was right.

Angels and demons. An imaginary friend from hell itself. It couldn't be true. It had to—

Pain. Sharp, shooting, acute. "Ow!" My hand flew to my bicep. My eyes bulged as I looked in Fauna in horror. She'd pinched me with bruising strength. "God damnit!"

"Did it help?" she asked. At my blank expression, she said, "You looked like you were in the middle of an existential crisis. I'm happy to pinch you as many times as you need. Or even if you don't need."

It was the tenth time in twenty-four hours that I'd forgotten how to breathe. I struggled to speak. "It's a little difficult to hear things that tear a hole in your understanding of the world."

"Marlow…" She chewed on my name.

My heart skipped an anxious beat as I watched the nymph, my eyes wide. "What now?"

She shook her head. "No, it wasn't a question. I was just tasting your name. It didn't make sense at first, but I think I get it now."

Heart still stuttering, I focused on my breathing while waiting with a quizzical brow.

"Driftwood—the meaning of your name. It seemed irrelevant. But now I see you in our waters, bobbing amid realms. It's quite poetic, actually. Human parents so rarely consider the implications of things when they name their children, do they? Yet here you are, floating between kingdoms."

"Call the kingdoms what they are. It's heaven and hell. That's what you're telling me. Oh my god, my mom was right."

Fauna made a face. "She was *barely* right. You're just leaving me and the other pantheons out? Rude." Then to herself, she muttered, "The narcissism of pretending they're the only two realms in the universe."

She probably had a few other choice words under her breath, but I was hung up on repeating a single word to myself over, and over, and over again.

Demon.

She spoke again, breaking my fixation. "Are we here for a history lesson, or should we go see Geir?"

I did, in fact, want a history lesson.

I wanted to talk about mundane things and bury my nose in books and ground myself in literature. I was almost positive that I did not want to meet a centuries-old Nordic creature of lore who'd sired Grandma Dagny. There wouldn't be enough room on any of my credit cards for the therapy I'd need to recover from such an experience. "No. Right now, all I want is to survive this coffee date. Then maybe I'll go back home, nap—since it's still too early for even the birds—and when I wake up this will all have been a dream."

"Shoot me straight," she said.

I sipped my coffee and used it as a grounding exercise. When having a panic attack, you were supposed to use the five senses. I tasted a well-brewed pour-over with honey. I smelled ground beans. I heard the clinking of cups and the espresso machine whir. I felt the warm cup. Everything was familiar, everything was anchoring, save for what I saw. Fauna was not of this world, and yet, here she was.

She parted what looked like petal-soft lips and asked, "Are you fighting this because you genuinely think you're crazy? Or are you pushing back because you don't want to deal with the consequences of accepting that there is so much more to life than you knew?"

She waited expectantly. My silence procured a smug look on her end before she took a satisfied slurp of her drink.

My eyes narrowed.

"Well, I know when I'm not wanted," she said brightly. She stood and headed for the door.

"Wait!" My still-inconsistent heart refused to pick a pattern as it slammed into my ribs at the fear that she was leaving. I panicked as I glanced around the coffee shop, realizing she was about to leave me completely and utterly alone. "How will you get home? I drove."

140

Her giggle was pointed, and I knew the laugh was an answer in and of itself. She was only present because she chose to be. She'd stayed with me because she'd wanted to. All she needed to do was step into the alleyway, away from prying eyes, and she could disappear.

"Will you come back?"

Fauna flashed a smile brighter than the moon as she said, "Are you kidding? With an angel sniffing around? You can't be left alone for more than ten minutes. You're stuck with us now."

Chapter Fourteen

I WAS STRUCK BY HOW MEDICAL IT SMELLED.

The chemical scents of astringent and dried blood filled my nostrils from the moment I stepped through the door. I'd expected dark rooms, leather jackets, skulls, and the sort of intimidating figure who might have stepped off the streets from a motorcycle gang. The music was a little too loud, but it was the sort of alternative rock I liked. Glass cases full of jewelry greeted me. Elaborate art dotted the walls. A girl with a swirly spike in her gauged ear and an inked sleeve of herbs and spices smiled at me as I entered. She was in a lovely shade of mustard and wore the sort of embellished, floral broach I'd seen only on grannies in their late nineties. She looked up from her phone and flashed me her teeth.

"Do you have an appointment?" she asked, voice chirping up over the bass that thrummed through the building, both music and receptionist fighting to be heard over the constant buzz from somewhere in the back.

"Do you take walk-ins?"

She nodded. "Can I see the size of your piece?"

I showed her and she offered me a reassuring look. "You're lucky," she said. "Nick is busy, but Mikey is scheduled for a regular who always shows up an hour late, and we've barely opened. He should be able to squeeze you in. But even if the piece only takes twenty minutes, we still charge one-hour minimum. Got it?"

She shouted for Mikey after my nod in confirmation. She slid a form for me to sign my life away before I lay down in Mikey's chair. He examined the folded piece of paper.

"That wizard movie?" he asked.

I closed my eyes in a soft chuckle, making an on-the-spot decision as to whether or not now was the time to grand-stand about ethical consumption of media. Instead, I landed on responding with, "Absolutely not."

"Sacred geometry, then? One of those chakra things?"

I made an apologetic face. He was trying, but I wasn't ready to be loose-lipped. "Not quite."

"This some demonic shit?" he asked. Mikey was a man in his late thirties covered in a series of disconnected patchwork tattoos, not unlike someone collecting Girl Scout badges.

We were surrounded by paintings, prints, and charts, presum-ably from the artists who worked at the studio. Some were intri-cate mandalas or lovely watercolors; others were big-breasted purple women with horns poking up from their glossy hair in 1950s pinup poses. An enormous mural of the four horsemen of the apocalypse lined one end of the shop, showcasing a skele-tal army of conquest, famine, war, and death. Maybe they'd be fine with devilry. I tore my eyes from the painting to look at the man who waited patiently for my answer.

I looked as nonchalant as I could. "It might be. Can you make the circle better? I did sort of a bad job."

"Are there any other changes—"

"No!" I said a little too forcefully, jolting up as I did so. I made myself relax before lying back down. He raised his eyebrows at me, so I calmed my tone before saying, "The only thing I want perfected is the circle around it. Other than that, you can't change a single thing. Not a line, not a shape, nothing. Okay?"

He shrugged as he dipped the needle in ink. "It's your tattoo, boss."

I swallowed as he lowered the humming piece of machinery to my arm, pausing on my forearm. He hovered on the flat spot just below my elbow crease.

"You ready?"

I didn't know, truth be told. I'd gotten little splashes of ink before; that wasn't the problem. The conversation-starting sun and moon on my opposing ring fingers that had connected Taylor and me on the streets of Buenos Aires had hurt, but the pain wasn't stopping me.

This wasn't a tattoo.

This was a folded piece of paper in the back of my pocket that had allowed me to see the Cheshire-cat smile of a parasitic entity. It was the sigil that had existed above my door for longer than I could possibly know. If Fauna was right, it was the very thing that had let me see Silas even in a basement of nightmares.

Maybe I'd need to bond myself to someone in order to lift the veil and see the things that existed beyond mortal sight...

Or maybe...

"I'm ready."

✦

"Remind me to make an adjustment to the wards so I can come and go. I did *too* good of a job on your doors and had to sweet-talk your doorman to let me up. On that note, he should probably be fired. He thinks pretty girls can't be hitmen? Sexist." It was Fauna's greeting as she breezed in like a tornado. Her outfit was a little different today—now in a cutoff, oversize band T-shirt that showed most of her midriff and something that might have been mandalas on her pants. They hugged the small of her waist, then tumbled in loose, hemp crinkles over her hips until they reached the floor. She looked like she'd just stumbled out of a music festival. I had no idea where this creature was getting her clothes.

She'd barely entered the apartment, her stolen rose-gold card still clattering to the island, before her eyes sharpened.

She sniffed the air once, then fixed her eyes on me with laser focus. She stormed toward me with the threat of a thunderhead, descending on me before I had enough time to do anything other than close my laptop and shove it on the cushion beside me.

She grabbed my wrist roughly and yanked the sleeve up over my elbow. I yelped against the yank of fabric on raw skin. Her eyes froze on the red, raised welt that stung below the fresh black ink. She stared at it for a long while with inscrutable emotion. When her eyes lifted, a small, appreciative smile tugged at the corner of her lips. She was quiet for a while before she said, "Maybe you're not such a dumbass after all."

"Will it work?" I breathed, looking from my swollen tattoo to her sparkling doe eyes.

"Lifting the veil without a bond? A true sight sigil still won't let you jump realms, but when it comes to seeing things humans shouldn't, there's only one way to know. Shall we test it out?"

I barely had time to grab my purse from the counter.

"Where are we going?"

"Where's your sense of adventure?" She grabbed my hand, and I followed in her wake as she tugged me from the building. The receptionist was an attendant from the original rotation and knew better than to interrupt my mayhem, so she said nothing as I was dragged through the lobby. Fauna led me to the parking garage and gestured impatiently for me to open the door. I obliged but frowned as I tapped the card to the garage.

"Can't you bring me with you? When you go places, I mean?"

She looked at me uncertainly. "I can go, but you'd have to stay behind. And as long as you're a person of interest for heaven, I don't know how wise it is to leave you alone. I assume you got the tattoo to circumvent the bond so you can see shit? You'll need an escort, but it's smart work, ace. Still, unless you connect yourself to one of the fae, you can't leave your kingdom on your own."

"And oh, what a mighty kingdom it is," I grumbled as I procured my keys. I unlocked the car and immediately regretted driving.

Fauna hadn't lost an ounce of her enthusiasm for the radio, the windows, the hazard lights. She also seemed to get a kick out of reaching around me to yank on the wipers.

"You're like a toddler! Stop touching things!" I smacked her hand as I eased out of the garage.

She gasped. "Excuse me! I'm a deity! You do not hit me; you worship me. Now, quick—make penance and I may yet be benevolent. I'll accept your sacrifice in the form of sweets. Can we stop by a candy shop? You know chocolate-dipped strawberries? Where can we find one?"

My irritation dissolved into a stifled giggle. "You're ridiculous."

With a dainty shake of her head, she said, "You think I'm kidding. Just you wait until I bring pestilence and suffering on the land."

I shot an unamused look over my shoulder as I took the on-ramp and changed lanes to head downtown.

"So, deity, where are we going?" I stopped her in the middle of her raised finger. "Other than strawberries. We can get those after you explain why you dragged me from the apartment. I assume we're on our way to test out the sigil?"

"Oh, right. Give me your phone."

"Absolutely not."

"Give it to me!"

With no regard for either of our lives or safety, Fauna nearly caused a four-car pileup as she lurched into my pocket, causing me to jerk the wheel into the neighboring lane. I overcorrected with a white-knuckle grip on the wheel. An angry Escalade driver lay on their horn until Fauna flicked her fingers with annoyance. To my surprise, the noise stopped.

"Did you do that?" I asked.

"Get on your knees later, peasant," she responded. "Now, what's your password?"

"I'm not going to—"

"Oh! I don't need it. You have a video call coming in."

"Don't!" But I didn't have time to stop her. She'd already accepted the call.

"Holy sh—oh my god. Hi, hi!" sputtered the startled voice on the other line.

"Hi, Kirby," I said dryly while I drove, not needing to see the screen to know exactly how poorly the interaction was going. "Meet Fauna."

"Um"—Kirby coughed on the word—"I guess I caught you at a bad time. Nia said you had a *friend* and I thought we were being left out, but I see you're busy, and, um." They continued their flustered rambles. I could practically hear their shade of crimson through the pixels.

"Kirby!" Fauna beamed. "What a quirky name. It's not one I've heard before, and I do love names. Thank you for giving me a new word on my tongue to play with." Fauna winked.

"It's not their real name." I rolled my eyes. "It's—"

"Tut, tut," Fauna cut me off. "Chosen names are the only ones I'll accept. Don't be handing out things that aren't yours to give." I glared at the cars ahead while she prattled on. "But Kirby, be a darling and tell me, where can we find a confectionary? Will you search for an address and text it to me? Marlow is uncooperative."

Kirby stammered. "You...you want me to find a candy shop?"

"One with chocolate strawberries, please and thank you. And make it close to downtown. We're going to be in the arts district, just past the university."

I arched a brow at Fauna's knowledge of the city before shouting to my friend, "Sorry. She's pushy. You don't have to look up the address of a—"

Kirby had already found a location and begun to give detailed destructions.

147

"You're an absolute treat," Fauna cooed. "Thank you, peaches. I hope we get to meet soon. Now I have to hang up before Marlow commits deicide." She ended the call and beamed at me from the passenger seat.

"Were you really just trying to get my phone to look up candy shop addresses?"

"I have a sweet tooth," she pouted. "Plus, I'm doing you a favor. And you hit me."

"I barely touched you."

She ignored my rebuttal.

"Now," Fauna said cheerily, "without being the rudest person alive and sharing a birth name, how did that doll come across the name Kirby? I'm still tickled. The only Kirby I've heard of was that round cutie from the show? Or the game? You know, the human game—"

I smiled sadly at the memory. "Yeah, that's why they got their name."

I changed lanes and appreciated Fauna's uncharacteristic patience as she waited.

"It's kind of a weird story. Are you sure you want to hear it?"

"We have time before our exit," she said, "and what's time for if not to collect stories?"

I made a face. I waited for a long moment, listening to the hum of the engine, the whir of the tires, and monitoring her perfectly still form from my peripherals before I released a weary breath. Eventually, I said, "It was my eleventh birthday, and it was a shitshow. I don't want to go through all the details, but I wasn't very popular growing up. I don't know why I'd thought it would be a good idea to invite all the kids in my class, but only ten showed up." I chuckled darkly, thinking of the seventy-two invitations I'd made on construction paper. I'd spent the entire day before decorating cupcakes with my mother and helping her clean the yard so we could play red rover or have balloon fights, with the naive optimism that the entire class might come.

"And you played the game?" she prompted, voice softening as she observed the slump of my shoulders.

I sighed. "Kind of. This girl, Nancy, she'd gotten me a present—well, her mom had gotten the present—and when I opened it, she decided she wanted it. It was a stuffed bear, and I told her she'd given it to me for my birthday and couldn't have it back. It was mine."

"Sounds like Nancy was a little bitch," Fauna mumbled.

I agreed, "Yeah, but that didn't stop my dad from spanking me in front of all of my friends while in my party dress for being selfish. Anyway, it freaked nine of them out so much that they called their parents to come pick them up. The party was over. I never celebrated my birthday again."

Fauna's jaw dropped. "Fucking gods and goddesses, Marlow. When you said it was a shitshow, I didn't realize you were about to traumatize me."

I urged the car to the right-most lane and shook my head, keeping an eye on the green exits. "It ended up being okay. Kirby was the only one who stayed. They'd brought their gaming system to the party, and we played that cartoon fighting game. I kicked their butt as ten different characters. As the princess, as the fox, as the spaceman—almost all of them. They chose the Kirby character over and over again. They had no fighting strategy. They'd just wiggle to the edge and try to spit me out. It was the only thing that made me laugh all day. And the next day when they called the house phone and my mom picked up, they said to tell me that Kirby was calling. Their nickname stuck."

It was the longest I'd ever witnessed Fauna be silent. She remained perfectly still for a long moment before she said, "I'm sorry that happened to you."

I shrugged as I'd been trained to do. One had to slough off tragedy quickly in order to keep conversation moving. "Pain builds character. Plus, we ended up dating a little in high school. Swapped v-cards and all that. But, it's better this way. We're more than friends now. We're family."

The skin around Fauna's eyes crinkled as she smirked. "Of course, your best friend is an ex. I love queer culture."

I kept my eyes on the traffic, smirking all the while. It was hard to argue. Staying friends after a breakup was something of a cliché. "Now, are you going to tell me where we're going? Right now, I'm just angling my car toward—"

"Oh, shit, that's right. Your trauma was distracting. Take the next exit. We need to pay a visit to a friend."

I was surprised and confused when she told me to wait in the car, until I realized she'd tricked me into taking her to the sweets shop first. I narrowed my eyes at the box in her hand, but she wrinkled her nose at me and informed me that grouchy car companions don't get strawberries.

The drive from the 1950s-style confectionary to her second destination wasn't long. Ten minutes later, we were hunting for a parking place. Fauna enjoyed how easily traffic made me curse, delighted by each new obscenity as I searched for a place to parallel park, yelled at assholes in luxury vehicles, and told one man exactly what I thought he could do with his own mother. Finding an open place on the street in the arts district was impossible, and she still hadn't told me why we were here.

Fauna practically leapt from the car before I'd even taken it out of gear.

"Grab the box!" she shouted as she took off.

I scrambled to unbuckle my belt and pour myself out of the car to yell at her, but she was already halfway down the block. I jogged to catch up just as she yanked open an aged, wooden door to what appeared to be a metaphysical shop. I paused just long enough to read the glass. *Daily Devils* had been stenciled over the window in large, gothic lettering. The shop had popped up over the summer in my searches for answers, but it had no online presence and hadn't listed a phone number. I might have visited it on my own, given enough time and frustration. Now I trailed behind Fauna as the tinkling of an antique bell sounded our arrival.

Crossing the threshold meant stepping into a cloud of incense. I blinked against the smoke while searching trinkets and bobbles and shelves for the source, but it seemed to be coming from everywhere and nowhere. Bundles of juniper and sage, rows of candles, and stacks of crystals lined the window. Every wall was cluttered tightly with brown, green, blue, and clear bottles containing muted liquids, oils, powders, leaves, and herbs. Enormous, thick curtains had been draped from the ceiling in bundled tufts, giving me the sensation that I was somehow under deep, dark waves. I'd barely had time to take in the store as the shopkeeper came out from the back. The tight curls of her short, peppered hair were a shock of silver on warm features. Warm, brown skin was lined with her years, speckled with spots from age and the sun alike.

Fauna whipped off her sunglasses just as the shopkeeper's face dissolved into a smile as radiant as the sun itself.

"Fauna!" She gasped, weathered hand clutching at her heart.

"Betty, you beautiful, perfect butterfly!" Fauna ran to the woman's side and snuck behind the counter, wrapping her in a hug.

"My goodness, what are you doing here?" Betty asked. "I haven't seen you in...what's it been?"

Fauna looked off into the distance while she calculated. "Has to be...one hundred and thirty years?"

Betty's eyes widened incredulously. "Has it really been that long?" She stepped out of the hug and beamed, slapping Fauna on the arm. "And yet here I am looking like an old bag of bones while you're even lovelier than the day I met you."

Fauna turned to me and said, "See? That's how you talk to me."

"She hit you too," I muttered as I approached, fingers still wrapped around the cardboard box of fruit and sugar.

"I brought you presents!" Fauna said, glowing. She wiggled her fingers for me to hand over the box, then opened the top for Betty's appreciative gasp.

151

"You remembered!" The woman sounded like she might cry while she eyed the strawberries.

"As if I could forget a single thing about you." Fauna said, looping her arm through the woman's bent elbow. "Betty, this is Marlow, my human tag-along. Marlow is a nitwit and has no hope of surviving in the world yet has somehow found herself in something of a conundrum. Marlow, this is Betty. Betty is perfect, has never done anything wrong, and is cooler than you'll ever be."

Betty's eyes sparkled as she said, "You're exactly as I remember you."

I struggled to understand the sight before me, but that was nothing new. I'd had trouble coping with most of what had occurred over the last several days. "How do you two know each other? Does she also...?" I stopped myself from asking if Betty had fae parentage. I didn't know what was and wasn't polite.

"Betty freed one of my sisters. She was running her craft in a seaside town in...Svalsbard?"

"Tórshavn."

"Gods and goddesses," Fauna exclaimed, "that's right! Time flies. Betty was in Arran two centuries ago. We are in *luck* that such a flawless treasure made it to your sorry city, Mar. Tell me, mythologist, why didn't you include selkies in your first book?"

I blinked in surprise. "Your sister was a...selkie?"

Fauna made a show of frowning at me. Not just her mouth, but her brows, the shake of her shoulders, the pucker of her cheeks all underlined her glare. "Selkies! The first *Pantheon* novel was all about Norse mythology, but you couldn't be bothered to include selkies?"

"They're more Scottish folklore..." I began to argue but snapped my mouth shut as Fauna's eyes became unimpressed slits.

"You're bad at your job," she told me matter-of-factly. "The Faroe Islands are every bit as part of the Nordes as I am. And if you know anything of selkies—"

I nodded, recalling the lore. "A human can hide their seal skin so they can't return to the sea. It's an old folktale people told to explain feelings about women being forced into marriages. It was a feminist tale."

The matching faces of disappointment looking back at me had me biting my tongue.

"See, Betty? She's hopeless. Yet here I am. And in need of a favor."

Betty patted Fauna's hand as she went to the shelves, scanning her bottles. "Anything for you, dear. Do you need something for your friend's intelligence?"

Fauna snorted.

I opted to speak up for myself. "I'm looking for someone."

The smug, self-assured look faded from Fauna's features. She watched my face thoughtfully.

"A...a friend. No, he was more than that. He was...is... so much more than that. And I asked him not to come back, and...I need to undo it. I didn't believe he was real when I said what I said. Not truly. I need..."

Betty turned to me, kindness in her eyes. She reached for me, clasping me in warmth as she held my hand with one of her own and covered it with the other. Tenderness coursed from her to me like the same warm honey I liked to stir into my coffee, turning bitterness into something sweet.

With a gentle frown, she said, "It's a mistake you'll have to learn from, Marlow. Names, commands, promises...they have power that those of us having a mortal experience don't understand. Humans aren't like fae, sweet one. We can lie. We can break our word. We don't need consent. Some suggest that the human kingdom is the true hell, and I often wonder if they're right."

The incense suddenly became too strong. I struggled to see through the cloud of smoke before I realized it was just the glaze of my own impending tears. Betty was the first human I'd ever spoken to about Caliban, even if I hadn't said his name—hadn't said anything, really. She'd validated

153

me. She'd recognized my experience and my pain all in one gentle piece of advice.

"Are you still working with Azrames?" Fauna asked. Her tone was gentle enough not to break my reverie, but there was a new edge to her question.

Betty's happy smile returned. "Of course I am! It's better in this lifetime than ever before. Business is abundant in the city. And the internet? I'm not even on the damn thing, but one client tells another tells another. It's remarkable."

Fauna propped her elbows against the counter and rested her chin on her hand as she looked at me, explaining, "Betty is one of the few witches I know who work with a demon. They make quite the team."

I balked at the sentence. Imagining the bartering of souls and the gnashing teeth of hellhounds, I couldn't stop myself from asking, "What could a demon want from a business partnership?"

Betty's lip pressed into a line. She gave Fauna a look.

Fauna complied, albeit impatiently. "Marlow, why might a detective arrest a criminal?"

"Um…because it's their job?"

I could tell she muttered *idiot* before trying again. Betty kept her polite chuckle to herself as Fauna continued, "It's not just for the money. You know human psychology better than this. Tell me what a detective gets out of solving a case."

"A sense of justice?"

Her face-framing curls puffed up in a cloud as she blew a dramatic huff of air. "*Satisfaction.* It's an orgasmic satisfaction to know that you were responsible for solving something complicated, for cracking a code, for tackling malevolence. Now, humans barter mostly in money or materials, but a lot of fae prefer a different form of payment. Like devotion, or kindness, or pain."

"He wants pain?"

"For the love of the deities, I cannot with this girl." Fauna threw up her hands.

Betty sighed heavily. She looked at me seriously. "I help women. Mostly those in abusive relationships, be it with lovers or husbands or parents. They come to me when they're in a bind, and Azrames gets the job done. The woman is set free, I pay my bills, and Azrames gets the victory of absorbing malevolence. The same way that a dam creates electricity from water or that we might get fire from wood. Malevolence does not feed malevolence. He's paid by taking one thing and converting it into another. Something new. Something better."

"Betty is the Patron Saint of Women," Fauna said with the click of her tongue. She'd folded her arms over her chest and was leaning against the shelves. "You are the Patron Saint of Frustrating Everyone Around You." Then to Betty she asked, "Would Azrames be willing to help us find Marlow's Prince?"

Her brows lifted, eyes alarmingly clear as she tested, "When you say *prince*..."

"I mean *Prince*."

Betty shuffled around the counter to lock the front door without another word. She flipped the sign from *Open* to *Closed* before beckoning us to follow her into the back room. I wanted to be alarmed at how quickly she'd reacted, but I had no basis for comparison. I picked my way through the shop, moving a curtain to the side as I ducked into her private office. I'd expected a round, velvet-clad table and a crystal ball but found merely a writing desk with a small, pretty—if a bit peculiar—altar. A number of candles, crystals, and one intricate, unfamiliar sigil decorated the space. A cup of tea sat on one side and a sealed, blue bottle of an unknown liquid rested on the other.

Betty lit a few of the candles. Low, ambient music continued to pipe through the shop. It wasn't the relaxing spa music I'd expect from a yoga session or crystal store but, rather, the low, haunting pluck of a mandolin.

"Get the light, would you?" she asked Fauna.

The electric bulb winked out with the click of her wrist.

155

Shadows filled any space that the orange glow couldn't reach. Betty gestured for us to stand back. We gave her space while she closed her eyes and settled into a slow meditation. When she called to the demon, it was not unlike me calling a friend on the telephone. She spoke to him again with a calm, patient informality, then waited. Thirty seconds of nothingness passed. My nerves heightened as if every cell were on its tiptoes. I held my breath as one minute stretched into two. Three minutes, then five, then ten and still, nothing had changed. The anxiety must have been clear on my face, since a squeeze on my arm from Fauna urged me to remain silent.

Fifteen minutes passed before the candles flickered.

My sharp intake of air was the first noise in the room. There'd scarcely been an inch between me and the wall behind me, but I jolted so suddenly that my head hit the plaster as I stumbled backward, putting as much space between myself and the newcomer as I could.

A young man, scarcely older than Fauna, tucked his hands into his pockets at the far end of the space. My eyes struggled to adjust through the gloom, but aside from the yellow flicker of Betty's flames, I could have sworn that the beautiful male was in monochromatic shades of black, white, and gray. He wore a black jacket rolled up at the forearms with a thin white shirt beneath. I swallowed, dragging my eyes away from the way the material left little to the imagination between the divots in his abs and curves of his pectorals. Large, thick silver chains in the form of one long rope lassoed into a single necklace, intermittently dotted with large, circular breaks in the chain. I'd intended to look only at the necklace, but my eyes traveled down the lowest rope to where a curious pendant—another circle with an interesting, complex sigil—hung just above the button of his pants. Even his steely skin was highlighted and shadowed as if he'd stepped from a world without color. Two obsidian horns, scarcely distinguishable above the youthful mess of his mussed, dark hair, poked up just above his temples.

"Hey, Az," Fauna greeted. "How's Hell?"

Chapter Fifteen

"FAUNA." HE FLASHED HER A COCKY GRIN. HE SMELLED OF ashes and smoke, and with his lack of color, that was precisely what he looked like. I could have imagined it, but Fauna seemed to pink slightly as she squirmed beside me.

"You two know each other?" I surprised myself by choking out a question.

The one they'd called Azrames started. His eyes flared in genuine surprise. While Betty's eyes remained closed, I didn't miss the way her head had tilted in disbelief.

His sooty brows lifted. "The human can see me?" he asked Fauna. He turned his gray eyes. I shrank under his gaze as he reiterated, "You can see me?"

Fauna answered on my behalf, which was a relief, because I wasn't sure I remembered how to speak. "It's why we're here. And it was sort of a 'two birds, one stone' situation. Glad to know her impulse tattoo is working. Betty's an absolute darling and was willing to help us get in touch with someone from your kingdom."

He clicked his tongue. "You know you didn't have to go through all that trouble, Fauna. I would have come for you."

I choked on my breath. The way he rested on the end of his sentence was borderline pornographic. My gaze shot from him to the fidgeting fae at my side for confirmation that

I wasn't reading into things. Oh yeah. She was definitely red. Perhaps it was my nerves edging me toward laughter, but I had to bite down on my lip to keep from making a sound. I'd never seen her uncomfortable before.

She cleared her throat to gather her composure before saying, "I'm sort of mortal-bound at the moment. I don't have the luxury of popping through realms while I have this little nuisance at my hip. Speaking of: Az, this is my friend. And, friend, would you like to introduce yourself?"

"I'm Marlow. Marlow Thorson—"

Everyone in the room, Azrames included, reacted. Even Betty, eyes still closed while she remained seated at her writing desk, shook her head in vehement disapproval.

Fauna punched me in the arm. "We've had this talk! Twice! You even threw in your family name this time? For fuck's sake, have you no sense of self-preservation?"

"What?" I demanded, my voice too loud for the occasion. "Am I supposed to lie to him? Do you want me to treat him like the barista and tell him to call me 'Your Majesty'?"

She made a contemplative face. "Actually, that helps me cut to the chase. Az, how's the Royal Family?"

His lips turned down. "How did you know to ask?"

I stiffened. To my surprise, so did Fauna.

"Why?" she asked slowly.

He shook his head. "Things are..." He looked at me, then back at her.

She jerked a thumb toward me. "This is the Prince's human."

I could have sworn his knees buckled. Azrames's hands left his pockets as smoky fingers ran through his hair, smoothing it out. He swallowed audibly. "This is..."

"So, you see why I can't exactly ditch her? It wouldn't look good for the Nordes' relationship with Hell. It'd be hard for us to stay neutral if we let a princess-in-waiting die on our watch—or whatever it was Heaven wants from her now that they know."

My heart hiccupped uncomfortably at her words. The shadows pressed in, everything suddenly seeming a bit too small, too smoky, too claustrophobic. I grabbed Fauna's arm for support, which she accepted fully.

Azrames took several steps closer. He examined me with cautious respect, then looked at her. "I didn't realize the Prince's human had fae blood. I thought it was just your scent when I arrived. It's been a minute since that chilly pine perfume…" He lifted a hand as if to brush her hair away from her face, then faltered. He lowered it again, dusting the shadows from his monochromatic clothes. He looked at me then and extended an open palm as he said, "It's an honor to meet you."

On instinct, I slipped my hand into his.

He pressed his lips gently to my knuckles, shooting painful nostalgia through me at the cool, soothing touch through my spine. He released my hand, then offered me an apologetic smile. "We haven't seen him. He hasn't come back from the mortal realms in some time. And if he isn't with his human—"

"Marlow," I corrected.

"With his idiot," Fauna said.

Azrames exhaled before amending, "If he isn't with Marlow, then I'm not sure where he is. Word is, he hasn't been in Hell for a while. I'm not high-ranking enough to have access to the information. You should speak to the King. He would want to help you. Not just for his son but for you, Marlow."

It was my turn to blush. All the air left the small room. I was no longer able to look at his too-smooth face, his mussed hair, or the way his shirt showed his muscles with just a little too much clarity.

Fauna's face scrunched. "She can't go into another realm unless she's bound. That's why I'm stuck in this flesh prison. And without the Prince to offer passage between realms…"

His jaw ticked while he considered her problem. "And I

159

suppose she doesn't want to bind herself to you because she's spoken for."

My stomach lurched. *Spoken for.*

Fauna popped a lip into her mouth. She sucked on it idly as she asked, "Is there any reason he might be hiding?"

His chuckle was humorless but not unkind. "Our Prince? No. There's no beast, curse, or deity that could send anyone in the Royal Family into hiding. He could merely..." Azrames snapped his fingers. "I strike down mortals. The Prince? He conquers deities."

She frowned up at him, batting her lashes more than seemed entirely necessary.

He rested a hand on the wall near Fauna's head, relaxing his weight into the space only inches from her while he considered the question. "Could you go as her intercessor? If she's a Norde, you might be able to act as her mouthpiece?" His eyes lingered on her lips as he said the final words.

"The girl has angels—well, one asshole in particular—sniffing around her," she said, allowing her gaze to similarly flit to the sensuous curve of his lips.

"Which angel?" he asked, eyes tightening.

"He's going by Silas these days. Do you know him?"

His dark laugh sent a thrill through me as he said, "We all know Silas."

"So, you get it. I can't leave her unaccompanied until we figure out what to do with her. Any ideas?" I could have been imagining the way Fauna's hips lifted slightly from the wall as if arching toward him, but I didn't think I was.

"Her fae blood?" he asked, voice dropping an octave as he practically purred inches from her ear. "Was her ancestor given anything?"

I knew they were talking about me and doing their best to be solution-oriented, but I felt like I was watching foreplay. Fauna bit her lip as she stared into the stormy sky within his eyes. His half-smile bore down on her, a sharp canine glinting in the candlelight as if ready to devour her whole.

"Mar?" Fauna asked breathlessly, not bothering to look at me while the nymph eye-fucked the demon lingering over her. "Do you have access to Aloisa's things?"

My mouth parted, unable to answer her. Though she was trying to help, I felt like I either needed to get out of the room before they started ripping each other's clothes off or splash Fauna in cold water. I stuttered through the first word, unsure if I remembered how to speak and too distracted to decide if I cared to try. I either needed them to kiss and relieve the tension for the entire room or remember that they were not alone. I wondered what Betty made of all of this. I shot a glance to the woman who still sat at her writing desk, then back to Fauna.

I squeezed my eyes shut, inhaling and exhaling before I was ready to respond. "There's a cedar chest at my parents' place. I know my great-grandmother's traditional clothes are in there. Her bunad is still safe."

Their sexual tension shattered as they pierced me with their collective attention. Azrames dropped his arm and Fauna angled for me. Her fingers bit into my shoulders as she grabbed both of my arms. "Is there a sølje pinned to it?"

The question was so specific, so bizarre, that it took me a moment to gather my bearings. I retreated into my memory bank and pictured the things from the old country that my mother had tucked away. I blinked rapidly before nodding. Yes, the traditional silver broach with ornate, spoon-like dangles was an important part of the classic woolen dress. The filigree jewelry was often passed down in traditional Scandinavian families as an heirloom.

Fauna's fingers tightened around my arms. "This is important, Marlow. If you've seen the broach or a picture of it, think carefully—what does the center look like? Is it like a crown? A flower? A pretty shape?"

It took me a second to conjure the image from my memories. I'd snuck away many a time to riffle through the cedar chest as a child, loving the scent of wood and imagining the treasures within as if they were my dowry. I'd always carefully folded everything and put it back exactly as I'd found it before my mother would catch me. But the silver broach stuck out with unique clarity. I shook my head slowly. "No... my great-grandma's was different. It was something odd...it always looked like..."

"A tree?" she asked breathlessly.

"A tree," I confirmed.

Fauna released me and looked to Azrames. "I wish I could stay, but..."

He extended his hand again as he'd done for me. When he kissed her knuckles, his lips lingered on her fingers, lifting only his eyes to burn into hers. Her tiny hitch of air assured us all that the gesture had been wildly effective. "I wish you wouldn't make me wait twenty years between visits, but then again, I know what you are. Only a fool would try to pin you down. Stay wild and free, Fauna."

With a backward step, he was gone.

The moment he vanished, Fauna released a long-held squeal. Betty broke her meditative state to spin to us. She shook her head with a knowing grin, saying, "Fauna, you really haven't changed a bit, have you."

"Breaking hearts and taking names." Fauna wiggled excitedly. She helped Betty to her feet as we made our way out of the shop. She was still dancing from the exchange.

"Sorry to interrupt whatever that was," I said, still reeling, "but what the hell does my great-grandma's broach have to do with anything?"

Betty looked at me. "It sounds like your heirloom is the gift of a thousand lifetimes. It'll allow you to walk with Fauna between realms, without needing to be bound to anyone."

"But why would I go alone? I don't know how—"

"I said the object will allow you to walk through realms without being *bound*," Betty said firmly. "I didn't say anything about not needing to be accompanied. Unless I'm missing something and you know how to jump realms as a mortal.

162

Though you could do worse than bonding yourself to Fauna." Then to my babysitter, she said, "You have your hands full with this one."

"Don't I know it," Fauna said. Still glowing from her exchange with the man made of ashes and smoke, she said, "Betty, I can't thank you enough. But you can do something for me?"

"For you? Anything."

Sincerity rushed through her as she said, "Be safe. The world is a better place with you in it, in this life and the next. Whether it's robbers or angels—"

"Honey, I know all about the worst the world has to offer. I have wards all over the building. I didn't skimp on my security system. I've got a Glock under the register for hooligans, and for Heaven? I have Azrames."

Fauna relaxed visibly. Her face softened as she squeezed Betty's hand. "And enjoy those strawberries."

We'd barely left the shop before I asked, "Were you talking about past lives? With selkies and knowing Betty and…"

"That's your first question?" She frowned at me as we fell into step along the sidewalk.

I lifted a single shoulder. I had a million questions, but every chisel at the marble of my understanding would do wonders for shaping my worldview.

She cast a sidelong smirk at me with the ever-present look of thinly veiled impatience before saying, "Some humans are evolved enough to remember each walk. Betty has been around for a long time, and we've been friends for her past three or four cycles in the mortal realm. She's the best."

I tried to respond but had nothing to say. I had reached my capacity for new, earth-shattering information. I'd reached my philosophical fill.

We returned to the Mercedes, me in stunned silence, Fauna in a combination of flattery over her shameless flirtation and nostalgia given her reunion with an old friend. We slid into the car, but for once, she did not immediately begin smashing buttons. Instead, she asked, "How long's the drive to your parents' house?"

My stomach dropped.

This was worse than summoning a demon.

This was worse than stepping on Legos, burning your tongue on your morning coffee, or learning your favorite TV show had been canceled after a cliffhanger. This was worse than a man in a white coat with a clipboard telling me that this had all been a long, vivid delusion.

She expected me to visit my mother.

Chapter Sixteen

I HADN'T SO MUCH AS TURNED THE KEYS IN THE IGNITION. I kept my hands wrapped around the steering wheel in stunned silence for what felt like an hour but was probably closer to six minutes. Fauna didn't push me to get moving. I suspected she knew a thing or two about trauma. She allowed me to drive back to my apartment with the radio off, cross the lobby, wait on the bank of elevators, and cross the hall in silence. She subdued her chaos marvelously until we returned to my unit.

I stepped out of one shoe, then the other. My purse dropped to the living room floor as I sank wordlessly to the couch.

"Do you want me to help you pack?" she asked, voice gentle.

"I haven't talked to my parents in four years," I said quietly. I wondered if I looked as pale as I felt.

"There's no reason it has to be a rush," she said. "The Prince can wait."

I looked at her miserably. "Is there any chance he's still in the human realm? Maybe he's chilling in the Maldives?"

Her expression softened. "Well, what's stronger? Your feelings for Caliban or your hatred for your parents?"

I said nothing.

"We don't have to leave the realm if you aren't ready."

"Yes, we do," I said at last. My stomach was filled with stones. This was my fault. I'd ruined his life and mine. He was the best piece of me, and I wanted it back. "I won't sleep until I undo what I've done. The morning after my attack, I woke up knowing I had to get him back. These past few months with him away have been worse than hell. If he can't come back first, then I have to find him."

Her usual cockiness was gone. Instead, a true kindness met me as she wrapped both hands around one of my forearms. "You won't be going alone. I'll be there with you the whole time. And I'm pretty hard to yell at, as I'm delightful."

My chest weighed a thousand pounds. I shook my head solemnly. "My mom will see through you."

Her smile faltered, and I saw the recognition behind her eyes. She knew I was right. Growing up, my parents, along with the church elders, had referred to the gift as the discernment of spirits. It was one of the fruits of the soul, according to biblical lore. While every believer was said to have a spiritual gift that furthered the kingdom of God, most of them were granted things like charity, generosity, the power to uplift, wisdom, understanding, or piety. The three rarest and most hotly contested gifts were scattered everywhere from the old book of Isaiah to the New Testament references in Corinthians. These abilities were said to be prophecy, the interpretation of tongues, and the discernment of spirits, though they were talents that God doled out with a careful hand.

These rare gifts had always sounded dangerously close to witchcraft, in my opinion. Looking at Fauna on the couch beside me, remembering the surprise on Azrames's face, the anger on Silas's, or the hunger on the Cheshire cat's had me reconsidering the gift of spirits. I could almost feel Caliban's fingers stroking my hair as I thought of all the times I'd told myself I was delusional, all the moments I'd denied what I'd seen, what I'd felt, what I'd known. The church would have told me I was meant to use the gift to see what is for the kingdom of Heaven and what is for the kingdom of Hell. An unscratchable place deep within my mind itched as I wondered how many humans with fae blood were simply trying to make sense of seeing through the veil and found their only validation within the church.

Finally, someone wouldn't tell them they were crazy.

It was a place where people like Lisbeth Thorson were not only terribly sane but lauded as special, as chosen and celebrated with the knowledge that their ability could be put to work for the Lord.

It had been an easy rabbit hole for my mother to tumble down and an even harder crumbling, claustrophobic dirt pit for me to escape.

But I'd never been alone.

✦

JULY 23, AGE 4

"What are you looking at?" My mother smiled. Her eyes stayed on her hands as she sewed.

My nose had been pressed against the window of our trailer house as I'd watched the neighborhood kids gather around a car. I tapped my pointer finger against the window as I counted them. I didn't know the big kids well, but I'd seen them around the trailer park. They were maybe ten or eleven years old. Their younger brothers and sisters were there dressed in shades of yellows and pinks and greens. Two girls who lived three trailers down ran behind the car, laughing as someone sprayed them with the hose. One of them was exactly my age.

I'd heard the music from my room and crawled on the brown, scratchy sofa that my parents had rescued from the curb. The cheap fibers bit into my scabbed knees—another in my collection of scars from falling or from being pushed. It depended on the day. The kid my age, a girl named Hannah, had always been nice. She'd given me half of her Popsicle once.

My mother scratched my back kindly from over my shoulder and smiled. "I'm just finishing up your bunny!" she said. She gestured to the kitchen table, where she'd been stuffing a hand-sewn rabbit, repurposed from the fabric of old shirts. She'd made it a blue dress and given it long, floppy ears. "If you want to go play with the kids, I'll be done by the time you get back."

I looked up at her uncertainly, then back through the window. "They're washing a car," I said. "I don't have stuff."

She'd made a dismissive noise and fished below the sink. She filled a fire-hydrant red bucket half full of soapy water and handed me a sponge too big for my hand. She popped a red baseball cap onto my head that matched the red shorts she'd made. So much red. Aside from my shoes and the value pack of white T-shirts, my mom made all my clothes. "Now you have everything. Go have fun!"

And so, I walked excitedly toward the children, red bucket in one hand, fingers digging into the sponge with the other. Though the music continued playing, the spraying water stopped as I approached. The laughter died down, and the playing stilled. My feet slowed, scraping against the sidewalk as I looked at them uncertainly. My eyes lifted to meet Parker—a boy two years older than me who'd shoved me to the ground and stolen my dinosaur toy only a few weeks prior. I hadn't spotted him from the window.

Life is full of firsts. The first encounter with the room going quiet upon your arrival is something you never forget. The first experience with seconds stretching into a miserable eternity, warping your sense of time and its passage, is hard to shake. When they happen at the same time, they burrow beneath your skin like a tick, sucking at you, draining you. At least, it did for me as I stood there, fingers tightening around the sponge, mouth telling me I needed a big glass of water, tummy feeling like I was going to be sick.

"You weren't invited," he said.

The girls stood quietly behind him. The others watched from the side, a happy chorus of songs from cartoon movies still playing, but the silence was so much louder than the music as no one spoke. I swallowed as I looked at them, wondering if anyone wanted me there, and quickly had my answer. They didn't look at me like they were sorry or like Parker was being mean or like they wished I would be their friend.

They looked at me like they wanted me to go away.

"Go back to your house," Parker said.

I stood on the sidewalk forever, feet frozen to the ground. Sudsy water trickled down the driveway, nearly touching the scuffed, worn sneakers. I stared at the bubbles and imagined the soapy water washing me away instead.

My eyes welled with tears. I didn't know what to do, except that I had to leave before they saw me cry. Big girls weren't supposed to cry, especially not at daycare, or at church, or in front of kids washing cars. I couldn't let them hear the bellyaching wail that needed to come out. Still, their eyes remained trained on me, freezing me, sticking me to the ground.

No, no, no. Please don't let me cry in front of them, I begged, remembering from my lessons that I could talk to God in my head when I needed to pray. And so I prayed for my sneakers to run. My tears to stop. Me to be safe in my bed. To be far, far away.

I don't think my legs would have remembered how to move if I hadn't caught distant movement. From across the gravel road of our little trailer park, an animal shot back and forth. My gaze pulled from the suds, from the children, from the cars and the torment as surprise momentarily made me forget about my need to cry. A white fox spun in a circle, then jumped, snagging and holding my attention. Even from across the road, I met the silver sparkle of its eyes as if it were looking directly at me. Under any other circumstances, I would have pointed it out to the kids around me.

But I couldn't breathe, let alone speak.

The best I could do was keep my gaze off the car, off the garden hose, off the boom box and quiet children, and fixed on the fox. It jumped again, hopping to the side until I pointed my body away from the children to follow it. I rotated to look at it just as it turned to trot toward my house. Swallowing against the threat of sobs, I turned to see the fox as it disappeared in the tall grass beneath our trailer.

Our trailer. The fox was at my house. If I turned and ran, I could be, too.

And so I did. I turned and pumped my arms, not caring how the water splashed and soaked my shirt and shorts as I gave it everything I had. I dropped my bucket and sponge on the landing just outside the front door. I'd scarcely made it through the door before I exploded in earth-shattering wails. My world swam; my throat hurt as the suppressed cry clawed through me. My mom was at my side in a second, sweeping me up and cradling me. She took off my baseball hat and stroked my hair, shushing me until she got me to explain what had happened. When I finally told her, she jumped to her feet with a fierceness I rarely saw. My mom had always been so pretty, but her face was twisted in goblin-like rage. Her baby had experienced her first rejection, and she wanted to make it right.

I begged her to stop, not to go, not to make it worse, and something about the desperation of my plea stopped her with her hand still on the doorknob. She struggled to pry her fingers from the handle and redirect her attention to me. After a long while, she picked me up and carried me to the couch and scratched my back, telling me how interesting I was, how funny I was, and how much they missed out. She told me over and over again that I was the most wonderful present God could have given her and that she knew that I, like her, was destined for great things. God had always told

170

her that I'd share her gift, she'd said, and maybe it was too powerful for dumb boys named Parker and little kids who didn't know how to spot something wonderful.

"Where's your dinosaur?" she asked, hand pausing on my back.

I owned so few things. My dad was a woefully unsuccessful salesman, and my mother, though educated, had forgone any career to be a good wife and mother, which meant she had entirely too much time to focus on her only child. My favorite toys had all come from the Christmas charity drives, though my parents had been too proud to go in. They'd sent me in alone. Given the state of my thrift-store jacket, which was thirty years out of fashion, no one had ever questioned the legitimacy of my financial status. The dinosaur I'd gotten—a Parasaurolophus, which had been a word I'd loved saying, both for its extra syllables and its uniqueness—was the best thing I'd ever owned.

"Promise not to get mad if I tell you?"

She studied my swollen, tear-stained face, then said, "I promise."

When I told her, she said she'd make me a dinosaur once she finished the rabbit. I shook my head and asked if she could make me a fox.

"Sure, I can get some red cloth—"

"Make it white," I said. "With silver buttons for eyes."

She made a curious face but agreed. The fabric and thread she'd used for the rabbit were white, and we had plenty of white T-shirts that were on their last leg, should she need more material. We had plenty of buttons.

"Sure, Marlow," she said, snuggling me. "Now, I thought I'd have more time to finish your rabbit, but why don't you go look at your book in your room and I'll come give it to you when you're done?"

I liked being alone in my room.

My *National Geographic* book of every animal and its habitat. It, *Goodnight Moon,* and *The Children's Picture Bible* were my three books. I sniffed away the last of my tears and disappeared, closing the door behind me. I flipped right to the arctic fox. Some of them were grayish in the summertime, but I smiled at the pictures that were as white and perfect as a magician's rabbit. It looked exactly like the one I'd seen across the street. I hadn't learned how to spell more than my name, but I knew from the pictures that they lived in cold, wild places. There were no images of foxes near homes or in trailer parks. Nothing looked like my city. The globe highlighted the parts of the world where the snow fox lived, and my mom had shown me our town on the map enough for me to know that the fox under our trailer was very far from home.

I jolted in surprise as it crawled out from under my bed. It stole my breath, but I wasn't afraid. The day and its pain melted at the sight of something so perfect, so stunning, so beautiful in *my* bedroom.

"How did you get in here?" I whispered, instantly aglow.

The fox approached me and rolled over playfully.

"Can I pet you?" I asked. I knew enough of animals to have been warned that some bite. This one seemed very friendly, but I still didn't want my fingers to get eaten.

It arched toward me, and I stroked its perfect, soft fur like it was an exotic housecat. It wrapped itself around me, taking my tears. I told it how beautiful it was, and it made a quiet squeaking noise as if it appreciated the compliment.

"Are you someone's pet?" I asked.

It sat upright, curling its tail at its feet, and tilted an ear. I remembered that foxes could not speak and giggled.

"You don't have to be my pet," I said, "but will you be my friend?"

It flopped to its side, head nearly upside down as it batted a paw at me.

I told it how excited I was to see it across the street. I told it that being with a fox was so much cooler than spraying a garden hose or listening to music or playing with dumb kids. I kept my voice low, hoping my mom wouldn't discover us and take away my new friend. She loved having a clean

172

house, and animals were dirty. She'd let me have a betta fish once, but it had died in its bowl, turning into a block of ice when we'd lost power and the house had frozen. We'd worn our snowsuits to bed, with me sleeping between my parents until they were able to pay the power bill.

"I bet you would have kept me warm," I whispered to the fox as I thought of our nights in the snowsuit and my long-lost fish.

It tilted its head toward me as if asking for scratches.

My head whipped around the moment a sound broke our happy reverie.

"Marlow, who are you—" My mom opened the door, finished toy in hand. Her mouth dropped open as she stared at me. I looked over to address the fox, but it was gone.

She'd scooped me up and driven directly to the church, face red, black smudges staining her cheeks as tears ran. No matter how many times I asked her what was wrong, she wouldn't tell me. She didn't carry me into the church but dragged me by the wrist while I demanded to know what I'd done wrong, fear coursing through me. I didn't understand why the pastor had been called, or the elders, or the water, or the men who pressed their hands on my head, my back, my shoulders while I cried.

I insisted she was wrong—the fox was good, the fox was a friend—but she couldn't hear my arguments over the strength of her conviction.

My mom changed after that day.

Her discernment of spirits had allowed her to see that her child had been visited by the devil, I'd learned. But through daily hours of prayer, dedication, piety, study, church visits, and purification, God would still lay claim on me. She tore the arctic fox page from my *National Geographic* book, leaving only the torn remnants of what had once been a pretty snow landscape and a perfect, furry creature in its memory.

I no longer had space for tears, as every night I'd hear my mother falling asleep sobbing as she begged the Lord to spare my soul.

Chapter Seventeen

OCTOBER 2, AGE 16

N O FOXES?" BECAME A STANDARD, CAUTIOUS GREETING between my mother and me.

Lisbeth Thorson, pillar of the community, wife, mother, pious, suspicious, anxious woman that she was, would say it before our bedtime prayers. She'd ask it before we entered church. She'd reiterate it as we brushed our teeth together, looking at each other in the mirror, like twins born twenty years apart. She was agelessly beautiful, her bright, blond hair dripping with evidence of Scandinavia, while mine favored my father's coloration, growing muddier as the years went on. Everyone from gas station clerks to babysitters told me we looked like sisters, which I'd always taken as a high compliment, even if my platinum locks hadn't stretched beyond early childhood.

For more than a decade, I'd dutifully respond, "No foxes."

I hadn't made the mistake of telling the truth again.

The memory was as painful now as the leather belt had been on my bare skin. Even as a teenager, I remembered her sobbing that the spanking hurt her more than it hurt me as I screamed, leather cracking again and again and again until the welts made it too hard to sit. She had to do it because she loved me, she cared about my soul, and she wanted me to go to Heaven. That was when I learned to lie. Never again would I mention the fox.

We left the trailer park within six months after the first incident.

Maybe it was the sort of thing I should try to let go, but I couldn't forget.

She'd convinced my father that there were outside influences battling for my soul and that getting a fresh start in the woods would be good for me. It had been the first time I'd looked at my mother with a question in my eyes, as I knew beyond a shadow of a doubt that she was wrong about the fox.

The fox was good.

But we moved. My father's commute to work was substantially longer, and my two-hour bus ride to school began at six thirty each morning, but a trailer in the forest was cheaper than one in the city. And so, for more than ten years, I lived with the flowers and trees. No streetlights interrupted my view of the stars. If I walked far enough into the woods and ducked under a farmer's fence, I could get to a small, babbling brook and play barefoot for hours. The birds, the snakes, the wild hares became my friends. My imagination flourished while I caught crayfish with my fingers and read tattered novels I'd smuggled from the school library in the crooked boughs of oak trees.

We remained too poor to live in anything beyond a trailer, but our new lot in the woods was quite the upgrade. It was still only two bedrooms, but over the years, we acquired a new couch and a television that played the VHS tapes my mom would borrow from the church or check out from the library. My mother had picked an eclectic antique theme of thrifted items to decorate the space, and my dad kept the grass short and the bushes trimmed. I'd always thought our excessive use of candles was a pretty choice until I was old enough to understand we were saving on electricity rather than living for aesthetics. Still, my parents were adamant that you didn't have to have a lot in order to be proud of what you had.

My clothes were never new, but they were always wrinkle-free. Our house was cheap, but it was quaint. My mother cleaned obsessively, scrubbing every inch, vacuuming, dusting, mopping, bleaching as if proving her worthiness.

"Cleanliness is next to godliness," she'd say.

"That's not actually in the Bible," I'd reply. It always gained a smile of approval from her. She liked that I was well read and could argue my verses. While other teenagers were getting boyfriends and going to parties, I was excelling as a student of the church, glowing each time I earned her approval. Her praise was like the sun after winter, cutting through the freeze-outs, the silent treatments, the punishments that frosted my misdeeds. But my mother went on washing as if she swept and sterilized and spruced to prove her worthiness, should anyone step into our home and witness our poverty.

No one ever did.

When I wasn't at school, I was in the woods.

For over a decade, I'd wait at my window until I saw a flash of white fur. If I didn't see it first, it would usually find me while I played with sticks, creating tiny corrals for boxelder bugs as I pretended to be a giant rancher, as I jumped from rock to rock in the creek, as I scraped my knees and palms on tree bark or read in the shade as I got older.

I was old enough to know that arctic foxes didn't live in the American Midwest, but it was as real as anything to me. Whether it was wild pet or imaginary friend, I loved it more than life.

If I was on a walk through the woods and I didn't spy it right away, it would chirp, wave its paw, or leap to get my attention. There was no feeling like the sun that bloomed within my chest, lighting me from the inside out when I finally saw it. Sometimes it followed me, listening to me as I babbled about my day or homework, or church. Sometimes it would lead me to a pretty flower, or I'd follow it to a bushel of wild strawberries. Other times, it would flick its tail in greeting. Then when I turned my head, it would be gone.

My mom couldn't know about my imaginary friend. She wouldn't understand. And I was no longer a child. Teenagers didn't conjure woodland creatures to keep them company. The fox would be a guarded secret. It made me happy. That's what mattered.

Very few students talked to me at school, though it was no mystery why. As I grew older, the librarian was one of the only friendly faces I saw at the school. She always had a smile for me and often set aside new or interesting books before other children could snag them. By age eleven, I'd read every fantasy novel within my reading level, and even those far beyond my grade. I loved history, poetry, and animals. I had my mom, the wilderness, the fox, Kirby, a library of books, and the Bible. I didn't need other friends. After all, she'd said, Jesus was the only friend I needed.

Jesus and her, of course.

She called what we had "friendship." We were best friends, she'd said, and I believed her, though sometimes I wasn't sure how much of our companionship was by choice. It was a solemn vow she'd say before singing haunting, beautiful songs with terrifying theology to lull me to sleep, each melody reinforcing fear over my soul and its eternal destination. It was a promise she made before coaxing my secrets from me. It was something she'd repeat before something I said or did ignited her rage. That was the pattern for years and years, and it worked. At least, it worked for her.

Everything was fine, until it wasn't.

In the weeks leading up to my sixteenth birthday, I stopped seeing the fox.

It was just as well. I was ready to stop seeing everything. The hot and cold desperation to please my parents, the unrelenting torment at school, the despair that no matter how I tried, I was always one imperfection, one sin, one short-coming away from crossing through the Pearly Gates. I broke

God's heart time and time again, so my mother said, and He wasn't the only one. Anguishing waves of disappointment from the way my mother looked at me, the sneers at school, and the disgust in the faces of the church elders—men who'd once rebuked a frightened little girl for seeing unclean spirits in the form of a white fox—made me feel like I was suffocating day in and day out. I wasn't happy, nor would I ever be.

I'd been crying so hard I nearly threw my back out. My nose was stuffed. My eyes were bleary. My ears rang. I'd kept my sobs as quiet as I could as I made my way from the bathroom to my bedroom. But I still heard a voice as clear as a bell when I reached for the bottle of painkillers I'd taken from the medicine cabinet.

Two male words came from the shadows.

"Drop it."

I choked on my final cry. Sorrow evaporated as fear took hold, shattering my bubble of isolation. The pill bottle clattered to the floor with thirty-odd tablets scattering across the carpet. I tore out of bed and grabbed the door the moment I saw movement in the shadows. Horrible words clanged through me as I tripped over my sheets and lunged for the door. Crime. Murder. Abduction. It was four long bounds from my bedroom through the living room to the kitchen. My mom was still awake, balancing the checkbook, paying bills.

"There's someone in the house," I gasped.

She jumped up from the table so hard that the chair clattered to the floor. She threw on the lights, checked under the bed, looked behind doors, and secured every nook and cranny in the rectangular tin can we called home. She didn't even notice I'd been crying. The woman had no sympathy. Worry turned to impatience as she informed me in no uncertain terms that our eyes played tricks on us in the dark, and I was almost an adult. I was too old to let my eyes play tricks on me.

"It wasn't a trick," I insisted, panic-stricken that there'd been a break-in and my mother wasn't taking me seriously.

178

"Then pray for protection," she replied, still irritated.

So I returned to bed with my covers over my head, struggling to breathe through stuffy clouds of carbon dioxide as I tried to outlast the quiet certainty that there was someone in my room. She was right. I was too old to be afraid of my imagination.

But I knelt and collected each of the pills that night from where they'd stuck between the fibers, then watched them swirl as I flushed them down the toilet.

Seven days passed before I saw the silhouette in my room. This time, I wasn't afraid.

"You were here the other night." I sat up in bed and held my knees against my chest as I watched the shape move from the corner.

"I was," replied the voice. It was a young man's voice, and it was decidedly gentle. I searched within myself for wariness, for a sliver of fear, for anything that told me to keep my guard up, but none existed. "I couldn't let you do it."

"I wasn't going to," I lied.

His answering silence hung heavy between us.

"Are you real?" I asked. I waited for my eyes to adjust to the dark in time to see a beautiful face, pale hair, and a lithe shape. Gone were the thoughts of a serial killer lurking in the shadows. My cheeks heated at the taboo of having a boy in my room. The warmth crept down my neck, flushing my chest and seeping into every part of me as my eyes traveled over his sharp jaw, over the broad shoulders, the ripple of muscle, the musical purr to the way he'd spoken.

"I am," he said quietly. "Though this wasn't how, or when, I wanted to meet."

"When?"

But the beautiful phantom did not elaborate.

For weeks that bled into months, my forest walks were not graced by a fox. I recognized the white hair and silver eyes as he moved in the ethereal form that could only belong to an angel. Instead, I'd wait up at night to see if the marble-hewn

179

vision would step from the shadows and join me. Sometimes I'd fall into a disappointed sleep only to have my dreams allow me permission and bravery to touch him, to breathe him in, to run my hands through his hair. On the nights he did appear, he remained on the far side of the room, leaving contact to my imagination. The beautiful anomaly usually asked me about my day, about friends, about life and thoughts and feelings, though he never stayed long after ensuring I was okay.

"Wait," I said as he began to shift his weight toward the shadow as he always did before departing. "Do you only visit at night?"

"I'm not sure if it's wise for me to visit when the sun's out," he replied cautiously.

"Why?" I asked.

He paused for a moment before saying, "I know you can see me now in the shadows, but it might alarm you in the light of day."

"Is that why you appeared as a fox?"

The question had been a risk, but I asked it anyway. I knew from the way his jaw ticked that I was right.

"Be not afraid," I responded quietly, thinking of the angels who'd appeared to the shepherds on the hill. I asked him if he was the guardian angel that God had sent, and he made an unforgettable smirk as he said he was there to make sure I had a good life. I thought of the first time my heart had shattered as I'd clutched a soapy sponge and the fox had kept me from breaking, and I knew he was telling the truth. He'd appeared to keep me whole, to keep me sane. I asked if everyone had a guardian angel, and his words rang through me.

"I can't speak for what everyone has, but I'm only yours."

It was one of the first times in sixteen years I'd felt special. I clutched the words as if he'd handed me a beautiful diamond necklace and slipped it around my neck, holding this secret close to my heart forever.

I asked him his name, and he said what I called him didn't matter.

"Gabriel is an angel's name," I offered, "If you're a guardian angel, would that be a good name for you?"

He made a face like eating blanched vegetables. It felt decidedly childish, but so was having an unseen friend. I giggled, and he said, "That name's taken. Can you think of anything you like that fits me better?"

I looked to the books on my piles from sophomore year and drifted to Shakespeare.

"Do you like Caliban?"

He smiled a lovely, perfect smile. It was prettier than the actors' in movies and far kinder than the plastered grins of the church pastor and greeters who forced me to shake their hand every time I entered the sanctuary. It was a little sad, the same way that my mom's smiles were often blue around the edges—the same way that *my* smiles were often tinged with heaviness.

"Do *you* like Caliban?" he asked.

I nodded.

"Then that's my name."

"Caliban," I repeated, his name a smile on both of our lips.

And so, I added him to my nightly prayers. I'd thank God for everything I had, I'd pray for protection, for salvation, for forgiveness. Then I'd pray for my parents, and without fail, night after night, I'd thank God for Caliban and ask the Lord to keep him safe. I'd fall asleep somewhere in the middle of my prayers, mumbling gratitude for my angel—the only friend I knew would never leave me.

That was when I made my next mistake.

"What do you think about guardian angels?" Months had gone by before I made a mistake. I asked my mother over a plate of overcooked spaghetti and red sauce straight from the jar. I swallowed a rubbery bite before vowing that I'd teach myself to cook.

My dad was either at work or at church. It was hard to tell, and neither of us cared. The modestly decorated home had no trace of a male presence. He was never home, and his absence was rarely felt. Besides, my mother was the intelligent one. She'd nearly finished her master's in biblical studies before she'd met my father and had to choose between supporting his dreams or achieving her own. Though she'd left higher learning behind for life as a wife and mother, she'd never stopped studying. She'd read everything, from theology and literature to geography and history. She continued to teach literature and loved to talk to me about the sorts of things that made me even less popular at school than I already was, which was fine. As the years went on, our relationship changed. There were times I even felt like she looked at me as if I were a peer.

She was nearly as friendless as I was. Perhaps that's why we clung to one another.

She swirled the spaghetti around her fork, chewing and swallowing her food as she called on a verse. "The book of Ephesians tells us that we're not contending against flesh and blood but against the principalities, against the powers, against the rulers of this present darkness. It talks about spiritual hosts of wickedness and heavenly places."

"And?" I asked. It was risky, but there was no one else I could ask. "Do you see angels or demons?"

She stiffened. Her fork was halfway between her plate and her mouth, but her eyes did not leave mine. Slowly, she asked me, "Do you?"

I forced myself to remain casual as I said, "I see my angel sometimes."

I was acutely aware of how shallow her breathing had become. I knew enough of her drastic mood swings, her intense temperaments, her bouts with depression and her quickness to anger to immediately back off. I'd been born into a house on fire, but through cautious steps, I'd learned to manage the source of the flames.

"I'm not a child. I know the difference between good and evil," I quickly amended. "I would know if I were seeing something bad. I would know if it's from God or Satan."

She relaxed, but only slightly. She twirled the noodles on her fork with no intention of lifting it to her mouth, eyes fixed on the slow, intentional movement as red-stained pasta coiled more and more tightly. It took her a long time to say, "You might have your mother's gift."

I looked up at her mid-bite. I wasn't sure what had possessed me to bring it up to her in the first place, but this certainly wasn't where I'd thought the conversation would go.

Her utensil clattered to her plate as she looked at me. "The discernment of spirits can be a very powerful gift, Marlow. It also means you have a great responsibility." She stood from the table and left the small kitchen, crossing into the shadows of our unlit living room. She fished a thick book from a high shelf and returned in several steps. She plopped it down on the surface next to me. "It's fiction, but it's about someone who can see angels and demons. They fight over our towns, our houses, our hearts as if each place is a territory. The angels are on the side of every believer. Demons want to drag us to Hell. I thought it would be too scary for you, but there aren't a lot of books that talk about what I... what we have."

I set my fork down, appetite evaporating. "You see demons? Like monsters?"

She made an interesting face I couldn't quite understand before saying, "Did you know that Lucifer was the most beautiful angel?"

I blinked. I knew the verses backward and forward, and she knew that. She wasn't asking because she expected an answer. Her question was heavy with some other implication as her eyes unfocused.

"He was a musician," she nearly whispered. "He played beautiful music and was one of God's favorite angels. A lot of people in the church translate his name to *Morning Star*, or *Shining One*. He was the dawn. A new day."

Looking back on that day, I remember only how cold the room felt, how dim the bald lightbulb overhead looked as I searched her face. The hum of the outdated refrigerator was too loud, too robotic for the seriousness required of such a topic. "You talk about him like you know him."

"He rebelled against God," she said finally.

I shook my head, then finished, "To bring evil into the world."

"No," she corrected, "because he thought he was equal to God. He took a lot of angels with him who no longer wanted to be under God."

I frowned and pushed the congealing pasta around my plate. The smell of cold food was beginning to make me nauseous. I couldn't keep the confusion from my face as I pressed, "This just sounds like people not wanting to have slaves and masters but be equals."

"Don't say that," she hissed, mood changing in a flash. She snatched my plate from me and crossed to the counter. It had yellowed over the years, the plastic peeling up from its corners. She found a stained Tupperware and dumped my spaghetti into it. She kept her back to me, shoulders tense as she began washing dishes.

"But"—I stood from the table, taking a step closer as I pushed—"it just sounds like the same people. If they were all angels, then they're still all angels, just on two different sides of the line—like the Civil War. One side who wants to keep things the same, and one side who wants freedom. If demons are just beautiful angels on the other side of the line, why do people think they look ugly?"

"Beauty is a trick," she said curtly, refusing to look at me. Every muscle remained flexed as if poised to fight.

I didn't understand why this was getting her so emotional. I was nearly an adult, and this was an academic discussion. As a scholar and a zealous theologian, she should have loved this conversation.

"If fallen angels are so bad," I continued, "why didn't God just evaporate them? Why create Hell? Why—"

She turned with wet, soapy hands and snatched the book

from where she'd left it before shoving the fictional novel on angels and demons into my hands. She returned to her chore before saying, "Go read the book. See if it resonates with you. Though, for your sake, I hope you did not inherit my gift."

I set my jaw as I said through gritted teeth, "I see angels."

She froze. The water continued to run for a long time, though her hands didn't move. After a long time, she turned off the sink. Rather than turn to face me, her eyes remained screwed on the individual droplets that clung to the faucet, dripping with rhythmic insistency before she asked, "What angel do you see?"

The words poured out of me before I could stop them. "Only my guardian angel. I pray for him, I—"

"No."

My mouth continued to move as if I were the sink faucet. "Mom, I pray to *God*. Just to keep him safe, to—"

"No!" she said, spinning with intensity. Her eyes, normally a bright shade of sky blue, were as dark as angry coal as she looked at me. "Nothing of God would ask you to pray to it."

I winced but stood my ground. I lifted my hands to brace against impact as I insisted, "You aren't listening. I don't pray *to* him, Mom! I pray *for*—"

"It's not a *him*!" she practically screamed. She stormed out of the kitchen and slammed the door to her bedroom so hard that the walls shook. I sank against the wall, pressing my ear to her door as I listened to her tearful prayers as she interceded on behalf of my soul. After that day I knew my angel, like my fox, would be something I'd never, ever mention again.

Chapter Eighteen

Please don't do this to me," I pleaded as I adjusted my grip from ten and two to something that more closely resembled nine and five. It was too early, and I was in no mood. The panorama faded from skyscrapers to suburbs to the dark emerald canopy of late-summer trees that lined the highway as we trekked north.

We'd loaded up the car and barely made it out of the city before Fauna revealed what she'd downloaded onto my phone in the night. Apparently, she'd figured out how to hack facial recognition software even while I slept.

"It's a nine-hour drive. It will be fun."

"It will be fun for *you*," I said miserably.

I was dressed as comfortably as I could manage for the road, but there would be no relaxing. No amount of well-worn childhood shirts or gray sweats filled with holes would bring me comfort for the nightmares she had in store. She dressed like a hippie once again. She wore a top that may have been a loosely fitting bralette or that may have once been a tank top that had lost its bottom half to craft scissors. The fabric of her olive pants was so wide and flowy that I'd mistaken it for a skirt.

Fauna pressed play on the audiobook. A woman's deep, authoritative voice boomed through the door as she said, "*A*

Night of Runes, by Merit Finnegan. Book one of the *Pantheon* series."

"For Christ's sake, please don't—"

"Hush." Fauna swatted at me. "I'm trying to listen to the story."

Despite my reminding her as often as possible that it was fiction, that I had been in college when I'd written it, that I'd learned and grown since then, she had no greater joy in the world than to talk over the book every time I'd made an inaccuracy regarding the so-called pagan gods, the cryptids, or the fae that had launched me into an unprecedented success. She informed me on more than one occasion that whatever such deity, entity, or being would laugh themselves into stitches when they heard what I'd said about them.

"Then don't tell them," I snapped.

"Frigg has already read it," she sang merrily.

I wanted to throw up. She referenced Odin's wife with the casualness as if she had been talking about an old pal. The most sovereign goddess in Norse lore should be a myth. And if she *wasn't* a myth, she sure as hell shouldn't know my name. "That's not funny, Fauna. You'd better be telling a really bad joke right now."

Fauna made a defensive gesture. "She's our great, protective mother of all! She was very curious to see what damage someone with a drop of our blood could do."

I white-knuckled the steering wheel, begging the highway hypnosis to lull me into unconsciousness as I stared at the dotted yellow lines that flashed between the road and the bumper. I was going to give myself blisters if I kept chafing my skin against the wheel like this, but I couldn't help it. The trees broke to reveal rolling hills and farmsteads before the woods returned with a thicketed vengeance as we approached forested northern areas where few dared settle.

"They're happy with you," Fauna said.

I took my eyes off the road to gape at her. "So help me, if you're—"

"I'm not lying. Look at the road. I'm too pretty to crash."

She pointed to the radio as if gesturing to a visual piece of history as she said, "We've had more converts to Norse paganism after the release of your book than we had in nearly two centuries. You drove a whole generation to seek answers. Tourism throughout Scandinavia skyrocketed. Now, I'd have to talk to our buddies along the Mediterranean to see if they saw similar results after book two, but even if you're a moron, you're one who's making a lot of friends in high places."

I couldn't have anticipated this response if I'd been given a million years of guesses.

"Did you go?" she asked.

I looked over at her, waiting for an explanation.

"Were you one of the tourists? You were, what, twenty-three when you wrote the second *Pantheon* book? Did you soak up the sun in Mykonos to celebrate its release?"

"No," I breathed quietly, glad for the change in conversation. I recalled the Thanksgiving release and the holidays alone in my apartment that had followed. Twenty-three had turned into twenty-four, but I hadn't left the house until Christmas had come and gone. It had been all I could do to push the sermons, the candle-lit vigils, the Nativity sets, the carols, the traditions into the furthest reaches of my mind while I sat in the dark, microwaving burritos and binging chick flicks.

A strange numbness made it challenging to feel the steering wheel, the pedals, the very vibrations of the highway as it hummed through the beige leather interior and into my body. I didn't dare flick my gaze to her in order to check her sincerity. I couldn't explain how, but I knew she was telling the truth. I'd done something...good. I'd sparked human interest. I'd made not just one god but *many*...happy with me.

"Hey, what happened?" Fauna asked, noting the sniffle I failed to subdue.

I shook my head.

She fetched my phone, punching the pause button on the

audiobook to frown at me. Her white and copper freckles bundled together like an earthbound galaxy as she pressed her back to the passenger door until she faced me fully. "Tell me."

I laughed at the absurdity of it all. How could I possibly unpack church psychology, two decades of religious trauma, or two thousand years of theology for her in a sentence?

"How much time do you have?"

She didn't falter. "All the time in the world."

Eventually, I settled on, "The first eighteen years of my life revolved around whether or not I was disappointing God. Every action, every move, every thought hinged on me saying or doing or thinking the right thing. Every decision I made was rooted in terror that a deity might be angry with me, or that I was letting him down, or that he'd be mad. As if I didn't already have enough mental illnesses before we factored in the shame and judgment... Just, give me a moment to process the concept that not one but multiple gods don't hate me." I used the back of my hand to wipe at a tear, grateful for the excuse of the road as I refused to look at her.

I'd expected her to laugh with me, but she didn't.

"He's a jealous dick," she said quietly.

I continued to stare at the cut between the trees, weaving between the dwindling number of cars on the highway as we crept farther north. I didn't say anything.

"At least the Nordes know Odin's name. We know where our loyalties lie. At least the Greeks can address Zeus. At least on Hell's side of the battle, they can speak to their leader. But with the angels..."

I didn't breathe. A long-buried part of me felt a pit in my stomach as if the heresy would cause the ground to swallow me as I was plunged into the fiery pits, vehicle and all. I waited for the plague of locusts, for the impending accident, for the earthquake that was sure to shake us. It didn't matter how long it had been, I was still terrified of speaking poorly of the God who ruled over the church—the one my mom had petitioned night in and night out for the destination of my soul.

"You know that verse in that book? The book you were raised with? It's from your Ten Commandments—thou shalt have no other gods before me?"

My frown took on a life of its own as blasphemous discomfort raked through me. I squirmed in my seat, ready to be struck by lightning. It took me a while to realize she expected a real answer, so I nodded. Yes, of course I knew it.

Fauna raised a brow. "No one considers what's spelled out there in the verse. If no other gods can come before him, he confirms the existence of other gods. And yet here we are. Look at the fae through your religious lens and call them whatever you want. Make them your angels and demons. But at the end of the day, pierce the veil and you're left with us. The Nordes more or less keep to ourselves. Then you've got the Greeks, the Egyptians, the Chinese gods—who, by the way, were really disappointed that you chose South America over them. Seems like you're neglecting the Global East, there, Miss Mythology. Next *Pantheon* book, eh?"

"I..." I swallowed before being honest. "I don't understand."

She frowned. "What *do* you understand?"

"Truthfully? ...Nothing."

That seemed to please her. She smiled as she said, "That's a good place to start."

The road highway hummed beneath me as I deflated. I knew nothing. My shoulders slumped. The shift in my mood must have been visible, because Fauna's tone softened before she prodded me again.

"Come on, you love to annoy me with questions. I haven't gotten you to shut up since we met. Ask me about something better. Ask me about the best lay of my life. Wanna know how good Azrames is in bed? Or what he can do with those horns?"

"Absolutely not," I said, face burning so hot I had to glance in the rearview mirror to ensure I was merely blushing red instead of the shade of violet that pulsed from my

190

discomfort at picturing that beautiful, gray-scale man using his horns in the bedroom.

She grinned and tried prodding me again. "Wanna know which goddesses I've boned? You know, people say the Mórrigan is a goddess of war, but—"

"Nope! Nope. Not sex. Not sex with you, not sex with the fae, not anything that's going to make me crash this car."

"Fair enough." She shrugged, as if agreeing that whatever information she'd relay would probably result in a crumble of steel, rubber, and aluminum on the side of the road. She resumed the book, pointing out inaccuracies and laughing at the way I'd painted certain characters and locations until it was my turn to ask something.

"Fauna? I do have a question."

She brightened. "Finally! It's about Mórrigan, isn't it? Gimme your queries. Let me make you smart."

I sighed before asking something that had been plaguing me for a long time. "No. Don't tell me jack shit about another deity's sex life. This is about..." I struggled to spit out the words, sorting through years of repressed memories. "It's about Caliban." I paused, closed my eyes tightly, then reopened them to accept the road before me. I chose my words again, saying, "It's about my life. It's... I just don't understand...he's been with me since I was a child."

She waited.

"He was a fox for years. I thought it was an imaginary friend, then a guardian angel. But I was a kid. I believed he was real at the time. When I was in the church, that is. Then I had to let it all go when I left my faith. He was just a coping mechanism, a hallucination, you know? Years later, here we are, with all I feel, with what we've done..." I let my question trail off.

"Oh, that's all?" She waved it away. "That's easy. I'll answer as soon as you get me gummy bears."

"But you already have—" My outrage was cut short. I made a sweeping gesture to the bags of snacks we'd gotten for the road. Every one of them was a ghost of candies past. There wasn't a trace of chocolate, sour worms, spicy cinnamon suckers, or sugar rocks. "How do you do that? Don't you get sick?"

"Nope," she said cheerfully.

I hedged for a moment, monitoring her from the side of my eye before I asked, "Don't most deer like saltlicks? What even are you?"

I wasn't sure if the question would offend her, but a smile tugged up the corners of her mouth. "You know, sometimes you remind me that you don't exclusively have cobwebs between those ears."

I didn't know what to do with her statement, so I waited.

"Your fae blood is Nordic, as is mine. Every pantheon has its heavy hitters front and center while its overlooked deities run the world in the background. Every religion has deities of forest or earth or wildlife." Then she muttered, "Artemis gets a whole temple for being a deer goddess and I get elf status, but whatever."

I stifled a chuckle before saying, "She's the goddess of hunted *and* the hunter. I'm going to go out on a limb and say you're just there for the wilderness, not the one doing the killing."

"Sure, I'm *just* there for the earth and a guardian for brainless bitches who fall in love with demon princes," she sighed. "Now, are we getting me that candy, or not?"

I glanced at the needles on my dashboard and supposed it wouldn't hurt to top off the tank. While I pumped gas, Fauna was bored enough to insist on ruining the lives of everyone inside the gas station for her amusement. She took my card in alone, no hat, no sunglasses, just brilliant, ethereal glory and a smile carved from starlight as she undoubtedly rendered all of the patrons speechless. I wouldn't have been shocked if speaking with her led the attendant of whatever gender to go home and immediately divorce their spouse in search of something magical. I'd just turned the nozzle to the pump when she emerged victorious, hoisting what had to have been seventy dollars of candy above her head like a deep-sea fisherman displaying their marlin.

She slammed the door. "Five hours down, four to go! Back to making fun of your book?"

"No," I said before starting the car. "You said you'd tell me about Caliban."

She kicked off her shoes and planted her heels on the dashboard. "Oh, yeah, that. It's just not a very interesting answer."

"I'm going to guess that you and I have differing opinions on what we find interesting," I said as I eased back onto the highway. I wasn't sure how comfortable I would be with her answer. I allowed her to empty the final sprinkles of powdered sugar donuts into her mouth, then cracked open a sugary soda before she started speaking.

She crossed one ankle over the other. "I mean, I don't know him, and I don't really know you. I haven't met him. But, if I had to guess, I'd just say he's done it before. Maybe a few times. Maybe hundreds of times."

I dared to steal a glance at the passenger's seat. "Done what?"

She cursed as she fumbled with a plastic bag. She tore at it with her fingers and teeth until I wiggled my palm for her to hand it over. I drove with my knee as I used the tiny, serrated edge to easily peel back part of the bag and hand her the candy.

"You're worse than a child," I said.

"But a child with answers!" she said triumphantly, shoveling tiny, red strawberry-flavored gummies in the shape of fish into her mouth. "I'm going to take a stab at it and say that he met you a few lifetimes ago. You were probably, I don't know, eighteen, twenty-five, forty, the age doesn't matter. The human cycle has been around for a long time. You could have been anywhere. You could have been anyone. You would have been more open-minded than you are in this

193

lifetime, obviously, if the two of you fell in this sort of love. Whatever connection you shared was important enough to seek out time and time again, even if it meant he'd have to find you in each of your lives. So, of course, he'd want to seek you out when you're a kid just to make sure you're okay."

I made a face, which strengthened her resolve.

She rummaged around in the bag as she continued. "Like, let's say you're married, right? You found your soulmate, and you're madly in love. You've been married for however many years, and then some witch's curse or sci-fi shit or something sends you back in time." She used a stray foot to push my shoulder. I wrinkled my nose down at her bare toes and narrowed my eyes at her, but she'd been kicking for emphasis. "So you woke up, and it was twenty years in the past or something. Wouldn't it be tempting to check on your soulmate and see if they were happy and healthy? To protect them? And if they were miserable or abused or suffering, wouldn't you want to try to make their life better, even in the smallest of ways? Because you love them?"

I rolled the hypothetical around on my tongue, tasting it, chewing on it.

She shoved another handful of strawberry-flavored fish into her mouth. She spoke through her mouthful as she said, "It's gross to imply there's anything romantic about a time-traveling wife saving her partner from abuse. You aren't time-traveling by choice. You're checking on them because you care. Don't make it weird."

I felt dismissed. "I'm not making it weird—"

"If you've known him since you were a child, I'm sure it was because he was doing what he could to keep you safe, to help you find joy, all that. Like yeah, he loves you, but love looks a lot of ways. How did he appear again? Ghost in the attic? An animal, you said?"

I knew it was unsafe to close my eyes while going seventy miles per hour, but I had to take a moment to myself as ten thousand memories sliced through me. On a breath, I said,

"He was a fox. When I was little, he was an artic fox. I didn't see him as a person until I was much older. He didn't talk to me until…"

She relaxed into her seat.

Fauna abandoned her tough-love bravado. After a long while, she said, "He's willing to wait by your side as a cute animal just to make you smile? Maybe that's why he's patient with you even when you refuse to acknowledge him, despite how frustrating it must be to watch you dabble with tales of deities and pantheons and know of angels and demons. It's all on the tip of your tongue, but you just won't say it. I guess if you waste this lifetime, he loves you enough to try again in the next. And the next. And the next."

"But…"

"But nothing," she said. "You can't apply human logic to a nonhuman situation."

"I'm human," I argued.

"Only mostly," she countered.

My lips parted. I looked down between my breasts to see if a physical blade pierced the space where my heart might be, expecting a dagger to protrude through my chest. Every rhythmic beat bled into the wound, exacerbating my injury. The idea of a love so deep, so patient, so…

"It's impossible," I breathed at last.

She shrugged. "It's your cycle," she said. "You're lucky. Caliban, as you call him—again, I like the name—has a solid reputation across the realms. Almost too sterling of a reputation for kindness and generosity. But, he is a demon. So, double-edged swords and all that." She paused for an unnatural length as if sorting through an uncomfortable, unspoken truth before saying, "That's a conversation for another time. Anyway, as I said, it's your cycle. You were free to waste it however you wanted, until the proposed bond with Silas."

"Because Silas is bad."

"What? No. By himself, Silas is morally neutral. But it's not like you could bond with him and then skip into the sunset. A bond to *any* angel would mean an entire heavenly kingdom would have access to you. It's the goose and the gander or whatever. You rarely get one without the other."

"He said they had a claim to me," I said uneasily.

She swallowed her gummies. "He and his master are referring to your baptism. Splash of water here, pretty white dress there. It's a bargaining chip to keep them in play at best. Heaven wants you—probably only because you're important to Hell—but you belong to no one until you decide."

There were so many pieces of her monologue to pick apart, but I remained fixated on the name. "What will happen to Silas?"

She played with the reclining settings on her seat as she wiggled her feet against my windshield. Her toes had been painted a pretty, shimmery shade of penny-bright copper. She bit into another fish, yanking its tail off, and responded while chewing.

"You know: war."

I was simultaneously exhausted at the prospect of all the things I didn't know and the need to understand it all. I hoped my doe-eyed plea would do the trick, and it did. She sank more deeply into the passenger's seat until she launched into her tale like the least reverent narrator a sloppy documentary could hope to scrounge together.

"He and Caliban are on opposing sides of what was once a united kingdom, obviously. Centuries—*millennia*—locked in a cold war like a bunch of losers wasting their time. A battle in which, for the record, *only* humans are on Silas's side...and even then, it's a limited number of humans. Every other realm is with Hell on this one. The defectors had every right to leave. They shouldn't have to live in servitude. We, on the other hand—the 'pagan gods,' as you call us—are the best. Well, most of us. Maybe not most. Some of us kind of suck. Anyway: the god of your church, the one who refuses to even give himself a name, since he prefers to pretend that no one else exists...he doesn't really believe in equality. So then, imagine, if you will, that Silas kills a parasite—oh, don't look so shocked. We all heard. I fucking hate those things. Parasitic entities?"

I gagged at the vivid memory. A horrific child, a scabby smile, the stink of pus, the grin of starvation. I wrinkled my nose both at her knowledge of it and at my reliving it.

"They're like leeches or ticks on humans, except sentient and persuasive. They take on a bunch of shapes and names throughout your scary stories and folklore. Creepy little bastards. Low-vibrational humans with dark inclinations have these openings; voids, if you will. Sometimes, parasites slip through the cracks and crank the volume to a hundred."

I attempted to reimagine Richard on our date all those years ago, wondering if a small child who bled blue had been standing at his side, whispering about their shared cravings. I'd trusted my gut so explicitly when it had urged me to run from him. I wondered if part of it had been—what had she called them?—my clairabilities sensing something nonhuman had been attached.

She shuddered, her entire body rejecting the image in the same way mine did whenever my thoughts drifted to the child with the cat-like smile. "Anyway, Silas kills a parasite, then gives his report to his boss. Silas gives the rundown about what he did and who was there. He gives the real name that you *insist on giving to everything and everyone.* It was sent up the chain fast as fuck, because by the time you got home, he'd already been given strict orders to take your deal. If you—*you,* miss The Prince's Love Across Lifetimes—were bound to an angel? Someone with Norde blood? It would be our fault. The King of Hell himself would be banging on our door."

Shades of green and brown and gray blurred on all sides as the world continued to open before us. She snorted as she switched to a vine of red ropes. I wondered how long it would take her before we'd have to stop for more candy. I also wondered if the fae had stomachs made of iron.

"So Silas…" I recalled the man who'd saved me, then

who'd knelt to tell me it was all a dream. I vividly remembered the gold flash of eyes, the hardened armor, the sword dripping in aquamarine pulp. I could still see the muscled arm I'd gripped in desperation as he contemplated leaving me in the basement to die. I needed something to do with my nervous energy, so I fidgeted with the air-conditioning. The chilly blast was doing an excellent job at keeping me wide awake.

"Same kingdom, babe. Probably grew up together... kinda. Eternity is a long time, so most of us get to know each other in whatever capacity. Silas is military, and Caliban is royalty. So. It would have been a fun slap in the face for the *heavenly* side if you'd bound yourself to a soldier over a prince."

I'd spent twenty-six years breathing without issue, but ever since meeting the fae, I regularly forgot to inhale until I grew dizzy. This was one of those times. The car jerked slightly until the tires hit the rumble strips. My Mercedes vibrated loudly and forced me to fill my lungs again. "When you say Heaven—"

"I don't mean 'the ultimate good place'; I mean their realm. It's literally just a word, sweetheart. Like I said, we're all fae. Silas, me, Odin, Zeus, Horus, Shiva, Caliban, your OG god: I'm using the word *fae* for everything. Every one of us who walks around behind the veil, who has home addresses in other realms, who wields superpowers. Heaven is just a word so humans understand we're talking about the realm on the side of this god, the one that a third of the world is sending their energy to during Sunday services. There you go. That's theology in a nutshell."

I couldn't stop myself from muttering, "Blasphemous theology in a nutshell."

She shrugged, ripping another rope in half with her teeth. Through smacking bites, she said, "Well, you're hearing it from a pagan forest deity—your words—so take whatever you want with a grain of salt. It's up to you. Believe me or don't. But, you got a sigil tattooed on your forearm. You've spent a shit ton of time with me. You've had a demon cock between those legs. I'm just curious—what would it take to convince you?"

As much as I hated to admit it, I conceded the point. She was right. If I wasn't fully convinced that everything she said was true by now, perhaps I never would be. And...I *was* convinced. But I wasn't comfortable with the truth.

I was glad the highway was empty as I glanced over my shoulder at her, and as I looked at the too-pretty being beside me, I understood my reluctance, at least in part. In a way, Fauna was my mother. She was the church. She was the Bible. She was a singular entity I would need to trust implicitly to redirect my reality. And I wasn't sure how comfortable I was with that.

But that wasn't something I was ready to say.

"Why does it matter? With Silas in play, I mean? I don't fully get why it's so important that now the Nordes are involved." I asked. I didn't have to look at her to see the way she stiffened. "I mean, I want Caliban back more than words can say. I've been so in love with him for as long as I can remember. It's consumed my thoughts and ruined my life for ten goddamn years. But it doesn't have to be ruined. He's real. We're real. I'm not crazy. I can let myself fully love him back. And I'm stressed as fuck knowing that Azrames doesn't know where he is. His disappearance is my fault, and I know it. But...things have been like this for thousands of years, right? I don't mean to be dismissive, but how much would change if—"

Gone was her levity. "Everything."

My stomach twisted at the way she'd said the word.

"Do you think humans will be spared once the stalemate is over? Gods ruled with iron fists on your soil. If the tide turns...if the war is over...everything changes. You don't get to be a normal human. Life as every person on this planet knows it is done." She turned so that her back was to the

199

passenger's side window, facing me fully. "And when that war is over, who do you want reigning on earth?"

She was talking about the Apocalypse.

I drummed my fingers against the steering wheel as I returned my eyes to the blur of pavement. Seconds ticked into minutes as I pictured the last book of the Bible: the prophecy of God bringing heaven to earth. It was a forgone conclusion that he would win. It had sounded like a wonderful thing.

And I could be the catalyst to the book of Revelation.

A concrete wall slammed down around my thoughts. I shielded myself from the implications as I decided in no uncertain terms that no, I was not ready for the world to end. And no, I would not be a tool in the last battle.

I wanted to sleep in, to drink coffee, to watch TV. I wanted to get drunk with my friends and have sex out of wedlock. I wanted to take mushrooms at the aquarium. I was unwilling to entertain the idea that it could all be taken away from me in the blink of an eye.

I changed the subject. "But that brings us back to Silas. He saved my life more than once. Shouldn't I be concerned about what happens to him?"

She flared her hands dramatically. "Who knows! Who cares? There are defectors all the time. Life is hard on both sides, so who's to say who has it better? They both believe in their cause, and in that way, I guess neither side is wrong. Ultimately, it doesn't matter. You're a Norde. If you wanna bond yourself to me"—she flexed her brows—"skip on over to our side, forget about your prince, let me be your goddess."

I took my eyes off the road again. The car vibrated against the rumble strips once more until I jerked it back into its lane. I wasn't sure what shocked me more, the jolt of the road, the threat of near-crashing, or her statement.

"Are you serious?"

The sound of her laughter was like silver bells. "Hell would be so mad. Bonds are forever, so there'd be no getting out of it. And then I'd have to answer to Odin. I have no interest in meeting up with the Aesir ever again."

I kept my eyes on the road while I waited for her to elaborate.

"You think you have family issues? He can be grumpier than you before coffee, except with more gore and viscera. Honestly, he'd probably cast me out and let Hell deal with me." It took a while for the laughter to dissipate. I'd almost thought she was going to press play on the audiobook again. Once her smile faded, she amended, "I would do it, though."

The joy between us died as a rare gravity colored her words.

"I would," she repeated. The air in the car felt thick as she said, "Not for me, but if you decided that you didn't want that life. If you didn't want Heaven or Hell, I'd take the hit so you could join your people."

The remainder of our drive was far less talkative.

Fauna resumed the audiobook. It helped ease the gravity that had settled with her message, but I no longer had it in me to whine, and she couldn't rally the energy to mock.

We had to stop several times, both for candy and for the restroom. I don't know why it shocked me that Fauna had a tiny bladder. Despite knowing she'd locked herself into a mortal form to go on this journey with me, her having human needs was still somehow surprising.

She allowed me my ever-growing silence as the clock wound down.

My anxiety swelled as the evening faded into dusk. We'd spent nearly nine hours in the car. The drive had been an eternity, but as the town neared, I wasn't ready for it to end. I needed nine more hours.

"My parents will be asleep by now," I said quietly when we were less than twenty minutes from the speck on the map where I'd been born and raised. There were no highway lights this far from their town. We were alone in the black. "They always go to bed early. We can't arrive at their house after dark."

"That's fine," she said. "We'll get a hotel tonight and go tomorrow morning to rifle through Aloisa's things. If you want, we can even wait until—remind me their names?"

"My mom and dad? John and Lisbeth."

"Great. We can wait until John and Lisbeth have left for the day and we have the house to ourselves. Okay?"

I breathed out a sigh of relief at the proposal I hadn't even considered. Of course we could break in. If things went well, we wouldn't see them at all. I might not have to relive our final fight. I might not have to see my mother's face after the condemnation, the damning of my immortal soul, the red face, the tears that had streamed down her face, the tiny droplets of spit that had flown from her mouth as she screamed. I could get in, get the sølje, and get out.

My anxiety remained a cinched corset, unwilling to grant me oxygen as the speed limit lowered from seventy to fifty-five to thirty. I eased into the small town and crept down Main Street, stomach churning against years of suppressed childhood memories. Fight or flight ticked through me like a clock as it turned back the hands of time, sending my hands clammy and creating a gentle bead of cold sweat over my forehead and upper lip. Fauna silently reached over from the passenger seat and wrapped a steadying hand over my knee, giving it a squeeze. She left it there as if to reassure me of her presence as we eased into a parking lot.

I left Fauna to the bags while I checked into the seedy motel, praying that we wouldn't get bedbugs. Amid the punching of buttons on an outdated computed, the clerk found the time to leer over my shoulder through the window at Fauna. I shot him a glare.

"Does the motel offer a military discount? My friend is on leave to celebrate her commendation with her family. Top marksman, that one. Better with a gun than anyone on the planet." I delivered the lie with enough cool believability to take the grimy receptionist's eyes off her.

Maybe it was that I was too exhausted to shower or wash

my face or protest. I'd scarcely been able to shimmy out of my pants and tug the bra off from beneath my shirt. Maybe it was that I'd driven for nine hours and something about being on the road was oddly taxing, akin to running a marathon. Maybe it was that she could smell my dread as thick as any perfume, but Fauna didn't take the other twin bed. She changed into one of my T-shirts and running shorts, lifted the covers, and tucked herself into the space beside me. Whether or not she could feel the way I trembled at the trauma I'd left behind or what it did to me to be near my parents, she didn't say. She merely turned off the light, gave me a squeeze in the dark, and, despite ten buckets of sugar coursing through her veins, was soundly asleep within moments.

I hadn't forgotten the SSRIs that made my life bearable, but the litany of other drugs I used to fall asleep remained untouched on the nightstand. The smell of the sea, the weighed quilt of her kindness, and the steady breathing of someone well on their way to sweet dreams pulled me under. And maybe it was that I knew it might be my last true chance at sleep in a while, I let myself sink beneath the waves and drifted off to join her.

Chapter Nineteen

(Kirby) Are you still with Fauna?

(Nia) You learned her name?! How do you know more than me! I just got one selfie!

(Kirby) I got to video-chat with her. She is a goddess and I am in love with her.

(Nia) Marlow, you'd better be on some awesome bangcation and that's why you're ignoring us. If you are: good. we love that for you, happy for you, yay! If you're not: fuck you, text us back.

(EG) I shouldn't have to tell you that your chapters are due tomorrow, but my spidey senses are telling me that you don't have them done. If there's something going on, you have to tell me.

(EG) Marlow, I'm trying everything I can to let Merit succeed. Let me help you. If we need to spin something, let's spin it, but you have to clue me in

(EG) Marlow, the deadline is passed. I made an excuse, but it was a lame out. No one bought it. Tell me what's going on, girl. Are you burned out? Do you need extensions? You just have to communicate

(EG) MERIT FINNEGAN. Your job is not the only one at stake right now. Text me back

I STARED AT MY PHONE FOR A WHILE, LETTING THE GLOW EASE me awake while Fauna slept soundly beside me. Part of me wanted to type useless questions into the search engine, like *how long do nymphs sleep*, but I knew any answer would be something I'd have to get directly from her.

I couldn't bring myself to face my editor or my deadlines. I had no idea where to begin explaining the chaos to my friends, but I was quite certain they were better off in the dark.

Instead, I tabbed over to my oldest social media app. I hadn't used it in years. It was the only one I hadn't bothered to block my parents on, even if they'd deserved it. Without the app, I wouldn't have known that my childhood home had flooded, forcing my parents to move into a "blessing" of a new property. The site was how I'd found out Grandma Dagny had died, though I hadn't been invited to her funeral. The smiling pictures of a girl flashing her diamond band were how I had found out my cousin had gotten married. Without the site, it would be like my family had never existed.

I navigated to the account that my mom and dad shared. It was their way of preempting infidelity, or whatever it was they told each other. My parents, despite their despicable flaws, were frustratingly attractive. It was what had drawn my ageless, graceful mother to a failed salesman whose paychecks barely supported his family. They'd been young, and it would have been sacrilegious to consummate their infatuation without a wedding ring. It hadn't taken long after doing the deed to realize that she was insane and that he was a deadbeat. He couldn't stand to be around her, and she didn't respect him.

But, to all the world, they were madly in love. Divorce was off the table, after all.

Given their belief in the sanctity of marriage, I remember asking my mother once if you could leave your husband if he hit you, and she'd said that no, you couldn't. If you picked an abusive man, then you made your bed and you had to lie in it. You could only leave him if he hit the children, and even then, it was only for their safety. God, she said, hated divorce.

It seemed like a pretty violent stance to take, but then again, the god of the Abrahamic religions had always been a pretty violent guy. Sometimes he wanted his righteous soldiers to pillage and destroy cities, leaving no man, woman, or child spared, like in the genocide of Canaan. Sometimes he murdered all of the firstborns just to prove a point. Sometimes he called fire from the sky to burn cities to ash, leaving nothing but salt, embers, and memories as in Sodom. Sometimes he flooded the earth because he was sick of everyone.

Of course, we were taught the deeply contextual literary and canonical concept of righteous anger. For a while, it seemed like an exercise in mental gymnastics to argue one side and clutch the other. Whether or not it was the lesson the pastors and elders and passages had intended to teach me, I accepted that some people had to die. Sometimes violence was okay. Sometimes there were shades of gray, and morality was more complicated than the world liked to believe. Maybe that was why I thought my parents should have gotten divorced. Maybe that's why I could understand them and keep them out of my lives but not hate them. Maybe that's why the thing that kept me up at night was never a guilty conscience.

I scrolled through their social media page to look at the evidence of their years. Something about people over the age of fifty came with a distinct inability to use aesthetics when capturing anything. If I had to guess, I'd say that every photo was taken with a tablet in poor lighting. There were a few blurry pictures of them with church members. My ever-youthful mother held a baby goat and smiled in another. My mouth dropped open when I reached an image of them standing proudly in front of a whitewashed brick home, arm in arm, dangling the keys.

So grateful to the Lord that after all these years, God blessed my husband with an excellent job and this beautiful home! Thank you for this answer to prayers! God is good!

I stared at the picture of the trimmed hedges, the new, glossy car in the driveway. It was a three-story home with black shutters on what looked to be at least two acres of property. They looked...rich. A tiny fire burned through me at the glib sentences. The religious community's fucked-up stances on how privilege equivalated the blessings of the faithful were steeped in problematic issues of supremacy. I wondered if God wasn't good when we lived in a trailer, when we had to sleep in snowsuits because we couldn't afford power, or when we crashed on my Grandma Dagny's couch and floor for six months between homes. Perhaps material possessions defined his goodness. Then again, I had a chip on my shoulder.

Fauna made a small noise upon waking, and I closed the phone. I wasn't sure why I did it. I wasn't hiding anything from her. Maybe I didn't want her first conscious thought to be a glaring phone screen or for me to be distracted. I guess perhaps I felt like she deserved...more.

I slid out of bed in my oversize T-shirt and my underwear and started the tiny hotel coffeepot, wondering as to the wisdom of using something that may or may not have been cleaned in the last six months. I kept it running just for the smell of coffee, which had her yawning, stretching, and smiling in moments. I watched her blink open her enormous eyes and felt equal parts happy and sad. I'd never let my friends sleep over. I occasionally allowed the people I dated to spend the night at my apartment, but more often than not, I would insist we hook up at theirs so I could bow out under the believable, and somewhat true, guise of insomnia. I'd missed out on an entire experience of human existence. Waking up next to someone you loved, making them coffee, watching the sleepiness tumble from their eyes as they rubbed away their dreams with loose fists, it was an intimacy I didn't even realize I was lacking.

Fauna sat up and realized I was staring at her.

She yawned. "Are you shocked at how ravishing I am first thing in the morning?"

"Kinda," I answered honestly. "It's offensive for anyone to look that good when they wake up. Fuck you."

"You should!" she said, merry despite her grogginess. "I'm fantastic in bed." She laughed at my slack-jawed surprise before asking, "Is that coffee for me? And what do they have for sweetener?"

"Oh, this will be undrinkable. I just like the smell. Let's get ready and swing by the bakery before we commit crimes."

She pumped a sleepy first into the air. "Doughnuts and theft!"

I abandoned her to shower, brush my teeth, and go through the motions of my morning routine. The fear of being in my hometown coerced me into applying an extra layer of makeup, lest I run into anyone from my youth. I wanted to look my best, should I bump into any of the girls who were mean to me in high school. Fauna was practically dancing with impatience while I picked out my clothes. I'd packed as if I were staying for a week rather than a single day, and I struggled to decide what would strike the perfect balance between successful, attractive, and conservative.

"Come on," Fauna urged. "We'll be in and out. Quick adventure."

I shot a look at her reflection in the mirror just over my shoulder. "You either underestimate how small this town is or how insecure I am. But I'll blame you if we go anywhere without making a killer impression."

I forced Fauna to take the bags to the car just to give her something to do with her energy, promising her that there were some hard candies in the glove compartment. I settled on a long-sleeve cream dress that gathered at my waist and fell just a few inches above my knee. The neckline offered just enough cleavage to pique the interest, without showing so much that it gave away secrets. It was conservative while it still hinted that I had money. The best part was that it had pockets. I paired it with heels, a watch, and a delicate designer necklace to inform anyone who recognized me from my youth that they'd been shortsighted for mocking our income disparity. I swept my hair into a ponytail with trembling hands and stared at myself.

My gray-green eyes were neither my mother's sky blue nor my father's hazel. I'd hoped it meant I was adopted and had a much cooler family somewhere else, but no such luck. I'd used a shaky hand to sweep a cat eye onto either side, then dusted my lids with a mauve and sparkly neutrals. Worry had turned me a sickly shade of bloodless, but a generous amount of blush put the life back in my cheeks. My mousy hair had never relinquished the final traces of gold that lit its occasional strands, even if I was no longer the pale daughter of Norway that had represented my maternal line for generations. I smashed my lips together, rubbing in what remained of the lip gloss before sighing, full mouth tugging down in a disappointed pout.

I looked great.

I looked successful.

I looked put-together, elegant, and mysterious.

I looked like I was one minute away from a breakdown.

A whistle cut through the air as I exited the motel. It was the first time I considered how Fauna and I were dressed as if we were headed to entirely different events. I was ready for an upscale board meeting, while she looked like she was about to sell me crystals and tell me that astral projection had changed her life. Her crocheted bralette top looked great with the giant butterflies printed on her flowing pants, but I struggled to picture her shopping for such an item. Then again, she had just scared a gas station attendant along the interstate over a gummy bear craving. Who knew what she was capable of achieving.

I approached the car and asked, "Where do you get your clothes? I never asked."

"My place!" She smiled.

"Your...excuse me?"

"I have a house in the mortal realm. You know, for funsies."

At this point, I wasn't sure why anything she said shocked me. If she informed me that she also had a husband, three children, and wore pantsuits from Monday through Friday, I probably would have found it just as ridiculous as everything else I'd learned. None of it had to make sense, I supposed.

"Where is it?" I asked, bringing the engine to life so I could get the air-conditioning going. The car was already stuffy, despite the early hour.

She waved the question away. "On the beach."

I waited for her to expand. When she didn't, I promoted, "We're nowhere near the beach. How are you getting clothes from there? Didn't you say to that Azrames guy that you were...mortal-bound at the moment?"

She shot me a side-eye, presumably at how I'd referenced the monochromatic demon. She said, "I'm limited in what I can do *with* you. If I want to stay present with you, I have to stay in mortal form. Personally, I can come and go from wherever I want. And once you have the søjle, we can stroll everywhere from the Celts to the Shintos to the Greeks without you having to bond. If you can spare me for two minutes while you think I'm in the bathroom, sometimes that's all it takes for me to blink in and out."

"I'll jot that down on my ever-growing list of worries," I mumbled.

"You'd love my place. Unless you hate the ocean, but no one hates the ocean. Being in it, maybe. But looking at it? Always enjoyable. Plus, the owner is fae, so he rents it out to a bunch of us to come and go as we please. We trade in favors, mostly."

I arched a brow.

"He's a eunuch, so they're not those kinds of favors, but I applaud your entrepreneurial spirit. Usually he just needs errands run around the world or between realms, but only once in a while. It's a pretty sweet gig. And since I'm an absolutely lovable gem, I'm welcome between most kingdoms…except Egypt," she shuddered. "I may have pissed off Osiris. But in my defense: I should never have been the one sent to deliver things to a god of death. We have incompatible personalities. Anyway." She tucked a curl behind her ears as if speaking of a boring Tuesday night before saying, "My landlord knows I'm indisposed for a while. I'm on a super-secret, very important mission to be stuck in a mortal body with a pretty blockhead so she doesn't make deals with angels."

I smiled as I relied on my memory to guide me to the bakery. "Oh, so we're adding pleasant adjectives before the insults now? I'm flattered."

She nodded. "I call it like it is. You make bad choices. But, this is the first time I've seen you dress up, and you're stunning. I can sprinkle all sorts of incentives before truths if it makes them easier to swallow."

"Like putting a dog's medicine in cheese?"

She made a contemplative face. "Whenever I don't understand a reference, it just informs me that I need to watch more television. When our very special mission is over, I'll dedicate three weeks to nothing but education in the form of reality shows."

"That's wise," I agreed.

The town was small enough that it took only two stoplights and three turns before I pulled into a spot directly in front of the bakery. She stepped out the moment I put the car in park. "Wait, your hat!"

"Nah." She shook her head, peering through the crack in the door as she bent over to wink at me. "They weren't nice to you here, and you look great today. I think we should give your small town something to talk about."

My fingers and toes tingled as if I'd been injected with Novocain. I struggled to get my breathing under control as I fumbled with my belt. My gut told me no, but it was hard to

211

argue with her logic. I'd dressed up because I wanted to make a statement.

The glass bakery door squeaked open on ungreased hinges. I led the way and walked directly to the counter, not realizing our mistake until forks clattered to their plates and conversation halted around us. Fauna looped her arm around mine and smiled at the person working the cash register before saying, "How many cream-filled doughnuts can I order before it's inappropriate?"

The cashier's eyes were too wide, mouth too open, lips too slicked with drool as he stared at her with his blank, catfish-like gaze.

I decided that we'd already committed to the bit, so I might as well double down. I tightened my grip around her arm and flashed a smile of my own.

"I'll have a black coffee with six pumps of honey. She'll have a latte, whole milk, with six pumps of sweetener, two pumps of vanilla, two pumps caramel, and squirt in some liquid cocaine if you have it lying around. Oh, and she'll have eclairs, please. All of them."

He continued staring.

"The last one was a joke."

"Ma'am?"

"The cocaine, not the eclairs. Though, if you have any coke..."

"We don't, ma'am."

Fauna and I shared a giggle. She was right. This particular brand of chaos was fun.

He swallowed. "Name?"

Fauna looked at me expectantly.

"Your Majesties."

✦

"Holy shit." Fauna eyed the house impressively as we pulled up the driveway. "I didn't think you came from money."

"I don't," I said, turning off the car. The Mercedes was a

212

very quiet car, but in the absence of air-conditioning, radio, and engine, the silence was deafening. "I've never gotten a dime from them, even when I desperately needed it."

She unbuckled her belt. "All the more reason to leave everything in your will to me."

"The moment the ink dried, they'd find my body mysteriously washed up on the shores of the river," I grumbled.

She wrinkled her nose. "They used to leave treasures at my temple. Now I get an eye roll. Now, what do we do about this house?"

A dull ache joined the shades of blue washing over me. The truth was, I didn't know anything about their new home. "If I hadn't checked their social media this morning, I wouldn't even know that my dad had gotten some fancy new job and they'd moved into the most pretentious place in town. Let's hope the cedar chest is easy to find."

She chewed on her lip as she leaned forward, peering out the windshield. "Well, looks like we have our work cut out for us. You take the boring rooms, I'll take wherever your mom hides her jewelry."

Her joke almost got a laugh out of me, but not quite. Walking up the driveway mirrored how I imagined it might feel to arrive at your own funeral. I realized I had no idea how to get into the house. I blinked in horror at the flaw in my plan. I didn't have to communicate my mistake before Fauna realized the problem.

"Hold on," she said. "Stay here."

I tried not to look suspicious as I waited between the immaculately trimmed hedges. I inspected the door, the window-box planters filled with geraniums, the frosted glass, the welcome mat that said "*As for me and my house, we will serve the Lord.*" Fauna disappeared around the corner of the house, presumably heading for the backyard. I assumed she had more experience as a cat burglar, and remained obediently on the doorstep.

A moment later, the front door opened.

"Welcome to my home!" She grinned, throwing the door open on its hinges and making a sweeping gesture inward.

I started to ask her how she'd done it but acutely remembered her stepping into my house from oblivion on more than one occasion. I suspected she'd only needed to round the house in case curious neighbors and their prying eyes peered through cracks in the blinds as the attention-grabbing ginger vanished into thin air.

I struggled to take a forward step.

"Are you coming in? Or should we head back to the city?"

"Is that an option?" I asked. I knew the answer. I wasn't just curious to find Caliban. I was desperate. He'd been my anchor in a life that had been nothing but storms. He'd kept me from losing my mind, even when I'd blamed him for my loose grip on sanity. He'd saved my life in more ways than one, and I needed him to do it again. I couldn't face the future—especially not one knowing that angels and fae and gods and demons lurked in every shadow—without him.

They're not even home, I inwardly cursed. *Don't be a coward.*

I entered and looked around at the utterly unfamiliar space. While a few small touches remained, it was hard to find any evidence that I knew the humans who lived here. I never thought I'd live to see the day where John and Lisbeth were upper middle class.

The gallery wall of photos and mid-century-modern furniture were the browns, beiges, and grays of an HGTV makeover. I knew exactly how much the cognac-leather couch and chair set cost, as I had looked at it myself before ultimately selecting to move into a furnished apartment. My gaze wandered over the books, the globe, the bobbles, the speakeasy-style light fixture, and the cowskin rug. An enormous, illustrated topographical map that looked like it might have been salvaged from a one-room schoolhouse hung as a focal piece on one wall. Brown wooden beams stretched over the ceiling, breaking up the white walls.

It smelled faintly of window cleaner and bleach, which were the main odors permeating my childhood. The sterile scent, however, was the only element of nostalgia. There were no family photos. It felt so staged, so fake, there was no evidence that anyone real had ever lived here.

"Do any of your gifts help you find things?" I asked Fauna.

"Um, if you'd like, I can grow a tree? Or call a few animals, if you think summoning a bunch of rabbits might help. Or bless the fertility of their garden so those peony bushes get some tender loving care. Or—"

"Fine, fine. Let's get looking."

Despite her threats to raid the kitchen, Fauna stayed by my side for most of our hunt. We began on the ground floor, peeking into the guest room and the office, the kitchen, and stately formal dining room with glass double doors. Fortunately, a chest was a challenging object to conceal, which limited its hiding places. For most of my childhood, it had been at the foot of my parents' bed. Now that they had space, it might not be something Lisbeth would want sitting out in the open any longer.

Fauna and I went into the basement next—a finished, carpeted basement free from parasitic entities—and it took less than two minutes of poking around to ascertain that aside from a large sofa, a flat-screen TV, fire-safe egress windows, and the boiler room, there was nothing for us down there. We mounted the stairs, and the second floor seemed a little more promising.

Every door stood open, which drew me first to yet another guest bedroom. I looked behind the bed, opened the closet door, and frowned at the very large verse painted in driftwood that hung on the far wall. I found a few of my things tucked into a storage container beneath the bed, which may or may not have been comforting, as I wasn't sure if hiding them was better than my mom burning them altogether. Fauna had quickly grown bored at my walk down memory lane and wandered away, leaving me alone with the only proof of my existence.

There was a musty scent to my things. It was the mildew of nostalgia, of a tin-can trailer home in the woods, of rainy days and walks in the forest.

I lifted a crinkled picture of my mother, father, and me smiling in front of a tent. Our thrifted clothes were so collectively outdated that the photo could have passed as a relic from the '80s. I remembered the trip. It had stormed so hard that our sleeping bags had soaked all the way through. We'd packed the tent in the pouring rain and used what little money we had to get a motel for the night. The three of us had stayed up late, eating junk from the vending machine, and watching an old western on the static of a box TV.

It was a happy memory.

I looked down at my chest to see if a physical thread was sticking out where my heart should be. I knew that while under their roof, I was a single tug from unraveling.

Fauna had been away from me for less than two minutes when I heard her triumphant noise from the next room.

"Did you find it?" I called, still kneeling over old grade-school pictures, report cards, and several childhood drawings of me playing with a friend with eyes as silver as diamonds.

"Get over here!" she yelled.

I folded up a drawing of my guardian and slipped it into my pocket. I joined her in the master bedroom. Despite Lisbeth's commitment to beige, it didn't look like the stuffy, over-priced room one might expect. She'd used vintage movie posters and spread statement wallpaper from the 1920s on one wall to break up the room. She'd always loved antiques.

If only I could have convinced my mother that homes should smell like something other than bleach.

"Fauna?"

"In here!" Her voice drifted from the walk-in closet. Sure enough, the little pirate had tracked down our treasure chest. She knelt between the rows of hung pants and pressed shirts over a large cedar chest. She'd already opened it and pulled out the wool bunad. "It's in great shape,"

216

she marveled, running her fingers along the red-and-blue woolen dress. It was strange to see it in color after years of having only the black-and-white picture on my fridge. "This has to be two hundred and fifty years old. Gods, it makes me emotional."

"Great," I said. It made me emotional, too, but not in a way that permitted us to linger. "Let's focus on finding the broach and get out of here."

I picked up a handmade quilt and set it to the side to reveal a row of wooden boxes. I knelt beside her and felt through the various containers, frowning at the concealed, orderly collection. One box contained a collection of old photographs. I passed it off to Fauna, who began to flit through them while I continued to dig. I opened the next box to find a leather journal wrapped in twine. I passed it off to Fauna as well, who immediately dove into Aloisa's diary, no doubt searching for salacious details about her friend Geir and the human-Norde sordid love affair. Another box was filled with handwritten recipes for various desserts and traditional dishes. Finally, I found the box I was looking for. I knew it before I even opened it. The moment I lifted it, the sound of shifting metal snapped both of our gazes into alert. Fauna huddled around me as we opened the box and looked at the delicate fabric of a handkerchief concealing something small.

She held the box so that I could move the fabric to the side, releasing a low, appreciative murmur as I gripped the edges of the dangly, silver heirloom as delicately as possible.

"That's it," Fauna breathed. "That belonged to Geir."

"And what is it supposed to do?" I looked over the antique and into Fauna's eyes.

"These are exceptionally rare. Every pantheon has their legends about gifts like this. He gave it to Aloisa so that she could move to and from the mortal realm to visit him on her terms. If she—"

A car door slammed, and just like that, our spell was broken.

"Shit, shit, *shit!*" Our eyes met in mutual panic across the scattered evidence of our breaking and entering.

I wrapped the sølje back in the handkerchief and shoved it in my pocket. Fauna was busy lining the wooden boxes along the bottom of the cedar chest with family heirlooms just in time for me to put the quilt, then the bunad where we'd found it. I rushed to the window just in time to see a woman in her early fifties walking up with a tall, broad man. Fear mingled with puzzlement as I tried to make sense of what I was seeing. The pair disappeared beneath the lip of the window as the handle to the front door rattled.

I tore my eyes from the pair to look at Fauna. "It can't be."

She met my wide-eyed disbelief. "Is your mother with…?"

"Silas."

Chapter Twenty

W HAT. A. BASTARD," FAUNA BREATHED BESIDE ME.
"Does she *know* he's with her?" I asked, voice
shaking.

Fauna shook her head. "I have no idea, but I doubt it.
The motherfuckers don't need to be seen to whisper their
persuasion. It gets the job done."

I wasn't a child caught with my hand in a cookie jar. I
wasn't at risk of a wooden spoon, a switch, or a leather belt.
She'd already done the worst thing a mother could possibly
do to a child. The clang of keys in the front door reverberated
through me like a guard opening a prison cell. I was a child
again. Years of buried wounds opened as if a scab had been
picked, fresh blood flowing freely. I struggled to calm my
breathing as Fauna and I navigated out of the bedroom and
headed for the landing.

"Can we jump out a window?" I whispered, words
scarcely audible over the pounding in my ears.

"Do you need your legs?" she whispered back.

The door was our only option. I straightened my spine,
swallowed the heart that seemed lodged in my throat, and led
the way. Fauna remained on my heels as I descended the stairs
to see my mother, arms crossed, beside a man who stood a
full head and shoulders taller than her even in heels.

She bloomed into view, a picturesque monster in a charcoal pantsuit with a large, white-gold cross resting against her sternum, just as it had always been. Seeing the beautiful, horrible woman who'd raised me was every bit as terrible as I'd anticipated. She hadn't changed a bit. Except now, she was in a costume to play the socially acceptable role of wealthy, as was I.

Like mother, like daughter.

Time moved in slow motion as I saw her for the first time in years.

The tiniest hints of gray lined her bright blond hair, barely visible amid the natural platinum that had always cascaded from her roots. Her face was free from wrinkles, save for the evidence that she'd once been a person who'd smiled. We'd always been able to trade clothes, and I expected she could still fit into the very cream dress on my back if she'd wanted. The primary change was a cold fire in her eyes. It kindled something dark in me, as someone who'd been raised in a burning house. It had been so long since I'd had a match held to my skin that I'd nearly forgotten the pain of its spark.

"Marlow Esther Thorson." My mother's voice sliced through the house, each word a blade.

Despite the revulsion, the misery, the sheer terror that soaked through the room, Fauna leaned in to say, "Your middle name is Esther? How biblical."

"I rebuke you," she said with icy indignation as I descended the stairs.

"Lisbeth—" I said her name with frost and warning. My gaze darted between her and the angel, his shoulders back, chest puffed out, wondering which feat to tackle first.

She looked past me and directed her rage toward Fauna. Trembling with anger, she said, "I rebuke your persuasion over my daughter!"

The hate had a somewhat soothing, comical effect. The tension snapped. I exhaled, pushing out much of my anxiety as I said, "Mom, this is my friend, Fauna."

Her eyes darkened as she looked at me. "I know exactly *what* your friend is—and now, thanks to your parade around town, everyone knows that my daughter is here on an escapade." She spat the word *daughter* as if it were an obscenity. "Do you know how many pictures I got of you arm in arm with this demon at the bakery? As if I didn't have to suffer humiliation when I was being sent pictures and videos of my daughter on her social media kissing another woman, now you bring one into my *town*? Into my *house*, Marlow? Not only have you walked away from God, but you're letting demons in your *bed*."

Fauna suppressed a chuckle beside me, which, despite the turmoil, I appreciated. Her dedication to irreverence was grounding.

"Fauna isn't a demon, Mom. She's—"

"She's not of God" came her sharp reply. "This house belongs to the Lord. I don't know what you think you can achieve here, but your demons are not welcome."

I reached out to grab Fauna for support, which infuriated my mother further.

"Could we try being calm?" I asked, looking between my mother and Silas.

"Explain yourself, Marlow. What are you doing in my home?"

I scrambled for an answer that would put this conversation to a stop and allow us a speedy exit. I shot a quick glance at Silas and caught his appraising, narrowed eyes before deciding it was a very, very bad idea to disclose that we were here for my great-grandma's broach. My mother clearly didn't know what the trinket was worth, but I wasn't willing to bet our escape on Silas's ignorance. He was sharp. And apparently the angel knew the one tool to wield against me that could genuinely hurt me: my mother.

At a loss for excuses, all I could say was, "She's my friend."

"She is not of this world," my mother retorted. "If you truly had my gift, then you'd have the discernment to realize

221

what you've done, Marlow. An angel of the Lord was sent to me to tell me about the spirits you've let into your life. I should have known when you began whoring—"

"Hey—" Fauna cut in, bristling at the word. She took a half-step as if to put herself between her mother and me.

"It's okay." I waved, urging her to stand down. My mother and I had had this fight on the last night I ever saw them.

It had been early June in my twenty-second year of life. I'd returned from Colombia with six thousand dollars in cash, and that had only been what I hadn't been able to wire directly into my account. Taylor had been right. Between Buenos Aires and Montevideo, there had been more than enough opportunities for a girl to get ahead. Once my visa expired and I gave up my life in Colombia, I'd needed a place to bridge the gap between my transition back into North America.

My mom had cried when she'd hugged me at the airport— the Prodigal Daughter returned, she'd said. I was finally home to live a good life, to turn away from sin and distractions and worldliness. I didn't have the heart to correct her.

In a fog of jet lag and reverse culture shock, I'd needed somewhere to crash while setting up the next phase of my life. They'd left my bedroom more or less untouched, save for the closet space that my parents had used to stash things that were better off out of sight and out of mind. I stayed at the time capsule in the woods for the better part of a week while scouring the web for my own place in the city. While I was on a weekend excursion apartment hunting, my mother had taken it upon herself to snoop through my things. She'd made no excuses for what had prompted her to go through my belongings—she never needed to. She was the parent, and I was the child, after all. She hadn't been looking for anything in particular aside from a satiated curiosity when she'd found the money in the lining of my suitcase.

I vividly recalled the cloud of dread and adrenaline that had descended on me when stepping back into the house.

My smile had faltered the moment I saw her sitting at the kitchen table, cash neatly displayed in front of her next to an open, glowing laptop.

She'd suspected drug trafficking, which, in hindsight, she might have preferred. Of course, she hadn't stopped at finding the money. The moment she'd uncovered her treasure, she did what any good mother would do and immediately went through every means necessary to further violate my privacy. She'd managed to guess my security questions to get into my email and read exchanges between myself and my clients—both those over the past with whom I'd met up in my final weeks in Colombia and the clients I'd already arranged for the city. While helping herself to my computer, she'd googled an array of terms based on the acronyms in the threads, like *FSSW* for full-service sex work, *GFE* for girlfriend experience, and had gone down a rabbit hole on findom. She had a few pictures of me, naked, face obscured, from my client thread open on the screen when I walked in.

I met the disgust in her eyes with speechlessness.

"I don't even know who you are anymore," she'd whispered.

It had been the Pandora's box of fights.

We'd said every cruel, hateful thing we could conjure. We'd launched missiles at one another, bloodying the other with our words until we were little more than shreds. My dad had arrived at the house just to hear the tail end of the screaming, including me shouting just how much money I'd made in the past three months alone and how I was happier, freer, kinder, and better off as a sex worker than I'd ever been in the church or as their daughter.

She'd told me they had no daughter, and that she'd miss me when they were in heaven, knowing I'd be rotting in hell.

It was a fight I'd relived on therapists' couches through boxes of tissues. It was a fight I'd used bottles of prescription medications to get through whenever panic attacks over my mortal soul strangled me. It was a fight that had forced me

223

further and further from Caliban, demanding that I put up walls, that I choose sanity, that I close myself off from the irrational hold on the fiction that my mother led.

And now…now the words tickled me as I thought of my Prince.

"I know all about your angel of the Lord," I said, glaring at Silas, "and he's a dick with an agenda."

She turned and looked at Silas—actually *looked* at him.

Fauna and I gasped simultaneously. Despite our years of conversations on seeing angels and demons, despite knowing that her fae blood was thicker than mine, despite everything I'd learned, witnessing my mother make eye contact with an angel was staggering.

"He told me what you are," she said. The tremble of her fury had passed. She spoke to Fauna now with frosty strength.

"Nice one, Silas." Fauna glared. Then back to my mother, she asked dryly, "Did he also tell you what *you* are? Though, to be fair, I think I speak for the Nordes when I tell you: we don't want you."

"And he told me who you've sold your soul to." She looked at me, ignoring Fauna's goad. "Do you think I haven't spent every day praying for your soul? Do you think I haven't spent every night on my knees petitioning God's angels to get you back? Do you think I want my daughter to spend eternity in the inferno? I love you, Marlow."

Love. I nearly laughed at the word.

"I told you." Silas spoke for the first time. His voice was quiet but firm beside her as he looked directly at Fauna. "We have a claim to her."

"Silas, you're a goddamn cocksucker," Fauna grumbled. "And you can shove that claim up your master's ass next time you're kissing it. We're done here."

She grabbed my arm and yanked me toward the door. I winced as if preparing to plunge beneath icy waters as we closed the space between my mother and me. Fauna pushed past the woman and yelped when a small, electric shock stopped her. The jolt was enough to send her stumbling back, eyes wide.

My mom backed away, not daring to touch the demon and the whore as she watched Fauna grab for the handle once more.

She reached out her hand and tried again, cursing as the shock assaulted her. She lifted her eyes to where, just above the door, a protective ward had been hung—not to keep out but to keep in. She took several steps backward into the living room, panic rising as she scanned for an exit.

"I can't get you out of here," Fauna said, truly looking like a frightened deer in a glen as her wide eyes searched me. "I can't get you out," she repeated, taking another panicked step back.

The comfort of Fauna's calm irreverence evaporated. All that remained in its wake was the sickening injection of cortisol as my heart thundered. The smell of bleach was overpowering. The home closed in on me as I demanded, "Can *you* get out? Can you go?"

"Yes," Silas answered for her. "She can go back to the Nordes. She can visit the Sumerians, the Greeks, or seek refuge with the Hindus. She can go straight to Hell if she wants. She can step into any other realm. But her guardianship over you is done."

She'd done it. My mother had successfully pulled the thread. I cracked as it released the pieces of me that I'd spent so many years pulling together and became a child once more. My heart bled against years of buried terror as, small and helpless, I shattered into a powder of nothingness before her.

"I have not given up on your soul, even if you have," Lisbeth said. "I will force the demons from your life, whatever it takes. Now the angel—"

I swallowed against the cotton in my throat. "Mom, you don't know this guy like I do."

"I'm a chosen, faithful servant. I've been speaking with angels of the Lord my entire life. He arrived as an answer to prayer. Neither the Lord nor I have given up on your soul, Marlow, even if you have."

"I'm still willing to make the bond, Marlow," he said quietly. He didn't look angry or hostile or violent. Fractals of sadness reflected in his golden eyes as he looked between my mother and me. "I'm sorry it had to be like this, but there was no other way to get to you. I won't let anything happen to you. I've already proven my worth to you. I've saved you three times already, and I'll continue to do so. Just"—he extended his hand exactly as he had that night in my apartment—"make the bond."

"Commit your soul to the Lord," my mother commanded as she looked between the angel and me. "God is always reaching out his hand to you! Can't you see that? How can you spit on this chance at salvation?"

"So that's it?" I asked. My voice sounded so far away. "I choose a realm right now? My decision is now?"

The silent, watery-eyed apology on Fauna's face broke my heart.

"Marlow." He repeated my name, his quiet plea the voice of reason juxtaposed against her rising hysteria.

Then, something clicked. The world stopped spinning. The suffocating, sterile smell of cleaning products vanished. The only sound was that of my own heartbeat. I looked at Fauna with complete certainty as I said, "Step into another realm."

Silas's golden eyes flashed at my command. The tendons on his forearm pulsed as he flexed his fist.

"I won't leave you." She planted her feet, voice swelling with her resolve. "I can't throw you to the dogs—"

The beats between seconds stretched like taffy as time slowed. My pretty mother with her ugly heart surrounded by the opulence of her blessings and her jackass of an angelic counterpart blurred as I focused on Fauna alone. The roar in my ears sounded like the ocean's relentless pounding as blood thundered through me.

"Do it, Fauna!"

"I'm not going to abandon you," she repeated through gritted teeth.

I plunged my hand into my pocket, fingers digging through the bits of handkerchief until they touched the cool, silver treasure. Her eyes shot to my pocket, then up to me, and I knew she understood. I said all I could with the intensity of my eyes as I shouted, "Then don't leave me!"

Fauna's hand was on my bare skin in an instant. I heard a deep, masculine cry as the angel dove for me, saw a glint of glitter, and watched my mother's eyes flare all at once.

Silas's gold winked out as the world went utterly black.

Chapter Twenty-One

THE IMPACT TOOK MY BREATH AWAY AS I LANDED ON MY hands and knees, crying out as I struck the cobblestones. Cold rain hit my face, my hands, my neck. Nausea rolled through me as pain-induced stars erupted in my vision. I rolled onto my side, wincing at what I knew would be enormous, purple bruises on my kneecaps. I lifted my eyes through the dark and shadows that pressed in around us to barely make out Fauna picking herself up and extending her hand.

She shouted over the rain. "Come on. Let's get out of the cold."

Gone was the smell of bleach, the clean daylight, the white walls, the beige furniture. My mother and her dickhead of an angel were nowhere to be found. I looked around at the enormous buildings that stretched on either side down the long, ancient street. Through chattering teeth, I asked, "Are we in London?"

"Ha!" She laughed, the sound a bright, genuine joy. "No, but you bet your ass I'm going to tell every English person I ever met that you said that. Let's get moving."

I grimaced as I took her hand and got to my feet. I took shaky steps, heels wobbling as one nearly slipped into the space between cobblestones. Iron lanterns lined the sidewalks;

dim candles flicked within them as if we'd stepped into the past. Against the overcast sky, the silhouettes of Gothic cathedrals and old-world stone buildings intermingled with the glass, marble, and steel of modernity. I grabbed her hand and allowed her to pull me down the street.

"Where are we?" I asked, using my free hand to wipe the rain from my face.

"Welcome to Hell," she said, grinning like a tour guide.

I stopped so fast I nearly yanked her shoulder from her socket. The floodgates opened as decades of Christian fear filled me. I whipped my head from side to side, searching for Cheshire-cat parasites, gnashing teeth, talons, bats, and venom. Nausea returned as my heart skipped uncomfortably. If it weren't for the cold, rhythmic rain dripping down my face, I wasn't sure I would have stayed conscious.

I was going to be sick.

Fauna released my hand and stepped behind me, placing both hands on my back as she forced me toward a reddish, neon glow. The fires of Hell. The inferno. The lava. The lake of sulfur. The humming glow of a crimson sign that clearly read Shadow's.

I was too paralyzed with fear to do little more than shiver at the door until Fauna reached around me to yank on the handle.

My lashes fluttered as I struggled to understand what I was seeing.

I flinched as she wrapped her fingers around the handle, terrified of the monsters and ghouls and torture chambers within. Instead, she opened the door to reveal a mostly empty pub. Fauna gave me another small shove, as I'd lost all ability to move, to speak, to breathe. I could barely hear the music over the frozen chatter of my teeth but was almost certain "Don't Fear the Reaper" was being piped in from an unseen sound system. A few patrons cast us looks as we entered, two pausing their game of pool to watch us cross the threshold.

"Gentlemen." She nodded at the men before escorting

me to the bar top. Dark wood floors. Dark wood stools. Dark wood tabletop. The buzz of neon bulbs. Glasses. Music. The lingering scents of some savory snack and spilled liquor. It was…just a dive bar.

She slid onto a stool top as the bartender sidled up to us. My lips parted in silent shock as I stared at the inky silhouette. The man had no face.

He was composed entirely of shadow, as if a black, obsidian void where a person might be. I blinked once, then twice, then a third time. His body reminded me of Silas's—built and rippling, every muscle visible under his tight, red long-sleeve tee. His messy charcoal hair broke up the darkness, red horns poking up from the hair.

"Looks like someone got caught in the rain," said the shadow. I had a sudden suspicion as to where the establishment had gotten its name. He leaned against the counter with the same hospitable familiarity I'd seen in every club, tavern, and bar in the mortal realm. "What can I get you ladies?"

She propped her elbows on the countertop and arched forward. Fauna's lower lip puckered in a pout. "How strong can you mix something while still making it taste like candy?"

"I know just the thing."

"Wait." I stopped him. They both stilled, wondering what I could possibly say before I responded, "Nothing candy-tasting for me. Beer? Can I order beer here?"

Fauna giggled. "Of course you can order beer, but I don't know why you'd want to. I don't know if you know this, but it tastes like gross bread soda."

The bartender asked me a few far-too-normal questions about how dark, hoppy, or bitter I liked my beers before selecting something on my behalf and sliding me a glass. He paused as he handed it to me, then looked to Fauna.

"Is she human?" he asked quietly.

"Only kind of," Fauna responded with the lift of a single shoulder. "She's one of ours. It *is* her first visit though, so let's do our best to scare her."

230

"Can do, boss," he said, offering a two-finger salute before he returned to his duties.

Fauna wrapped an arm around me, chafing my damp sleeve with her hand to stop my shivering. "I'll get us a place to stay. But we couldn't very well stand out in the cold and keep you trembling like a wet Chihuahua while we figured things out."

I had no idea what it meant to figure things out in Hell.

I looked at the patrons playing pool. One appeared to be a handsome, fully human male. Unlike the bartender's aspect of shadow, or Azrames's grayscale pallor, he had rich, dark skin with cool undertones. If it weren't for the thin, forked tail that snaked up behind him, I would have sworn he had no place being in Hell. Beside him, the neighboring patron looked like he'd stepped off the set of a 1950s mob movie. He did not share the preternatural beauty I'd seen on so many faces but instead sported a serious expression and a portly belly that made his suspenders strain. The only prop he lacked was a cartoonishly oversize cigar.

I sipped my beer, eyebrows lifting in surprise.

"Good, huh?" she asked.

I nodded. "It's...smoother. Better, somehow."

"The humans have great junk food, but Hell really nails booze. Maybe if you're lucky, one of these days I'll show you what the Nordes do best. So, go ahead."

"Hmm?"

She gestured to the bar. "You're in Hell. And all you ever do is ask stupid questions. At this point I'm pretty sure it's your only personality trait. So do it. Get them out of your system now before we're in front of someone important and you embarrass me."

My teeth shattered as the rain chilled my bones, but there was only one thing on my mind. "Hell is evil," I said.

Her face, posture, and general aura sloughed in deadpan exhaustion. "Fine," she said. "I'll humor this question until I finish this drink, because every pantheon is exhausted with

231

the topic. And be warned, I'm drinking fast. So, tell me, why is Hell evil?"

I wasn't sure what she was asking. There had to be a double meaning. She knew of faiths and religions and angels and demons. She knew of churches and beliefs. It didn't take me long to offer, "What do you want? Old Testament or new? Weeping and gnashing of teeth. Realm of the dead. Eternal fire. Punishment. I don't remember any verses about playing pool and drinking beer."

She squared her shoulders and took a sip. "Okay, church kid, ready for the final word on theology?"

I wasn't sure if I was pleased or offended that a Norse pagan fae was about to lecture me on church culture, but I wasn't in a position to argue. I thought briefly of a piece I'd read on a physical burning pit beyond the holy city being conflated with the concept of Hell. "Are you going to make the Valley of Gehenna argument?"

Fauna's long-suffering exhaustion wore heavily on her as she said, "No, but I appreciate that you're halfway there. *Sheol* was the original Hebrew translation, the realm of the dead."

"You speak Hebrew?"

"I speak everything. You have three sips until I'm done with this topic. Are you done interrupting?"

I bit my lip to keep from interjecting.

"You're getting your imagery from *Paradise Lost* and Dante's *Inferno*, which is fine if you want to base your worldview around dead white guys who wrote religious fanfic. It was thousands of years after the establishment of the religion you grew up in. One sip to go."

It felt obscene to argue theology in another realm while speaking over classic rock and clutching a beer, but questions waited for no one. "But the verses—"

"Can I ask *you* a question?"

I wasn't sure if I was mad, cold, or confused. I may have nodded, or perhaps it was just a rain-soaked tremble. I was

232

uncomfortable in fifteen different ways and had no idea where to start.

"Cool." She made a satisfied, smacking sound as she drained the cup. "If your big bad Devil was forced to do things for God, wouldn't that mean he was still in servitude? Like a prisoner of sorts, doing Heaven's bidding, serving faithfully by punishing bad guys or whatever? And if he's a faithful servant, then did he commit treason? Because either you buy in to the idea that he's a fallen angel because he rebelled and rules his own kingdom, or we believe he continues to serve his original king by faithfully punishing people and continues to be a good little lap dog for the King of Heaven. Have it one way or the other."

I shivered again and Fauna sighed. She slid the dredges of her candy-apple-green beverage to the lip of the bar and walked to the far side of the counter. I watched her exchange a few words with the shadow before he nodded. He procured a large stone bowl from beneath the bar and walked around to our side of the counter. He set it at our feet and flicked his wrist, setting a controlled, roaring fire ablaze. The heat was utterly delicious. I hadn't realized I'd still been clenching every muscle until my blood began to thaw.

"Oh!" he gasped, onyx fingers outstretched as if he'd dropped something. I froze, worried I'd done something wrong. I gave him my most attentive concern before he said, "I brought the fire, but I forgot the brimstone. Shall I...?" and though he had no face, I could feel him smile.

"You're terrible," Fauna said, offering a starlit grin.

"Holler if you need anything else," he said. I allowed the flames to defrost the rain and cold, marveling at the magic that caused the fire to hover within the bowl without any observable source aside from the bartender's will. I listened to the music with the beer to my lips and choked at a repressed memory.

"What?" she asked, eyeing me over her bright-green music.

I shook my head, "I just…my mom was right. She thought rock music would send me to Hell, and she was right. They're playing Kansas. I expected ominous orchestral music, heavy on the organs."

"Well, you can find that here, too. But you can also find that on Earth. Preferences are preferences wherever you go. I bet there's a cute demon cowboy listening to country while doing the two-step somewhere in the city. Honestly, all our kingdoms thrive on their diversity, like anywhere. Maybe not so much in Heaven. They're a lot stricter. They keep their ducks in a row and all that. Don't get me wrong—there are still some cool guys there. And some good music. It's not all bad."

"You'd said Silas wasn't that bad, and he ended up being the biggest prick of them all." I glared over my drink, distracted from Fauna only long enough to appreciate the tacky, illuminated art behind the bar. The neon-red outline of a pinup-style devil lit half of the wall, setting the entire bar aglow. Save for our fire and two dim, naked bulbs dangling from the ceiling over the pool tables, her crimson light was one of the only things separating us from shadows.

Fauna shook her head as she laughed, damp hair already drying as we enjoyed the firelight. She made a curious face, mouth quirked between hushed conspiracy and amusement as she said, "Silas isn't a total prick. We went on a date once."

I had to set down my beer to keep from dropping it to the floor. I banged on my chest, coughing so hard that it drew the attention of the other three in the room.

"Oh, don't be dramatic. He took me to a nice place in Heaven. He paid and was a perfect gentleman. But talking about kingdom conversion on the first date? So uncool. I did not take him up on his offer for a second, but honestly, he wasn't a dick about it. We run into each other occasionally, and he's usually friendly. He even apologized for coming on too strong. It's fine; I can't blame him. I'd also want to lock this down." She clicked her tongue and shot finger guns at me.

"You can switch kingdoms?"

She gestured broadly to the bar.

"I knew Hell had a lot of fallen angels and—"

She slurped loudly enough to cut me off. "They didn't just go to Hell. Some defected to other realms, too. A handful of pantheons have former citizens of Heaven."

"I just can't believe…"

"What? Is it the realm-conversion thing? Or is the look on your face over angels dating and marrying? It's even in that Bible, right there in Genesis. Maybe more book of Enoch. Pick your poison. They even wed humans from time to time, which might be part of why Silas is less of a prick to you. You're cute. Pretty privilege and all that."

"That's what you consider being less of a dick?" I gaped, consciously sidestepping her implication.

Her lips pinched to the side. "This was our first time interacting in a business capacity, and I will admit, I like him a lot less when he's on the job."

"On the job, being, coercing me into a bond by involving my mother?"

She swirled the tiny straw in her drink. "He doesn't get a lot of say in what he does. They have real hierarchy issues over there. His master is a really controlling guy. But I have a theory."

I looked at her expectantly.

"Maybe he's doing you a favor by insisting he's the one on the job. Any angel could have showed up to talk to your mom. There was no reason it had to be him, unless he's requesting the task. And if he is…"

"If he is, is it a good thing or a bad thing?"

She chewed her lip. "That depends on his motives for doing so. It's certainly curious. Then again, he's a curious guy. Like, I admire his balls for asking me out, but he had to know I'm not angel material. Nymphs, fae, deities, and demons, though…" Her eyes drifted to the bartender. "Well, love isn't out of the cards for us, but…"

"You're going to say something gross, aren't you."

"We fuck."

My exhale was heavy with amused exasperation. As ridiculous as she was, I was fond of her particular brand of nonsense. "I don't know why you bothered finishing your sentence."

She smirked into her drink and made a come-hither expression to the bartender so he'd bring her another. The muscled shadow looked up from whatever he was doing and acknowledged her beckoning.

"How are we paying for this?" I asked. "I doubt they take credit cards."

"You paid for things in the human realm. I'll take care of things when we're out of the mortal kingdom. Now, go ahead, ask your next stupid question. I can see a few more clanging around in there, and I can tolerate them while getting drunk. But I think I should get a few questions in return."

"Fine." I was only halfway through my beer, but Fauna was well on her way to finishing her second green drink. There was something remarkably normal about the tit for tat of two friends exchanging questions over drinks. It put me at ease, even if the topics did not. I hedged for a moment before asking, "The horns?"

"Oh, that's a pretty good question. So, when the kingdom split, it was the whole brother-fighting-brother thing. Or like, what do you do in human sports, when hot men get sweaty and half-naked?"

"Shirts versus skins?"

"Yes! That's the one. Anyway, it's just easier for the rebels to spot one another if they're out and about. Maybe in the human realm, maybe in battle, whatever. The war is asinine, and at this point it's most comparable to your Cold War. Lots of espionage and covert operations. No one has the time or energy for horsemen and swords and blood."

I chewed my lip, considering the information. "Okay, and that cat-child that Silas killed? He was a demon, right?"

"The kiddo? Ew, no. Like I said, he was a parasite. Nothing to do with demons, though to be honest, parasitic entities are what most humans think of when they hear the word. Every realm has them. We've got them with the Nordes. The Hindu realm has them. They're big in toteism. Malevolent entities are like rats in the age of bubonic plague—"

"You don't have to relate every example back to a human experience."

"I am being a good teacher and you're being ungrateful." Then to the bartender, she turned and said, "Sweetheart? Can I have one more for me, and another beer for my friend?"

"You're putting them away a little fast, aren't you?" I adjusted my body so the fire warmed a new side.

She nodded, sliding the empty glass toward the man. "Liquid courage, babe."

"Courage against something scary?"

"Yes, something terrifying."

I shifted uncomfortably, wondering what precisely could be unnerving enough to put Fauna on edge.

"It's my turn now," she said. She propped her elbow firmly against the bar, gesturing until her drink sloshed as she asked, "You never suspected?"

I slumped in my seat, frowning.

She elaborated. "All of this. Even Lisbeth knew she was seeing something real. She's oversimplifying things, but at least she's acknowledging what she's seeing. I'm sure you've been noticing shit your entire life. You didn't at least think you were psychic? Or experiment in witchcraft? Or...?"

It took me a moment to gather my thoughts, and she didn't rush me. After a while I said, "Maybe I would have, if my mother weren't who she is. Maybe she's fae or psychic or whatever, but she's also cruel and crazy. And it's a lot easier to put it all in the same box, you know? If she's nuts about five things, it tracks that she's nuts about the sixth, too. Does that make sense?"

Fauna considered this. "But you saw Caliban in spite of her, not because of her. He didn't—"

"I think it's my turn to ask another," I said. The lyrics to "Wanted Dead or Alive" wove through the bar, filling the space as she smirked. She raised her glass for me to continue.

"Okay...is it always dark here? In Hell?"

She guffawed. "It's nighttime, dumbass."

"Hey!" I grumbled. "It was daytime when we left Earth. Or is this not Earth? Oh my god, I'm getting a headache."

She shook her head, damp silver and copper tendrils reflecting the firelight. Even the little white freckles were brighter somehow as they caught in the flame. "Time moves differently in every realm. Next one."

"Fine," I sighed. "Electricity?"

She frowned. "What's the question?"

"I...I just didn't expect..."

"Oh! Yeah, that's a really stupid question too. Oh my god, Marlow. We're immortal beings, and you think we want to stay in the stone ages? Life is long! When we see something nifty, we incorporate it. You humans have decent ideas sometimes. Half these demons are traditionalists. You could probably pop next door and find someone sitting in the dark who only makes his calls through silver bowls of fresh goat blood. Life, joy, and adaptability all go hand in hand."

"Then why do you come to the mortal realm to watch TV?"

She giggled into the bright-emerald drink. "You think we're going to debase ourselves by doing the dumb shit you do on your shows? No, that's uniquely human. It's marvelous. I hope people never stop. Okay, so, we covered modernity, hopefully? I knew some of your questions were going to be brick-brained. I think that earned me at least two in return."

"Fine," I grumbled.

She flashed me her most dazzling smile. "On a scale from one to ten, how breathtaking am I?"

I gave her my most deadpan stare. "You're unbelievable."

"Is that because I'm an eleven?" she asked.

I wanted to fire back with something clever, but it was a night for transparency. "Honestly? You're gorgeous."

She wiggled with delight.

"But you're also an enigma. You are equal parts king and clown."

It was her turn to interject. "Hey!"

I made a show of relaxing into my chair. "I'm just shooting you straight. You have no respect for anything, you have the taste buds of a four-year-old, you've dated an angel, apparently you seem to have no problem taking a stand against Heaven, you—"

"I get it. I'm mysterious and cool. But mostly I'm pretty. Now, I had another. Try to make your answer interesting."

I wondered if she was still being playful or if something I'd said had truly struck a nerve. I looked into my bubbles and waited.

"Caliban."

My eyes shot up. I looked from left to right, panicked that someone might overhear.

Fauna was unbothered by the disinterested crowd of distant patrons. She set down her drink and looked at me seriously. "You didn't even believe in him. Now you're on this vigilante mission to find him. Why?"

I made a weak attempt at deflecting. "You mean other than because he's even hotter than you?"

"Beauty is subjective," she mused, "but yes, I've heard he's a fox."

Fox. The word set me on edge. It was like swallowing a burning coal. It scalded going down as I considered her question, then sat heavily in my stomach, roasting me from the inside out. "I don't know where to start."

"Is it cliché to say 'the beginning'?"

One corner of my mouth flicked upward for the barest of moments, eyes returning to watch the slow climb as carbonation escaped my beer and popped. "Yes," I said quietly. The writer in me was mildly amused, but the wounded child in me was stronger. "Because he's the only person who's ever truly seen me. And fuck, I've been so madly in love with him, even when I didn't think he was real. I've fought it so goddamn hard. To learn I could have given in long ago? That I didn't have to make my life this difficult? It's torture."

Copper waves tumbled to the side as she tilted her head. "You have friends. You've dated. It's not like you're alone."

I shook my head. "It's not like that. He understands me so well that it was easy for me to convince myself that he *was* a projection of my subconscious. He gets my sense of humor. He's so fucking clever. But I thought he was the part of me that loved myself, you know? Like, my self-loathing was so palpable that I had to create an external figure that didn't judge me, that helped me think through things without making me feel bad about myself. He was the part of me—well, what I believed was the part of me—that thought I was worth keeping alive. And he did."

Her expression changed.

I kept my eyes on the bar top. "My sense of self-preservation has been…low."

I felt her soft fingers before I realized I was about to cry. She gave my hand a squeeze.

I bit my lip to keep in the emotions until the first wave passed. Then I said, "People have seen my value for what I can do for them. My parents saw me as an extension of them—a chance to do better where they'd failed. When I was an escort, my value was as an accessory. I was professional arm candy. One who could keep a conversation going, who could read moods, who could offer an experience so that someone might get to feel that high of dating and lust for a night. Now that I'm successful, so many people see me as a sort of feather in their cap. But with Caliban, I was just me. And he never pushed me to change, you know? My journeys were mine to go through, and also mine to reflect on, with his support. And sometimes that support was just being held all night while I was convinced I was crazy. The only thing he

240

wanted amid all of it was for me to be happy. And I just want him back. I want him back so much it hurts."

"Who knew you were such a sap?" She squeezed my hand once more before releasing me. "Being sane is so boring. All the coolest people are crazy."

I breathed a half-laugh.

"Plus, he's a demon. The sex has to be—"

I jerked to alertness, looking around with far more intensity. "Can you not?"

She gave me a tired look. "Riddle me this: sharing drinks with an escort who is too much of a prude to discuss a good lay."

"Maribelle did that," I said quietly. "I have very distinct boxes for the personal versus the professional."

She softened ever so slightly. She balanced her chin on her fist and regarded me. "Fine. I think it's your turn. Any other inquiries you need to get out of your system?"

"Two more," I said with some certainty. "The first is, now that we're here, how do I find Caliban?"

The shadow slid two more glasses in front of us. I wasn't sure if he'd anticipated our needs or if Fauna had signaled him while I was lost to my reverie. She thanked the bartender and took another long sip before saying, "We'll go to the palace and look for an audience with the King. We'll do it tomorrow once we've cleaned off your rain-smeared face, and we'll get you some clean clothes. Now, last question. Hit me with it."

"What are you so afraid of?"

She sighed. "I'm working up the courage to call us our ride. We need somewhere to sleep for the night, don't we?" Fauna abandoned me to talk to the bartender. He offered her what was unmistakably a cell phone—or at least the black, glassy equivalent of what one might have in Hell—which she accepted. Fauna turned her back to me while she made a call. She thanked the bartender and rejoined me on the stool.

Her anxiety was contagious. I flinched against the question before whispering, "Who did you call?"

"Azrames."

Chapter Twenty-Two

"I F IT ISN'T THE GODDESS HERSELF GRACING SHADOW'S WITH
her presence" came a charming call from over our shoulders. I turned to watch the black, white, and gray demon
approach but didn't miss Fauna's creeping blush as she took
a deep, steadying breath. She'd seemed so self-assured when
they'd flirted in the back of Betty's metaphysical shop. Maybe
it was a little harder to keep her act together on his turf.
"When I told you not to wait twenty years, I didn't realize I'd
said the magic words."

Azrames leaned onto the bar beside Fauna, resting his
weight on his arm.

"I don't want to jinx it by asking to what I owe the honor.
Who am I to question fate? How about it, sojourners? Can I
get you another? Fauna? What about you, Marmar—who I
hope knows better than to say her full name out loud down
here?"

A knot in my throat made it impossible to swallow as the
man casually dropped an adorable nickname. "I...no. No, I
haven't."

"Atta girl," he said approvingly.

My soul left my body. I turned away to conceal the open-
mouthed shock and accompanying flush. I couldn't blame
Fauna. The man dripped sex. He'd shoved his jacket up to

his forearms, revealing thick, muscled arms and large, strong hands.

Azrames ordered a round for all of us. My head was already ringing pleasantly as the buzz crept into my limbs. I usually drank only while writing. Ah, shit. Writing. I needed to message EG back…though something told me that my phone would not work from another realm. Hopefully, two international bestsellers would buy me the grace to play hooky for a little while.

Fauna still hadn't spoken, so Azrames carried on for the three of us.

"Last time you were in Hell…"

She turned a violent shade of scarlet. If I had caught the arch of her back and curl of her toes, I was sure he had, too. He positively sparkled at her reaction.

"We're on business this time, Az," she said breathlessly. It was the first time she'd spoken since he'd arrived.

"And…," he tested, "can the business wait until morning?"

I could have written poems on the way Azrames's eyes stayed trained on Fauna's face, amazed and intimidated all at once by the burning intensity of his unwavering gaze. Mine, on the other hand, flickered once more to her tell-tale toes.

God, these two were incorrigible.

I finished my beer, sipping as I watched the speckled smartass fumble with the dredges of her candy-apple drink and struggle to speak. I would have exchanged glances with the bartender if he'd had a face. Instead, I waited as the handsome demon laid out the red carpet with a little more shameless flirting before it was time for us to leave.

"You ready, Marmar?"

I pointed to myself with a little too much surprise. I'd almost forgotten I existed amid the intensity of their two-person play.

"She's fine." Fauna waved without looking at me.

"Off we go." He winked.

Azrames waved goodbye to the shadow before plucking

a dark umbrella that I hadn't realized he'd rested against the wall upon entry. He pushed the door open with one hand, sheltering Fauna and me with the other as he escorted us to a slick, black vehicle.

A renewed confusion coursed through me. I'd expected to be led to a hearse, a hellhound, a horse-drawn carriage. Instead, he led us to the most expensive car I'd ever seen in my life. The black night of driving rain couldn't obscure the star-striking anomaly at the curb. The man drove a goddamn Bugatti. My gaze shot between him, Fauna, and the sports car. I didn't know much about Hell, but I knew money when I saw it.

Azrames didn't seem to notice my open-mouthed shock at what would have been north of a two-million-dollar vehicle in the mortal realm, with some models topping out in the fifteen million range. I gulped against the display of wealth, vividly remembering a client's gripe about the race cars. He'd claimed he'd love to buy one but that the elite ones sat only two, and he had a wife and children to consider. He'd claimed he was unwilling to consider humiliating himself with the four-seater models. I'd recognized it for the bluff it was. The top models cost anywhere from five to fifteen million. He was a first-time client, and I knew from the way he'd tipped and cut the evening short that it would also be his last meeting with me. When it came to Maribelle and Bugattis, the man could afford neither.

I'd refrained from mentioning that "considering his wife and children" should begin with the ethics of hiring escorts rather than where they'd sit. I was a single working woman. They were the ones going to Hell. Or...perhaps I'd have to come up with somewhere worse for the bastards to end up, as Hell seemed far too cool for them.

I remained beneath the protective canopy, rain thumping overhead as I tried to calculate what one would have to do to own a Bugatti. While my cogs continued turning, Azrames busied himself opening the front door for Fauna first, then the back door for me. The doors lifted skyward, making me feel like an accomplice to a Bond villain as I slid in. The rain quietly dripped down his hair as he held the umbrella over her, then me, protecting us from its chilling bite.

I was pretty sure I was in love with him.

I scooted to the middle of the back in case I needed to be included in conversation but immediately felt like I had turned on the early dialogue to porn, which did nothing to lessen the star-struck crush I'd grown on the couple in the front seats. I didn't know how to click out of the screen. The actors were already delivering their lines.

"It's still the hottest chain I've ever seen," Fauna said, four strong drinks clearly working as she ran a finger along the silver, rope-like necklace that had been draped around him like a lasso in four distinct tiers, intricate sigil dangling from the bottom.

"It would look better around your neck," he said, "particularly once we get you out of your wet things."

"But I didn't get we—" She stopped in the middle of her sentence, squirming as his meaning clicked. He grinned, sharpened canines catching in the dimmed light from his chariot.

I was caught between wanting to disappear and being unable to look away. I wasn't sure whether or not I wanted them to stop or if I was buzzed enough to ask them to let me watch the inevitable conclusion of their entanglement… Maybe if I'd been shooting whiskey instead of drinking beer…

Some part of me remembered a proverb about two wolves fighting within every person. One was for light, and one was for dark. I chewed on my lip as I considered the outcome. I was in Hell, after all.

It was a twenty-minute drive from the bar to Az's place. While he kept one hand responsibly on the wheel, another rested on Fauna's knee, his thumb working idly over her thigh.

We stayed put when he parked, equally speechless. If

Fauna was too stunned to speak, then it was out of the cards for me entirely. She didn't even look over her shoulder at me as he rounded the car to open her door, extending his hand to help her out of the passenger's seat.

The walk from the vehicle to his apartment was the single, tensest moment of my life. I might have been imagining it, but Azrames seemed to have lost a bit of his swagger as he unlocked the large, black door to his place.

I pulled my lips inward as I battled the urge to make a curious face. Was he nervous?

Ever the gentleman, he ushered us into a home so grand that it turned my eight-thousand-a-month unit into comparative squalor. He tossed his keys onto the island and told us to make ourselves at home while he moved into the kitchen and poured glasses of water for everyone. I appreciated how well he'd decorated the large, upscale space, even if it was a tad masculine. The furniture, though expensive, remained stiff with a certain coldness. The art was tasteful, the place was enormous, and the entire floor was filled with the arousing smells of fire, authority, and the same incense that had burned in the metaphysical shop. I considered the scent and the memory of my trip to *Daily Devils*. Perhaps Betty had been it solely for her demonic business partner.

He offered me a glass of water, voice husky as he did his best to address me, though his attention was clearly divided. "Mar, you can stay in the room at the end on the left. It has its own bathroom. I'm pretty sure the items in the closet will fit you."

I scarcely had time to react.

He turned to Fauna, but she didn't give him a chance to say another word. She planted her hands on his chest and pushed him backward toward a bedroom that she obviously knew very well. His grin returned as he picked her up, scooping her into his arms with an unmistakable growl until her legs wrapped around his waist, cinching them together. Her mouth was on his with claiming intensity before I had the chance to look away. They'd barely closed the door to his room when I heard the unmistakable tear of fabric and the first of what would be two carnal hours of many, many moans.

If I were a better person, I would have politely ignored them.

But I'm not a better person.

I was very curious to know what someone might look like in a world devoid of color without the hassle of that sinfully thin white T-shirt, the cuffed jacket, the dark jeans. I would have clicked on a vanilla thumbnail of the two of them based on the visual curiosity of a gray, horned man and an impossibly beautiful woman alone, but something between the gasps, the yelps, and the distinct metallic sound of chains told me that whatever was happening behind those doors was premium content.

I made my way to the guest room and crawled atop the mattress.

I stripped free of my things and allowed the auditory erotica to wash over me with drenching intensity. Az would have soaked anyone's panties, but hearing him unleash himself was a memory I'd have to tuck into the back of my memory for lonely nights. The hedonistic music of their ravishing carried from their room into mine. The banging headboard created an excellent bass for the high, rhythmic sound of slapping flesh against flesh. It set the perfect tempo for the circular stroke of fingers after my hand wandered south. My right hand moved in company with their sounds, my left working my breast until it landed on my throat. My back arched off the bed in coordination with the snarls, and the loud, climactic screams of the grand finale happening on the other side of the wall.

I helped myself once, then twice.

If they didn't want my adjacent participation, they shouldn't have made their sexual chemistry such a palpable problem. I came harder than I had in months and fell into a deep, dreamless sleep on the silk sheets of an impossibly soft bed.

✦

It took me a while to realize where I was.

My fingers stretched out against the black, butter-soft sheets. I'd fallen asleep naked with the luxurious material caressing my skin. God, these sheets were *amazing*. I almost made a mental note to ask him where he'd bought them before remembering that Azrames and I didn't share a Bed Bath & Beyond.

I slipped from the bed and walked naked to the bathroom, bare feet warmed by luxuriously heated floors.

His enormous, bronze tub reminded me of a witch's cauldron. It was gorgeous and I wanted one for my home, though I supposed unrequited envy might be a common theme down here. I smirked, recalling the seven deadly sins as my fingers dangled in the running water until I was satisfied with the temperature. I allowed the tub to fill while I investigated my surroundings. The tub was nearly the size of a one-person swimming pool, which gave me time to find an offensively soft towel, an antiqued silver mirror that seemed to be whispering breathy compliments, and a robe fit for a queen.

My lower lip puckered at the mysterious array of products.

As things hadn't been bought in bulk at the nearest supermarket, the bottles lacked labels. I opened a variety of glass jars, all in uniformly aesthetic shades, sniffing and testing them until I ascertained that Azrames had provided shampoo, conditioner, soap, perfume, and a bright, minty liquid that had to be mouthwash. I wasn't exactly expecting Old Spice, but I was still surprised that the hair products smelled nothing like the ash incense that he exuded. Instead, the delicate floral notes were distinctly feminine.

Then it was time to luxuriate in my personal spa.

I sank into the waters as I experimented with different

soaps and things, mostly for the experience of bathing in Hell. Fauna had spent what may or may not have been the most animalistic night of her life only a few feet away. If I wasn't going to get laid, I felt I at least deserved a sumptuous soak and a good meal. When I'd finished my bath, I wrapped my hair in the nicest towel a human could ever feel, slipped into the robe, and dabbed some of the perfume on my wrists. There was something vaguely familiar about the scent. It reminded me of the ocean and the forest all at once, though I couldn't quite place it. Once again, it seemed like it belonged to a woman.

I rolled my eyes as I recalled a comment Azrames had made the night before. He'd suggested I might find something clean that would fit me in the closet.

The shampoo and conditioner, the perfume, the clothes all made sense. Of course, the ultimate fuck boy would have the sort of pussy parade that ended in a veritable treasure chest of clothes from which a guest could choose. I left wet footprints from the bathroom to the closest, ready for something dark, sexy, and sparkly. Perhaps I'd meet the King of Hell in lacy black lingerie.

I opened the closet and frowned.

My eyebrows bunched against the confusing array of neatly hung shirts and pants. Loose, flowy pants…crocheted tops and cropped band tees… My frown deepened as I leafed through the clothes as if paging through a book.

Everything was unmistakably Fauna's.

I pulled a long, thin, white tunic free from the closet and stared at it. Intricate green and silver threading of beauti-fully stitched leaves ran along the collar and the sleeve cuffs. I returned it and grabbed something else—a loose, black shift dress with Nordic rosemaling embroidered along the hem.

Holy shit.

I took a few steps back from the closet and looked at the time capsule of their story.

Azrames was not some demonic fuck buddy. The perfume…it was Fauna's.

249

This room was the shrine of a man in love.

I sank to the bed, closet doors still open as I stared at the evidence. I wasn't sure how to pick something of hers to wear, not only because she'd managed to dress like a hippie for centuries but because it seemed wrong, somehow, to disturb the things he'd kept safe over the years as she'd transitioned from Scandinavian forest maiden to nomadic yoga fiend.

She'd changed, and he'd let her.

It was all I could do to keep from crying out when the door opened.

I shouldn't have been surprised that Fauna didn't knock before letting herself in, but I still jumped as if I'd been caught in the middle of breaking the law. I blinked out an apology.

"Oh, good," she said cheerily, oversize button-up shirt grazing the tops of her thighs, hair tousled, and with the glow of someone who'd just gotten laid. "You're awake! And you found the clothes." She went to the closet and selected a few comfortable things, then gave the clothes a hard shove, forcing them to the far end of the rack as she fished for two zipped-up bags at the back of the closet.

"Here." She tossed me a pair of cozy sweats. "Unless you want to wear the robe until we get ready for the palace. I do keep some nice things here. Just in case." She winked.

"Fauna..."

She stopped what she was doing to look up at me.

"Who is Azrames to you?"

She blushed again, which confused me. Before, I'd thought it was merely the sexual chemistry pinking her cheeks. Now I recognized it as something else entirely. "What do you want to know?" She lifted a single shoulder in a half-shrug, though she fought too hard to keep the gesture casual. It was utterly unconvincing.

I unwrapped my hair from the towel, absorbing the remaining dampness as I looked at her. "Well, clearly the sex is terrible and you hate each other, so, being cagey about it makes sense."

She sank against the wall, crossing one ankle over the other as she looked at me. "Tell me, wise and powerful Marlow, what would you have me do?"

I gestured to the lavish life around me. "Move to Hell? Be with him? Be in love? Be happy?"

"I am happy."

"He said you hadn't seen him in twenty years!"

She began to unbutton her shirt to change into her sweats. Given her silence, I took my cue to do the same. I slipped the robe off my shoulders, feeling guilty for letting such expensive material puddle at my feet. I stepped into a pair of Fauna's baggy pants and the short-sleeve shirt she'd offered me. There would be no bra or panties in Hell, it seemed. I supposed that was okay, as long as everyone in the house was fine knowing I was cold.

"Tell me something," she said, exhaustion tinging her voice. "Truly, Marlow, I want an answer."

I straightened and looked at her, preemptively defensive.

"If someone adores you for your chaos, what's the best way to honor that love? If they treasure your rootlessness, if they celebrate your anarchy, if they love you as you are, do you think they'd be dancing in the streets if you gave up the very essence at the core of your being that made them fall for you?"

I folded my arms over my chest, both to cover the chilly evidence beneath her thin, white shirt and to shield my discomfort.

She pushed. "Humans do it all the time. I swear to the gods, it's the norm in your realm. And how often does it make them happy?"

I shook my head as if to argue but had no defense.

"Besides," she said, levity returning to her voice. "Hell doesn't fit my aesthetic."

"But then..." I didn't know what to ask, except, "Why did you have to throw back four drinks to work up the courage to call him?"

She snorted. "Az is wild in bed. He's amazing, but you'd need a few drinks too after a long break from that kind of ride."

I opened my mouth to respond but snapped it shut again.

I couldn't begin to comprehend a nymph and demon's parameters for kinky sex, so I began to unzip the bag to see what had been hidden at the back of the closet. Searching for something to break the haze of my confusion, I asked, "Why did we need Betty to call him?"

"That one is your fault. We needed a safe space to prove the efficacy of your ink outside of your sigil-painted apartment," she said, snatching the bag from me. She shook the bag free and procured a stunning gown. "Thank the gods and goddesses we got our hands on Aloisa's sølje; otherwise I'd still be mortal-bound just to keep you safe. It really ties my hands. And not in the fun way..." Her mind seemed to drift, one hand idly tracing the bare skin of her wrist.

I cleared my throat.

"Anyway." She handed me the dress, snapping to attention. "I think this one suits your coloring better. I'll wear the green one. Let's have a relaxing day, so don't worry about changing yet. Tonight, we meet the King."

Chapter Twenty-Three

"How'd you sleep, Marmar?" Azrames was cursedly shirtless as I emerged from the bedroom. It was an act of cruelty and violence that someone with such an impeccable body would walk around his own apartment with sex-mussed hair in only boxers. Of fucking course the hot man was covered in tattoos stretching from a single pectoral to his shoulder as the piece snaked down his arm. What a cliché.

My gaze had initially begun in ongoing shock that his skin was truly shades of iron and steel, as if watching a movie from the fifties, or staring at someone who's stepped out of a turn-of-the-century photograph but living in a fully saturated world. Somewhere between the line of demarcation in his abdominals and the thick tree trunks he had for legs, I'd forgotten what I was doing and neglected to look away.

"Ow!" I gasped, jerking to see what had accosted me.

Fauna had pinched my ass while walking by. She grinned as she pranced, barefoot, into the kitchen. "Wanna borrow him?"

These two were going to be the death of me.

There was no pride to salvage. I covered my face with my hands and shook my head before joining them in the kitchen. "Do I smell coffee?"

"How do you take it?" he asked.

"She likes her coffee like she likes her men," Fauna responded, hopping up backward onto the counter and letting her legs dangle off the ledge. "Hot."

He chuckled as he slid a tall, black cup of coffee on a tray that included a tiny, bronze cup of cream, a little pot of sugar cubes, and the fanciest, littlest spoon I'd ever seen. It wasn't honey, but I could make do. I looked around the apartment, if only to take my eyes off the demon. I hoped she'd never bring up my question about Hell and darkness, particularly the beauty of the morning light as it streamed in through the windows. It caught on the coppers and metals that accented his apartment, offering a shimmering quality to the entire space.

"So, working with Betty pays well?" I mused, remembering what Betty had said about converting malevolence the same way a hydro plant turned water into electricity. If that was the case, Azrames must have been the Hoover Dam.

He slipped a hand behind Fauna and sipped on his own coffee while nodding. "Centuries of smiting assholes has proven lucrative."

Fauna kissed him proudly atop his head from her countertop perch but had no smartass remark to add. I recognized the twinkle of admiration in her eye and was once again struck with how easy he would be to love. Not only did he adore her, but she clearly respected him. He'd dedicated hundreds of years to ridding the mortal world of abusers and setting women free. If I had to sleep in a demon's house, this seemed like the place to be.

"Ask him about his tattoo," she said.

He'd begun to protest, but I took the bait. The scalding packaging had made it easy to forget how formidable he was, the shadow in the dark, the last thing a violent man saw before he died. I'd taken it for a cohesive piece, but my eyes lingered on it long enough to spy the way the dark tendrils were separated. Given the context of her remark, I thought of teardrop tattoos as I looked at him. "Your ink? Is each section from a kill?"

He lifted his arm as if remembering the piece was there. "These? No, the kills are not worth remembering. I make sure they deserve it, and I never look back. These aren't for deaths, they're for lives, Marmar. Every mark represents someone who was set free. It helps me remember why I do what I do."

"The income doesn't hurt either," Fauna added.

For fuck's sake, this man. Maybe I *did* want to borrow him. How was I supposed to function in the human realm after this? I was pretty sure I'd never find joy topside again.

Breaking my pre-caffeinated existential spiral, Fauna asked, "Az, would you be a peach and see how we can get word to the palace that we're here seeking an audience with the King?"

Azrames nodded as he sipped. "Way ahead of you. I don't run in royal circles, but I phoned a friend of a friend. I don't think it's going to be hard to get Marlow in front of the King once he knows she's here. The challenging part is getting the news to him."

"Can I ask a question?"

They both perked, but my attention was on Fauna. "This isn't your kingdom. Why do you call them the Prince and the King? Don't the Nordes have a royal family? Wouldn't they be your princes and kings?"

"Can I ask *you* a question?" she responded. "Did you print your diploma off from a shady website, or did they actually let you graduate?"

Maybe if they hadn't kept me awake for hours with their screaming, I wouldn't have been so cranky. I narrowed my eyes. "You're such a goddamn bully."

She didn't just roll her eyes but flopped her entire head backward dramatically. "Remember that hot pop singer who divorced the leader of France—Nicholas something or other? What's the leader called there?"

"Oh, Carla Bruni!"

"You're a nerd for knowing that."

I clicked my tongue. "You're a nerd for asking. Yeah, she was married to the president of France."

Fauna slurped her syrupy coffee loudly, blinking at me with her large, mockingly innocent doe eyes before saying, "Are you sure you don't want to say she was married to *a* president? He wasn't *your* president."

I hmmphed. She wasn't the gentlest teacher I'd ever had, but she did get her points across. "Fine. I get it." I looked around the apartment, admiring its lavishness in the morning light. "So, what does a day in Hell look like?"

Azrames unraveled himself from where he'd remained connected to Fauna. He planted his large hands on the island and leaned forward. I wished he hadn't. It was deeply inappropriate to lust after your friend's wealthy, muscled, powerful, kinky lover.

Probably.

He raised a brow as he said, "You mean, between the torture and dismembering?"

"Oh," Fauna chimed from over his shoulder. "Should we do a tour of the Lake of Sulfur?"

"Go fuck yourselves," I muttered.

He chuckled. "There actually *is* a lake of sulfur. Well, that's what it's named, anyway. It's a mineral hot spring and a great tourist attraction. If you're looking for a spa day, you could certainly tell your friends that you boiled in the Lake of Sulfur."

"Lisbeth would *love* that," Fauna said. Then to Azrames, she explained, "Az, her mom is a hardcore fan of the other side. Doesn't her name mean something extreme like 'God's oath'? No beating around the bush with that one. Anyway, Az: Mama Marlow's fae blood has given her way too much free time to chat with angels. She's putting her psychic abilities to obnoxious use. A real stick up her ass, that one."

"Speaking of talking to the fae." Azrames's voice quieted as he reached across the island for me. I froze as he gently straightened my arm, lifting it from the elbow so he could look at the sigil I'd had tattooed. He lifted his eyes to mine, marvel in his voice as he asked, "Look who has some ink of her own. How did you find this?"

I exhaled slowly at the decompression of fingers against my forearm. I kept my eyes on the ink as I said, "It was above my door. I didn't see it for a long time. Not until after Silas was in my apartment. It was the last night I saw Caliban."

"Caliban?" He repeated the name, sliding a thumb over the still-healing tattoo to feel the scab. As his touch passed, so did what remained of the wound. Only perfect ink was left in its place.

My heart ached at the memory of that horrible night and how he'd kissed my hand, healing the cut I'd acquired in my scramble to survive. I bet Richard was the sort of man Az would have loved to have killed, and I wondered how different my life would have been if he'd been the one to respond to Richard's mark. Maybe if they stopped making fun of me for my questions, I would ask how a human was marked and how another might respond to its call. Instead, my thoughts were focused on Caliban.

"The Prince," I said, answering his question.

"I like it," Fauna added. "It fits him, don't you think?"

Az considered it before asking, "Did you give it to him?"

I nodded, recalling the way Caliban had smiled at the name all those years ago.

"Speaking of Caliban," I said, "if he's not in Hell, why do we think the King will know where to find him? Or why he'll help?"

The pair exchanged a meaningful look. Az said, "Trust me, he'll want to help you. As for how they'll be able to find him: call us legion, for we are many."

"The parasite said the same thing," I mused.

"I know," he said. There was no amusement in his voice. "It's their line to start with. But since it was accredited to demons, we don't mind the catchphrase. We've got manpower, we're well connected, we're everywhere."

257

"Like the KGB," Fauna added. Then, "Because of the Cold War demons and angels—you know what, never mind. My magnificent references are underappreciated."

Between his interesting piece of information and Fauna's chatter, I'd been too distracted to realize Azrames was still holding on to my arm until his phone—or, what I could only describe as a phone—rang. He released it to pick up the device. Much as in the mortal realm, it was a glassy, black rectangle. It didn't appear to have buttons, a screen, or any harsh, white glow. He lifted it to his ear and stepped away, heading to his room as he began to speak quietly into the shape. He disappeared around the corner.

"He's dreamy," I said, complimenting Fauna as our eyes trailed his shadow-like wake. "Are you going to explain what that exchange was about? Is there some reason the King will want to see me that I should know? Or is this all..." I hesitated before spitting out what felt like the most ridiculous end to the sentence. "Apocalypse talk."

"Well sure; now that you're involved we've all got the end of the world on the brain. But more importantly: of course Az is dreamy. I have impeccable taste," she agreed. "But sometimes I just do things for the plot. So, you know, you gotta fuck a centaur for the party anecdote."

I didn't have time to ask if she was serious before he returned. To both my relief and dismay, he'd slipped into a pair of black pants and a white tee. "Company is on its way. Fauna, did you ever meet Ianna?"

Fauna's prolonged whine told me that she did not like the individual in question.

I missed the days when I had answers to things. Instead, I sighed as I asked what felt like yet another in an endless string of questions. "Who's Ianna?"

Fauna grimaced. "She a lillith."

A bolt of lightning shot through me. "Lillith is coming to your apartment?"

"Not *the* Lillith. *A* lillith. More of a miscellaneous femme fatale. It means shriek owl or night monster depending on the text," Fauna said, correcting me before answering his question. "Yes, she was at that party we went to in 1360. She was an absolute bitch. Call someone else."

He made an apologetic face. "She still is. And I'm afraid there's no calling anyone else this time, Fauns. She's already on her way, and she's my only in."

Fauna hopped down from the counter and began to riffle through his cabinets, frowning at the lack of food. She settled on a box of cookies and addressed me with a crumbly mouthful of what looked like sugar-crusted cookies with caramel chunks.

I raised a finger. "Can I go back to *a* lillith?"

Fauna waved one hand while tearing through the box with the other. "It's a thing. Nymph, vampire, valkyrie, angel, lillith. Throw a dart at the board: it's all real. Google the specifics on your own time. Just—"

Azrames interrupted her long enough to give her a chance to chew. "Listen, Faun, I know you don't like her, but she can pull strings, and she owes me a favor. She'll be here in twenty."

Fauna sucked her teeth. "A *favor* favor?"

"Indeed," he confirmed. The word seemed to have some deeper meaning, but neither of them offered to elaborate.

She sighed while riffling through the box. "In that case, thanks for wasting your favor on us. I'll keep what I think of her to myself. Probably." She then offered me a cookie, and I took one. "She's a stylist for the royal court. It isn't exactly a royal title, but she comes and goes from the palace and can definitely get us an audience." She ended her explanation by extending the box to Azrames.

He shook his head. "I hate those things."

My mouth opened, the uneaten cookie falling onto the plate where I'd left the dredges of my coffee. It had been abhorrently sweet. I shoved it away as I asked, "Then why do you buy them?"

"In case my little sugar goblin stops by," he said, ruffling her hair as he passed in a return to his room.

She smiled happily as she popped another cookie into her mouth.

My heart squeezed painfully as I looked at the place where he'd been only moments before. *Twenty years.* He'd kept the pantry stocked for twenty years, just in case she paid a visit. Just as I was about to scold Fauna for not appreciating his love, I thought of something she'd said to me in the car when I asked why Caliban had stayed with me.

If you waste this lifetime, he loves you enough to try again in the next. And the next. And the next.

And because I didn't have the emotional capacity to deal with half of what I was going through, I did what I did best: I compartmentalized. I shoved the pain into a little pocket and decided to distract myself.

I kept myself busy by poking around the apartment while we waited for the arrival of a lillith. While most of the home was beautiful in its simplicity, he did have a number of antiquities that made the mythology enthusiast in me drool. A row of interesting candles had metallic threads where a wick should have been. An intricately carved dagger with a passage written in ornate Latin rested behind a glass enclosure, propped up on display. A black book with writing that may have been Sanskrit sat upon what could only be described as a small pulpit, opened to a single passage. There was a piece of pottery with, if I wasn't mistaken, *his* form, arms outstretched as men knelt, presumably pleading for their lives.

The sound that rang through the apartment to signal someone's arrival wasn't the familiar, robotic buzz of a delivery man. Instead, an ominous, haunting note slithered through the building.

My heart caught in my throat as I nearly knocked over the priceless antiquity I'd been gingerly fingering. It had to be the lillith. The night creature. The royal stylist. The bitch from 1360.

I scrambled to the kitchen to refill my coffee cup just so I'd have something to do with my trembling hands when she entered. I pressed my back against the furthest cabinet and braced myself for gnashing teeth, for Cheshire smiles, for whatever talons might grant someone the title of shriek owl.

Azrames opened the door, and my eyebrows lifted in surprise.

Given Fauna's description of the woman, I'd readied myself for one of two extremes: either a shriveled monster or a towering figure in a golden, drapey gown. I thought I'd meet the ancient Sumerian Morticia Addams in black and lace or the imposing reincarnation of Cleopatra. Instead, a bored-looking woman with horns that started at the crown of her skull and curved around her ears stepped into the room. She wore pointed stilettos and tailored, high-waisted black pants with a semi-sheer black bustier tucked into her pants. She removed enormous, angular black sunglasses and folded them in half, tucking them so they dangled between her breasts. She looked like she'd come straight from a private jet after a fashion week in Milan. She pursed nude-painted lips as she gave me a once-over.

"This is the girl?" she asked, crossing her arms. She dangled one hand in my direction, manicured nails pointing at me.

"It is indeed," Azrames confirmed. Then to me, he asked, "Would you like to introduce yourself?"

All three looked at me expectantly as I clutched my coffee cup.

"Merit," I said. I didn't think I was imagining the way Azrames visibly relaxed. Fauna's proud grin from the far side of the room was unmistakable.

"And you can call me Ianna," she said.

I didn't miss the careful wording. I was curious who, if anyone, knew her real name. I idly wondered how the fae-like-creatures in the room had chosen the names they gave freely, before asking the same question of myself. I was

261

a woman of three names in a single lifetime. Maribelle had earned me an ocean of money, and then Merit had outshined her ten to one. But I hadn't come to Hell seeking riches. My aliases had done well, but hopefully Marlow would be the one who found herself a prince.

Azrames shut the door behind her, politely offering coffee.

"Don't be dull," she said, perching delicately on his black leather chair. "Offer me a real drink."

"Sky's the limit, and I only carry top shelf," he replied, no hesitation at the hour. "What would you like?"

She asked Az to make her a martini, which I found utterly fascinating.

"Onion or olive?" he asked.

"Bitters," she said as if it were the most obvious thing in the world. "It's breakfast."

Gin and vermouth made for a quick cocktail. He procured the citrus and peeler seemingly from nowhere and finished in a flourish.

"Ianna, you remember Fauna?" he asked, handing her the glass carefully garnished with a fresh curl of lemon. Ianna made a dismissive gesture, to which Fauna rolled her eyes.

Watching this woman—this *demon*—tuck her hair behind her curling horn as she elegantly sipped gin at nine the morning was a stranger fiction than anything I could have dared to imagine for the mythological world within the *Pantheon* series. The morning light refracted on the glass, breaking the sunbeams into tiny rainbows on his furniture.

"Merit," she said with the sort of clipped authority that I expected from a CEO, "why are you standing in the kitchen? I didn't come across the city for you to shrink like a mouse. Assert yourself."

I swallowed and hurried obediently to the couch opposite her. The others watched with mixed curiosity and amusement from where they loitered. Fauna stayed near the island while Azrames leaned against the wall.

"I'm looking for the Prince," I said, deciding against giving her the name I'd ascribed to him. "And in order to do that, I'm told I need to speak to the King."

She looked from me to Azrames, then back to me. "You're lucky I didn't have the option to say no. There's no use asking why, just as it's fruitless to understand why neon was ever on the runway or why the mortal realms keep trying to make salmon mousse palatable. It's a fish, for fuck's sake. You can't force taste." She sighed. "That said, Merit the Neon Salmon Mousse, you're our Prince's human. I wanted to see you with my own eyes before I made any calls, and now that I have..." she tsked, then looked to Fauna. "Do you have anything in your closet worthy of the royal family?"

I didn't miss the loathing in Fauna's eyes or the apology in Azrames's as she stalked into the hallway. She reemerged with two gowns.

"Oh!" Ianna brows raised in surprise. "They're shockingly not horrible. It's hard to believe you own them. No offense, darling."

"Everything about you offends me, but this isn't my trip to Hell," Fauna said, tossing the gowns onto the island.

"Yes, well." She sipped her martini before saying, "As lovely as they are, you can't go in black tie." She procured a smooth rectangle like the one I'd seen Azrames use and lifted it to her ear. "Lyviane? Darling, how are you? It's been an age. Yes, yes," she cooed. "Listen, I'm going to need assistance. It's for the royal family. Ha! Don't I know it. Mhmm, mhmm. Yes, he called in an outstanding favor. Azrames. Yes, that's the one. Tell me about it. We all go through it. Mhmm, yes. There's three of them. Two feminine bodies, and one masculine. What do you have for me?" Her eyes went to me, then to Fauna. "The Norde might fit into sample sizes, but the human certainly won't. That shouldn't be an issue with your abilities. Yes, darling. Oh, you're too good. I'll see you in an hour. Yes, kisses."

Ianna finished her martini and set the glass down on the side table.

263

"I have one more call to make, but before I do, tell me something?"

I frowned expectantly.

"How does a human girl lose the Prince of Hell?"

✦

I'd felt like a dog on the way to the park as I remained glued to the window, gaping in excited awe at Downtown Hell. I'd seen the silhouetted edges of Gothic churches and sleek buildings but had no idea how ancient and modern a single city could be. Black, gray, stone, blue, and steel seemed to be recurrent themes, avoiding bright eyesores or the Global West's architectural dark ages of distasteful, perfunctory buildings. Everything was visual candy, from the restaurants and businesses to the people and things strolling the streets.

Fauna had offered to sit in the back with me, though she made it clear to everyone in the car that she'd done it to keep me company, not to give Ianna preferential treatment.

"Your Norde is a real treat," Ianna said, the backhanded compliment thick with judgment.

"She's the whole cake," Azrames agreed with a cool smile.

I looked at Fauna for a reaction but barely caught the upward tick at the corner of her lips as she remained carefully positioned to look out the window for our drive.

The walk from Az's Bugatti to the designer boutique was just as distracting. I had an impossible time looking at any one thing, as every detail was more interesting, more marvelous, more engrossing than the last.

I had to put out my hands to stop from plowing into Fauna as I skidded to a stop, so lost to my marveling of the confusing amalgamation of historic decay and flashy modernity that I hadn't realized we'd reached our destination. I planted a single hand between Fauna's shoulder blades, whipping my head up just in time to see the door open, revealing the curious creature who had been on the receiving end of Ianna's phone call.

I tried to tell myself that it would be just as abhorrently rude to stare in Hell as it would be to gape at a curiosity in the mortal realm, but I couldn't help it.

Our host for the morning, Lyviane, was a rich, purplish mauve with ink-black hair.

It surprised me, only because I'd seen femme red and purple devils portrayed so often on tattooed sailors or tacky posters that no part of me imagined a demon might actually possess such features. In lieu of horns, she sported the same thin, pointed tail I'd noticed on the pool-playing patron at Shadow's. When she spoke, I noticed the forked, serpentine flick of her tongue. Quintessentially demonic aesthetic choices aside, she was every bit the vision of a tasteful, frustratingly attractive woman in her early thirties with sleek, voluminous curls.

The gentle thrum of lyric-free electronica pulsed in the background as she beckoned us inward. I called on Maribelle, the part of me who knew how to handle foreign, posh social situations as I took in my surroundings.

The designer's workshop had white walls, white ceilings, and white floors.

I knew enough to understand the statement made with white floors. It said: no speck of dust or filthy shoes will sully this upscale building, nor will anyone lowly enough to blot my pearly reputation cross this threshold.

I could be pearly. At least, Maribelle could.

I scanned the enormous studio for any further clues as to how I should act in this entirely alien realm. The only patches of color were the antiqued frames around the mirrors. which matched the same purplish shade of Lyviane's skin. As if she'd selected candles to complement her coloration, soothing lilac filled the space in a calming, all-encompassing grip.

"Ready?" Fauna gave my bicep a squeeze as she breathed the question into my ear.

I did little more than nod. I wasn't sure I had any other choice.

An hour later, I smirked to myself as I looked in the full-length mirror of Lyviane's studio. As it turned out, the devil did not, in fact, wear Prada. Prada was too pedestrian for an ancient, egotistical shriek owl. That said, she had not picked the flashy prints or statement pieces that would have made me blanche. She slipped us into Hell's finest.

"Yes," Ianna purred behind me. "True power is understated."

I agreed wholeheartedly.

When I'd first begun escorting, my volcanic eruption from poverty to privilege loved the way attendants would scurry to my side when I walked down Rodeo Drive. They'd eye my shoes, my bag, my clean, expensive clothes, and offer me something that had been withheld for more than twenty years: respect. While raised with holes in my snowsuit, I'd slipped into the skin of someone who could breeze to the front of a line and have the velvet rope clipped to the side as my pieces spoke for me.

Raised in a state of hyper-awareness given the quickness of parental mood swings, I was extremely perceptive to every shift in energy, every micro-expression, every twitch of the eye or tightening of the mouth. Through trial and error, I learned both through meeting clients and from the appraising eyes of the hostesses that they felt one way about the golds, the prints, the brands and another way entirely about classic neutrals and clean lines. One look screamed new money, and the other whispered old.

Once the books had taken off, the dams had burst and the money had flowed, but the desire to be perceived did not keep up.

As delicious as it had been to taste fawning and gawking, it wasn't what I'd wanted. No amount of thin, gold chains with tiny desirable logos on them had brought me joy. I certainly didn't revel in uncomfortably tall heels with brightly colored bottoms. All I wanted was what I'd been denied—a life without worrying about bills, a life where I could stay in my pajamas and order sushi, where I could sleep peacefully, where I could breathe without debt sitting on my chest like the fabled sleep paralysis demon.

I looked at the demons in the room and silently amended my thought to *sleep paralysis parasitic entity.*

The entire room had undergone a glow-up.

Azrames somehow looked hotter every time I saw him. As if his white T-shirt hadn't already destroyed any chance of platonic thoughts, Ianna had dressed him in the most well tailored gem-blue suit I'd ever seen, complementing his shades of black, gray, and white.

My eyes drifted to my friend. I'd been a petty bitch to assume that the lillith would do Fauna dirty. Somehow, Ianna had managed to capture Fauna's style while upgrading it. The chaotic Norde was still permitted loose, flowing pants in a deep brown, though now the pleats were structured and intentional. Cream heels with ballet-like laces wrapped around her ankles, paired with a structured cream top. Lyviane's face wrinkled in concentration as she manipulated fabric and clasps with the wave of her hand to fit Fauna. I would have referred to Fauna's top as a bra, as it covered her tits, her sternum, and little else, but something told me that Ianna wouldn't have been thrilled with my lack of fashionable vocabulary.

"And for the princess-in-waiting," she'd said, smile on her lips.

I thought of Caliban's diamond eyes and the hair so white it might have been woven from moonbeams as I stared at my reflection. Ianna and Lyviane had collaborated to fit me in a sleeveless, purely white jumpsuit. The top was cut in dramatic geometric shapes, collar plunging toward my belly button on one side while remaining just modest enough to earn my admittance into even the most political of functions. Around the center of my neck was a single, choking band of pearls.

I procured the silver sølje from my pocket. It raised

eyebrows from the demons but a gentle smile from Fauna. I looked to her as I asked, "Can I wear it?"

"You can, and you should," Fauna said, voice quiet with pride. She crossed to my side as she helped me slip the family heirloom, the evidence of my blood, just above my breast. I wasn't sure if I wanted to meet Ianna's gaze, but much to my surprise, there was no disapproval in her eyes.

Perhaps broaches were in season.

After kissing me delicately on each cheek and making whatever empty promises for future brunch, Lyviane examined the three of us approvingly. "And now," she purred into my ear, close enough that I could smell something that, to my shock, I recognized exclusively from the human realm. She leaned in near my face with the unmistakable perfume of Chanel No. 5, stroking down the length of my arms as she postured behind me, "You're ready to meet your king."

Chapter Twenty-Four

PILLAR. GLASS. LIGHT. PLUSH. PERFUME. LUXURY. PALATIAL. Feelings. Thoughts. My brain tossed a word salad of nouns and adjectives between its tongs as my eyes struggled to land on anything. I knew now was not the time to be myself. I tried my best to conjure Maribelle, to keep my mouth closed, to keep my chin high, to act like nothing was too incredible or unbelievable.

I wondered how the royal families of the mortal realms would have felt about taking decorating pointers from Hell. I visualized the images I'd seen of Buckingham Palace and juxtaposed them against the incredible structure before us.

I hadn't breathed from the moment we'd entered.

The palace was an architectural marvel. While its bones were older than time, elements of magic, of fresh originality, of clean lines, of beauty beyond comprehension kept the air from my lungs.

I counted on my legs to work on autopilot, following the others in our small group as I gaped, and remained grateful that I was not alone on this mission. Quickly upon our entering, Ianna checked another box in my ever-growing list of reasons I admired her.

I understood Fauna's and Ianna's clashing personalities.

Half of Fauna's charm was her devil-may-care disregard

for convention. Yet nothing about her irreverence had a snowball's chance of garnering the respect of the posh lillith. Ianna's sweet tooth for power and deference was as forceful as Fauna's was for candy. The two were never meant to be friends.

I, on the other hand, found Ianna spectacular.

I'd never want to be pals with the demonic stylist—*god*, no—but I watched her as if glued to the television, like marveling at a panther sinking its teeth into a gazelle as she led us into the palace and directly to the receptionist. The polished man with small spikes on each of his temples recognized Ianna immediately. He reacted with wordless respect and led us to what, in the mortal realm, would have surely been elevators.

Except, these were no elevators.

My pulse quickened as I looked to the others, struggling to keep my calm.

We approached four large squares of sparkling, black space, as if we were meant to step into the stars themselves. Everything inside me told me to turn on my heels, but the others had remained utterly calm.

To my gratitude, Fauna didn't roll her eyes when I extended my hand for comfort. Instead, she looped a reassuring hand around my waist with her free arm while holding my hand with the other, effectively wrapping herself around me. The assistant stepped into the swirling void, followed closely by Ianna.

I took a half-step forward, wincing against the knowledge that I had to follow the others into oblivion. I was right on Azrames's heel when he caught me off guard by stopping.

My mouth dropped open as he dropped to a knee and reached for my hand. Fauna released me as I blinked, dumbfounded, at Azrames.

I didn't breathe as I looked between his serious eyes and the milky fingers caught in his steel-dark palms.

"Marlow," he said with quiet urgency, "I know Fauna

270

teases you, so please hear my worry that you might not be taking her seriously. Listen to me when I tell you that you are not to give anyone, not even the King, your name. Don't make any deals. Don't make any promises. Don't even say *thank you*. Semantics are incredibly important. Even if you reigned Hell as our princess, you'd be bound to your name and your agreements in a way I'm not sure you understand."

"Az—" I stammered.

His stormy eyes burned with intensity. He squeezed my hand for emphasis as he said, "Clearly you're special enough that our Prince has risked lifetimes to be with you. Fauna loves you. I don't need more convincing than that. You have my loyalty, Mar. But you have to promise me."

"But, I—"

"Tell me you understand." The anchor of his voice weighed me to the bottom of the sea. I wanted to look away but couldn't.

"I understand" was all I could say.

"*Promise*."

I swallowed. "I…" I looked between him and Fauna, equal parts surprised and perplexed to see the matching mask of hope and worry on her face. I looked back at Azrames before asking, "Is this the first test? I'm not meant to promise?"

The side of his mouth twitched slightly. He squeezed my hand again before getting to his feet. He dusted his gem-blue suit, brushed a kiss to Fauna, and disappeared into the void without another word.

"What the fuck," I mouthed, throat constricting around the words, rendering me unable to vocalize my shock.

My intestines climbed into my chest cavity, wrapping around my heart, making me nauseous and dizzy at the same time. My pulse thundered in my ears. I couldn't believe I'd been so swept up in the fashion, the glamor, the beauty, that I'd forgotten I was in another realm. I'd been utterly naïve to let my guard down as I'd confidently trotted to meet the King as if I were stepping into a five-star restaurant for a hired evening with a politician.

271

I'd been wrong to try to summon Maribelle. This was not her territory.

"Am I going to be okay?" I asked, feeling ever the part of the child as I looked desperately at Fauna.

She offered me the ghost of a reassuring smile as she said, "You have no other choice."

Without waiting for any signal of readiness, she wrapped her arm around me once more and urged us into the glittering, celestial galaxy of diamonds and darkness. I flinched, holding my breath as if plunging underwater. I regretted it one second later when we stepped into an upscale room stitched of the same dazzling, obsidian marble that had sparkled in the vortex. The high, palatial ceilings were vaulted by perfectly smooth onyx pillars.

I wasn't lost in space. I was somewhere so, so much worse.

From behind a glass desk, a new assistant smiled.

I looked into the unfamiliar face and dug my fingernails into Fauna's bicep.

The hair on the back of my neck prickled as I stared in unblinking alertness at the receptionist. The new woman had white-blond locks that tumbled far below the lip of the desk. Her pink mouth, blue eyes, and porcelain skin hummed with an eerie, doll-like beauty. Everything about her, from her perfect white teeth to the slow tilt of her head screamed of death. I couldn't explain the dread that swarmed within me as I finally saw something worthy of the terrors I'd spent my life affiliating with Hell.

This creature was the nightmare that lurked in the closet.

The first receptionist—the polite, horned man from the atrium—introduced us. Ianna dropped her brusque demeanor as she was announced. She offered a slow, closed-eye nod to the receptionist. Azrames did the same when the receptionist gestured to him, announcing him to the doll-like woman. When the pair of receptionists focused their attention on me and Fauna, I nearly clawed my way back into the rectangle of the space-time continuum. I was confident I'd be better off

272

risking my chances on the streets of Hell than locking eyes with evil personified.

Fauna seemed to sense my need to bolt. Her grip tightened, anchoring me in place.

The young man introduced Fauna of the Nordes, then hesitated at me. He frowned, turning to Ianna for an explanation.

"This is a very important human to the royal family," Ianna supplied. "One in possession of Nordic fae blood, thus the mandated escort from her realm."

Ianna turned to me and met my doe-wide eyes. Her cold gaze turned to something else entirely. Her face tightened in a way I hadn't seen. For a single moment, I understood the look of true fear on her face as she asked, "Would you care to introduce yourself?"

I held Ianna's controlled terror for a fraction of a second before looking into the porcelain woman's uncanny face, the chilling tilt of her head, the curious widening of her too-large eyes as I grasped at straws.

"Maribelle," I breathed, Fauna's fingers flexing against me reflexively. "You can call me Maribelle, and I am..." I struggled with the right words. I didn't know how to say what I needed to say in order to convey my worthiness, my right to stand before the most threatening being I'd ever seen. "I'm the Prince's human," I said finally.

Fauna's squeeze was one of unmistakable approval.

The room relaxed with the barest signs of relief, save for the doll.

"Can I get you anything, Maribelle?" the woman asked, voice airy and beautiful. "Is there anything I can do for you?"

Yes. I was thirstier than I'd ever been in my life, though I suspected most of that was a result of nerves. I wanted to crawl into a hole, if she happened to have one available. I would have liked her to excuse herself from the room and leave us all alone. But instead, I just said, "No, I'm all right. How kind of you to ask."

273

In front of us, Azrames wrapped his hands behind his back. To everyone else in the room, he would have been clasping his wrists with formal grace. For us and us alone, he flashed a single, very human thumbs-up.

"One moment," said the blond, rising from her chair. She wore the loose, flowing gown I'd imagined on the banshees of Celtic lore. Her pale, ethereal curls hung to the middle of her back in perfect, glossy waves.

The moment she disappeared through two tall, thin doors, Fauna whispered into my ear, "She's a Soul Eater."

I swallowed against the title but didn't ask her to elaborate. I didn't need to know anything further. We were already in Hell. Anything that struck terror into demons was truly an entity I never wanted to see again.

No one moved a muscle as we waited.

The Soul Eater breezed back into the room a minute later with the same perfect smile. "The King will take an audience with Maribelle and her escort. Allow me to accompany the rest of you to our luxury room for refreshments while you wait."

Her loose, icy curls disappeared through the swirl that may as well have been the Milky Way Galaxy, followed by the receptionist, then by Ianna.

"Good luck," Azrames whispered before following them into the stars.

We turned to the doors that had been left ajar for only Fauna and me.

I'd expected to feel relief after the Soul Eater departed. Anxiety glued me to the floor instead at I stared at the sliver of white light that separated the atrium from whatever rested behind the heavy palace doors. If she had been the precursor, I wasn't ready for the main event.

"I don't want to go," I said, allowing fear to speak for me. I was a child again, a leather belt, a Bible, a pastor, a crying mother punishing me with threats of Hell, of Satan, of souls. If the pretty phantom assistant had filled me with the worst fear of my life, I wasn't ready to meet the King of Hell. I didn't want to enter the room. I wanted to go home, to write the third *Pantheon* novel, to drink myself sick, to see a new psychiatrist, and to check myself into the sort of ward that could convince me through enough therapy and medication that I'd hallucinated this entire trip.

"You're not going alone," Fauna said.

I looked from where my fingernails had unintentionally been chewing into her skin and then up into her eyes. They so often gleamed with mockery, with taunts, with laughter and obscenities and chaos, that the soft, kind seriousness melted me.

"You're going to have to lead the way," I whispered, "because I don't think I remember how to move my legs."

Fauna took half a step, then stopped. She whispered an abbreviated form of my name, getting my attention as she asked, "Hey, Mar?"

As if I weren't panicked enough, the concern on her face sent sickly fear through me. I recalled a film from my youth where a superhero had a painful, liquid metal injected into his veins. I didn't recall the point of the film, but I remembered how he'd screamed. I felt the metal now as it hardened in each of my limbs, settling in my thumping, leaden heart. I was afraid enough that I was on the brink of tears as I asked, "What?"

"Az was right. Everything he said was right, but there's more," she said, each word scarcely above a whisper.

My eyes shot to the cracked door awaiting us, then back to Fauna.

"You don't have to do this," she said. "We can leave now. Or, we can go in there, hear what he has to say, and reject it. You're a Norde," she emphasized. "Az is right about a few things. I tease you, so I'm not sure that you take me seriously. Before we go into that meeting, I want you to know that I wasn't kidding. You don't have to choose this. If you don't want Hell, if you don't want any of this, I'll do it. I would bond myself to you if it's what you wanted. My philosophy has always been to ask for forgiveness rather than permission, after all."

I tried to give her a grateful squeeze but was too numb to feel if my hand responded to my brain's command.

"I have to see him," I said.

She dipped her chin. "I know you do. But I needed you to know."

"Hey, Fauna?" She cocked her head, copper and silver strands cascading over her shoulders and doe eyes looking at me with curious concern as I said, "Don't make this weird, but I'm pretty sure I love you."

"I love you too, loser," she said.

With that, she led us forward to meet the King of Hell.

Chapter Twenty-Five

M ARIBELLE!"
I didn't even have time to identify the source of the voice. I was crushed in a hug that snatched me from Fauna and swept me off my feet. I felt like a startled kitten cuddled by an over-excited toddler. I lost my equilibrium as the unidentified speaker twirled me in a tight circle before setting me back down on my feet. The man held me at arm's length to drink me in, but I'm sure all he saw was a mouth opened in shock.

I struggled to understand whose presence I was in.

While other demons had opted for horns or a tail, the person before me had enormous, feathered wings. Their wings were so black that they refracted the rainbow irides-cence of an oil slick. I almost missed the thin, silver ringlet of his crown contrasting against his golden-brown skin. Had it not been for the crown, I wouldn't have realized that I was staring into the pale, sapphire-blue eyes of the King. They sparkled at me with true joy as he gave in to the urge to squeeze me once more, crushing me against himself with more intensity than I could possibly understand. This impossibly beautiful, ageless man with wings larger than life was the first person I'd met who looked the part of a true fallen angel.

When he finally released me, the smile didn't leave his face.

"And you must be Fauna," he said, catching her hand and clasping it in both of his in a warm, friendly shake.

My brain tipped and whirled as I tried to make sense of events.

The man was too happy. The gigantic, modern-Gothic room with silver filigree on the ceiling and dangling chandeliers was too beautiful. His sleek, black suit was too perfect, its chain, his watch, his crown too chic. His irises were too blue, particularly starkly contrasted against his features. His youthful skin was too golden. His smile was too white, too even, too kind. Even his eyes crinkled with too much gentleness and joy.

As I looked at him, I was thirteen years old and in my kitchen all over again. My mother's question rang through me, chilling me as I regarded the King.

Did you know that Lucifer was the most beautiful angel?

Was this him?

"I'm sorry, I..." I hedged in honest confusion. I shook my head, not in rejection but in utter lack of comprehension. I'd expected a throne. I'd been ready to fumble through a botched curtsy while I trembled in terror. I'd expected a swimming pool of blood and a harem of Soul Eaters.

"Of course," he said, leading me away from Fauna as he pressed a hand to my lower back. He gestured to include her as he led us to a collection of tufted couches, ushering me to my seat before settling into the chair beside me. "We did meet once, nearly two thousand years ago. I don't suppose you remember, but of course, why would you? Most of those caught in the mortal loop don't. You weren't ready to join us at the time, and my son is not one to rush perfection. He's my better in many ways. But, by the powers, you're as splendid now as you were then."

I wasn't sure if I'd ever had a glass of water in my life. My tongue was made of paper and sand. I blinked at him without a drop of comprehension and tried to remember what my therapist had taught me about grounding myself when the world spun out of control.

I was supposed to name the five senses.

What could I see? I saw the loveliest man with the loveliest wings and the loveliest...office? What was this? A desk, couches, a chandelier—no, *three* chandeliers—pillars, floor-to-ceiling windows...yes, this had to be an office.

What did I smell? Well, there was Fauna's scent of winter and sea. There was the lingering smell of Chanel No. 5. There was something sweet, like pomegranate maybe, or dates...

I heard laughter. I felt soft, comfortable fabric. I tasted sticky dehydration as I attempted and failed to swallow.

My therapist had been wrong. The spin hadn't ended. I was not grounded. I would be requesting a refund for her services.

"Sorry," the King amended. "I apologize, Maribelle, truly. I can imagine how overwhelming this is for you. I know some experiences are more enlightened than others. I can't tell you how hopeful I was when I learned you had fae lineage in this incarnation. To not just be able to see him when he reveals himself but even of your own accord... It was the bridge we've needed for millennia."

I looked to Fauna, but she only offered an unhelpful shrug.

"Of all the names you've given my son," said the man, "Caliban is one of my favorites. I'll add it to my repertoire! He liked Kit, Vulpes, and Nyx the best. Oh, and the cycle where you named him Fluffy! I'm almost certain it was before your people at the time crossed the Bering Strait, though I get the dates mixed up. Of course, the Qawiaraq word for 'fluffy' you used was...what was it? No bother. Was that the one where he remained a beast and never took one human form? Oh! Do you remember when you were in Haiti—no, of course you don't." He shook his head in jubilation, tilting it back as he let another long, happy laugh escape his belly.

"Maribelle, sweet Maribelle, the joy of our kingdom, *please*, tell me you've come to join us at long last."

I had no idea what to say. The ringing in my ears was almost too loud for me to hear the King. To both my surprise and my relief, Fauna spoke on my behalf.

"If you'll forgive my intrusion, Your Highness," she began.

Her politeness and formality were enough to wake me from my stupor. I blinked the shock from my eyes as I trained my eyes on their exchange.

The reluctance at shifting his attention away from me was unmistakable, but the King was a gentleman. He turned to her cordially.

"Unfortunately," she said, "her fae lineage in this cycle has led to a few complications. I'm not sure what you know of Maribelle, but with a clairsentient mother who has strong feelings for the opposing side of your war, Your Grace, Maribelle has gained an angelic tracker. It's part of why I've been unable to leave her alone for more than a minute. She's at risk."

The joy smoked out. A chill settled over us. At first I thought it was my imagination, until I saw the goose bumps on not only my arms but on Fauna's. Even the arched, picture windows that belonged in a sanctuary showed the bright, blue day as clouds crept in to cover the sunlight. Gray light filtered into the room.

Gravity weighted his question as he repeated, "An angel is tracking her, and my son is not here with her?"

Fauna emphasized her seriousness by remaining reverently still.

I could nearly see the puff of her breath when she spoke through the chill. "Yes, Your Majesty. I can't speak to her former lives, but I don't expect her other forms have been at risk of bonding with an angel. You know as well as I what this would mean for her cycle. If the angel succeeds…"

"Which angel?" he asked, voice low as an oath.

"He's going by Silas. You may have known him as—"

280

He held up a silencing finger as he looked from her to me.

Despite the grandeur of the room, everything felt too small, then too large. At first it pressed in on me, making it difficult to get the air or space I needed. In the next breath, everyone was too far away. I was so alone, so distant from Fauna. If I fell through the couch and tumbled into the awaiting galaxy, I wouldn't be able to grab anyone for help. I chafed my arms for warmth, hugging myself for comfort in more ways than one, wishing Fauna were beside me. I longed to have her arm around me while I tumbled into the impossible, unable to connect with reality.

He exhaled slowly as he said, "I'd always expected that when you were ready to leave your mortal cycle, you'd join us here. Now you're here with a Norde and, if she's to be believed, which"—he patted her comfortingly on the hand— "I do entirely..." He frowned. "This could be your last cycle, Maribelle. And not for the better."

The spinning intensified.

Against my will, a hand went to my chest, as if to feel for the thread of yarn that my mother had always been able to pull, unraveling me into my childhood. I'd grown up hearing the petition, the dream, the plea that our souls would only continue amid the heavenly hosts after we passed. Now at twenty-six, I was hearing that such a life-long prayer might be answered, but as a punishment.

Fauna had said it before, but hearing it from the King took the air from my lungs. I'd fallen in love over and over again with the same soul—connected to him through time, through body, through country, through language, since the sands of time had flipped from BCE to AD. I wasn't sure if I was honored or horrified. The room swam, filigree bleeding into the black around it, furniture wiggling, floor rising up to meet me as if it were little more than the celestial whirlpool in the lobbies. I grappled within myself for stability. Nothing about it made sense. Nothing about it—

"Oh." Fauna leapt to her feet in the same moment the

King grabbed a vase that had to be worth more than Azrames's Bugatti and shoved it in front of me just as I emptied the coffee, bile, and crumbles of cookie into the beautiful piece of priceless art. It took a second attempt for her to catch the rest of my hair, removing what still dangled near my face as I retched a second time. "Mortals," she said apologetically to the King as she patted me on the back.

"I'll take responsibility for that one," he replied. "I should know better by now. It's just not every day I get to see..." He stopped himself from reigniting the same fire that had set my belly to curdling. I apologized weakly through humiliation and twisted guts before my third and final emission, relinquishing whatever tiny bits of liquid remained in my stomach. The muscles in my neck, back, and abs all strained against the effort as my body lost the battle against the supernatural. "And with the Prince absent..."

I wiped my mouth with the back of my head, burning with humiliation. The King had already snapped his fingers and the sullied vase vanished. He procured a handkerchief and glass of water, both of which I was almost certain hadn't existed a moment before. I made the snap decision to do what I'd spent twenty-six years doing and ignore literally every piece of information that had been offered to me so that I could plow forward as a functioning human. Unable to engage with a single topic the man had spoken, I straightened my back, rallied my courage, and did what I'd done best for years as a sex worker: I acted.

"So," I said, feigning as though I hadn't just vomited in front of them both, "you're Caliban's father?"

His expression softened. "You don't have to pretend you're okay with this. We value sincerity."

Well, there went my plan.

I scrunched my face, closing my eyes. Sensing my struggle for normalcy, the King did me a favor.

"Yes, yes. I'm the king of the freedom fighters. My son—your Caliban—is their prince. As I've said, I am surprised to see you here at long last without him. He's been in the mortal realm for some time now... Time"—he stopped, waving a hand to indicate his aside—"moves a little differently here than it does there. That said, he generally checks in when he isn't with you. Princely duties and what have you."

"Maribelle," Fauna said carefully, "I think it would be wise for you to share what you said to Caliban with the King."

I shook my head slowly before I even realized what I was doing. No? Was I saying no, I was refusing information to a monarch? To Caliban's father? In direct disregard of Fauna's request, when she'd never led me astray?

They both frowned at me before it struck me.

Shame dropped my words to a barely audible register as I said, "I'm embarrassed about what I said."

Fauna blew out a breath and interpreted. "Maribelle here wasn't quite familiar with how literal promises are to citizens of the nonmortal realms."

The King shared a sad sigh. "That's the blessing and curse of mortality, isn't it. Your life is short, so you're allowed to live it with little rhyme or reason. You can pay penance in your next life, or the one after that. When you live forever..." He looked out the window, gaze unfocusing as he regarded the blacks and grays, stone and steel, glass and iron of his city. Clouds continued to roll until they'd become bottom-heavy thunderheads. "You can't say things you don't mean. Words have consequences."

"Tell him," Fauna prompted once more.

I closed my eyes as if it would make the memory any less painful. I returned to the last night I'd seen him, to the smell of the forest, the cool rush of his skin, the chill of his kiss as he brushed his lips against my neck. I felt him hold me in those final moments as my shock melted into anger. My refusal to understand our earlier agreement—one wherein he'd bound himself to my verbal consent before any action in my life—had tied his hands from intervening.

"It was three-fold," I said, eyes still closed. "I'd spent my life convinced he wasn't real. I needed to believe I was crazy. I didn't want to see him anymore, and so I didn't. He continued to visit for years, but he was no longer visible."

The king chuckled quietly at the loophole, but the laughter was not unkind.

"Then we made a deal that he couldn't do anything, he couldn't intervene, he couldn't so much as lift a finger without my expressed permission. To be fair, it was his counteroffer. I'd told him I couldn't do any of it anymore, and rather than lose us altogether, he'd allowed me to sequester him into a permitted box. And then, someone tried to murder me."

Neither of them so much as breathed as they listened to my story.

"An angel—Silas—showed up at the last second and killed the human. I barely made it. He'd...been unable to intervene. He couldn't help me beyond marking the would-be murderer. I don't fully understand those implications, but when I'd learned he was there, that he saw everything, that he stood right there and didn't help..."

The king patted me on the leg until I opened my eyes.

"He loves you deeply, Maribelle. To put out the sort of mark that even an angel could take is a harbinger of urgency and desperation that no one could pass up. The risk he put himself in..." He removed his hand, looking into the middle distance. "You haven't seen him since then? Since he put out the mark?"

I frowned. "What does it mean? The mark, that is?"

Fauna twisted her mouth, but at the King's forlorn look, she seemed to decide she would spare him the pain of speaking. "You know Azrames's work? How it isn't for money, the way mortals work?"

I nodded slowly.

"Marks are for favors. Azrames had answered a mark for Ianna, which is why she had to help us when he called in the favor. And if an angel responded immediately, I assume he'd valued the favor really, really highly."

I swallowed, meeting the worry in her eyes. "If he owes the angels a huge favor, why would Silas still want to bond with me?"

After a long silence, the King said, "The war, Maribelle. Because you may be the pawn they've needed to turn the tide."

Chapter Twenty-Six

I T TOOK MERE MOMENTS FOR FAUNA TO INFORM THE KING that no, I hadn't had protective wards around my house until she'd arrived, and anyone could walk in or out. He had me describe everything about the angel down to the minutia, as well as the parasitic entity that I'd met on my second encounter with the heavenly host.

"I struggle to believe that the Prince would have left you vulnerable. I suspect Caliban removed your wards when he marked your attacker so that someone else could respond," Fauna mused. "Then after you banished him, he couldn't put them back up."

The King was quick to action. The next moment, he had his back to us, looking out the window as he made a number of calls. I didn't dare open my mouth while he spoke to person after person. When he returned, it was with a serious face.

"He's not with Heaven."

I looked between Fauna and the King. "That's good, right?"

The King met my eyes. "Another pantheon is rumored to be involved."

"But the Nordes—" Fauna began.

"It isn't Nordic. Reports are unclear. But it isn't Heaven."

I felt ready to crawl out of my skin. Nothing made sense, and I said as much.

"A parasite like that should have been a tier-one favor," he explained.

Fauna rose from where she'd been seated and slid into the space beside me.

"They're easy to kill. They require almost no skill. Hell, even a nymph—" He shook his head. "I'm sorry, Fauna, I don't mean to be diminutive. That word isn't even of your realm."

She offered a polite scoff, "I am many things, Your Majesty, but skilled in combat is not one of them. Nothing you could say regarding my inability to fight would insult me."

I hadn't even realized that I'd been bouncing my legs anxiously, twisting my fingers between my knees while they spoke. Fauna slipped her fingers into mine, resting her forearm on my knee to still my restlessness.

"A tier-one?" I asked her quietly, not wanting to interrupt the King. He was so lost in his distress that he appeared to have forgotten we were there all together.

Her face was not one of impatience but of concern.

"You know how Azrames works, right?"

I nodded.

"His work is in energy between man and fae, and he has a pretty sweet deal. He rarely works with other immortals. But for many of us… Well, many put out contracts that can be claimed across realms—contracts in favors. It's risky to enter into deals, even small ones, with someone…even someone from your own realm. A first-tier favor could be something like trading jobs or doing remedial tasks. It's busywork. A tier-one favor that's sent out for any realm to grab could be more dangerous. If a mermaid calls in a level-one favor to a fire sprite and asks her to help her brush her hair…"

I didn't want to touch the introduction of new fae with a ten-foot pole, so I just said, "Even though it's a small task, the sprite would die."

"Open-realm favors are unwise. They're reserved for the

rarest of circumstances." Fauna looked from me to the King. "And from your tone, Your Majesty, I assume the bounty on this entity and its host was not marked as tier one."

He sank into the leather chair and slipped his hands into his hair. His ageless face suddenly bore the weight of thousands of years as he said, "No. No it was not."

✦

"I don't understand what happened in there," I whispered, eyes panicked as Fauna dragged me from the building. Azrames hadn't spoken since she yanked him from the waiting room. His face remained tight with concern as he got us to the car. "Fauna, what happened!"

"Az," she said, ignoring me, "how fast can you get us back to your place?"

He bit down, a muscle ticking in his jaw as he began to drive like the proverbial bat out of hell.

"Fauna!" I gripped the shoulders of the two front seats and leaned forward.

She whipped around, true anger in her face as she said, "You would have been fine! If you had died in that apartment, you would have resumed your mortal loop. Twenty-six years from now you could have been a *different* idiot. But your precious Caliban couldn't leave good enough alone. Apparently, whatever you were going through was too terrible for him to allow you to endure. Gods and goddesses, has he only ever let you die healthy and of old age? No wonder you're caught in a mortal loop refusing to learn any lessons. Personally, I would have let you die."

"You don't mean that..." I struggled to breathe. Only an hour before, she'd held my hand in the palace and said she loved me. I'd begun to believe we were truly friends. I mouthed her name again, the question a wordless plea as tears threatened me. The gray streets blurred, both from the wall of emotion and the speed with which Azrames wove through traffic. Our twenty-minute drive would easily be finished in six.

"Five, Marlow! Tier five!"

Azrames reacted so suddenly that he almost jerked the vehicle into a horned demon on a motorcycle. His gray knuckles turned white with his grip, muscles tensing. My stomach lurched against the g-force as he pushed his foot on the gas pedal, cutting the six-minute drive into four.

I shook my head, eyes wide as I said, "I don't understand..."

"Five means whoever you are, whatever you are, come right the fuck now and I'll do whatever you want."

I lurched with the car as Azrames took a hairpin corner. I gripped the seats in front of me as I let my eyes do the begging, pleading with her for answers.

"Anything!" she practically shrieked. "It means Silas can ask for *anything*! He wants Caliban to rip his soul out and serve it up on a platter? He wants unlimited access to come and go to Hell's palace? He wants the King to choose between surrender or the death of his son? It is within Silas's right to ask! And he got the favor from the fucking Prince of Hell! This isn't just bad for him, Marlow. This is bad for *all* of the realms! Think of what it means for the Nordes! The Greeks! The Egyptians! The—" She gasped, balling her fingers in her hair. "Every kingdom will be thrust into chaos if Silas calls in this barter. Marlow, do you hear what I'm saying? This is really. Fucking. Bad."

The tendons on Azrames's neck flexed as he said, "That's it. Heaven wins." He swung into the parking spot, little more than a blur as he moved. He'd sprinted to open Fauna's door before she could even leap from her seat.

"And?" I gasped, tumbling from the back. "What do we do? How do we help?"

She spun on me, jabbing a finger into my sternum as she burned. "Silas wants *you*. It's the only thing he's harped on since meeting you. It's why he showed up at your apartment. It's why he involved your mother," she said. "As far as we know, he hasn't called in the favor. In fact..." She calmed herself, forcing a long breath in, then pushing it out. She made her fists unclench as she relaxed her face from the uncharacteristic panic and fury that had burned through her. "As far as we know...he hasn't told anyone what cards he holds."

I looked between her and Az.

"And what about the other pantheon?" I asked.

Azrames stiffened. "What other pantheon? Heaven doesn't have any allies."

"It doesn't make any sense," said Fauna. "The King's intel could have been wrong. He seems to believe other gods are at play."

"Then..." Azrames's posture changed. "Whoever it is, they may have bought us some time."

None of this made sense. "How?"

Azrames clarified with low intensity. "Silas can't have told anyone in Heaven that he has the power to end the war, or it would have happened already. Hell would be swarming with angels. Clearly, their king knows you're the Prince's human, but that seems to be it. Silas must have reported his fight, explained who you were, and gotten his orders from there. If anyone knew about the deal...things would be very, very different."

I swallowed. "Could he ask for me? As the favor?"

"Only if you had bonded yourself. He could have asked for Caliban to hand over your bond, and the Prince would have had to comply. Heaven would own you right now," answered Fauna.

"And?" My eyebrows had climbed so high that I was positive they'd disappeared into my hairline. "What do I do? How do I fix this?"

She gripped my shoulders, looking between me and the sølje still pinned to my chest. "You get to Silas first."

We were in Azrames's apartment within a moment, the luxury of his space feeling ominous as the backdrop of Fauna's fervor. I'd never seen her move with such intensity. She zigzagged through the apartment like a deer bolting in the forest. I had to stop her from tearing the designer bodice from her chest, as it looked like she was seconds away from shredding thousands of dollars in fashion in her haste. She left her clothes in a rumpled pile at my feet as she stepped into the comfortable, harem-style pants she'd worn the first night we'd met. Her heather-gray shirt, cropped like the others, had a Nordic rune in the center, antlers intersecting it through the middle. Fauna yanked another shirt and pair of pants off hangers and chucked them at me.

"Wear these," she commanded, then left me to my own devices as I shimmied out of my jumpsuit and unclipped the broach.

I stepped out in curious, skin-tight leggings that seemed to have been made from rust, forest, and gold. I'd never owned anything that could have been described as steampunk, but no other word came to mind as I blinked at the buttons that ran along the seams on the outside of the pants, contrasted against the indecently thin, white shirt she'd thrust on me. I understood a nymph's incentive to champion the *free the titties* movement, but I wasn't sure unbound D cups were the most suitable attire for seeking an audience with an angel. I looked down at the perfectly black tattoo, the only mark on my otherwise exposed flesh, and felt my chest tighten.

It was the sigil that had turned me into Alice as I free-fell into Wonderland.

Except with Alice, after she'd returned home, she'd been able to pretend it was all a dream. I was marked in more ways than one. There'd be no coming back from this. I shook the thoughts from my mind like eliminating cobwebs, ridding myself of old patterns of thought as I abandoned the bedroom.

"Is Az coming with us?" I asked, watching her tear things from his shelves as she appeared to chaotically search for something.

Her back remained to me, hands scouring his things as she said, "He can't come."

"Why not?" I asked.

"Yeah" came Azrames's voice as he joined us in the living room, tugging the shirt over his muscles and running his hand through his hair. "Why not?"

She growled as she spun on him. "Az, where is your—oh. Never mind." Fauna ran to the glass container I'd marveled over only one day prior and placed a hand on either side.

"Don't break the—" He stretched out a hand to stop her, but she'd already tossed the glass to the side. The tinkling shards of ten thousand diamonds filled the apartment as the case shattered to the floor.

"There was a latch, Fauna."

"Whoops." she said, ignoring him entirely. She shoved the Latin-inscribed dagger into its silver sheath and turned to him. "Find me a leather holster, Az. Make it cute."

He narrowed his eyes slightly, looking from the shattered evidence of her carelessness, then back to her. He disappeared, returning a moment later with two loose, leather belts. He fitted the first to her waist as he asked, "Now, why exactly can't I come?"

"It's too dangerous," she said, still too distracted to truly look at any of us as she wreaked havoc on the apartment.

"What's too dangerous?" I had a million questions and no one was giving me answers. "Are we killing Silas? What's the plan here?"

"That depends entirely on what Silas has to say," Fauna replied. "But with this favor hanging over the Prince's head, the clock is ticking, and we have no idea what we're really up against without understanding why he hasn't let anyone know that he has the key to winning the war."

"Maybe he has," I said quietly. "Could he have told a different god?"

"Stand still," he said, grabbing Fauna by the back of her shirt as she readied herself to dash into some other room and reeling her in. She danced in place with impatience. He cinched the belt with a final tug, bringing her up on her toes slightly. He hooked his finger between her hip and the strap, then spun her around. "You know Silas, Fauns. Could he be a defector?"

She pinched the bridge of her nose. "I have no idea."

"So, we don't know his motives, and, just to be clear," he said, voice dropping from its gentleness to a low growl. He bent his forefinger, tucking it beneath her chin and forcing her to calm down long enough to look into his eyes. "A sugar goblin and a human won't let me, the centuries-old demon assassin, come on their fight because it's too dangerous?"

"I…"

"You love me." He grinned, releasing her. He began to fit himself with the other weapon, then opened a door in the hall that I was almost certain had never been there before. He procured a scimitar, a thin silver rope that he clipped to his waist, and a leather roll of god-knows-what clinking metals hid within. Much to my surprise, he procured a small, golden pistol.

"Really? Demons use guns now?" I gaped.

He shoved it into a holster at his hip and shrugged. "No use fighting the times." He moved into the kitchen and began to scrawl a note, leaving it on the island.

"What are you writing?" Fauna asked.

"An apology note for the maid, since I'll be busy battling it out in the mortal realm when she arrives." He then looked at me, as if seeing me for the first time. His lips tugged up in a smirk before he looked back at Fauna. "You're really going for the angel's balls with that one, huh?"

Fauna shrugged, saying, "He wants her. It's probably just a war thing, but, just in case he's thinking with his dick…"

My eyes widened in horror as my hands flew to my chest. "You picked this on purpose!"

"Relax." She rolled her eyes. "You have very cute nips. He'll love them."

My skin was unbearably hot. I could feel my pulse in my very cheeks as if my blood were trying to escape through my face. I switched my position, folding my arms over my chest rather than cupping my breasts before saying, "Okay. We find the angel. How, exactly?"

"Well, he can't come to Hell, and at the moment, Fauna's the only one of us who can get into Heaven," he said. "We'll meet him in the mortal realm. He'll come when you call, Marlow." Azrames's gaze darted to my chest, and my eyes widened in shock. To my relief, he merely asked, "Where's the sølje?"

I unfurled my hand to reveal it, lifting it to my shirt. He shook his head.

"No, leave it hidden. We don't want it ripped from you. Those pants don't leave much to the imagination, so we don't get the luxury of pockets, but pin it on the inside of your waistline to ensure it doesn't fall out. Plus, it'll remain pressed to your skin that way."

"Aw," Fauna said, grabbing the cookies before she joined us, "look at you idiot-proofing Marlow's hold on the broach. Come on. We have to get going."

"Shouldn't I get a weapon?" I asked, looking from Azrames's battle-ready attire to the soft, looping leather that held Fauna's ornate dagger.

"Sure! What have you trained in? Can you lasso things? Have you taken fencing classes? What are your archery skills like?" The look she gave me told me to grow up.

My frustration was so palpable it nearly had a flavor.

"You'd be a liability with a sword in those hands," Azrames said apologetically. "Your mind, words, and influence are the best weapons you have."

Then to me, she said, "See, I thought he understood you, but apparently he's forgotten you don't have two brain cells to rub together. Now, are we ready to get going, or are we going to let Mister No Other Gods Before Me begin to topple his dominos and ruin every realm from the Slavs to the Mongolians thanks to someone who was apparently too pretty and special to die in her apartment? I like my life with the Nordes, but if Hell falls and I don't get to sleep on

294

those sheets again…" She pouted, looking over her shoulder at the ultimate loss in the battle between Heaven and Hell: her sex life.

I was strangled between apologetic and frantic. My ignorant fuckup could destroy Caliban completely, and it was already too late. I'd destroyed him, the realms, the world as we knew it without even understanding the veil. He loved me; that love had been his biggest mistake. "I had no way of knowing—"

"You remember how I said Frigg liked you? You wanna keep it that way? Then make your people proud and fix this. Az, Mar's apartment is invite-only." She extended her hands toward both of us, one to me and the container of sweets toward Az.

"You can't bring the cookies," Azrames said, plucking the box from her hand and setting it on the counter. I slipped one hand over the callouses of his large, gray fingers and interlocked my other with Fauna's soft hands to ensure they could both get past my warding. Before I could say another word, the world smeared into black, red, white, and gray, silver streaks blinding me as they seared into my vision. Then everything went dark.

Chapter Twenty-Seven

I GASPED FOR AIR AS IF EMERGING FROM DEEP UNDER WATER. My knees buckled, making me painfully aware that they were still purple from when I'd tumbled to Hell's cobblestone streets. If I hadn't been clutching two powerful beings, I would have crumpled to the ground once more. It took me a fraction of a second to recognize the couch, the television, the enormous windows with the distant view of the river, the orange glow of warehouse lights twinkling as they refracted in the late-summer night.

"Are you going to ask if it's always dark here, too?" Fauna taunted, untangling her hand from mine as she moved about my apartment. I wasn't sure what she was looking for, but Azrames shoved his hands politely into his pockets.

"Nice place," he said appreciatively, and I knew he meant it. It was a nice place. It wasn't centuries-of-assassination-compensation nice, but I'd done very well for myself. And in the absence of friends or hobbies outside of those that existed in my phone, I'd invested my expendable income in things that made me happy.

Oh shit, my friends.

My hands flew to the skin-tight pants on instinct before I realized that the last time I'd seen my cell phone, I'd been in a cream dress sprawled across the cobblestone streets of Hell. I'm sure it was in the gutter of some other realm, a relic of mortals sitting in Satan's sewers. I ran for my computer and scrunched my eyes against the tongue-lashing I knew awaited me.

I didn't even read the messages from EG before responding.

(Marlow) Hey EG, I know it was uncool to disappear for a
few days. My phone fell in a gutter on the same day
that I ran into an old friend, and I took it as a sign from
a universe that I needed to take a mental health break. I
should have told you. I'm sorry for worrying you. Please
send it up the ladder that none of this is on you. I am
going to need a few extensions. At the moment, I can't
give you a new estimated time of delivery until my
friend leaves town. She could be here anywhere from fifteen more minutes to a few more days or a week or so.
I wish I had better answers for you, but this is as honest
as I can be. I just wanted to pop my head back up from
the ground before I go back in the earth again—I still
haven't replaced my phone and probably won't for a
minute. Sending love and regrets.

I winced against the hundreds of missed messages from the group chat. Something about them seemed…wrong. I frowned as I began to scroll, looking at the missed messages, then at the slow decrease in frequency. I clicked on one of Nia's obscenity-laced messages to expand it, and my frown deepened as I looked at the date and time of delivery. I couldn't believe the coldness in the last thing she'd sent.

(Nia) I called your bio-mother. Believe me when I say it was
my last fucking option, and even then, you think I'm going to take the word of the abusive woman who put you
in seven thousand dollars of therapy debt? The police
were not thrilled with me, nor was she when she chewed
me out for having to give a statement. Your car is at her
place, Mar. Apparently you brought your lady friend to

your hometown? And honestly, Mar, I'm really goddamn disappointed. I thought you cared about us enough to let us know before you fell off the face of the earth. I am your family. Me. For your sake, I hope you're fine.

I minimized her message and my eyes went to the corner of my screen, where once again the date and time showed something very, very off.

My hands began to shake as I lifted my face to look at Azrames, still quietly admiring the apartment from the middle of the room. He looked utterly at home in the shadows, his shades mixing flawlessly with their gloom.

"Az?" I whispered.

He rotated toward me, arching a curious brow.

"What day is it?"

His face softened at once. He took two steps close to me then squatted to eye level so that he could meet my face while I remained on the couch. An apologetic sadness pulled his mouth, his eyes, his very energy into a shade of regretful blue as he said, "Time passes differently between realms. What day did you leave the mortals?"

I swallowed, eyes darting to the corner of my laptop again. The cold, white letters and numbers hurt my eyes with their cruel impossibility. I shook my head slowly. My hair tickling my arms was the only sensation that cut through the numbness. "I was only in Hell for a little over a day," I said with certainty. "Less than that. We got there in the middle of the night and left the next evening. It's been eighteen hours at the most. It's been..." But my eyes remained trained on the screen.

"How much time did you lose?" he prodded.

I looked into his face again, struck again by seeing his horns, his skin and coloration made of something entirely *other*. Fauna and her ethereal beauty had been hard enough to accept, but having Azrames in my apartment was the key I needed in order to accept that, yes, this was all happening to me.

298

"It's…September. It's been two weeks," I said quietly, suddenly realizing that no excuse to EG or the publisher would be enough. No bangcation or hot girl or retreat into the countryside would make Kirby or Nia forgive me for the nightmare I'd put them through or for the betrayal of holding me while I'd cried, mourning my family for years, only to have my own mother be the one with the answers.

My mother.

I wondered what tale she was telling. For that matter, I wondered what tale she'd been told.

Fauna clicked on a light in the hall, which broke my spiral. I called out to her, "What are you looking for?"

"Az!" She shouted from the next room. "Come help me with something."

He sauntered into the hallway. I closed my laptop and followed him with my face creased in confusion. She was on her hands and knees as she peered under my bed.

"Explain yourself," I said calmly, leaning against the frame of my own bedroom while a Nordic nymph and shadow demon helped themselves to my personal space.

Az flattened himself on the floor, sliding his long arm into the dark space beneath my bed. He emerged a moment later, hands wrapped around a small…something.

"Explain yourself *faster*," I said, eyes widening in surprise.

Fauna sighed. "Like I said, Silas wants you."

Azrames extended the object to me. "It's for sympathy," he said. "In witchcraft—"

"It's a poppet," I said, breathing out the fear-laced word torn from fairy tales. I turned over the tiny golden figurine. It had the unmistakable curves of a human shape. I dug my fingernail into the metal, and my eyebrows lifted in surprise at the nearly imperceptible indentation that confirmed that it was, in fact, gold. I turned it over to see a curious combination of swirls, circles, intersecting lines, and curves etched into it.

He nodded, though it was riddled with his frown.

"Almost. Poppets are generally for hexing, and this is more for connection."

"He's looking for his in," Fauna said, crawling onto my bed. She crossed her legs before saying, "Can I just say something?"

We both looked at her before I answered, "I'm confident you will anyway."

"I think this is a really good thing," she said, voice lowering until it was scarcely more than a whisper. She looked at the tiny shape in my hands, then back up to me. "Knowing what we know...he could have forced our hands. Instead, it looks like he's trying to get you to want this."

I almost dropped the figurine. "He wants me to choose, what? Heaven? The bond? *Him?*"

Azrames pinched the bridge of his nose. "Maybe all of it. Maybe he just knows how this will shake out the moment the heavenly hosts find out and hopes you'll take the step of your own free will before you're forced into chains. After all..." Azrames looked at his feet, eerily quiet as he said, "He and I both know what it's like to serve that god."

I threw the figurine onto the bed. "What sort of free will is that?" I demanded, quoting years of theology about accepting the faith of my own volition.

"I had the free will to rebel," Azrames responded. "And as a result, I'm locked out of Heaven. There were consequences. My choice to fall cost me friends, brothers, a kingdom, and family. I'm engaged in thousands of years of slaughter with smaller numbers on our side and a ruler who values equality, which also means he's less likely to sacrifice us. Which is great, except when it means—"

"That you might lose the war," Fauna said, reaching up to squeeze his arm. "You won't," she promised. "I mean, you probably would if it were up to Marlow alone, but I'm the wheel steering the ship, here. I'm not going to let her do anything stupid."

I wanted to argue, but she was right. Everything I'd known

about Heaven, Hell, the pagan realms, Norse mythology, and international deities had been like Plato's blind man in a cave. I'd done my best to make sense, then fiction, based on my limited understanding. I was not qualified to wage war.

The tightness in my chest worsened. I wanted Caliban back. I wanted him safe. I wanted him with me. Instead, not only had I sent him away, but he'd gambled with his life, his kingdom, and with every single pantheon by putting out a mark to protect me. He'd been willing to burn it to the ground, and I'd sent him away. Now his soul and the lives of everyone and everything—mortal and immortal alike—rested on my shoulders.

"Will Silas know that you're here?" I asked.

Both looked at me skeptically.

"I don't want to wait. He didn't bring anyone with him when he came to my apartment or when he involved my mother. If you truly think he's trying to keep other angels out of it—"

Fauna winced.

"What?"

"Your mom…" she said slowly. "If she's been praying, and knowing the level of her clairvoyance, she may have been spilling more to the angels than we'd want them to know. Now, hopefully this doesn't change things. As long as Silas kept his mouth shut about the contract he took, your battle is with him. But your mother may have made things harder. She could have told them about me, about our visit, about our disappearing act."

"Shocker," I breathed. I shook it away like a dog drying its coat before saying, "Fauna, we smell alike. Even if he smells you here, he might think it's my fae blood, or just the time we've spent together. Az…" I looked around before reaching for the book of matches behind my bed. "Time to light every candle in my apartment to mask the smell of your smoke."

Fauna nodded with a slow, proud smile. "Maybe we'll burn something on the stove?"

"We'll cover it all," I agreed. "And then, I'll call him."

"What will you do?" Fauna asked.

I exhaled slowly before gesturing to the still-sheer shirt. "Maybe I don't know the rules about giving my name to gods and fae, or about making deals, or about the realms. But I know a thing or two about men, and when it comes to weapons, mine is sharp as a goddamn needle. I'll do what I do best."

"Which is?"

"He's a man, right? I'll do what I've always done. First, I'll make him think he has the upper hand. Then, I'll get him talking."

✦

How long had it been since I'd stood in my doorway after returning from the sulfur and blue pulp of the Cheshire-cat massacre only to see an angel in the middle of my living room? I remembered him extending a hand, making a joke about how anything could be lurking in my closet in the moments before Fauna stepped from behind the shadows. I focused on that memory, calling on it to comfort me. He hadn't known she was in my apartment then, and surely he wouldn't sense it now. I prayed—though to who, I had no idea—that Fauna and Azrames would remain concealed as I settled on my couch. Then I'd knelt, as I had in childhood when talking to God. Finally, I'd taken to pacing.

Candles flickered around my apartment as if I were holding a séance. The entire unit clashed between the fragrant vanilla, the cinnamon bun, the fireside, the balsam, the pumpkin pie, and the fireside embers I'd stocked and stored around the place, fetching them from every closet, every bedside table, every dusty hiding place under the sink until they were all ablaze. Hopefully, the smells would be as overpowering for him as they were for me. The room danced with shadows, while every piece of furniture, every belonging, every nook and cranny reflected orange in its dim light. I knew that meant he'd be able to see me, my every expression, my smiles, my frowns, my uncertainty, my pain, my fear, all with perfect clarity.

Clutching the sympathetic poppet in my hand, I followed an indiscernible intuition and pressed it against my heart. Without knowing why, I squeezed my eyes closed and whispered his name, inviting him in.

Perhaps it was my fae blood, perhaps it was cowardice, but the instinct to close my eyes was right. The room filled with a painfully white light for the briefest of instances. Perhaps if my eyes had been open, I could have written it off as the gripping claws of an ocular migraine. Instead, I knew it for what it was.

I looked up, and there he was.

"Marlow." He said my name as if it were an apology. I'd forgotten how golden his eyes were, and a tiny tug of curiosity wondered if those magnificent irises had been the birthplace of halo lore. They darkened, the glittering light behind him folding in on itself as his muscled shoulders slumped slightly. He was in the same cream-shaded armor he'd worn before, and, knowing what I did about his rank and the controlling nature of his realm, I wondered if he was in uniform.

I took a step backward from the towering man and held up the figurine. "What is this?" I breathed, horror and offense plain on my face. I didn't need to fake my outrage.

His eyes went from the golden statuette in my palm to me. Guilt wove itself through his features. The glitter around him gave way to the flicker of candles as he said, "I...I'm sorry. I'm doing everything I can."

"What's that supposed to mean?" I asked, voice trembling.

"Listen, Marlow, it's more complicated than you realize."

My fingers tightened around the poppet as I made an angry fist. No, it wasn't more complicated than I realized, despite his condescending assertion. I understood so much more than he gave me credit for. I bit my tongue as I fought the urge to spit his words back at him, resisting my temper in favor of information.

"Then help me *realize.*" I failed to keep the venom from my words but decided it was fine. It was honest, at the very least, which I'm sure he could sense. So far, nothing I'd said or done had been an act. "You nearly left me to die in a basement. I had to beg you to get me out of there. Now, you're everywhere. You're in my apartment. You're in my family. You're leaving tiny gold statues under my bed!" I couldn't help the involuntary response as I chucked the poppet across the room. He flinched as it hit the wall as if the impact caused him physical pain. I stirred my voice into equal parts confusion and desperation as I begged, "What do you want from me?"

"It's about you, and it isn't." He blew out a breath. He ran his hands through his hair, and between the boyish gesture, the defeat in his voice, and the collapse of his posture, he looked positively...human. "It's not fair that you're caught up in this, Marlow. It isn't. But here we are, and we can't change the dice that have been cast."

I took a step closer and watched him soften sympathetically as I approached. The thieves' oil scents of frankincense and myrrh were strong enough to overpower the candles that burned throughout the apartment. Everything about his tone, his posture, his message confused me. I was ready to be angry. I was ready to be *furious* as I plied him for information. I'd prepared a variety of tactics that had proven endlessly useful in my career of getting industry tycoons, actors, financial experts, and old money to open their wallets in conjunction with their lips. I sat on a vault of secrets nearly as powerful as my well of savings.

They'd prattled on to a pretty, polite, blank canvas. I'd smiled, nodded, and touched their arms supportively while they'd projected their fantasies onto me. I was a friend. I was a lover. I was a bimbo. I was an empty vase, a static television, a college girlfriend, a confidante, a nobody. Nothing they said to me had mattered, just as I hadn't mattered. I'd mirrored their anger, their excitement, their indignation, their pleasure, persuading them to give more, share more, reveal more. And with each secret, each whisper, each coin of information, I'd slipped it into the bank within myself and accrued more and more until I could buy myself a kingdom built on knowledge as its stones.

"Are you going to ask where I went when Fauna and I disappeared?"

He closed his eyes. "You went either to the Nordes or to Hell. I don't know how you did it, but you did."

I nodded slowly. "Are you going to ask what I learned?"

He took a step toward me, and I watched his hand reach for me just as it had when he'd offered the bond. It rested briefly on my shoulder, sliding down my arm with the barest of touches before he dropped it altogether. He turned his head as he looked to the wall.

"Why haven't you told anyone?" I asked.

He met my gaze then, golden eyes flashing. I knew in my core that he understood my question. We'd cut through the bullshit. We'd skipped the pleasantries, the dances, the guessing games until I asked what I'd summoned him to ask. He'd responded to the most urgent of tiers, and he'd done nothing with it.

"Why hasn't Heaven—"

He raised a hand to silence me, and I complied. Maybe it was the way he stiffened or the quick intake of air, but I knew with immediacy that the truth of my question couldn't be spoken aloud. I realized my foolishness in a moment. If Azrames, Fauna, and Silas could be in the same apartment, then so could anyone. Thanks to the ink marring my skin, I'd be able to see them whether or not I was within the unit. If they loitered just beyond earshot, though, I might unravel the good Silas had done by keeping my secret.

"I called it in" came his low response.

My blood chilled. My lips parted, pulse quickening. I

blinked rapidly to try to bring moisture to my eyes, but I couldn't. I wanted to study his face, to search for answers, to ask what he'd done, but all I could do was focus on the shallow breaths that barely kept me alive.

He'd called in the favor.

It was too late.

My lungs weren't filling. My panting grew quicker until it was too late. I took a backward step, buckling against the pain of my bruised, purple knee as it gave out from beneath me.

Silas had his arms around me in a moment, hand under my head just before it smacked against the obsidian floor. He scooped me up, pressing me into chest and muscles and frankincense and spice as he relocated me to the couch, muttering a low string of agitated curses. I groaned against my own weakness, hating my stupid, swollen knees for failing me.

"Don't say anything," he said, voice low. "If you know, then you know. Don't say it out loud." I looked up at him, confusion widening my eyes. He still hadn't released me, warm hand cupping the back of my head as his arm remained around me. He eased me to a seated position as he said, "Just nod if you understand."

Though I'd spent some time with Fauna insulting my intelligence, I understood that wasn't what was happening. He wasn't questioning my ability to understand; he was asking whether I comprehended the gravity that my words might have. I nodded slowly, and as I did, he released me. He moved away, but only slightly. His knee bumped mine and I winced, hand flying to the goose-egg-size welts that decorated each kneecap from my collapse into Hell.

He frowned down at my outfit as if seeing it for the first time. His gaze went first to my knees, but I didn't miss how they traveled up, snagging briefly before meeting my face. Even in the candlelight, I could see the blush creep into his cheeks.

"Are you hurt?"

I shook my head. "I just banged my knees when I...I don't know. Jumped realms?"

His gold-brown brows bunched as he lifted a large hand. "May I?"

My lower lip lifted in a pout. He didn't wait for an answer before his hand touched one knee, then the other. The warm, tingling sensation radiated from my joints through my body, filling me with a decadent, downright sinful pleasure as something far more indulgent than healing coursed through me. I nearly choked on it, eyes closing, lips parting in a gasp as the tingling ended. When I looked back at him in shock, his mouth was quirked up in a half-hearted smile.

"I'm glad I could make you feel...better."

I swallowed. I wanted to be angry, but it was hard to feel anything through the haze of dopamine. I didn't have to glance down to know that my breasts had pebbled against his nearly translucent shirt. I bit my lip, shaking the treacherous chemicals from my mind as I tried to look at him through the haze.

"Silas," I meant to say seriously, but his name came out a bit too sensually. I coughed and didn't miss the smile. "Silas," I repeated, this time managing to lasso the gravity the situation required. "You called in the bargain. You have to tell me—"

"Minor entity." He cut me off loudly as if speaking for the room to hear. "Made for an easy bargain. There's been a job out west that a handful of the faithful have been petitioning us to take. I haven't wanted to tackle it, as it's below my rank—but their prayers have grown annoying. One pagan deity or the other is making the agriculture in this town thrive like it's eighth century BC. I was made aware of it months ago, but I knew it would start shit with the Phoenicians. I thought it would be easier to make Hell take the hit. It's a small gig," he said, voice a little too heavy as he landed on the final sentence. His eyes burned into mine, begging me to understand.

My lashes fluttered rapidly.

I did. He was announcing for the listening walls—whether

Heaven, Hell, or all the realms, that he and Caliban had a low-level bargain to deal with a minor pest problem. His raised tone rang a curious note. I had no idea whether or not he was telling the truth, but he clearly wanted to be heard.

But...the Phoenicians? I knew the pantheon as the bad guys from Sunday school stories. Could an angel really be talking about the Canaanites, the Philistines, Carthage, and the cut-and-dry biblical antagonists around the Euphrates?

I reached my hand toward where his rested on his knee, wrapping my fingers around the top of his hand and squeezing for emphasis as I asked, "Did you really?"

He flared his eyes in warning. His tone changed, lifting his pitch to an arrogance I hadn't heard before. His gaze remained unchanged, golden gravity fixed on mine as he said, "If you think he can't handle a Phoenician nuisance, then perhaps Hell's lost its touch. It's just outside of the town of Bellfield. Typical deal: idyllic town seems too good to be true because it is. Be my guest if you think he needs backup. Tell Hell thanks for squashing our cockroaches so we don't have to get involved."

Cockroach. I knew how Heaven felt about this pantheon in particular.

My mind flashed to horrible thoughts, feelings, and pictures of Sunday school. I was flung immediately into the memory of a scratchy dress and a cold, metal folding chair, surrounded by other children. The teacher used a flip book to illustrate the very graphic retelling of the Canaanite religion of the Old Testament that had been Yahweh's main rival. The teacher had laughed as she had shown cartoon images of a scene so violent and horrifying that I'd mentally buried it until I began unpacking religious traumas on my therapist's couch.

She'd told us about the infamous competition between Yahweh and Baal.

She started the story on the smiling, kindly face of Yahweh's favorite prophet, Elijah. In the next picture, he pointed an accusatory finger as he issued a challenge to prove Yahweh's superiority over Baal's. They would both sacrifice a bull on an altar, but they would not light a fire themselves. Instead, the priests and prophets would pray to their respective gods, and the winner would burn the sacrifice.

The next pictures had been so red. Drawings of large, dead cows, of pools of blood, of knives and gashes in the arms of strange men. Baal's priests had cut and harmed themselves, mutilating themselves in humility while they begged for his intercession. They were things children weren't meant to see.

The Sunday school story told that, though they'd prayed day and night, nothing happened.

The teacher's eyes had twinkled with victory as the story had taken a turn. She'd flipped the pictures to show the room crowded with children in their nicest church clothes the next scene in the story. In an act of showmanship, Elijah had asked the people to fill barrels full of water and soak the altar until the wood, the bull, and the trench were so saturated that it would be impossible for a fire to burn. When Elijah had prayed, Yahweh had answered, consuming the sacrifice, the wood, the stones, and the water until nothing but ash remained. Then, he blessed the land with rain.

When I'd asked my parents why God had stopped doing miracles, they'd raised their hand as if to hit me for such a heretical question. Working through their tempers, my mom had explained that He did miracles all the time—they just didn't get written down anymore, since the Bible was finished.

Perhaps it shouldn't have surprised me to hear that, thousands of years later, Heaven and the Phoenicians continued to hate one another. But it left a much bigger question in its place. When it came to Heaven and its enemies and allies, the Phoenicians may as well have been Hell.

Traumatic memory had snatched me from the present. I thought of the fires consuming the water-soaked bull in the story as the flickering candles drew me back.

I realized my hand was still on Silas's in the same moment

it took him to turn his palm upward, snatching my wrist before I could pull away. He pulled me in. His free hand brushed a strand of hair away from my face as he drew unbearably close, reminding me of the serotonin that had gushed through unspeakable parts of me at his touch only moments before. For a terrifying moment, I thought he might kiss me. He left his free hand on my cheek, lips brushing my ear as he whispered, "I did you a favor. I don't know how long he'll be there before others find out. Look to the Wild Prairie Rose. Get to him first."

He pulled from my ear and planted a gentle kiss on my cheekbone as if it had been his intent all along. Heat radiated from the place where his mouth had met my face, and this time I had no one to blame but myself for the tell-tale way my body responded below the flimsy cloth. He noticed, too.

Silas squeezed my hand and stood. He looked to where the poppet had tumbled near the far wall, then back to me before saying, "Keep it on you. You know…should you need me." With a confusingly charming wink, a flash of white light, and the barest edges of residual glitter, he was gone.

Chapter Twenty-Eight

S ILAS HAD BARELY LEFT MY APARTMENT WHEN FAUNA WAS already upon me, snatching the laptop from my hands. She was a flash of copper and white, a blur of metal, and the glow of a screen. I shuffled closer to her to see she was searching the town of Bellfield. Azrames leaned against the wall and frowned at me.

Maybe she didn't need to talk about the encounter with Silas, but I did.

"Since when are the Phoenicians on the board?" came my bewildered demand.

"Since ten thousand BCE," Azrames said with a shrug. Though the gesture was casual, his energy was anything but.

Fauna's fingers continued flying over the keyboard. "What is Silas playing at?"

I rubbed my arms for warmth as the blur of possibilities chilled me. "It can't be a coincidence."

"It isn't," Fauna said without looking up, "but I'm inclined to trust Silas."

"You were calling him a cocksucker not too long ago!" I could barely contain my emotions. "Now you trust him?"

She looked up from the computer and jutted a thumb toward Azrames. "Az was also an angel, until he wasn't. I can't say that's what's happening, but this is weird, Marlow. This is really, really weird."

I wanted to question this radical leap in conclusions, to push back on their willingness to trust that Silas was not the enemy, their confidence that Caliban was in Bellfield and that they knew what they were saying and where we were going and what we would do when we arrived. I wanted to interrogate an assassin with thousands of years of knowing people and combat and situational awareness and push back against the forest deity who'd watched the first plants bloom and commanded the wild animals, but arguing with them was every bit as silly as recognizing that they were living, breathing, powering things.

I was Alice, twirling through the looking glass, and the world was mad.

Worse still: I was a child in church all over again. To accept one piece of this new reality meant to accept everything, except there was no barometer, no good book, no teacher save for those around me. I was six once more, looking at my mother, my elders, my pastor to tell me right from wrong, only now I was looking into the eyes of a nymph, blindly trusting that she wouldn't lead me astray.

The urge to question everything softened with the knowledge that the answers didn't matter. Either I'd be bludgeoned into submission or lied to, or she was telling the truth and I was meant to follow her.

I believed her, or I didn't. I would follow her, or I wouldn't.

And as odd and erratic and blunt as she was, I believed her.

I numbed any human questions that would be answered with nonhuman logic, and she led the way.

Azrames's frown deepened while I wrestled with my agnostic paradigm. I'd witnessed an array of emotions out of the demon in our time together, but his face reminded me of a loading screen from an early computer. I could see the pages process on his face, though each new thought seemed to bring him greater trouble as the tabs in his mind opened.

"What?" I asked him, studying the expressions flickering across his face. "Do you have something to say about Silas?"

He shook his head. "It's not that—it's…"

"Here!" Fauna turned the computer around to show us what she'd found. A gallery of beautiful images transitioned from one idyllic picture of an orchard. The images continued to dissolve steadily as one picture bled into the next, from the blossoms on the trees outside their barn to the amber waves of wheat and barley that rippled in the surrounding fields. Deeply green knolls surrounded the town with picturesque uniformity. Pretty pictures of a blessed town danced across the screen, showing brick buildings, wooden homes, and the ever-running presence of lovely, green hills. "Next stop, Bellfield. Grab your purse, Mar."

As the images began to loop into ones I'd already seen, I looked back to Azrames. I'd abandoned my phone and wallet in Hell, and my feet carried me to my bookshelf. I didn't have to look at the small book that had been cleverly hollowed out to possess a tiny hiding space as I fetched my backup card and ID. My good purse was missing, but I grabbed a slim leather belt bag from the hook and clipped it around my waist. It had been an impulse purchase as I'd thought it made me look like Indiana Jones, and it had proved rather useful at the book signings when I'd needed to pop anti-anxiety meds at all hours of the night and day in the crowds. Perhaps now I had more reason than ever to play the part. I slipped the cards into the belt bag, and just for safekeeping, I scooped up the golden poppet and dropped it in after them.

Fauna made an impressed noise at my inventive failsafe, then returned to the screen. My eyes didn't leave the demon. "What is it, Az?"

"It's the Phoenicians," he said, brows bundled so tightly that lines creased his forehead to underscore his confusion. "Silas said it was a minor entity. The only thing in the Phoenician realm known for benefitting crops or that would be of any use to agriculture would be Dagon."

313

"Or Niki," Fauna offered without looking up.

"Niki is more Sumerian—"

"Wait." I stopped them. "You're talking about...gods? I thought he said it was a small problem, like a parasite from their realm."

Fauna's eyebrows lifted. She immediately clicked out of the orchard's site and toggled to the map. She zoomed in repeatedly until a satellite image of the city filled the screen. "Well," she murmured, "I'll be damned. I've never seen anything like it."

Azrames straightened suddenly. He ran to my kitchen and began to tear open drawers and slam them closed. His teeth set with determination. Intensity burned as he growled, "Marker. I need a marker."

I nearly tripped over my feet as I stumbled to the table where Fauna had set down my marker the last time she'd been in my apartment. I didn't even have the chance to properly extend it to him before he snatched it from my hands. He bit off the cap and kept it in his mouth as he ran to the door and began to draw a shape. I watched with wide eyes as he disappeared into my bedroom, then the guest room, returning at long last to the tall window.

"It's a permanent marker..." I muttered weakly as he drew with a speed I didn't understand.

"I can't believe I didn't think of this before," Fauna muttered, running her fingers through her hair and leaving them bundled against her scalp. "My invite-only wards aren't enough."

"Silas wanted to be overheard," Azrames said, cap still in his mouth. "We don't."

He recapped the marker and breathed a sigh of relief as he stepped away from the elaborate design resting just beneath Fauna's graffiti. His words were cryptic, but his actions were easy enough to understand. Whoever might want to eavesdrop on my apartment no longer had the ability to do so. I looked between my door and window to confirm that the same thing had been emblazoned on both access points. If I had to guess, I'd assume that every window in my apartment now displayed a bizarre combination of what looked like little more than triangles and intersecting lines. Two symbols of the occult per entrance seemed imbalanced. If we were going to keep defacing my property, I'd have to ask them to add a third.

Now was not the time to worry about getting my deposit back. I hated that they were sitting on their hands while, if the angel was to be believed, we knew where Caliban was. "Okay, let's go! What are we waiting for?"

Az's voice was every bit as troubled as his face as he said, "Dagon's credited with gifting farmers with the plow. But he's mer. A Philistine fish god."

"Mer?" I repeated incredulously. "You're telling me this tiny town has a merman? And, just to be clear, a merman was put in charge of agriculture?"

"A mer *god*," Fauna said appreciatively. "Look at the town." And sure enough, at the center of the town was an enormous circular lake. Its perfect edges informed Marlow and the others in no uncertain terms that it was man-made.

"Wait," Azrames said, stealing the computer from Fauna's lap. His lips parted. I could hear the shock escape from him as air left his lungs. The gray of his skin shifted to a nearly silver pale. Every troubled thought seemed to click together all at once as horror crashed over him. "Holy shit." He turned the screen, eyes wide. "Fauna...I can't let you come."

"What do you—" Her eyes widened as she saw it. She gaped at the screen for a few more moments, jaw slackening. She shook her head, "No, Az, *you* can't go! If this is strong enough to hold a god—if this is keeping the Prince—"

"Is someone going to tell me what the hell is going on?" I hadn't meant to yell, but panic bubbled over as I sucked in the palpable stress that pulsed between them.

Fauna opened her mouth to speak, but only a squeak came out. Her finger touched the screen, running along the circular lake. From there her delicate nail traced outward as

315

a green line on the satellite image ran from the water like a spoke from a wheel. She continued to follow the path as the green line widened into a thick hill that curved into a small, unbroken mountain range of perfectly connected hills. The dark, intermittent cluster of trees on the satellite image had kept me from seeing its uniformity until her finger carved the path through the trees. The knolls ran through town in squiggles, hills, and intersecting lines.

I swallowed, hardly able to believe my eyes. The circle had to be miles wide. There would have been no way to see it without a bird's-eye view. Within the concentric shape were several small hills, each mound creating dots and lines of ornate, intentional patterns. The only thing it had in common with my tattoo was the circle and the eerie sense of other-worldliness. I looked between them, realization dripping through me. "The town is a sigil?"

Voice as low as an oath, she said, "The town is a trap."

The world fell out from beneath me as I asked, "Silas sent Caliban into a trap?"

No sound beyond our near-silent breathing interrupted the windless night.

After a long time, Azrames said, "I've never seen anything like it. To be strong enough to hold a god…"

"Why would he tell you?" Fauna whispered.

"What?"

Her freckles burned like constellations as they furrowed, face bunching in her confusion. "If Silas was trapping Caliban, why would he tell you where to go? Why would he give you the town name? Or the pantheon? He could have left the Prince imprisoned. This gets weirder by the gods-damned second. If it's kept a god stuck in a town—"

"She can come and go," Azrames said. "Marlow remains unbound, so the seal won't affect her. If anyone's going to be able to save him…"

"But with what power?" Fauna demanded. "How the fuck is a human supposed to save him? How—"

316

"With a shovel," I said.

They both looked at me. Azrames folded his arms over his chest and rubbed his chin while he considered my words. Fauna's fists went limp at her sides.

"Why can't I just break the seal? Wouldn't that render it useless? I mean, if Silas is some dark-horse hero who tipped me off to where he stashed Caliban, and it just happened to be a place where only a human can come and go? It's fucking crazy, but it's every bit as insane as your existence in the first place. So, if I were to dig a crack into the hills around the town…"

Azrames nodded. "We'll go now."

Fauna shook her head. "Let her go," she said. "She's human. The seal won't hurt her. If Caliban is there, she'll be safe within the seal. We can wait on the other side for her."

It took him three steps to plant a kiss on Fauna's head. He reached around to envelop her in a hug. "You stay here, Fauns. I'm not going to let you go into combat in a town you can't escape. Besides, Marlow may be an eighth Norde, but she's also the closest thing Hell has to a princess. I can't let her go alone."

She looked up with him larger doe eyes than I'd ever seen her use.

He exhaled into her hair. His hands began to unravel from their hold as he said, "I love you."

With his final, distracting words, he accomplished two things.

I watched with a silent gasp on my lips as the fingers of one hand wrapped around the hilt of her Latin-engraved dagger. With the other, he reached for me. She must have felt the tug as he plucked the blade from her holster, for in the second it took him to grab me, the last thing I saw was Fauna's wide-eyed fear before everything disappeared.

Chapter Twenty-Nine

AZRAMES ROTATED AS WE FELL THROUGH TIME AND SPACE, absorbing my rough collapse in the last instant. He grunted against the blow as his back struck the grass with a dull thud. I apologized as I scrambled out of his arms and looked around.

"Where are we?"

Stepping from one place to another in the same realm wasn't as disorienting as jumping between Earth and Hell, but it still came with a head-spinning confusion. I'd expected to appear outside of the red barn in the photos or on the edge of the lake at the town's center. Instead, we rolled to our feet in a perfectly ordinary neighborhood. The high-pitched yip of a small dog cut through the night as a crusty, white shih tzu alerted the world to our arrival. I made eye contact with the dog through the bay window of its home. It had pressed itself between the window and the curtain as it howled its angry alarm.

Its owner cursed at it to shut the fuck up from somewhere within the house, loudly enough for the world to hear.

I looked around for Caliban as if we should have appeared at his feet, but he was nowhere to be found.

Az gestured to me to follow as he made his way to the sidewalk. I waved at the dog and caught my tattoo, realizing that people would only be able to see me—not my demonic escort. The tattoo was the best one hundred and fifty dollars I'd ever spent. I crossed the yard to catch up to him.

"Where did you take us?" I asked, keeping my voice low. Knowing that I'd be perceived as a lone woman in an unfamiliar town, I couldn't afford to draw more attention by loudly conversing with myself. It was bad enough that I was still bra-free in a thin shirt that Fauna had specifically selected for the wandering eyes of an angel. The chill of the late hour did not improve upon my self-consciousness. I folded my arms across my chest as I examined the copy-paste normalcy of suburban homes.

Azrames shrugged. "I wanted to get us as close to the business district as possible without drawing eyes. We can't have a human appearing out of thin air in front of a hotel. People might see you."

"How thoughtful," I mumbled.

"Listen," he said, voice serious. "People can't see me, but I'm as stuck here as you are. I can't go back to Hell. Whatever we do from here on out, we do together."

"How do we find Caliban? Do you still have...whatever abilities you have?"

"I believe so," he said, "except for movement. We don't have the luxury of jumping through space, even within the seal. And no, I can't track him. He's royalty. He's untraceable. If Silas hadn't told us where he was, even the legions couldn't have pinpointed his location. But this seal is trapping something. The threats have to be within it. We only have one lead."

"And our lead?"

"Dagon."

The god.

"How do we know he isn't the bad guy?"

The way Azrames's brows met brought me no comfort. "He certainly could be, but it's his lake in the trap's center. My guess is that he's as much of a victim as the Prince and I are."

319

He remained silent, which was even worse. I frowned at him as we continued to walk. "Fauna was right," I said. "You should have let me come alone. You're stuck in flypaper with whatever nightmare awaits us. And if I already have to go door to door, house to house to find him as if we're both helpless humans, then the only thing I've accomplished by bringing you here is ruining your life."

He laughed, voice light. "You're a good soul, Marmar. You're also perfectly useless, even if you have a fighting spirit. I, on the other hand"—he tapped the silver lasso on his hip lightly—"am far from useless."

I frowned down at the object, realizing it wasn't a rope at all. Quite like the layered necklaces he wore and their sigil, the weapon at his hip was more than it appeared. A large, spiked sphere dangled at its bottom. "What is that?"

I caught the wicked gleam of his smile in the streetlights as he said, "Have you ever heard of a meteor hammer?"

Azrames apologized at least three times for the length of our walk. It took roughly forty-five minutes until an aged sign announced we were approaching the Bellfield Inn.

"We can't get a hotel room," I practically spat through my surprise. "The clock is ticking, right? We have to be looking."

"Silas said we should start with the Wild Prairie Rose, right? We have no idea what that is or what it means. We need to get the lay of the land and formulate a plan that isn't: wander the streets and hope for the best. We'll need to speak with Dagon, and we can't call upon him until morning. He's a daytime deity."

I struggled to believe that deities kept certain hours, but as much as it pained me, we headed toward the check-in office. The moment I cracked open the door, I wanted to leave. Though it had been years since I'd watched *Psycho*, I couldn't help but feeling like I'd walked into the Bates Motel. If a demon known for protecting women hadn't been at my side,

I don't think I would have been able to confidently withstand the ogling of the man behind the counter.

The interior had yellowed with cigarette smoke and decades of neglect. From the gaunt of age and the creases of his face, the man might have been around for its grand opening back when the dinosaurs roamed the earth. He rubbed discolored fingernails along his jaw as he eyed me, asking a few too many questions about why I was here and who I might be seeing.

"One key or two?"

"Two, please," I said. No part of me wanted this man thinking I was alone.

His eyes lingered on my bare ring finger before asking, "Will your boyfriend be joining you?"

"I expect him any minute," I replied tersely.

He made a sound to let me know that he didn't believe a word. He flashed me a smile, and I wished he hadn't. The odors of inflamed gums, age, and decay rolled from his mouth.

Azrames's loathsome glare brought me comfort as I handed the man my credit card.

He swiped it as I booked for a room for two nights, but the moment the man turned his back, Az swiped his hand through the tech, and the computer blinked out of use just before the machine finished processing my payment. I concealed a smile while accepting my card with one hand, the other still folded over my chest. The man passed me a metal key, which was all the confirmation I needed to know I'd stepped into the past. I hadn't stayed at a motel that didn't use electronic cards since my family's failed camping trip.

The moment we entered the room, Az held up a finger. I'd thought he looked angry in the lobby, but that was before I saw the burn of true hate. I caught how lupine he looked as his lips pulled back in a snarl. It took him exactly six seconds to locate the cameras and microphone that had been drilled into the wall, hidden in the vent, and propped behind the

321

painting. I stood speechlessly in the middle of the room as he short-circuited each of the pieces of equipment.

"Don't go anywhere," he said without looking at me. I almost gasped at the shadowy hate in his eyes as he brushed passed me. I swallowed as he disappeared out the door. I took a seat on the bed and watched the clock, heart racing. Five minutes turned into ten. Ten turned into sixty.

The deluge of exhaustion hit me like monsoon season in the tropics. I crawled backward onto one of the twin beds and slipped my legs beneath the starchy sheets. If the clock was to be believed, it had to be almost four in the morning. Given our walk from the neighborhood and calculating the time I'd spent in the apartment before Silas's arrival, I tried to count how many hours I'd been awake. The math was something like counting sheep, as before I'd reached a final tally, the rhythmic raindrops of fatigue lulled me into a deep, terrible sleep.

Leave, and don't come back.

I stood in the middle of a body of water so large it could have been the ocean. There were no mountains; there was no land, no signs of life. The clear ice ran as thick as cement as Caliban stared back at me. The ice fractured under the weight of his broken heart at my words. Thousands of white lines spread from where he stood as the sea was cut from top to bottom. The once-perfect glass was now covered in a spider-web of white. The wind howled as I looked at him.

Leave, and don't come back.

A white fox cocked its head at me before taking one step back, then another. I looked around in search of friends or family but saw no one. I was alone in the whipping winds of subarctic temperatures. I reached out to touch the snowy fox, but I'd issued it a command. It continued to step away.

"Wait," I said quietly, but it couldn't. Bound to my words, it had no choice.

The wind kicked up until snow surrounded me. I hadn't felt the temperature before this moment. As the fox disappeared, the crippling cold sent me to my knees. I huddled against my pain, fingers, toes, and ears turning red as frostbite bit into my flesh.

"Come back," I said, but the howling wind stole my words.

I was completely and utterly alone.

Chapter Thirty

I SQUINTED AGAINST THE MORNING LIGHT.

Starch—not the bamboo sheets of my apartment, not the luxurious black silk of Hell—stiff and scratchy cotton was the first sensation that pricked through my skin. My eyes flew open as I realized where I was. I shot up and soaked in the surroundings. The cheap brown-and-beige filigree of the polyester comforter thrust me into the present. I looked around, searching the tiny motel room with adrenaline bypassing any need for coffee.

The first smell to fill my nostrils was something like chlorine and dried urine.

"Morning, Marmar," Az said, voice low enough to respect the early hour. He sat upright, legs outstretched, hands in his lap. He'd crossed his ankles on the remaining twin bed as he'd rested his head against the wall. It looked more like he'd been meditating than sleeping.

"What happened last night?"

"Well," he breathed out, "we're in Bellfield. We're in a god-catcher. Caliban's somewhere in the city. I've spent the night thinking about it. If Silas were betraying him, he wouldn't have told you where to find your Prince, which is the only reason I didn't shake you awake at six to start our hunt. Also, I have a few presents for you. Is there anything human you have to do before we venture out?" His nostrils flared with controlled temper before he added two strained words. "You're safe."

I swallowed at his meaning before I decided that, yes, I did need a few human moments. I showered off the stress of the night. I scrubbed my skin free from the evidence of my roll in the grass and raked my fingers through my hair. When I emerged from the bathroom, I had one word on my lips.

"Presents?"

He smirked, a small piece of whatever agitated him fading as he said, "You and Fauna have more in common than you realize."

He used two fingers to beckon me forward as he led us from the motel room. The morning air was refreshing, which would have been pleasant if it didn't feel like my world was ending. "Even if by some miracle the angel is secretly on our side, there's something wrong with this town. He wouldn't have told us to go quickly if everything was fine."

He considered my words silently. We rounded the hall that wrapped around the building's exterior and descended a set of stairs. He led us into the now-empty lobby and bypassed the desk to where the former night's clerk sat listlessly in the corner. Azrames went directly to the man's closet and gestured.

"Choose a sweatshirt. We need to cover up that tattoo of yours. Until we know who made the town's trap, we can't risk eyes on you. And with a demonic sigil..."

My gaze shot between the closet and the glazed eyes of the man who rested in the corner. If his chest didn't rise and fall with signs of life, I'd have sworn I was staring at a slack-jawed corpse. I couldn't keep the concern from creeping into my expression.

He smirked. "Oh, give me some credit," he said. "Go ahead, call the motel."

I blinked in confusion. He pointed to a small, greenish, seventies-era landline with a tightly coiled cord that had to have been sitting beside the man's bed for decades. I looked at him with confusion.

"It's zero. Press the button."

I wasn't sure what was more disconcerting—his casual energy or the bizarre instructions. I crossed obediently, wrapping my right hand around the phone and lifting it to my ears. The consistent note of the dial tone blasted my eardrums until I hit zero. The second the phone in the lobby began to ring, the clerk jumped to attention and walked swiftly to his station. Though only a few feet away, he answered with total oblivion.

"Bellfield Inn," he said politely. "How can I help you?"

Azrames nodded expectantly.

"Um." I swallowed, eyes going between the back of the man's head and Azrames. Though only feet away, the clerk acted as though I'd never existed. Unsure of what to say, I kept the conversation as normal as possible. "I'm in room 305. I just wanted to ask for maid service to be suspended today? So I can rest?"

"Absolutely, ma'am," he said. "No one will bother you. Is there anything else I can help you with?"

I shook my head, still looking at Azrames. If I wasn't mistaken, his gray-black eyes flickered with shades of red and hellfire. I didn't look away from Az as I responded, "No, that's everything."

"Have a pleasant day, and please let me know if there's anything I can do," he said before the line disconnected. The moment he hung up, the clerk returned to his chair in the corner to resume his blank, listless stare.

I returned the phone to its receiver. I mainlined adrenaline, cortisol shooting straight to my heart as I stared at the demon. He leaned against the wall with perfect, unmoving gravity.

"What the hell did you do?" I whispered.

"I won't tell you that you're welcome, because you're responsible for neither knowledge nor gratitude for the removals of evils of the world, but I do serve a very specific purpose in the mortal realm. I'm glad I was with you last night." He closed his eyes slowly as if the thought pained him. "I wish I could be everywhere, for everyone. I'm not omniscient. Betty helps me find those who deserve it, but..." He shook his head as if clearing it of cobwebs. "Now, find something to cover that arm. Let's go."

I sucked in a shocked breath, but it wasn't one of disapproval.

I wasn't aghast at the vileness of the world.

I wasn't startled, or even disappointed, that a gross, gaunt man in the dead of the night had filled my room with cameras and undoubtedly observed countless women without their knowledge or consent. I was dismayed, of course, but not for the reason one might think.

I was upset for every moment that I'd existed before knowing Azrames.

I understood his quiet frustration as his words had drifted off. The look on his face was one of a man who would do his job without pay—not for the luxury apartment, the beautiful vehicle, the soft sheets, or the sugary cookies that he doubtlessly had to replace every week just to ensure they were never stale.

If I could go back in time, I'd grab every escort I'd known by the shoulders and beg her to wear the same sigil that dangled from Azrames's lowermost chain. He was the dark angel who lurked in the shadows. He was the one I wanted when my back was against a wall.

"Az?"

He raised an eyebrow from where he leaned near the closet but said nothing.

"If we had made a deal...one where you said you wouldn't do anything I didn't explicitly ask for..."

His shoulders slumped slightly. He removed a hand from his pocket and gestured to the man. "I know what you're asking. I couldn't have done any of this. This was your life, and your night. If we'd made a deal? Then, if you hadn't explicitly asked for me to handle him, I wouldn't have been able to act of my own accord. You would have had to tell me to destroy the cameras, to go from room to room throughout the motel to ensure every woman was safe, to erase decades of footage so that anyone who looks at it sees only static, to infiltrate the wiring of his brain..."

My eyes nearly popped out of my skull. "You did all that?"

"Free will isn't always a two-way street," he breathed. "But when I have it..."

I wondered if he could hear the way my heart thundered in my ears as I weighed his words. Fauna was right about several things. Above all: I was an idiot.

His lips pressed into a thin line before he said, "Don't make deals unless you want them honored, Marlow. And then when someone adheres to the parameters of your agreement, understand that it's something you asked for. Now, are you going to choose clothes, or do I need to do it for you?"

I didn't want to fight him on the issue. I didn't have the energy to learn more about binding verbal contracts. Instead, I grabbed the closest long-sleeve plaid shirt and shrugged into it. I rolled it up to the middle of my forearms, ensuring my tattoo was covered, and left it unbuttoned for the late summer warmth. I looked to the clerk once more but knew without having to ask that he would never be a problem again.

Whatever gratitude I'd felt was being replaced by my rising tide of anxiety that we hadn't made any strides toward finding Caliban. We got to the lobby before I asked Azrames to explain our plan.

He shoved his hands into his pockets before saying, "If the town is a seal, then someone's responsible for its existence. I suspect it's tied to the orchard Silas mentioned, but we can't go in half-cocked. If we want to figure out what's going on? I recommend our first stop be to the lake."

"To the merman?"

"To the god."

328

Perhaps if the clerk hadn't deserved the living death he'd been issued, I would have felt bad for our theft. We'd robbed him clean, taking all of the alcohol, the glass, the honey, the cash, and the fruit we could find. Azrames wiped off a silver platter and smiled when he realized it was genuine. He handed it to me to add to my tote—another stolen item. I grabbed the clerk's car keys from his bedside table and cast him a long, cautious look as a single stream of drool ran down his face.

I almost wanted to ask Az what else he'd learned about the clerk.

Almost.

Instead, I shuddered in disgust as we left the motel, slamming the doors on his chipped compact car from the mid-nineties. The smell of the soiled fast-food wrappers that covered the floorboards permeated the air. I gagged as I rolled down the windows. With a sympathetic flex of his fingers, Azrames's scent of smoke filled the vehicle in a welcome, overpowering relief. I shot him a grateful look as we pointed the borrowed car toward the lake.

Terrible clerk aside, the town was stunning.

Every home, every shop, every building hummed with an old-world picturesque charm, as if plucked from time and perfectly preserved. The windows all seemed too clean. The people were too smiley. The grass, the bushes, the trees were all so green that they'd be more believable as transplants from a movie set. Under normal circumstances, I would have been thrilled at the chance to stroll through a small, idyllic town. Instead, seeing the emerald, grassy hills that prevented any straight shot between the motel and the park at the heart of the city filled me with dread.

The bright-green hills crawled lazily throughout the little city, and shops, roads, and bridges had been built to accommodate the unbroken shapes. Because I knew how the sigil looked from the top down, everything about them went from quaint and unique to ominous. The snake-like knoll stayed to my right as I followed the road to the lake. The frown rippled from me as I drew nearer to the sparkling, man-made body surrounded by perfectly manicured trees and lush, vibrant gardens of grasses and flowers. Thomas Kinkade couldn't have painted a more unnaturally radiant lake if he'd tried.

Its banks were too round. The water was too blue. The draping willows that tufted gently in the perfect weather were too storybook. I unbuckled my seatbelt and grimaced at the heavenly park, hating it with every fiber of my being.

"Bellfield is the worst place in the world," I said to Azrames.

He chuckled. "I think the residents of this little slice of heaven would disagree."

I narrowed my eyes as I stared at the glittering water through the filthy windshield. "Isn't Heaven your enemy?"

"Yup."

Even with the smoke and the fresh air streaming in through the windows, my stomach roiled against the nausea of a night with little sleep, a morning without coffee, and a world where women had to sleep mere feet away from terrible men. The clock read just after nine in the morning when we pulled into a parking lot.

Not caring if someone stole our only means of transportation, I left the windows of the vehicle down. I wholly understood the side-eye from passersby as they caught a glimpse of the garbage that filled my vehicle and didn't possess the sass to snap at them. I was glad Azrames had made me cover up the tattoo, given the number of classist stares I was already drawing because of my outfit and the vehicle.

"Okay," Az said, clapping his hands together as he took several steps away from the car. "Time to find a piece of the lake without pedestrians. Mortals will be no more able to see him than they are to see me. I'm most concerned with you looking crazy and having the authorities called on the raving lunatic in the park, so do your best not to talk to me when anyone's looking. I think if we aim for those trees"—he gestured to the far side of the lake—"we should be fine to make our offering and see if Dagon really is in these waters."

The park-goers in their athletic apparel thinned as we rounded the lake, and I realized I had no idea what day of the week it was. It didn't have Saturday energy, for which I was grateful. It seemed as though the overly ambitious members of society had jobs to get to and lives to live, leaving Azrames and me with the park more or less to ourselves. By the time we reached the far side of the lake, I watched the final car pull out of the parking lot. Maybe they were fleeing my presence.

Azrames wasn't overly chatty, which made me miss Fauna. He seemed to talk only when he could improve upon the silence, whereas I was confident she would have been chirping like a warbler at dawn. I nearly asked him how the two of them had found one another, just for something to talk about, when the seriousness of our situation pressed on me again.

My understanding of the world had changed so wholly after decades of telling myself I was crazy that I'd found it easy to bob in and out of states of lucidity. Sometimes, I completely forgot that the handsome demon in shades of iron, smoke, and ash, with small black horns poking up through mussed, black hair, was someone—or something—that I'd written off as fiction before the day Silas intervened in my apartment and made Richard choke on his own tongue. Prior to that, I'd spent years telling myself that Caliban...

"How do we find Caliban?" I asked quietly.

He nodded. "That's our top priority. If Silas was telling the truth, then the Prince must be here. Like me, Caliban won't be able to leave or move within the seal, save for on foot. Dagon might be able to tell us who created the seal in the first place."

"And this mer god—Dagon—is your ally? I know Heaven and the Phoenicians are at odds."

Azrames twisted his mouth to the side. "It isn't that simple. We have a healthy respect for each other. But realms don't really do...allegiances. Not like that."

We left the smooth asphalt path and crossed the grass toward the water's edge. Part of me felt like I'd prefer the uncomfortable odors of piss and stale smoke to the curated perfection of floral blossoms, the magnificently green leaves that brushed against one another as if to sing a charming greeting, and the grass so soft that it might as well have been carpet. Everything about the park set off an indescribable alarm bell within me.

Before now, I would have told myself I was paranoid... but I thought of the dread that had descended over me the moment I'd broken into Richard's house, and an idea pricked me. I wondered how much I was able to sense of an otherworldly presence given the diluted fae blood sparkling in my veins. Perhaps my irrational intuition was just what Fauna had spent weeks calling clairsentience. I was too distracted by the bright-blue water, the expensive scent of exotic flowers, and the warmth of the cheery, blue day to catch the underlying implication of Az's words.

I stopped at the water's edge, looking at him as I realized something with horror. "What if Caliban isn't here at all? What if Silas was just lying to get you trapped here?"

Azrames didn't look concerned. "If that's the case, we'll get you that shovel. Besides, I'm not important enough to trap."

"I beg to differ."

I looked beyond the lake to the hill and balked at the sheer size of it. This would not be a few hours of digging through a hedge. This would be a month of unbroken excavation. Not only would I have to dig longer, farther, and deeper than I could have possibly fathomed, but I'd need to find a place in the town where I wouldn't be jailed for a very perplexing crime of vandalism. I wondered what stories residents told themselves about the emerald bluffs, or what the police thought of the interesting landscaping that carved through their little city. I couldn't imagine any excuse making sense once they found me elbow deep in a mountain of destroyed property.

He sat down on the edge of the lake but didn't touch the water.

"All right," he said. "Make your little altar."

I didn't have to be a practitioner to understand what he meant. I'd done enough and seen enough to understand the rough configuration of my offering. In addition to the food, crystal decanter of liquor, and the roll of bills, I arranged a few candles and procured a matchbook with *Bellfield Inn* emblazoned on the side.

"I don't know what a merman is gonna need cash for," I mumbled as I lit the candles.

"It's not about the money; it's about the sacrifice. And please, for the love of the gods: if Dagon shows up, don't call him a merman."

I didn't want to snap back at Azrames that I wasn't stupid, because the truth is, I was. However, I was an idiot with a literature degree and an international reputation for fictional works in mythology. Perhaps I didn't know anything about the ancient Canaanite religion of what would be modern-day Lebanon, but I understood that gods weren't djinn. I wasn't summoning a lake genie to grant a wish; I was compiling an offering of gratitude to thank him for intercession on my behalf. In this instance, hopefully Dagon and I would share a common goal.

The candles burned, and we waited.

And waited.

And waited.

"Az, what if—"

He lifted a finger to his lips to shush me, then pointed to the clouds. Just on the edge of the horizon, the calm sky broke into cumulonimbus towers. The enormous clouds moved forward on a gust of wind, blowing out what little remained of the candles. I lurched to grab the offerings, but Azrames snatched my wrist to stop me before I touched the items, allowing the fruits and bundle of cash to blow into the water. I looked to him with growing concern as the clouds crawled through the air with incredible speed, snuffing out the midmorning sunlight to a day so dark it might have been dusk.

Wind whipped across the lake, stirring up tiny whitecaps. As the air turned harbor-gray with the churning weather, the waters dropped into a menacing shade of charcoal. For the first time, I smelled fish and seaweed and the silty soil of lake bottoms rather than the manicured gardens. I squinted as the wind whipped my hair into my eyes, wincing as the world abandoned logic and reason for the sort of meteorological anomaly that one could only describe as an act of God.

Don't be scared, you coward, I begged myself. *Azrames isn't afraid, and he's sitting right next to you. You're fine, you're fine.*

But it was a lie. Chills raced across my back, my arms, my neck, pebbling every inch of my flesh with fear and adrenaline. My mouth dried out as the water began to ripple, stirring from the center of the lake. I was one crack of lightning away from wetting my pants. I jolted halfway to my feet at the shock of movement as a thick, white mist crept in on either side, but once again, I was yanked to the ground and urged to remain still. Azrames kept a tight hand around my forearm this time.

"Be reverent," he hissed.

Reverent. Right. I nodded, swallowing. I'd spent years on my knees in church. I knew how to prostrate myself before a god. Only, my god had never answered my crystal decanter of liquor with mist and thunder. My heart raced as the fog thickened until I could barely see Azrames.

Then just as soon as it began, the wind died, giving way to utter silence. The thunderheads, the mist, the tangible feelings of dread remained.

I heard it then. At first it sounded like a fish jumping out of water. The sloshing noises of steps filled the air, and then, we were not alone.

Chapter Thirty-One

D AGON.

My heart stopped at the sight of the man beside me.

I forgot to breathe as I looked at him through the mist. From the straight, black beard to the rainbow scales of his robe, I knew beyond the shadow of a doubt that this deeply ancient deity took no pleasure in modernity. He would not be the TV-watching, candy-eating goblin who waited in my living room, nor the demon with a luxury sports car.

He was history and culture and language. He was the Epic of Gilgamesh, the sands of time, the tectonic plates shifting as Pangea broke apart. He was deeply and terrifyingly eternal.

He stood in front of us, feet planted in the lake. He did not possess the fishtail of a merman but thick, muscled legs. I understood the storm and mist the moment I looked at him. Even if someone else had possessed my sigil or the ability to pierce the veil, they couldn't have seen through the impenetrable curtain of fog that concealed him.

Azrames rolled from his sitting position onto a kneel. He didn't bow his head but dipped his chin once in respectful acknowledgment as he propped his elbow against his knee. "Dagon, Your Excellence, I'm Azrames of Hell. I think I speak on behalf of all of us when I apologize for your hands."

I was still in the process of copying Az's posture, steading myself on one knee, when my eyes shot to the fish lord in the lake. Each wrist bore a thick, terrible scar, as if his hands had once been severed.

At long last, he returned the acknowledging dip. With a terrifying and unfamiliar accent that screamed of his agelessness among eternity, he responded, "The enemy of my enemy is my friend."

I waited for Azrames to have me speak, but he did not.

"How long have you been kept here?" he asked.

Dagon's eyes sharpened with vitriol as he asked the present year. "Hmm," he said slowly. "Two hundred and fifty-two years they've kept me here. She could have had it all without me, but if your civilizations crumble, and your temples fall to ruins…if your people forget your name and you're unwilling to return to your realm…if you demand a kingdom of your own in a world that has forgotten us, what better way to do it than to capture a god?"

"Who, Your Excellence?"

He looked over his shoulder, through the mist and into the inky waters, bitterness seeping into his words as he said, "If humanity would no longer do her will, if they ceased to build her altars and offer her sacrifices and speak her name, then to become a god's god…that was her evolution. To contain a god who would yield the most excellent crops, who would make her kingdom flourish, who would bless its very soil, so long as I remained fed. She didn't want my son here. He'd step on her toes, and that would not do. Not for one seeking to be on top."

Beside me, Azrames's mouth dropped open. "So, this seal, this trap, are you saying it was made by…?"

"America…" He tasted the word as if it were sour on his tongue, upper lip pulling in a sneer. "Of all of the places to summon me, it had to be where the people are so divorced from the old ways, so lost to history and culture and creation that they'd never suspect…"

"And Baal—" Azrames prompted.

336

With cold calculation, Dagon said, "Why would she desire his presence in her kingdom if their powers are one in the same? She would spend no more time in the shadows. Furthermore, why would he enter to save me when he knows she would not let him leave?"

"Who?" I whispered at long last.

Dagon turned to me as if noticing me for the first time. He stared at me—*into* me—before a slow smile began to tug at his lips. "You're exactly her type," he said with chilling slowness, each word penetrating me like a bullet.

"You're not the only one trapped here, Your Majesty," I said quietly, doing my best to sound respectful as my mind went to Caliban. "There are others here from other realms. Anyone who enters..."

"Including her," Dagon said, cutting me short.

Azrames's eyebrows went up. "She's caught in her own seal?"

"The traps we lay for ourselves are the most difficult to escape."

"*Who?*" I asked again, rallying as much authority as I could muster.

His dark eyes returned to me. Dagon began to sink into the lake with glacial slowness as he said, "She is the one who conceives but does not bear. She was the Most High, and it's the title she'll retain, no matter the cost." The water lapped around his knees, then his waist as the wind picked up once more, drowning his words. The rainbow scales of his robe were scarcely visible through the fog as he spoke. "Her sacred tradition is to prostitute in her temple; the selling of sex is more delicious to her than the gifting of souls. Find her in Venus."

Dagon disappeared, but the heavy, soaking mist remained. My hair felt damp against my face. I tugged at the plaid shirt to button up against the immodesty of my wet shirt. The lake quieted as all traces of the god, including our small offerings to him, disappeared entirely.

Azrames stood and held out his hand.

"Who the fuck are we going to find?"

"Astarte" came his worlds-weary sigh. "The goddess of sex, love, and war."

✦

I would have felt guilty that the storm had whipped the fast-food wrappers from the car and littered the streets, except that, seeing that the town was evil, I thought it probably deserved far worse.

"You didn't even ask about Caliban!" My temper flared as I slammed the car door.

"The Prince can't be tracked. If we're meant to get to him before others know he's here, then our first task should be finding out what's going on. We can't unravel a web we don't understand."

I jammed the key into the ignition. The engine coughed and sputtered to life. I wanted to fight Azrames on his rationale, but as agitated as I was, I believed he knew best when it came to speaking to ancient, powerful mermen. I eased the car out of the parking lot and plucked the first question that came to mind.

"What were you saying back there? About his hands?"

Az chuckled darkly. "He and the King of Heaven got into an altercation in about five hundred BCE over the Ark of the Covenant. It's in your book of Judges if you want to become a biblical scholar later."

"Isn't that funny?" I asked, not waiting for an answer. "Mister No Other Gods Before Me talks about other gods in his own book all the time, and the modern church thinks it's all witchcraft and nonsense and gibberish. There's only one god. Everything else is demons or make-believe."

"See, I knew you were familiar with your Bible."

"It's not my Bible."

"Sorry. No intentions of offending. I just know you weren't raised on The Agamas or The Vedas."

338

"What about the Satanic Bible?" I asked.

He laughed. "I'm confident you weren't raised on that either."

"No." I rolled my eyes as I guided the beat-up car through the winding streets, resisting the urge to ram it headlong into a stupid green hill. "Is it accurate? Like a good way to...talk to Hell?"

He quirked an eyebrow. "The Satanic Bible is more philosophical than religious. It's mostly about loving nature and Epicureanism, or being a stabilizing force in your own life. It didn't show up until sixty-nine, so, take that as you will. Plus, our king isn't as interested in dogma."

"So, if I want to learn about Hell...?"

He shrugged. "Then just ask."

We pointed the car back to the hotel and idly chatted about our intentions to eat the rest of the clerk's food and use his computer once we arrived. Since I still had no phone and Azrames had his hands magically tied, we need to figure out what the fuck Dagon had meant when he'd told us to find Venus.

If he was going to continue to disregard my calls for a manhunt to track down Caliban outright, I had a few begrudging alternatives. I suggested we go to a planetarium, followed quickly by a suggestion to drop acid. Azrames found the first suggestion useless but was more open to my second one, though not for the purposes of the mission.

"What if we just bypass Astarte altogether and I rent an excavator?" I rambled on about what I thought was a rather brilliant plan as I pulled into the parking lot. "How hard can it be to operate heavy machinery? Gimme ten seconds to break the seal, and then zap me out of here once it's done so I don't get arrested. I just drive the yellow dinosaur to the knoll and—"

My thought died, the rest of my sentence catching in my throat.

Azrames saw it too.

It was him.

The world stopped spinning, my vision vignetting as I saw only the lightning strike of silver fire leaning against the chipping pillar in front of the motel.

I hadn't found him.

He'd found me.

When Darius had proposed to Nia, she'd claimed she'd turned to see him down on one knee and had blacked out until the ring was on her finger. Lisbeth had once said that mothers forgot the pain of childbirth entirely, remembering only the joy once the bundle was in their arms. I'd heard similar stories where events were so shocking, so wonderful, so life-changing that they short-circuited the brain until it turned off completely. I supposed that that was what had happened to me, and I could only be grateful that my heart remembered to beat, my lungs remembered to breathe, my blood remembered to flow—at least, I hope it did.

I didn't remember throwing the car in park, though I must have. I didn't recall grabbing the keys, or Azrames's comment about disappearing, though he probably said something to the effect. I operated on autopilot out as my feet flew across the pavement, ears ringing, tears spiking my eyes until I crashed into his chest. Strong arms wrapped around me. Moss and rain and gin were as powerful as safety and longing and sorrow. My knees buckled beneath me as I began to cry, but he had me.

I had no idea how he knew which room was mine.

I had no recollection of going up the stairs or of the door opening.

I didn't remember anything until my back was pressed against the wall, cool hands raking through my hair and fingers brushing away my tears as Caliban said, "I am yours, and you are mine. And whether it's in this life or the next, we will always find each other."

340

✦

Chapter Thirty-Two

I 'D NEVER WANTED ANYTHING SO BADLY IN MY LIFE.
My body was hot and cold all at once. My fingers tore
at him, digging into him as if, perhaps if I could burrow
into him, he'd be unable to leave. He caught me, scooping
his hands under my ass just as I hopped up to wrap my legs
around his waist, kissing and tasting and touching any part
of him my mouth could find. I moaned as he growled the
name he'd called me from my first memory against my throat,
arousal rushing through me like a flash flood as years of the
longing I'd denied myself crashed over me.

He wasn't just real.

I was his, and he was mine.

I wrapped my legs tighter as he slammed me into the wall
with a demand, a claim, a desperation that I'd needed more
than water, more than life. I gasped between pleasure and
pain as the world spun. He moved me to the bed, yanking me
up with strong arms so my head crashed against the pillows,
propped up like the princess he'd always wanted me to be. I
scrambled for his shirt, craving his skin, his tongue, his cock,
but he gathered my wrists into a single large hand and pinned
them above me.

"I've missed you more than air," he breathed, words
moving between our lips and tongues.

I hooked my legs around him once more, and his low, appreciative chuckle did more to me than I could ever understand.

"How did you find me?"

"Love." He said it like a prayer. "I always know where you are. Imagine my surprise when I felt you step into my kingdom without me. And then to feel you so close…"

"I'm so sorry, I—" I began, the apology pouring out of me as I dug my fingers into him. I'd been crawling out of my skin for months. Knowing that he was real, Caliban was an addiction for which I wanted no cure. Desperation seeped from me. He released my hands as they shot to his face, to his hair, apology filling my eyes. "What I said, what I did, I had no idea, I would never have—"

"Shh." He rolled his mouth toward the hand that I'd left against his cheek and pressed a kiss into my palm. "Why are you blaming yourself for what you didn't know?"

Even his kindness was sending me into a tailspin. I was so overcome with waves of conflicting emotions that I didn't know what to do or how to feel. I didn't want every memory he had of me to be me crying. I exhaled slowly as I asked, "Was I this stupid in all of my lives?"

He relaxed his body into mine, and I felt so secure beneath the pressure of his weight. He wrapped an arm around me as he said, "You're brilliant. You're as quick and clever in this life as you've been in all of them."

"Fauna would disagree," I murmured.

He smiled softly. "If I had to guess, I'd say you've found a Norde."

I realized with a sharp stab that, though I'd been living and working with Fauna and Azrames, spending every waking second talking about Caliban, he hadn't heard a word about them. I distinctly recalled Azrames saying he'd never met Hell's Prince, as he wasn't important enough to run in such circles. I wondered what Caliban would think about me having a demon as one of my most trusted friends.

"So much has happened," I said, intensity cooling as I memorized his features. His eyes burned with the incomprehensible silver of starlight. His hair was the same white as the fox that had kept me from shattering, my friend and guardian when I'd had nothing and no one. His chest was broad enough that I could disappear into it as he held me, lost in the mossy scent of the forest.

He asked me to tell him about it, and so I did.

His fingers continued to work through my hair, grazing gently against my scalp and moving my strands around with slow, methodical motions. He didn't stop touching me as I explained the witches I'd called or the sigil I'd found above my door. He drew a thumb around the black ink that contrasted against the skin of my forearm while I spoke of the parasite and my second encounter with Silas. He stiffened ever so slightly when I explained how Silas had offered the bond, and then he relaxed once more when my story turned to Fauna.

He traced relaxing patterns along my back while I told him of Betty and Azrames and hearing about the cycle of mortal lives. He cupped the back of my head when my conversation drifted to my mother and her cruelty and then bunched in my hair with a smile when I told him of my time in Hell. His teeth glistened with true joy at the way I described his father.

"He's loved you for more than two thousand years," Caliban said. "You're his daughter-in-waiting in his eyes."

"That's a long time to wait," I whispered. A switch within me flipped at thoughts of his father. "Caliban…you risked his life. You risked your kingdom. Your people. The *war*. The end times."

His laugh was short and breathy. "If you wouldn't burn the world to the ground for the one you love, are you even in love?"

"You should have let me die," I said quietly. "Fauna said that if Heaven wins, every pantheon will fall. Heaven and his angels will reign on earth. Eight billion humans enslaved while calling it worship. I'm not worth the goddamn apocalypse."

"I can promise you: you are." He pressed another kiss into my hair, tucking me against him even more tightly as he said, "I'd wait two thousand more, you know."

I wormed away just enough to look up at him as I said, "I won't."

He arched a cautious brow.

"Bond with me," I said, voice breathless.

His smile faltered. "Oh, Love."

"I end the loop then, right? Isn't that what everyone's been trying to explain? If we bond, I won't be born again as a human. I can stay with you. We can—"

"We're already bonded. What we have is more than the formality of realms," he said quietly. "You don't need to hook your soul to mine."

"I want to," I pressed, and I meant it. Maybe I'd spent my life insisting that he was a perfect figment of my imagination, that I'd created a best friend, a guardian, a lover, a beautiful puzzle piece for the hole within me. Maybe I hadn't known about realms or kingdoms or fae for long, but I'd known Caliban since my very first memory. I'd known of him and his goodness since the day I stood with soap running around my sneakers and a sponge in my hand. And after Fauna's words…

He exhaled, ferns and mist on his breath. "Even if we were to finalize the bond, it can't be now, Marlow. You know where we are? What this town is?"

My cheek rubbed against the impossible soft fabric of his thin black tee as I nodded. "It's why I'm here. Why Az and I—" I looked over my shoulder as if Azrames would be in the corner. "We're going to get you out. I'm going to get you out."

"Once you're bound, you won't be able to leave. It's a—"

"God catcher," I finished quietly. "Have you met her? Astarte? We were supposed to go find Venus, whatever that means. I was ready to knock on every door in Bellfield to find you, but apparently, this goddess and some random planet were the key to figuring out what the fuck is going on."

He made a short, frustrated sound.

"I've found her," he said, "and Venus was a way to hide in plain sight. I've kept a low profile while I plan my next steps. She'll know something is amiss after today's display with the weather. I expect she'll be on alert. She's kept Dagon here for hundreds of years, and I know there are others. I can smell them." He inhaled my hair, and I wondered if he was breathing in the distant salt and pine from the splash of fae within my blood. "I don't know whether they stumbled in on accident, or how they've come to be, but this city is a spider web. No one from any of the realms can come to save us."

Anger lanced through me. I pushed myself out of his arms and into a sitting position. "How could Silas do this to you? Does he hate you that much?"

Caliban moved into a sitting position, facing me as he smirked. "I think you might be surprised at the answer."

My muscles tensed as I waited.

"I could be wrong, but I think he sent me here specifically *because* no one else could come for me. No angel or deity is going to intervene here. I don't know what he's up to, but...many of us were angels once. We're brothers of the same kingdom cleaved in two."

I swallowed. "Are you implying that he...?"

He shook his head. "I wouldn't stake my life on him defecting, but even if the best we get out of him is that he doesn't agree with the war? Then we've made a powerful ally."

A new, fresh anger surged through me as I balled my fingers into a fist and hit him as hard as I could in the arm. First surprise, then delight shone through him. I got up from the bed as I glared.

"We haven't fought in *lifetimes*." His eyes sparkled, far too amused by the rage that filled me. He swung his legs over the side of the bed as he eyed me.

I was ready to fight. "What the fuck is a tier-five favor? Why would you do that! You didn't know who would respond! You didn't know what they could call in! You didn't—"

"Love—"

"No! It wasn't just your kingdom or your people. *You* could have died! I could have lost you!" I cried out and swung for him again. He caught my fist this time, so I switched arms and tried to hit him with my other hand. He was on his feet in a flash, snatching it just as easily before it made contact. I spun to break his hold, but it backfired terribly. He twisted with me until my back was pinned to his chest, arms pressed to my sternum.

"We really should have been working on your self-defense," he murmured in my ear.

"I'm mad at you!" I said while trying to drive my elbow into him. Unable to so much as see my target, I failed once more and he tightened his hold, running his teeth along my neck from behind me. "Don't be sexy! I'm angry!"

"Can I help it if your rage is a turn-on?" came the vibrations against the back of my ear.

"Fuck, Caliban." It came out in a gasp strangled between lust and fury. He tightened his arms and bit down on the soft spot where my neck met my shoulder until my growl gave way to a gasp. My body was a traitor. "Wanting you doesn't make me any less enraged," I said, but my hips rolled as if to contradict my words.

He only needed one arm to keep me pinned to his chest while the other ran idly down to my hips, forcing me against him so I could feel the precise effect the fight had had on him as it pressed into me.

"I need a few things from you," he said in my ear.

I swallowed and closed my eyes, leaning into his voice.

"First, I need you to set me free from the limitations you've put on me in your life. You've roped me into the smallest of corners, and I respect you, Love, but I'm not one for a cage."

My breathing came in ragged pulls, wanting his hand to go farther, to touch me, to cup and stroke and enter me. I nodded.

"I'm afraid you're going to have to be the one to say it, Love."

"What do I say?" I repeated, lightheaded as I scarcely remembered to sip the air.

He tsked. "If I feed you the words, it defeats the purpose of free will."

"Do it," I said, voice so airy I wasn't sure if he could hear me at all. My head swam in memory, in hope, in past and present and future. We weren't in Bellfield, or in a hotel, or Heaven or Hell or the mortal realm. We weren't anywhere. We existed between place and time that had been created just for us.

"Do what?" Caliban asked, crushing me to him.

"Anything. Everything. It's all yours. I'm yours."

Chapter Thirty-Three

I CAN ONLY ASSUME AZRAMES MEANT TO MAKE A BETTER FIRST impression on the Prince of Hell, but the moment he saw my face, he burst out in a laugh so cruel that I wanted to punch him. I had the worst case of blue tubes in the history of womankind, and I was ready to make it everyone else's problem. "*Now is not the time to fuck, Marlow*" and "*We have a goddess to defeat and a sigil to break*" and "*Stop trying to stroke my dick or I'm going to make you pay for it later*" were followed by "*Now I'm going to make you pay for it much later and add a new day of deprivation every time you're difficult.*"

I'd stomped like a brat from the hotel room to the lobby, which I knew Caliban found infuriatingly charming. I could feel his grin all the way behind me as I blazed an angry, sex-denied trail to where my partner in crime undoubtedly waited. Azrames was on the computer when I walked in. He jumped to his feet and choked on his laugh, doing his best to swallow down the particularly rude brand of humor he saw in my pain. Despite his best efforts, I could still see it brimming in his eyes like tears as I glowered.

I threw an angry, introductory hand between them.

"Az, meet the Prince of Hell. I call him Caliban, but I'm thinking of changing his name to Cocktease. Caliban, this is Azrames. He's the Patron Saint of Women, or something."

Azrames cleared his throat and made a tense bow. "Correction: I *work* with the Patron Saint of Women. She's called Betty in this cycle. I can't take credit for her work."

Even under the ugly, flickering lights, both men could have been gods on the runway. Az's skin should have been greenish in the light, but alas, I doubted the man ever had so much as a bad hair day. And Caliban…well, I was still pretty frustrated over how badly I wanted him to rip off my clothes. Looking at him now, chiseled from starlight itself, I had trouble staying mad. Still, there was work to be done, though being sandwiched between two of Hell's finest made focusing a challenge.

If the men saw the drool dripping from my lower lip, they pretended not to notice.

Caliban's brow lifted. He tasted the name. "Azrames… Did you go by Farefax in the first century? I want to say it was until…"

Az's face lit. "Ten sixty AD! Yes!"

I folded my arms over my chest. "Have you two met?"

Azrames looked like he'd met a celebrity. His glow was almost sweet enough to distract me. Almost.

"No, no. I was still going by Farefax when I met Fauna in the Viking Age."

Pride glinted off of Caliban's smile. "You were well known and deeply valued. I was wondering why I hadn't heard anything." He extended a hand.

Az's eyes widened.

Caliban fought an obvious smirk at Azrames's reluctance to take his hand. After a comical pause, the men shook.

"I already liked you, Farefax, but now that I know you've been taking care of Marlow and know her Norde—"

"*Know*," I snorted. "Oh, sorry. He *knows* her in the biblical sense." I giggled at my own joke as I looked between the demons. "Anyway, they're star-crossed lovers. I'm not totally sure what Fauna is to me, other than my sugar-addled bully of a Nordic nymph, but apparently Hell and the Nordes have excellent…relations."

Caliban's smile remained as he released Azrames's hand. "Hell has good relations with all realms but one. We're either lauded as partners or politely ignored, which is how we like it." He jutted a thumb to the catatonic clerk staring blankly at the wall over our shoulders. The man hadn't so much as blinked since we'd entered. "That your handiwork?"

Azrames dipped his chin. "Indeed, it is."

Caliban clapped him on the shoulder once. "Then I know he deserved it." He frowned, then slipped his arm around my waist as if to comfort himself. It seemed to work, if only slightly. "This isn't how I imagined the day Love finally wanted to end her mortal cycle, but alas, here we are, and we have a lot of day ahead of us. Shall we stick around this little haven? Or do you want to meet the Phoenician goddess standing between us and a good time?"

It was my turn to frown. "Could you two do what Fauna does? Step into mortal bodies?"

They exchanged looks. Azrames shook his head. "I can't speak for the Prince, but I don't have that ability. I'm strictly behind the veil, as you'd say—between your sigil and fae blood, you're the exception, Marmar, not the rule. Nymphs and the like are known for the corporeal forms. Fauna's lucky that way."

Caliban nodded slowly. "I can, but I don't think it's a good idea. I...stand out. Right now, we're trying to evade the public eye."

"Won't the goddess be able to see you?" I asked.

"Undoubtedly. But I've kept a low profile so far, and we don't need the entire town buzzing about it before we get there."

As I was the only human visible to the public eye, I would, of course, be driving. I escorted us to our beat-up chariot. Caliban opened my door whether or not the world around us noticed, which made me bite my lip.

He was real, he was real, he was *real*.

I would never get sick of those three words.

He leaned across my lap and buckled my seatbelt for me before closing the door, and I knew it had little to do with my safety. I couldn't speak for my other lifetimes, but I'd never let him interact with me outside of the darkened shadows of my dream-like states in this age. I'd never given him free rein over me. He was making up for lost time. He wanted to touch me every bit as badly as I wanted to touch him.

Azrames, to his credit, was the sort of person—demon, entity, fae—who could be comfortable in any situation. Normally, in such close proximity, I'd be able to smell his smoke. Instead, there was only the fresh perfume of the forest. Az slid into the back while Caliban took the passenger's seat, relaxing his hand behind my headrest as I pulled out of the motel and pointed the compact car toward downtown.

Once again, I found myself disturbed by Bellfield's too-perfect charm. I glared at each grassy hill as if it were my personal enemy, blaming every uniform blade of grass for what it had done to Caliban—and simultaneously faulting it for the reason I couldn't get laid. I couldn't fathom what stories the residents told one another as to why their city had the most bizarre landscaping in North America. Maybe they thought it was quirky to live in a blessed, lush small town with perfect weather and a cornucopia of produce every season. Perhaps they'd grown attached to their little dots and lines and bumps.

I frowned as I drove, listening to Caliban's cool delivery of driving instructions with one part of my brain while contemplating the seal with the other.

While it had taken a minute to see it on the satellite image, I knew that we lived in a day and age where most people had searched their home from space at one time or another. Airplanes existed throughout the state, even if Bellfield lacked a major airport. I'd been warned about the orchard, but the grain fields had to require agricultural planes. Surely, people had to have seen how peculiar the shapes were from the top down.

"What's on your mind, Love?"

I blinked twice. The first was over my surprise that he'd been able to read my emotions, and the second was that I'd been dense enough to be surprised. He knew me better than anyone, in all forms and shapes and lifetimes.

Without fighting the logic, I exhaled and shook my head. "The residents—the humans, that is—they can't be ignorant to this shape. It's enormous. It's unmissable. And even if it just looks peculiar from the ground-level, it'd be ignorant to assume none of them had seen it from the air. What story have they been told?"

I looked up into the rearview mirror in time to see Az's eyes darken.

Apparently, I'd brought up an excellent point.

We didn't have time to discuss the answer before Caliban gestured toward the sort of driveway that could have existed in a horror movie about a haunted asylum. Except...it wasn't. While the gate was wrought-iron and protected by gargoyles, and though the ostentatious fountains, exorbitant stonework, and manicured lawn hearkened back to old money, the building was entirely modern. Sterile, even.

I was suddenly aware not just of how cheap the car looked but of how poor I looked.

I'd grown up in poverty. I was used to the looks, the sneers, the sniffs as someone told me with their eyes that I wasn't worthy to breathe their air. I'd left that life behind the moment I'd met Taylor and sworn never to return. I should have been pulling up in my Mercedes while wearing clean, bespoke lines. I wished Ianna had dressed me for this place. Instead, I was still in a thin tee, leggings, and the button-up of a filthy motel clerk. His compact car was the icing on the cake. It was the trailer park all over again.

We idled three rows from the entrance and eyed the building.

Wild Prairie Rose: A Venus Clinic.

"It's a hospital?" I asked breathlessly as I stared at the

352

building. It had to be ten stories high and made of steel and glass. It angled out with sharp, modern architecture. Even from the parking lot, I could see the elaborate art within the lobby—the only floor that had not been mirrored for privacy. It wanted to be seen.

"It's a private fertility clinic," Caliban said quietly. "One of the most exclusive in the country."

Venus. I pictured a naked woman, covered only by her impossibly long hair, standing in a clam shell while angels and humans alike tended to her. The second pantheon novel, *Kingdoms of Salt and Sand,* had been a conflation of Greek and Roman mythology. Venus was the goddess of love, beauty, desire, and, of course, fertility.

The breath left me as I remembered Dagon's words. I repeated them quietly. "Astarte. She is called the one who conceives but does not bear."

Caliban nodded gravely. "She's a fertility goddess."

My heart was doing odd things in my chest as I looked into the rearview mirror to see Azrames's pained expression. The Phoenician had an element of violence that her Roman counterpart did not. I looked to my companion for confirmation. "Sex, love, and war, right?"

Caliban squeezed my hand. "I don't know if I can let you go in there."

I stared back into his silver eyes as I remembered the uncomfortable way the fish god had eyed me as he'd told me I was just her type. "Her priestesses were prostitutes," I said, hating the way the word felt on my tongue. We'd barely begun to call it sex work in the modern era. She wouldn't see it any other way.

I threw the car into reverse and left the grounds faster than either of the men could blink. I gritted my teeth as I pushed my foot to the accelerator.

"Love—"

"Mar—"

"If I'm just her type? Then it's time to live up to the role."

I'd spun out of the clinic and torn through the town, Monaco Grand Prix style.

I scrubbed from head to toe in cheap hotel soap, then wrapped myself in a towel, hair still dripping as I used the room's phone.

"Hi, Venus Clinic? Yes, my name is Merit Finnegan. Mhmm. Yes! I'm glad you love the series. Oh, yes, it's always so fun to meet a fan. Mhmm. I've just popped into town and would love to be seen. No, it has to be today. Yes, I understand she's very busy. Would you be a doll and give her my name? Tell her who I am and then see if she still needs me to make an appointment."

I stepped back into my filthy clothes and raked my hair out with my fingers, leaving the phone wedged between my ear and shoulder. Classical music scored my short wait until the receptionist was back on the line.

I used Merit's clout and Maribelle's authority as I said, "Oh, how kind of her to extend office hours. I'll be there at five on the dot. Yes, yes. That's right, South American lore. Oh, thank them for me! That's so sweet. Mhmm. Yes, yes. All right. I'll see you at five."

My escorts asked no questions as I led the charge. The men talked quietly to each other—whispered battle plans on angels and Phoenicians and fertility—but seemed most interested in what I was doing as I marched them from the motel and back to our car, eyes set in determination. We were at the precipice of something terrible, and here I was, leading the charges. They kept curiously quiet as I navigated through the town.

I parked and walked past three shops until selecting one that looked precisely pretentious enough to be monochromatic and overpriced.

The saleswoman may have narrowed her eyes at me when I'd entered the store, but it took one moment of my posture and bored superiority complex for her face to flash with attentiveness. I was a veteran to the game. Excuses were weakness. If I wanted to enter her establishment with wet hair and my tits out, that was her problem. I put her in her place with a look that could drop the temperature in any room. I flicked out my card, holding it nonchalantly between two fingers.

"I need two changes of outfits, a bag, and black heels."

"Price range—"

I sneered as if her question offended me.

"Right away, ma'am."

"And your perfume?"

She gave me a worried look.

"Do you have anything that smells less...cheap?"

I'd appraised the town well. The picturesque qualities reminded me of my findom days in the upper-class resort town of Vail—of meeting wealthy clients on their wealthy ski chalets while their wives and children waited at home. They'd buy me cashmere and order the nicest vintage and I'd play the role required, holding their elbows as we walked from shop to shop, each more exorbitantly priced than the last. The more money I spent, the more important they felt.

This town may not have been surrounded by mountains, but I understood its bones. It was built on prosperity; whether through the blessing of an ancient god or the exclusivity of a wealthy clinic, money flowed through the city. Perhaps Azrames and I had found the only shitty motel in the entire vicinity simply for the long-term rentals of the staff employed by the elite. The Bellfield Inn reminded me more of my childhood than any kid wanted to admit. But even the poor needed a hovel to be shoved into so that the affluent could wander about prosperously.

The jewelry shop gave me the same disgusted look when I entered, which changed to profuse apology when I picked out the first pair of diamond-encrusted pearl of earrings and handed them my black, metal card with no expense limit. Maribelle's expression remained on the razor's edge of dark and bored.

"Shall I wrap them up?"

"I'll wear them out," I said coldly.

The ATM around the corner sucked up my card and spat out my cash advance before returning my precious piece of metal. Fortunately, the blowout bar and makeup artist down the street required neither appointment, nor attitude adjustments. It was the sort of place that played pop music, painted yellow geometric shapes on the wall, and had *Blow Me* in neon pink scrawled across the far wall. They pushed a mimosa into my hand as I took a seat. I assumed the ambience was a pandering way for the well-to-do women of Bellfield to recapture their vitality.

My need to talk down to snobs would never extend to those in the service industry. That's what sex work was, after all, and we had to stick together. I dropped the act while my hair was shampooed, blown out, and curled, chatting away while my face was painted. While I didn't regret buying the overpriced perfume from the saleswoman, the gentle scents of cucumber that had gone into my scalp massage were more my preference. We kept it light, funny, and open as we gabbed about the world. Everything was honest, save for my name and the date of the information. I had them call me Maribelle, and we discussed my life and theirs right up until I left the country for South America. Before that, I was just one of them.

While my stylist gave me the spiel about how long she'd been pressuring her boyfriend for a ring, it made me examine my own nails. I wished I had time for a fresh manicure, but time was of the essence. Fortunately, my existing gel manicure, though a bit grown out, was unchipped and clean.

I caught Caliban's eyes any time I wasn't looking at my stylist. I ate up his look of approval like it was oysters and fois gras and caviar.

He loved every second of it. He leaned against the polished shampooing sink in his short-sleeved shirt of darkest black, crossing his arms and eyeing me with predatory evaluation.

356

He winked at me from where he watched me, devouring me with his gaze from directly across the stylist's chair. If she noticed my prolonged stares into open air, she said nothing. I nearly went into cardiac arrest when he casually approached to run a finger along my forearm, up my bicep, onto my neck. Chills covered my body.

The stylist stopped at my sharp intake of air. "Is everything all right, hun? Are you cold?"

He shot me a wink and returned to lean against the sink as I choked through an incoherent response.

I made a mental note to ask him to tell me about our interactions among humans in other lives, but whether we'd done it in the previous life or never before, the thrill on his face at watching me switch between skins was invigorating. Azrames was equally impressed, though I'd assumed he would have been desensitized to watching women jump through hoops to have their humanity acknowledged.

From the chair in the salon, I held Caliban's gaze, loving that no one else could see the silver twinkle in those diamonds. I extended my hand and did my best to imitate Fauna's doe eyes as I asked to borrow the stylist's phone. She didn't fight me on it, remarking on how often she shattered hers or dropped it in the toilet. I searched the only car rental in town and made a call. The man on the other end went from sounding bored to surprised to speaking with me as if I were the president himself.

"Steven, is it? Yes, that's fine," I said smoothly. "No, I want the upgrade. Is that the best you can do? No, upgrade. And how soon can you get it here? And tell me, Steven, how much does that number change if I tell you I'll give you two hundred in cash to be here in the next fifteen minutes? Excellent, you're a doll. See you soon."

I tipped my stylist and artist three times their rates, offering parting hugs as if we were old friends. I used to say there was a special place in Hell for those who mistreated those who worked in service but was once again confronted with the turn of phrase. Perhaps I should start saying there was a special place on the bottom of the ocean, or in the Antarctic, or perhaps Ohio.

I stepped from the salon as a nervous-looking attendant in a polo handed me the keys to a champagne-colored BMW. I flashed him my most radiant smile and touched his arm, just for the joy of confusion, while I slipped him his promised tip.

"Now," I said to my companions, "I have a fertility goddess to see. Time to get me pregnant."

Chapter Thirty-Four

W E CAN'T GO IN THERE WITH YOU," AZ SAID, VOICE LOW. "The moment Astarte sees us—sorry, *Doctor Ayona*." Then to himself, he muttered, "Little on the nose with that one—our cover will be blown."

"I propose we set the building on fire," Caliban said.

I wasn't sure if he was kidding.

Once again, I'd parked facing the entrance so that we could watch people come and go. The BMW's display screen told me I had roughly ten minutes to pull myself together and walk into the clinic. I now looked the part, and with my name firmly at the number one spot on the *New York Times* bestseller list and after having made the Thirty Under Thirty list of self-made women, I knew that, not I but Merit Finnegan could do this.

When no one took him up on his proposal for arson, Caliban explained Astarte's chosen moniker. "The name has a few meanings, and all of them are egotistical. 'Eternity,' 'princess,' 'fertility'…she's really challenging anyone to come find her. But the cage works both ways. It keeps her in, yes, but no one who knows this is a terraformed seal would ever enter."

My heart felt heavy as I asked, "Then why did you come?"

He offered a half-smile as he said, "I had no choice. Silas

called in his favor, and it certainly seems like he sent me into a box for safekeeping. It could have been worse, by a lot. But Love, I really don't want you going in there. I'm much more comfortable setting the clinic ablaze."

"Stop with the fire thing."

"No..." Azrames looked contemplative. "He has a point."

"You're both being insane. We're going for intelligence. Besides, fire wouldn't kill a goddess, right?"

"No, no. Very few objects and beings alike can end a god."

"So it's settled," I said with finality.

He wasn't telling me not to go, nor was he offering an alternate solution. He was the same man who'd issued a tier-five contract to ensure someone arrived to save me, no matter the cost. "I know. I'm not afraid."

Caliban's eyes tightened. "I am. Let me gamble with something else."

"Sure, sure, put your kingdom on the table again. Risk the lives of...what's the population of Hell? Plus planet Earth? And every other pantheon?" Then more seriously, I said, "Let me do this. I'm just getting a feel for her. I'll be right back."

His fingers slipped over my knee, squeezing my thigh. I hadn't realized how hard I'd been gripping the steering wheel until his touch distracted me. I relinquished my hold on the wheel and exhaled slowly.

"What's your plan?" Azrames asked.

I closed my eyes and said, "She loves sex work, money, and praise. I have the first two and can manufacture the last. I'll explain that I'm ready to have a baby and don't want to stick around and wait for a man to do it." I looked between them and asked, "Do you think she'll meet with me herself? What if I go in there and it's just an intake sheet and a nurse and a demand to come back later?"

Caliban's lips curled up at the edge as he said, "Then do what you showed the world today."

"Fake," I said dryly.

His terse laugh didn't make sense to me until he said, "No, that you understand the world around you so innately that you can put on whatever mask you need for whoever you meet. It takes incredible empathy, awareness, and psychology to do what you do, Love. You observe, adapt, and respond in the time it takes most to breathe. There are layers to your skill that can't be taught, not to humans, not to demons or fae or anyone."

I squeezed the hand on my leg and said, "When you meet Fauna, can you please repeat all of that?"

Azrames's lips twitched supportively in the rearview mirror.

My eyes went to the clock. Four minutes. "Any parting advice before I go?"

"Yes," Caliban said, voice serious. "You're just going in to meet her. Observe what you can. See if you can get a sense for who else in her company might be a citizen of another realm. She could have surrounded herself with humans or be sitting in a castle of demigods. It might be good to casually mention your Nordic blood, as it might verify anything *off* she senses about you, should your clairsentience be discernable, without setting off alarm bells. Never give her your true name. Even if she somehow knows what's on your birth certificate, her seeing it online or hearing it secondhand is different from you giving it to her. Sign nothing. Don't make any agreements. Don't even say *thank you*. Don't—"

"Right, right, fae rules," I said dismissively.

Caliban stopped mid-sentence.

From the back seat, Azrames said, "I gave her a similar speech before she met...well, your father."

He laughed, but the sound wasn't quite happy. "Wise man" was all he said.

"Here." Az leaned forward and handed me the dagger he'd stolen from Fauna in their final moments. "I'm pretty sure it won't do you any good even if you do need it, since you're probably as good at wielding a knife as I am at writing popular fiction, but I can't let you go in there without anything pointy. Stick it in your purse and pray you don't need a dagger."

Etiam di mori.

I knew the word *death* when I saw it, regardless of the language. I thanked Azrames for the murder stick, and he responded with a sad smile. I slipped it into my black bag, glad that I'd selected the larger cross-body purse.

Caliban gave Az a look of gratitude before returning his full attention to me. He tucked his fingers behind my ear, weaving them into my hair before cradling my jaw in his palm. He touched his forehead to mine. "Would you believe me if I told you that saying goodbye to you gets harder each time? Every life, it kills me more and more to not be beside you."

"Well," I said, trying to keep my voice light as my lids fluttered closed, "let's make it through this so this can be my last life. I don't want to say goodbye again."

I'm sure he meant to kiss me tenderly. His lips were soft, his hand clutching my face closer to his, but there was nothing gentle about the way he embraced me. His hand slipped through my hair to the back of my head. His tongue swept over mine, the hand on my knee slid up my leg, his body leaned as close to mine as the vehicle allowed. Something about the kiss cracked my heart. A knot formed in my throat, tears lining my eyes as I severed the passionate moment, breaking the kiss.

He kissed me like I was about to die.

"I love you," I said quietly.

He pushed his lips to the place where my hair met my forehead as he said, "I've always loved you."

I unbuckled my belt and escaped the car before Caliban could see me cry.

I left the men to discuss war plans and gods and city-size seals while I walked confidently toward the glassy, modern fertility tomb.

✦

I wondered if the Soul Eater had another name and whether or not that name was Jessabelle.

While the receptionist who greeted me had been exceptionally lovely—the sort of beauty that belonged immortalized in marble and preserved behind glass—I hated her from the instant our eyes met. I had a few moments to decide upon a strategy as my heels clicked into the luxurious lobby decorated in whites, pastels, and creams, a gargantuan chandelier overhead making me feel like I was steps away from the Champs-Elysées rather than in a tiny, pagan midwestern town. While reflective vases overflowing with interesting, pale-apricot roses flooded the lobby, I couldn't take my eyes off the receptionist awaiting me.

I knew she was aware of me the moment I entered, but her gaze remained politely averted until I was close enough to address her. Behind her sleek, modern desk was an antique that belonged in the Louvre, not in a private clinic. To the side, a grand staircase rose and slowly spiraled as it doubled back onto the second floor.

"Merit." She smiled at me as she stood from her desk. Her skin sparkled with warm Mediterranean shades of bronze and copper, though her eyes were a shocking shade of olive green. I didn't miss the subtle points on her perfectly white teeth. While I'd spent a few years in the company of the wealthy, even I struggled to calculate the worth of the clothes on her back. I recognized her jewelry from an actress who'd worn something similar at a red-carpet event. If I was right about her snakelike bracelets, each diamond and platinum ouroboros one cost upwards of thirty thousand dollars, and she wore five. "I'm Jessabelle," she said smoothly. "Doctor Ayona is expecting you. Please, take a seat and fill out the form."

I accepted the pen, paper, and sleek clipboard. Before I turned away, my gaze went between Jessabelle and the cluster of pale rose-like flowers on her desk. Their scent was closer to aromatic tea and apricots than anything floral. I kept my expression neutral as I said, "I might be mistaken, but these smell like..."

"Juliet roses?" she completed appreciatively. "You have a good eye, Merit Finnegan. Please just let me know when you're finished. Can I get you anything? Herbal tea? Sparkling water?"

"Water would be great," I said quietly. My mouth was so dry I'd need a gallon of the life-saving liquid just to continue functioning. I was sure not to thank her as she passed me the carbonated glass with its delicate mint and cucumber flourishes but dipped my head with appreciation.

I perched on an expensive-looking cream couch but couldn't examine the loose-leaf forms just yet. I scanned the room again and did my best to conceal my shock. Juliet roses were one of the most expensive flowers in the world. I knew because a particularly boastful client had offered me one at the start of our date and then launched into a seven minute monologue on their rarity and how lucky I was. The clinic was filled with their delicate peach scent, the entire lobby overflowing with the living art. There had to be ten thousand dollars of flowers alone, and given how quickly fresh-cut bundles wilted and needed to be replaced...

It was exorbitant, wasteful, and most notably...no one else was here. Who would witness her ostentatious display of wealth? And of her clients, who would identify the blossoms for what they were? Fear crawled slowly from my toes up my legs, chilling me into a shudder as it reached my spine. I knew in theory that I shouldn't be shocked at an immortal being's wealth, but even the King of Hell hadn't bothered with shocking displays of his excess.

I looked down at the form and frowned.

Name.

In any other office, I'd have filled it out without a second thought. Now, the personal details, the signatures, the dates, the agreements all took on a sinister edge.

The airy trill of a phone call broke the otherwise-gentle

music that piped through the lobby. Jessabelle accepted the call, and after a few polite agreements, she returned the phone to its resting place and stood. "Merit? The doctor will see you now. You can finish your form after your appointment."

I gulped down my water before following Jessabelle up the stairs. The second floor did look less like an art gallery, but only slightly. There was no nurse's station, starchy curtain, or fluorescent overhead lighting. There wasn't a stitch of carpeting to be found or a single pastel nineties painting I'd come to expect in hospitals. Everything oozed of lavishness. Jessabelle paused at a door and offered me one final smile before gesturing me into the office.

I caught her olive-green eyes in the moments we passed and felt a sickening emptiness consume me. I broke the contact quickly enough to blink away my terror as I thought once more of the Soul Eater. Perhaps it was less of a name and more of a title—apparently the sort that every high-ranking monarch and deity needed to play guard dog for outside of their sanctuaries. Hopefully, it was a category of fae I'd never have to meet again.

Until I entered.

It took me three seconds to decide I preferred Jessabelle over the being before me.

"Merit." The woman behind the desk smiled.

The room flooded with natural light, bathed from top to bottom with the gray exterior world as windows lined the office. Unlike in Hell's palatial rooms, I continued to feel like I was wandering through an annex of a Parisian museum with elements of Mediterranean flare. Modernity wove itself like a common thread through every piece, uniting the antiques with angles, glass, steel, and corners. For every historical painting or sculpture was the latest and greatest piece of furniture or technology.

Inarguably, the woman—fae, deity, whatever—had impeccable taste. Despite the room's intricate grandeur and the intimidating, femme bodyguard in a cross-armed power stance in the corner, I had eyes only for her.

Goddess, my brain corrected, repeating the word over and over again as if it had been tapped into my brain's wiring and was looped through my internal sound system. *Don't underestimate her. You're fucking with a goddess.*

While Jessabelle had been beautifully tan, Doctor Ayona was made of true gold. She wore a thick statement necklace and a fitted dress under her white lab coat. Like Jessabelle's serpent bracelet, the doctor wore the golden ouroboros around her neck. I blinked against the visual in an attempt to see human shades of tawny skin instead of the glistening topaz and sparkling sands of ancient Mesopotamia before me. Her ink-black hair had been slicked into a high ponytail, then twisted into two coils that wrapped in a unique and captivating braid disappearing behind her shoulders. Her eyes— rimmed with coffee brown and dissolving into gold around her too-large pupils—her berry-dark mouth, her hands, her shape...I struggled to articulate my words. I had a feeling that one look at the doctor would cure even the straightest woman of her heterosexuality. I lost focus entirely and partially blamed Caliban for my inability to clear my thoughts by helping me get laid earlier, as all I could think about was her hands...her mouth...her body...

Fuck. Goddess of sex was right.

I needed to say something. I needed to say hello, to greet her, to rub my remaining two brain cells together and spark a thought.

My gaze flitted to the corner of the room where a similarly stunning woman in a well-tailored suit stood with her arms folded across her chest. Unlike Doctor Ayona's, the stranger's night-dark hair was unbound, cascading to her hips in luscious, onyx curls. Between her dark eyes, her evaluating stare, her pointed stilettos, and her unmoved expression, it felt like she'd stepped off a set after playing the role of assassin.

My eyes returned to the doctor, and I crossed the room to accept her outstretched hand.

A tiny spark shot through me when she touched me, and I recoiled as if a snake had bitten me. Attempting to recover, I laughed awkwardly. "Static," I mumbled while sliding into the chair on the opposite side of her desk. Over one shoulder, I glanced out the floor-to-ceiling windows to see the parking lot. I swallowed at my discomfort at realizing she'd positioned herself to monitor the comings and goings of clients. I would have assumed anyone of importance would want to observe the gardens, fountains, or trees. I didn't let my eyes linger, though I caught the darkened reflection of the BMW's windshield and said a silent prayer into the void that neither Caliban nor Azrames had been spotted.

"Mmm," she responded calmly, smile still playing on the corners of her mouth. The bright smell of peaches and apricots wafted from the lobby into her office as Juliet roses filled the space. She eased back into her chair and said, "Why don't you tell me what brings you in today, Merit Finnegan? Big fan, by the way."

"Thank you." I did my best to return the smile, whether or not she was just being polite. "I'm glad you've liked the books. The next one will focus on South American pantheons and deities. Its primary anchor will be Brazilian lore."

"Oh, I know." She continued to give the sort of smile that looked like it bloomed from a secret. She flitted a hand to her bookshelf. Sharing her wall of framed Ivy League diplomas was a set of well-decorated shelves. Beside numerous medical texts were the spines of my novels.

It would have been disingenuous to hide my surprise, so I allowed the shock to shine through. "I wouldn't have taken you for a fan," I said.

"Who doesn't love ancient worlds?" she asked with warmth. She folded one arm over the other as she leaned on her desk with feline regalness. With the conversational tilt of her head, she asked, "Any plans for book four?"

I nodded, dipping my toes in the water. "I'm heading east; I'm just not sure how far east I want to go. The Shinto gods, maybe? Or perhaps something in the Middle East... closer to Mesopotamia. Of course, I'm nowhere near ready," I said. "I'd need to spend hours in libraries before I would feel confident to tackle the lore. I'm tragically ill-informed on many of the world's religions."

"Religion," she replied, the word almost a purr. "Not mythology. How curious."

I wasn't sure whether she was pleased or suspicious. I dared a glance at the stoic woman posturing in the corner, but she did not react. I kept my tone light, forcing myself to stay relaxed as I monitored her for a response. She offered me nothing.

"Truly," I went on, "I had it easy with my first book. My maternal family is from Norway, so I grew up with most of the mythology and lore. My mother's side has always been deeply interested in Norse mythology, though perhaps we'll never know why. Interweaving my lived experience was half of the success. I should have dedicated the book to her."

I thought of Caliban's warning as I saw Ayona relax with an almost imperceptible ease. I hadn't realized her smile was stiff until the microscopic shift in her eyes, in the corners of her mouth, in the way she held her shoulders. Yes, bringing up Nordic blood had worked in my favor. I wonder what it was about me, if she could smell the same sea and pine that I smelled on Fauna or if was something else entirely.

"Your maternal line, you say?" she said. "That explains the deeply Irish surname, I suppose."

I laughed as if I were on a morning talk show, slapping on a forged ease and gabbing inauthentically with the host. "I don't think my father has a drop of Irish blood, though who's to say? He's a sixth-generation American, and no one on that side of the family can verify a country of origin."

It was a fictional backstory, of course. My father's family was from Oslo. But she didn't need to know that.

"Well," she said with the cooing voice of a mourning dove as she changed the subject, "parents are an excellent segue as to what led you to a fertility clinic. Why don't you tell me what's brought you in today, Merit?"

I wished I had the ability to freeze time. Fear was going to get the best of me if I couldn't calm down and look for answers. Anxiety clenched my muscles, hitched my breathing, and tightened my eyes. My palms grew clammy as I wanted a moment to gather my thoughts, to ask about the wildly intimidating, shockingly gorgeous bodyguard in the corner of the room, to examine my surroundings without looking suspicious. It didn't seem fair that I was expected to answer her questions, to think rationally, to have my wits about me while flanked by a tiny army of gorgeous women. It was with a chill of horror that I realized the doctor's personal Soul Eater might remain outside the door, triangulating me between immortals.

A solution came to me all at once.

She was a client, and I was her very expensive date.

I decided to look at her like she was Josh, her office was the overpriced omakase restaurant, and her degrees were the Rolex watch. She was used to having people fall at her feet, to succumbing to her every whim, to her worship. I may not know the right or wrong moves with ancient Phoenician goddesses, but I'd learned how to put myself on equal playing fields with powerful people.

I removed Doctor Ayona entirely and replaced her with the open-mouthed chewing of my last terrible date. I allowed her desk to become the table, the comforting sounds of the luxurious office to transform into the too-loud mastication of the man who'd mixed wasabi directly into his soy sauce. Her designer dress, her supple curves, her hypnotizing face became little more than another rich, mediocre John. I pictured Josh snapping at the waitress for the bill. I added a few flourishing details, like leaving one of his buttons undone, a piece of sesame in his teeth, and the annoyance I'd felt at wasting my night on a date when I could have been home watching *Fire and Swords*.

I wasn't sure what it was that the goddess Astarte had loved about escorts, but perhaps it was this—our ability to slip into skins, to find an advantage, to become peerless. After all, Dagon had said I was exactly her type.

Fear evaporated as I eased into my chair and spoke to Josh.

"I love what I do," I said casually. "I work from home. I could support a family of ten if I wanted. And I've always loved children."

Two out of three was a pretty good truth-to-lie ratio, I told myself.

"Besides," I added, "why should I need a man to accomplish the things I want in life?"

There, now we had three out of four truths…mostly. Caliban wasn't a man, after all. Not really.

She smiled again at that. My gaze flitted to the corner of the room at the unsmiling, statue-still figure, then back to the doctor. The doctor's smile faltered and she half-turned toward the bodyguard, then stopped herself, returning to me. She cleared her throat and bent to fish something from a drawer within her desk. She procured a thin, glossy binder and slid it to me.

"This is for our elite clients," she said. "You may not be old money, but you certainly are special."

I fought my eyebrows' desire to pull together in confusion as I flipped open to the first page only to realize she'd slid me a book of suitors—of semen. The men in the book were the finest humankind had to offer, fashioned after Adonis himself. Their perfect, disarming smiles, their flawless skin, their postures, their pedigrees.

I paged through the first three.

Liam, 25
University: Brown, M.S. Engineering
IQ score: 157
Family heritage: Polish, French
Sperm count and motility: 50,000,000 / 60%
Family medical issues: None
Special mention: Proposal for hydroelectric power plant has been accepted on the borders of Argentina and Uruguay

Theodore, 28
University: Princeton, Ph.D. Economics
IQ score: 162
Family Heritage: Dominican, Kenyan
Sperm count and motility: 45,000,000 / 55%
Family medical issues: None
Special mention: Pioneered developmental model for precise evaluation of political expenses and their effects on the public

Ji-Hoon, 23
University: Columbia, M.A. Architecture
IQ score: 165
Family Heritage: Korean
Sperm count and motility: 60,000,000 / 70%
Family medical issues: None
Special mention: Youngest architect to design a national art gallery

She had given me a shopping menu. I leafed through the meat market of men, pretending to imagine what my offspring would look like if I bred with any of them. They were all gorgeous, educated, healthy, and accomplished. I wondered what most others had to do to qualify for access to the elite binder of men. I continued to page through the book as I considered what the mid-tier and lower-tier book of men looked like.

Even without the money and the reputation, I knew that

if Doctor Ayona had stayed after five o'clock for me, it was because she was booked out too far to discuss an appointment. I hadn't looked at the costs of her services or inquired as to the price of anything from consultation to in vitro fertilization. I left the book open to the laughing face of a bright-eyed actor from Spain as I looked at her. Caliban had told me to come in and gather intelligence, nothing more.

Despite what Fauna loved to shout from the mountain-tops, I wasn't a simpleton. I understood that he knew more about the immortal realms than I did and wasn't about to take my chances with her Soul Eater just because I wanted to prove a point on independence.

"What are our next steps?" I asked.

"That depends entirely on your budget, comfort level, and desire to start a family." She smiled easily. "Here at the Venus Clinic, we're not focused solely on traditional methods of hormonal injection and artificial insemination, but instead, we pioneer research in human fertility. If you'd like, we can begin with the methods that have been preached and carried out throughout North America and most of the Global West at a twenty to thirty percent success rate. Or, you can partake in the unique and often unorthodox combinations of scientific breakthroughs, holistic medicine, elements of Western convention, and the natural procreation process, and I can guarantee nine in ten odds of impregnation."

Nine in ten.

I worked hard to control my face.

She was Josh. Josh was telling me about his job, thinking too highly of himself, obsessed with his own importance. Picturing the man at the omakase restaurant helped once more as I said, "Well, numbers like that don't lie. It's hard to argue for conventional medicine when they fail more often than not."

Her smiled widened. For the first time, she reminded me of the Cheshire cat.

"How badly do you want to be a mother, Merit Finnegan?"

I swallowed. "More than anything."

"And that's exactly what I'll give to you."

Maybe it was my wish to freeze time, or my prayer that I'd slow the world around me so that I could absorb every detail, but the cogs in her word choice clicked together, churning as they started a new and wholly startling realization within me. *Natural procreation process.* In the absence of priestesses, this was how Astarte satiated her need for prostitution, for escorts, for the sexual exploitation of bodies worshipping in her name.

I decided to keep my voice as light as possible as I joked, "Depending on how unconventional your methods, I have to say, these men are easy on the eyes."

"They're easy on more than the eyes," she purred.

A chill wrapped itself around my spinal cord, slithering into a space within my vertebra and puncturing my column, filling every hollow space within me with ice.

When I'd stepped into sex work, it had been for agency, for freedom, for choice. Every date had broken my chains from poverty, bringing me comfort, security, wealth, and the ability to build the future I wanted.

What Astarte wanted...

Discomfort took root. The apricot smell became stifling. I wanted to leave.

My eyes flitted to the bodyguard once more before I asked, "I'm sorry, is she present for all appointments?"

Doctor Ayona opened her mouth as if to answer, but only a thin wisp of air escaped.

"Is who..." She looked over her shoulder long enough for her and the woman to lock stares. She looked back at me with wide-eyed confusion for a moment before her face tightened. The warmth, professionalism, and medical mask dropped from her in an instant. I was struck again with the terror of her ancient power as I knew beyond the shadow of a doubt that, without knowing how or why, I had made the worst mistake of my life. The doctor's teeth set in a grit. As she snapped her fingers, the door opened, and I didn't have to turn to know Jessabelle had entered from behind. The bodyguard took another step closer.

"Jessabelle, Anath," she said coolly as her eyes narrowed on me.

I didn't have to know more of Phoenician etymology to know I'd fucked up. I gripped the arms of my chair, knuckles turning white as I turned to look over my shoulder. The world collapsed around me as the Soul Eater approached me on one side while the bodyguard came at me from another. Whatever I'd done, I was no longer safe. I stood and backed up against the window. I pressed myself into the glass, knowing it was mirrored and that Caliban wouldn't be able to see me.

I'd failed them. I'd been in here for thirty minutes, and I'd failed them.

"I'm sorry, I—"

The women flanked me on either side, each taking an arm. The Soul Eater gripped an elbow while the bodyguard grabbed the other.

"How?" demanded the woman in the black suit.

"How *what?*" I gasped.

"Search her, Anath," said the doctor with a wave. I expected them to go through my purse, but instead, the one called Anath grabbed the collar of my shirt and yanked.

"No pendant," she muttered. She shoved my sleeves up to the middle of my forearms, stopping just short of my tattoo, before saying, "No pendant, no bracelet, no rings. I don't know how she's doing it."

I realized with horrifying clarity that they were looking for the true-sight sigil. That was it, then. I hadn't been meant to see the woman called Anath while she kept vigil in the corner. I'd tilted my cards, and they knew I was no mere author. My mind raced as I looked for a solution. I felt like my finger hovered above the channel button, pressing it at lightning speed as I flipped through station after station, desperate for a reason, an excuse, a—

"Do you know a Norde called Geir?" My question came out in a rush.

Anath's hands remained on me, but her eyes lifted to meet mine. I looked back to the desk where the doctor now leaned, perched on the edge of her station. I wasn't sure where I was going with my tactic, but I'd gained their attention. The Soul Eater leaned in as if to use her glinting teeth to puncture the tender flesh of my jugular. I wasn't sure if vampires existed but had no idea what she was doing until she inhaled deeply.

"She does smell of it," said Jessabelle, "but it's so faint..."

"Wait, let me show you." I tried to yank my elbow free. The women resisted for a moment, then released me. It was working—*what*, I didn't know, but it was working. I wasn't willing to show my demonic sigil, but I had one more card to play. I took a few cautious steps to where my purse remained on the chair, angling my body so no one could peer over my shoulder. I opened it up, looking at the five precious things inside. A credit card, an ID, a golden poppet, a knife, and a silver sølje. I plucked the broach from the purse and held it up.

"See?"

Doctor Ayona closed the space between us, and no longer could I smell the lovely apricots of the Juliet rose. The woody scents of burnt sugar, smoked sage, and sandalwood were deeper and more powerful than a perfume. It was an ancient and ominous smell, wonderful and terrifying all at once.

"May I?" she asked.

My heart stuttered again as I remembered Azrames yanking me on the shores of the lake.

Be reverent.

I had no idea if my choice was clever or foolish, but I had no cards left to play. I swallowed as I handed it over. She raised a speculative brow as she eyed the bauble.

"What is this Norde to you? Geir, you said?"

I swallowed again. *Great-grandfather* would make my blood too thin for the clairsentience I'd need to satiate her anger, but *father* wasn't believable for my delicate scent. "He was my grandfather," I said, hoping that the extra quarter might make my gift for seeing through the veil believable. My mother and her quarter blood certainly appeared to have no trouble communing with angels.

"Truthfully," I said, looking at Anath, "I have no idea who you are. Please don't take that as disrespect. I came to the clinic because it has the best reputation in the country for fertility and because..." My throat bobbed once more as I looked for ways to word what I was saying so they wouldn't detect dishonesty. It was true. I hadn't known who Anath was, and they could see the earnestness on my face. I did my best to play into her suspicions, heeding Caliban's advice by acknowledging my fae connections. "I'm an unconventional person who was raised knowing of my grandfather's people. I'm seeking...unconventional solutions. I think we might be a good fit for one another."

The doctor turned the broach over in her hand gently, allowing the tiny, spoon-like dangles to clink together delicately. She eyed the ornate tree in the center.

I was surprised when she returned the broach to me. Some part of me thought she'd close her fingers around it and melt it down. Instead, after a terrifyingly long pause, she gestured for me to take a seat once more. The panic subsided as quickly as it had flared.

"My apologies, Merit Finnegan. Clairsentience is a rare gift, and my clients have been almost exclusively human. I hope you'll be gracious enough to understand why it might make us...cautious. Please, Anath, offer your apologies."

Anath released me slowly. "Are you harmed?"

I shook my head numbly, sinking back into the chair. Fear was appropriate, so I didn't try to hide it. She stepped away.

"Your apologies, Anath," the doctor repeated. "Miss Finnegan is a VIP client in more ways than one."

The woman's jaw remained set, her expression dispassionate as she said, "I extend my regrets."

And because I was still reeling, the best I came up with was "No problem."

The worst had happened, and I'd overcome it.

This was working out even better than I'd hoped. She'd detected no lies when I'd told Anath that I was ignorant—whether the woman in the tailored suit was a demon, fae, entity, or angel, I had no clue. If I was lucky, Doctor Ayona would assume that the only thing I'd acknowledged was an understanding that, because I was a citizen of a different realm, the fertility clinic might provide answers that I couldn't get in the mortal world.

"How exactly did you hear of me?" Doctor Ayona asked at last.

Unfortunately, her compatriots stayed uncomfortably close.

Jessabelle remained on my side of the desk while Anath rounded the desk to stand behind the doctor. The intimidation made it difficult to grasp for something believable. The same sensation of flipping through vivid blurs of colors and sounds as I searched my memories blinded me before I pieced together as many half-truths as I could into a Frankenstein of an answer.

"From a demon," I said hoarsely. "My friend—a Norde—is partnered with a demon."

She didn't have to know that those two statements were not connected. It might just be enough.

Doctor Ayona looked over at Anath. "I wasn't aware the demons knew of our operation, though I suppose if it had to be anyone... How are our relations with Hell?"

Anath furrowed her brow. "Do you mean the realm in its entirety or your kingdom here, Astarte?"

I had assumed from the moment I met her that I was speaking with Astarte, but hearing it on Anath's lips was something else entirely. Her mighty kingdom of Bellfield, with its elite, private fertility clinic, her captured god, and her terraformed seal.

Astarte narrowed her eyes slightly, which prompted Anath to continue.

"Our relations are nonexistent. We are neither friend nor foe."

"Let's keep it that way," Astarte said. Anath offered a shallow bow in acknowledgement. The doctor turned back to me and repainted her face with professionalism. "There are defectors all the time, Merit. If the Nordes haven't claimed you, then allow me to welcome you to my little kingdom. I understand, of course, that a bestselling author has a life to live and that life requires motherhood. I think we could strike up a bargain, if you'd be so inclined?"

The word stabbed through me.

I could almost see Caliban's silver eyes glint like chipped ice as she tempted me to violate one of the few things he'd made me promise. I fought the urge to look over my shoulder and peer out the window at the BMW.

"What do you have in mind?" I asked, wanting to stay both conversational and noncommittal. I assumed it was fine that I no longer sounded relaxed. They had to realize they'd just struck me with the terror of a goddess's wrath.

"Global recognition," she said with a smile. "Your fourth book. I want my name known—the one the masses have forgotten. Will you do that for me, Merit Finnegan? Put my name on human lips once more. Make them sip from the cup of my histories. Tell the story of my conquests. Fill my temples. The temple of Astarte."

My mouth parted at the absurdity of the offer.

"I can't fill temples..."

"Nonsense," she said. "You are a goddess in your own right." She propped her elbow onto the desk and flashed me her pearly teeth. "Every realm has a creation story. You create. You speak things into existence. The first *Pantheon* novel sold more copies than the Edda. The old gods of your people have cups overflowing for the first time in centuries. Word has spread of Odin's and Frigg's prosperity since your short human life began. And it's being done in a way so that they never have to step from the shadows to harvest what you sow. The Hellenic pantheon didn't need the boost your second book brought, but the Greeks won't deny what you did for them. That's what I want."

"And what do I get in return?" I asked, regretting it immediately.

Astarte laughed as she leaned back in her chair, interlacing her fingers. "You create life? So do I. You give birth to the written word. I'll grant it within the womb. I just need you to do one thing for me."

"What's that?" My question came out as a rattled breath.

She pulled a pen from a cup that looked like a golden honeycomb and snatched a leaf of loose paper from immaculately stacked documents beside her. Her calligraphy soon filled the page with speed and grace. When she was finished, she wrote her name at the bottom and slid it over to me.

"Just sign this for me. And this time, don't use your pen name."

Chapter Thirty-Five

A FTER A LONG DAY AT FIRST GRADE WHERE THE KIDS FOUND a hole in my shirt and spent every hour after lunchtime trying to slide things through the rip in my clothes without me knowing, I was sent to the after-school program to do crafts and play until my mom finished work. The daily activities were generally sparsely populated, with me and other low-income students whose parents couldn't afford private daycare. But having poverty in common didn't make the others any kinder. If anything, it gave them more to prove in establishing a hierarchy.

At least, that's how I saw it in hindsight. At the time, there were only the bullies and the underlings.

The rec room was in shambles as boys toppled over a toy kitchen and chucked Legos at one another from across the room when the supervising teacher sat down and cried.

It was jarring enough that we all stopped what we were doing to watch her, cross-legged on the floor, face in her hands, as she cried. We'd broken her.

By the tender age of six, I knew I never wanted to have kids.

If she couldn't survive children for a few hours after school, I wasn't sure how I could handle it every hour of every day if I became a mom. Besides, I never wanted to bring a life into the world who would have to go through the rejection, the cold nights, the spankings, the torn clothes, the jeers, the punishments, the pain I'd gone through. Society didn't need someone new to kick.

✦

SEPTEMBER 2, AGE 26

I thought of my lifelong vow to be childless as the technician wrapped a band around my bicep, preparing me to take vials of my blood. I smiled at the woman in her bright white scrubs, knowing Caliban would slap the needle out of the woman's hands if he realized I was volunteering blood to a god. Then again, given the events of the appointment, I was confident this wouldn't be the only thing that would make him angry. I'd failed him on roughly every promise I'd made.

But I'd been the one who'd insisted on meeting Doctor Ayona today since I was *so desperate* to get pregnant, so it would have raised more than a few eyebrows if I'd refused standard lab work to establish my current health and wellbeing. I could write a book on the ancient Canaanite religion as my fourth novel. Perhaps she'd done me a favor by taking the guesswork out of my future project. I'd had no choice. She hadn't even needed to coerce me. I would either blow our cover or do whatever was required to get us what we needed. Besides, bloodwork was standard practice in any boring, human clinic. It should be fine...right?

"Make a fist for me?" the tech said, voice calm as gentle rain.

Cartoon pictures of Baal's priests slicing themselves open in his honor flashed through my mind, my feelings about Sunday school were not unlike the traumatic flashes of a war veteran. Crimson illustrations filled my eyes as she pierced my skin. I inhaled sharply but did not flinch. I watched her fill one syringe, then another, then a third. She labeled them carefully with my name and case number.

When the technician finished with me, Jessabelle was waiting in the hall with a smile. Gone was the feral terror that'd been instilled in me in the moments her boss had called my intentions into question. I wasn't sure if I'd been quick-thinking, lucky, or profoundly stupid. I guessed only time would tell. But for now, Jessabelle gestured for me to follow her down the stairs.

"We can't tell you how excited we are to work with you," Jessabelle said, voice practically glittering. Not only was she no longer trying to scare me, but even her professionalism had melted away into something that resembled fawning. "This means more to us than you could possibly realize."

"Don't mention it," I said thickly. I didn't want any of it. I didn't want to have children or to have made deals with a true devil. All I'd wanted was to break the terraformed seal and set Caliban free.

Fauna was right. I was a goddamn idiot.

"We need twenty-four hours to get a few selections here," Jessabelle said as she escorted me to the door, "but we'll send planes for all of them to ensure you have the optimal experience. We'll be ready for you tomorrow at five. Wear whatever makes you comfortable. We'll provide alternate attire upon your arrival."

"Sure, sure, five," I agreed without looking at her. I just wanted to leave. At the rate of my recklessness, staying another minute longer would probably result in me bonding with Astarte and pledging my undying allegiance to the Phoenicians.

Unseasonable warmth hit me as I abandoned the air-conditioned museum to the Dumbass Formerly Known as Merit Finnegan. I tried to focus on my breathing, on the sound of my heels on the glittering black asphalt, on the absence of suffocating Juliet roses as cut grass and the distant scent of a freshwater lake wafted on the breeze. There was no way I'd get my pulse under control before I had to face the others.

I did my best to keep my pace normal as I walked back

382

to the car, shooting a glance behind me to ensure Jessabelle had closed the door before I reached the car. Fortunately, the luxury vehicle had deeply tinted windows. I slid into the car and my eyes widened.

I exhaled slowly, closing my eyes.

"Where's Caliban?"

Azrames leaned forward and rested his elbows on his knees, smoke and ash the only scent in the car. "Hello to you, too, Marmar. Don't worry; the Prince is just doing reconnaissance for exit points as a fox on the property. He's pretty sure he can reverse-engineer their wards if he can figure them out from the exterior. I'm confident he'll be able to sniff them out. How'd it go in there?"

I swallowed, voice trembling slightly as I said, "Caliban's going to be really mad at me."

Az's voice went from friendly to strained in a second. "I have a feeling that I am, too. What did you do?"

I started shaking before I could even spit it out. Each breath came out more jagged than the one before as fear pricked through me. "I fucked up, Az. I fucked up."

"Tell me."

I closed my eyes as I explained what had happened and what I'd done.

"Fuck," he swore, flinching away from the information with closed eyes. He didn't reopen them as he said, "You're hers."

"No," I insisted. "It wasn't a bond; it was just lab work and a book agreement—"

"You're hers, Marlow," he repeated.

"*No,*" I emphasized, agitated that he wasn't listening. "I'm just going to write a book. That's all! I have to write a book on mythology anyway! It's my career! So *what* if it's about her? It doesn't matter. Maybe I would have done book four on them anyway; who's to say? And bloodwork is standard practice. It doesn't mean anything. It—"

"You're hers."

Thrice. It took three repetitions for me to truly hear him. I fell silent for the next few minutes, staring at the gray assassin in the back of the car. I hadn't even started the car. Instead, we let the quiet press down on us until the passenger door opened. I jumped. Caliban slid into the seat and immediately to me, scooping me against him as much as he was able between the two front seats. He released me and frowned.

He cradled my face with one hand again, but I wouldn't look at him. I couldn't. His voice stayed low. "I was coming back with a good report on the back staircase, but something tells me you do not have good news, Love."

From the back seat, Azrames said, "What are the two ways to break a terraformed seal?"

Caliban frowned. He looked at Az, confused at the change in conversation. "Either someone who could freely come and go would have to destroy the seal's integrity, or it would have to be done by the seal's maker...one way or another."

Azrames nodded slowly before saying, "I hate to be the one to tell you this, but we're down to one option."

It was worry, not anger, that filled Caliban's voice as he his eyes fixed on me. "What did you do?"

"I'm so sorry," I said, face falling into my hands to cover my shame. The car crunched in on me, suffocating me, enveloping me in pain and darkness as I hid from Caliban, disappearing into my own self-loathing.

From the back seat, Azrames said, "I hope you're ready to kill a goddess."

✦

I handed my keys to the valet driver of the downtown hotel I'd spotted while readying myself to meet the goddess. When a bell boy inquired about my bags, I informed him that I traveled light. The concierge had me checked in and sent to my room within a few short minutes. If I only had a night left of freedom, I sure as shit wasn't spending it among the mold and dried cum stains of the Bellfield Inn. If we

384

hadn't arrived in town on foot, without a phone, and in the middle of the night and stopped, I wouldn't have allowed us to settle for the first bed-bug-infested site we'd found. Still, I supposed it was a good thing we had. Thanks to the human roach's encounter with Azrames, the clerk's reign of terror had come to an end.

Tonight, I would sleep on clean, soft sheets.

Tonight, I would order bacon cheeseburgers with extra fries through room service and drink four bottles of beer from the well-stocked mini fridge.

Tonight, I would draw a bubble bath and drift off in the water while resting against someone who was very invested in keeping me alive. At least, that was the plan. I wished the others could see what I saw reflected back in the glossy, golden elevator banks as I approached in my designer clothes flanked on either side by gorgeous, otherworldly men. I was having a celebrity moment, and the pedestrians were missing out.

I punched the button to summon an elevator and sighed when the glow of the red device informed me that the elevator was on the twelfth floor. I missed my apartment and the always-ready modes of transportation.

"Well, lovebirds," Az said, breaking the quiet. He looked at a human couple patiently waiting for another elevator, and I knew he was advising me not to respond. "I'd love to give you two some alone time, but as much as I know you want time together, I suspect you also want to survive the next forty-eight hours."

Caliban slipped his arm around my back, resting his hand on my hip. He rubbed a thumb on my hip bone while he said, "Planning comes first." Then to me, he said, "We have nothing but time after that."

I opened my mouth to argue, but he squeezed my hip to remind me that it wasn't in my best interest to talk to the air. I narrowed my eyes, disagreeing. I was quite confident that talking to the air was exactly the right move to get the human couple to select a different elevator. The moment the elevator dinged, I decided they couldn't tell me what to do.

"I can't wait to stand on the roof and talk to the birds," I said to myself, "and sing them all of my favorite songs!" I saw the couple beside me halt as I pressed the button to close the door. "In fact, I think I'll practice those songs now. *Doe, a deer, a female deer...*"

We'd been so tense that the single act of ridiculousness broke us. Azrames snapped like a rubber band, nearly crying as he laughed at their bewildered faces as the doors shut behind them. Caliban nipped at my cheek as he gave my ass a squeeze.

"This might be my favorite incarnation." He smiled at me, moving my body so my back was against the elevator wall.

"Is it the fae blood?"

His chuckle rumbled against me. "I think the blood is working in my favor. But this is the first time you've chosen me like this." The elevator dinged, and Azrames slipped out like a shadow, shooting an apologetic grimace. We occupied the elevator for a few more seconds as he said, "I've never let you hurt. I've never been able to stand by and let you suffer. Every time you pass, it kills me. Then I hold my breath and wait. But if something happens to you this time?"

"Nothing's going to happen to me."

The elevator doors closed, but the box stayed put.

He rested a hand on the wall beside my head, leaning his body toward me. My heart skipped at how close he was in the clear, bright light of the small space. I licked my lips and did my best to focus as he spoke. "I can't take the risk, Love. What if this life is our shot? *This* is the life where you know who and what we are to one another, and we want the same thing? It will break me if the next cycle..."

His free hand followed my curves. I knew I wasn't supposed to be turned on—this was serious, and no time for thinking of him picking me up and fucking me against the elevator wall. It was no time to envision those sensuous lips on my neck, my breasts, between my thighs. It wasn't the time to wish he'd slide the free hand to my throat, or to the bundle of nerves that he knew better than anyone. My toes curled in my shoes as I focused. Recognizing a saddened emotion on his face brought me back to reality. His frosted brows gathered in the center, bundling against a deep wound. I felt like this might have been a pain he'd endured before. Perhaps not to this extent, but I recalled his father mentioning a cycle where he'd remained a fox for the entirety of my life. To love and be loved in return, to spend each lifetime making someone fall in love with you all over again, and to finally have her choose you back, only to have her life cut short...

"Nothing's going to happen to me," I repeated seriously as I returned his stare. I felt guilty for how selfish my body had been while he used those diamond eyes to look into every version of me who'd ever existed. Now was not the time for this moment. I brushed my hands across his face, appreciating how he looked in the luxurious lighting of a hotel elevator. No shadows. No dreams. Just him, real, mine. "Now, let's go chat with the assassin. He's pretty qualified to kill people."

Caliban slipped his hand over mine as he punched the button to open the doors and we joined Azrames in the hall.

"Damn, Marmar," Azrames said, following me into the suite. It was the sort of place I'd grown familiar with frequenting when clients would take me upstairs after dinner and drinks. With the gold-and-crimson wallpaper, the leather furniture, the thick curtains, and the enormous art, it looked like every Four Seasons: overdecorated and overpriced. Az murmured appreciatively. "How much *do* you make?"

My laugh wasn't entirely humorous. "It isn't Bugatti money, but I do all right. I think I may have had some help."

Azrames lifted his brows and Caliban gave a loose, two-fingered salute. "I may have called in a few favors, but

Love is immensely talented. She wrote the books and did the work. I just made sure it wasn't ignored when it got on the desks it needed to get on. And I may have…influenced the advance and royalty rates. Because she deserves it."

I blushed.

He'd always been so generous. Even when I was convinced he was evidence of psychosis, he'd been a wishful manifestation of all the good things I hoped might happen for me. He was the reason I believed in my ability to make it, despite my conviction that it had been a result of the law of attraction or whatever the new age documentary had told me about self-actualization.

Azrames flopped onto the bed and cut to the chase. "So, Marmar here made a binding contract with Astarte, and the goddess is currently in possession of her blood offering to cement the deal."

I felt the way Caliban flexed beside me against the flash of anger. We'd gone over this in the car, but apparently it would be the sort of regret I'd need to relive a few more times.

"I was backed into a corner," I apologized breathlessly. "Once I'd recognized Anath, they came for me, physically. I did the only thing I could think to do to deescalate the situation. The agreements seemed so harmless. I'm so sorry—"

"You did what you had to, Helen," Caliban said with a controlled laugh.

I blinked at him. "Helen?"

He nodded, "Of Troy—the most beautiful woman in the world, before you, of course. You're the lynchpin about to set off two kingdoms into war."

"War?" I repeated breathlessly. I seemed to be responsible for the echo in the room.

"Astarte is the goddess of sex, love, and—"

"War," I said once more. "You're already at war. I don't need to have a PhD in history to tell you that split battlefronts rarely come out victorious."

"Sure," Azrames agreed for them both, "but that's human history."

388

I kept my eyes on Caliban. "If you don't let her have me…"

"Anath is her sister," Caliban said. "I don't know who Jessabelle is in their realm, but her name suggests she belongs to Baal. When we stand against them, it won't be a minor spat between civilians. This wouldn't be like Fauna killing Az."

"Fauna's tried, but that's a story for another time. Our Prince and their goddess? That's royalty versus royalty." Azrames finished for us. "Honestly…"

We both looked at him speculatively.

"Well, I was thinking, if it were anyone else in the realms, we might worry about them looking for a partnership with Heaven in a bind like this. Heaven has no friends, but they're getting creative in looking for paths to victory. Thank fuck it's the Phoenicians. Even if you kill their goddess, they won't ally themselves with Heaven. Next to us, the Phoenicians are Heaven's longest-standing rivalry."

Caliban rubbed his brow as if a headache had blossomed behind his ice-white skin. "Thank fuck indeed. So, a split battlefront it is."

Az interlaced his fingers behind his head, horns nearly brushing against the headboard as he kept his eyes unfocused toward the ceiling. "Our war with Heaven has been espionage and subterfuge at best. I acknowledge you know far more about the war's inner workings than I do, Prince, but with the Phoenicians…I don't know. Astarte has Dagon prisoner. There's a chance they won't mourn her."

Caliban was unconvinced. "She's Baal's consort, and he's the highest god in their realm. He won't be pleased."

Azrames pushed back. "But Dagon is Baal's father. And for whatever reason, Baal hasn't joined her here. When it comes to what's left of the Phoenicians and their reactions, it might be a coin toss."

"Anath—" I said, but Azrames cut me off.

"Is Astarte's sister," Caliban explained. "Some sources suggest she and Baal also had a thing, but it's unconfirmed.

389

Anath is almost exclusively prayed to for war. She's like a…
more powerful, singular Valkyrie. In your Norse mythology
authorship terms."

"It seems like the Canaanites were predisposed to
violence," I mumbled, trying not to take offense to how often
everyone had to simplify things for me.

Azrames let out a singular laugh. "Yeah, good job on that
one. You had to give blood offerings and sign a contract with
Astarte, didn't you? You couldn't have made a bargain with
Lord Mahavir?"

I winced against my own ignorance. I turned to Caliban
with an apologetic face.

"Jainism," Caliban whispered.

Ah, yes. The most nonviolent religion in the world. I
suspected Lord Mahavir would not have backed me into such
a corner. Or have opened a fertility clinic to rule over an
earthly kingdom because his pride felt neglected in his respective realm. Or capture an agricultural god to force blessings
upon his wealthy town. Or coerce couples into sex…

"Wait," I said, remembering something Jessabelle had
said. The men looked at me as my forehead creased. "I think
she means to bring in a meat market tomorrow."

Caliban looked like I'd splashed him with cold water.
"Excuse me?"

I nodded for emphasis. "Men. I think she's bringing in
men. She handed me a binder to look through potential
sperm donors. Then she started going on about how artificial
insemination and Western medicine has a low success rate,
and her methods were unconventional…but it was something
the receptionist said at the end. She said it would take a day to
get them here. *Them*. I didn't consider it at the time, but…"

Caliban went statue-still. "But if she's honored through
prostitution…"

And in this case, I agreed with the use of the word.
Prostitute was a slur. We both saw the extreme distinction
between prostitution and sex work. My life as an escort was

390

empowering. I'd been the queen of my domain. I'd built an empire, set myself up, and established my power over men. I decided who I saw and could charge them more and more if they so much as annoyed me.

But self-import wasn't what made gods crave prostitution as a devotional offering. Gods of sex, love, and fertility wanted bodies in submission to them. Astarte wasn't looking for agency or union or lovemaking. She was looking for the power of intimacy in taking our innermost expressions of being and making them her own.

"She means for you to get pregnant tomorrow with one of her whores," he said, voice cold. I thought of the binder and its smiling faces, their numbers, their statistics, their ascribed values. I thought of Jessabelle's comment about finding something for me to wear. "If I'm not wrong, she'll want to be...present."

"Present?" I repeated, voice hoarse.

"Come on, Mythology," Azrames said from the wall. "Tell me you don't know enough from your book on the Greek and Roman gods to understand group sex as a favorite brand of pagan worship. And yes, before you ask, I read your books. Very steamy stuff, Marmar."

"You really think Astarte—no, she can't! She's posing as a doctor! She has to at least *play* the role of professional. She's done this with other people...she—"

"I don't know the extent of her involvement," Azrames said as he shrugged. "I'm not saying she's going to strip down and ride your face while you're getting railed—"

"Hey," Caliban warned. The friendship they'd built evaporated for a single, tense moment. All the blood in my body rushed to my cheeks, cooking me from the inside out with its embarrassed heat.

"Sorry, sorry." Azrames made a face, apologizing with his hands. He seemed to remember who he was talking to. He amended, "As a medical professional, she might be able to justify her presence in the exchange as an overseer, to add legitimacy. Sexual studies have been done throughout human history. It's not out of the question, or even out of the realm of mortal science. This might not raise as many brows as you'd think."

I turned red as I stammered, unsure of what point to address first. In the end, I was too flustered to speak directly to him and settled on the definitive statement. "I don't want to get pregnant."

Caliban's humor returned, if just barely. With a single, mirthless laugh, he said, "Yes, that's a common theme with you. I have to say, in all your lives, I never would have put my money on you selling your soul to have a baby. Quite the twist."

I balled my fists. "I don't want a goddamn crotch goblin."

"The deal is the deal whether you want it or not. But I might have an idea."

Azrames and I both looked at him expectantly.

He shook his head and said, "Obviously we can't call for reinforcements. No one knows we're here, and it's best we keep it that way. More flies in a web won't kill the spider. But I think we can fix this from the inside." Looking at me seriously, he asked, "Do you trust me?"

And I didn't need a single heartbeat to consider my answer.

"Implicitly."

✦

I didn't think I'd be able to sleep a wink that night. I got my cheeseburger, but something about room service always ruined the flavor. Burgers were meant to be eaten out of greasy wrapping paper on top of picnic tables that had been welded into parking lots. Fries needed flickering streetlights and the hum of traffic and the late-night pleasant feeling of coming home from the bar. Five-star hotels, with their jalapeño jam, their bacon chutney, and their Wagyu beef, took the magic out of a good burger.

I'd taken longer than necessary in the shower, knowing Caliban and Azrames had things to discuss. They'd had very little time together since I'd dropped the bomb that I'd ruined all hope of breaking the seal under the radar. I would not be taking a shovel to a secret hill and disrupting the integrity of the trap. We would not be escaping without bloodshed.

I managed to finish two of my beers, but the men took the others. I realized with some disappointment in myself that Fauna was constantly eating in my presence and that I should have been more considerate of their needs, but they assured me that, as they weren't in corporeal form like my Fauna, they did not operate the same. Alcohol was a common offering to spirits regardless of the realm. And with a toast, Azrames had taken the far bed and I'd crawled beneath the covers to face the blank wall.

The dark was not comforting.

Caliban wrapped his arm around me, enveloping me in the heavy hold of strength, of the forest, and of affection. I felt safe, I felt loved, and I felt the most profound regret I'd ever experienced in my life.

I'd spent eighteen years in a physically and emotionally abusive household, rarely granted compassion. I'd rejected the only companionship that had been consistent in my life until it was too late. And when we had each other at long last, the first thing I'd done was fuck it up.

He must have sensed the painful spike as my emotion shifted.

Wordlessly, he used the hand that held me to brush away my tears. I snatched his hand from the shadows before me and pushed a kiss into his palm, feeling the way his body tightened around mine, encompassing me wholly. And though I'd been certain I'd lie awake in a fit of stress and worry, I was swept up in calming visions of a misty forest, of deeply olive ferns, of moss-covered logs and the calming smells of gin and cypress, and I fell into a deep and dreamless sleep.

Chapter Thirty-Six

I 'D ONLY ASKED HIM ONCE.

"I just go in there and…wait for the cavalry?"

Pain painted itself across his expression. "I truly can't tell you, Love. Not because I don't trust you with the information. Quite the contrary. But I am confident my plan will work. And if it doesn't, I will hack my way through every man, woman, and child who stands in my way."

"So violent." I tried to smile.

"I'm serious," he replied. "I don't want you to go at all, but we have one shot at breaking this bond, and killing a goddess is no small feat. We need her guard down. Not only hers, but everyone around her. Like I said, we have—"

"One shot."

My throat worked as I struggled to swallow. He was serious. I tried to picture Astarte's stunning form and spotless, medical coat full of bullet holes as she looked back at me with lifeless eyes.

And though I was desperate to know what he and Azrames were plotting while I stepped like a child into a den of vipers, I didn't press him. She may be a serpent, but I ran with wolves.

"Astarte needs to believe everything is normal. Better than normal. I've seen you in a number of masks, Love. This may be the greatest acting role to date. It's...I wouldn't be able to do what you can do. I wouldn't be able to look her in the eye knowing what I know. You have a gift far greater than mine. Don't underestimate the value of your skill."

"So I carry on with the procedure as if I'm just there to get knocked up and write a book. Got it."

My tone may have been light, but my soul was anything but. My unshakable faith in Caliban and Azrames didn't make things any less stressful for the anxiety-ridden control freak in me.

He'd kissed me more times that morning than I could count. Cool, gentle kisses against my shoulder had woken me up in the morning light. Tender kisses on my mouth, on my neck, on the notch at the bottom of my throat had made me loop my leg around him to pull him closer. He'd accepted my bid for affection, crushing me against him as his mouth claimed mine.

"Fuck later" came Azrames's grumbling voice from the far side of the room.

"Prude," I replied.

He laughed and shook the sheets from him. Shadow-dark muscles in little more than night shorts, he ran a hand through his hair and walked past us for the shower as he said, "You don't want Astarte smelling Hell on you."

Azrames disappeared into the bathroom, and a steam of hot mist escaped the shower a moment later.

"He's right," Caliban agreed. "You'll need to scrub off any sign of me."

"Join me?" I asked, biting my lip as I rolled my hips against his.

His voice stayed low as he growled against my cheek. "That would defeat the purpose, Love." Goose bumps raced from my scalp down my back at the rumble of his words. He traced his fingers up and down my spine as we waited for Azrames to shower, and my heart squeezed for him. I wondered how much harder this was for him than I could ever realize. I tried to fathom lifetimes with a person, only to have a window of understanding after two thousand years. The moment the window had cracked open, it had been slammed shut. It was hard to believe a love like that could exist. It was even harder to believe I could be worthy of it.

"Caliban?" I whispered.

"Mmm?"

"Can you tell me about the first time we met?"

He inhaled in a way I didn't quite expect. It was more of a sadness than a laugh. His hand tightened on the back of my head as he tucked me in closer, and I knew intuitively that our story was a tragedy.

"The King..."—I cleared my throat as I rested my face against his chest—"your father, I mean...he said we met two thousand years ago, he and I. Is that when you and I met?"

"No," he murmured, patting my hair. "We met several cycles before that, near the Dead Sea."

I pictured a map of the world, zooming into desert, salt, and sand.

"What happened?" I asked.

He shook his head. "I don't think you need to hear."

"Caliban—"

"Today will be hard, Love. You are strong. You've been strong from the moment I met you. And you shouldn't have to be. You shouldn't have to be this resilient lifetime after lifetime. It's a blessing to forget."

"Please?" I asked.

He continued to stroke my hair, the motion matching the rhythmic noise of the shower from the next room. With his chest and shoulders blocking out the light, I nearly thought I would fall back to sleep. I tried to picture the Dead Sea and wondered if it was truly crystalline around the edges from salt deposits, aquamarine water, and burnt-orange mountains like in the pictures I'd seen. Most of what I knew of the Dead Sea had been from my upbringing in the church.

"Was..." Something uncomfortable scratched at the back

of my brain. It was almost a tickle, like something I couldn't possibly soothe with fingers. I could feel the way my face bunched as clearer, sharper images of the white salt beaches and pale blue shores stretched in my memories. A loud noise filled me like the memory of a dream. Anger. Yelling. Pain. My hair was tugged. I was dragged. My throat was raw from screaming. My eyes stung. I saw the blue of the water, of the sky, of the line where water and air dissolved from one to the other.

It was a nightmare.

"Was I killed there?"

Caliban pulled away from me to examine my expression. I was surprised by the sudden absence of my face against his skin, but something about the alarm in his expression stirred me. "Why would you ask that?"

Even as the concern on his face deepened, the sound from deep within the buried parts of me grew louder. I could see faces. I heard the crunch of bone before I felt it, and I knew he could see me wince against the pain. Their voices continued, but mine stopped the moment the crushing began. I was no longer willing to give them the satisfaction. I stood until I could stand no longer, then I knelt, then I lay, then I crumbled. The hot, coppery taste of blood filled my mouth. The turquoise water turned a shade of lavender as a ruby stream ran from its salty shores into the crystal-clear sea. The sounds stopped, but I continued to stare at the lavender, watching the blood bloom into pretty, floral roses and dilute into the sea.

"I was stoned to death, wasn't I?"

"Love," he said, voice low with concern. "What are you seeing?"

I didn't know how to answer him. I'd never done or seen or felt anything like this before. I wasn't afraid as the sensations washed over me. It felt like recalling a movie I'd seen in my childhood—disconnected, unimportant. "I don't know," I said honestly. I knew Caliban was in front of me in the

397

town of Bellfield, but I continued to watch the gentle purple color as sun scorched my skin. It burned, frying my cheek, my shoulder, my calves. My dress had torn, though I wasn't entirely sure where. I tried to move my body but couldn't.

"I cried out, to no reply," I said, speaking to the memory. I didn't know what I was saying, but hushed words tumbled out, one after the other. It was nonsense, and yet... "I needed him. He didn't come for me. He didn't answer me. We were told he'd be there. He let me—"

"Shh." Caliban wasn't silencing me but reassuring me of his presence as emotion bubbled through me. "I know, Love. You were on Heaven's side. You have been a few times, and it rarely goes well. We met in nine hundred BCE, and your family was very devout. And when you were accused of blasphemy—"

"They killed me."

He cupped my chin. "They tried."

"How did I... How did you know how to find me?"

It took him a while to answer, as if sifting through painful memories. Eventually, he said, "The battle was much bloodier in those days on both sides. We've used the mortal realm as our middle ground. And when an atrocity is committed in the opposing party's name..."

My brow furrowed, not quite understanding his meaning. I wasn't angry, just quiet, still so far removed from the grainy vision as I asked, "I would be, what? Propaganda? An example?"

The seconds ticked between us. I felt his arms around me in the hotel as fiercely as I felt the heat on exposed skin, not quite like a dream after waking. It was like living two realities at once. My fingers flexed against him to anchor myself to the present.

"Yes," he answered honestly. His hands continued to move comfortingly against my hair as he spoke. "You would have been an example when we still tried to persuade others to defect. Seeing the bloodshed, the gore, the cruelty committed on one side of the battlefield under the banner of righteousness…sometimes that's what it takes for another angel to fall—that's what you call it, anyway. Falling."

I saw the turquoise water ripple. A vulture landed on a sun-bleached branch.

"So?" I asked in a whisper. My muscles remained stiff, but not with fear or distrust. They hurt as if recovering from the impact wounds of a long-forgotten memory of a daydream. I wasn't sure what pressed me to ask anything further. He was in my bed. I was in his arms. The rest should have been unimportant. And yet I asked, "What happened to your plan?"

I wondered how often he thought of our meeting. It seemed from the wounds in his voice and his reluctance to answer that it was a memory he tried to bury. His voice was thick when he said, "You reached out and touched my face. I was so surprised you could see me, but then again, your time between life and death was evaporating quickly. Sometimes it makes the veil thin. For a moment, we weren't human and other. We were just us. The only two in existence. And you said three words."

"Which three?"

He closed his eyes, and I could sense the way the memory flooded him. Emotion colored his voice as he saw the day when he recited: "*Don't leave me.*"

The baking sand, the taste of salt, the excruciating blood and pain crashed over me once more as I felt a cool touch. Scavenger birds joined the others, their shrill cries piercing the air when a face blocked out the sun. I was picked up in arms and carried to one of the caves that lined the shores. Maybe they'd think my body was taken by the wild dogs. Maybe they'd never check on my corpse and leave me for the buzzards. The sun died as my bones knit together, my swelling calmed, the ringing in my head settled into the quiet sounds of the desert.

I'd clutched at my heart when I'd seen him. The blood

was dried and stuck to my hair and clothes, but there were no wounds to be found. The pain had dissipated, leaving a pleasurable humming in its wake. There was no fire, yet I had no trouble seeing the phantom-white man who'd shared the shadowed space in the sea cliffs. It should have smelled of dust and blood, but it didn't. There was a freshness, a beauty I didn't recognize.

"Are you an angel?" I'd asked.

He'd shaken his head sadly at the fear on my face, but his answer had been simple enough.

"No."

Something between panic, horror, and confusion had torn through me as I'd stared at the beautiful man. I'd rejected the day as if I'd imagined it, but looking at my clothes, I knew it had all be real. I should have been dead. "I needed God. I didn't denounce him, and—"

The crystal-white hair had been such a shock, like the moon itself had joined me in the cave. He'd looked like a star had been knocked out of the sky to heal me. "I know," he'd said, voice quiet. He'd extended his fingers for mine, then stopped himself, hovering just above my hand. He withdrew slowly. "He didn't deserve your loyalty. Your refusal to turn your back on that which ignored you…it broke something in me."

"But, I waited for him, and—"

"The deities you call aren't always the ones who answer."

That had been it.

I looked at him now in my hotel room as the memory faded like smoke, twinkling stars from the gap in the sea cave evaporating into the speckled decorations of the luxury hotel. He was even more beautiful now than he'd been in the gloom of the cave. I whispered, "I made you promise me, didn't I? I'd been abandoned by Heaven. And then I met you and…I asked you to never leave me alone."

He breathed out slowly, tufting my hair with his chilling breath.

400

"I chose you then," I said. "Cruelty and pain and neglect, and then you were the first person—first anything—that didn't let me down. You answered my cry when I was left for dead. I chose you the moment I knew you."

His laugh was quiet, almost imperceptible. "And I, you."

"How do I...?"

"How do you remember it?" He moved his head slightly, not quite shaking it against the pillow. His lips twisted. "You've never done that before. I want to credit your fae blood, but... I don't know. I think it's your openness. Every day you step closer to accepting the universe might have new impacts on the world you knew before."

I tumbled into his eyes, confident that he'd looked into mine a thousand times before, but never with the hope he held now.

The high squeak of a knob followed by the abrupt end of the shower cut our conversation short. Azrames didn't need the shower any more than he'd needed the beer. Some pleasures were indulgent whether or not you were in mortal or immortal form. Obviously, a good steam was one of them.

"You're up next, Love," Caliban said, tucking a lock of hair behind my ears.

"But—"

"I made a vow that I intend on keeping, for two thousand three hundred and fifty reasons. But first, we have to get through today. When you come out of the shower, Azrames and I will be gone. I don't want Astarte to have any reason to sense us on you. But I made you a promise that I've never broken."

"Caliban—"

"You're never alone."

Azrames emerged from the bathroom with a towel wrapped around his waist, water glistening off of his horns and dripping from his hair. "It's all yours, Marmar. Go get ready. We have a deity to kill."

✦

I hated emerging from the bathroom to see that they were, in fact, gone.

I hated that they'd opened a window to banish the smoke and moss from the room, leaving only the garden-fresh smells of the idyllic town beyond. I hated changing into the only other pair of clean clothes I'd purchased at the boutique, and I hated the bitter taste of coffee from the lobby. I hated wasting my day on the hotel's business computer googling ancient Canaanite civilizations, Phoenician gods and goddesses, religious practices, and pagan fertility rites. I did kind of enjoy the scowl I gave a nosy, middle-aged onlooker with bobbed blond hair when she peered over my shoulder.

"I'm just looking up sacrificing rituals," I said to the woman.

She glared at me as if I'd just flashed her my tits and told her to take a picture.

"Human sacrifice," I clarified. "It's a favorite topic of mine."

The woman disappeared with a loud huff and a look on her face that told me that the hotel manager would be hearing from her.

My thumb slipped a time or two and I found myself searching for pictures of the Dead Sea, but memories did not return.

I promptly returned to hating things.

I hated choking down an overpriced cuban from the hotel's restaurant and pushing the fallen bits of ham and spare chips around the plate until I eventually signed my name to the room. I hated flipping through the television with nothing to watch, staring at the clock as the hours crept on. I hated that time moved slowly when I didn't have my phone to scroll or my laptop for work.

I hated walking down the street to a coffee shop and seeing the chocolate pastries, wishing Fauna were here with me. I opened my purse to pay and frowned. I was down an item.

My broach and poppet clanged together in the loose bottom of the bag as I reached for the credit card, but Azrames and Caliban must have taken the knife back from me while I was in the shower.

I wouldn't have been any good with the weapon, but it was hard to swallow that I'd be going in truly defenseless after all.

And once the clock hit half past four, suddenly it felt as if there'd been no time at all. I could never have prepared myself for the emotional turmoil of the drive to the clinic, or the way my heart thundered so hard in my ears that I thought perhaps I'd crashed the BMW into the car in front of me when I'd eased into a parking spot. I shouldered my purse and walked on unsteady feet toward the lobby, but Jessabelle was there to receive me before I reached the glass door. Her smile was one of appreciation and something that almost looked like…veneration.

"Merit," she cooed. "We've been counting the seconds all day."

"Me too," I said honestly.

Abandoning all sense of decorum, she looped her arm through mine as she escorted me forward. Instead of taking me to the stairs, she turned to a row of elevators and hit the downward arrow. Given the height of the building, I hadn't expected so many subterranean floors, but from the tiny dashes indicating the negatives before each number, it appeared that it extended into the earth nearly as deep as it was tall.

And as the elevator began to pull us down, down, down, I couldn't help but wish we really were going into the pits of Hell. At least Hell had good booze.

Chapter Thirty-Seven

DESPITE BEING SWALLOWED BY THE EARTH, THE ELEVATOR opened into a room so bright it could have been filled with natural light. I stepped out of the elevator, and my lips parted in surprise. I didn't try to hide my confusion from Jessabelle.

"Beautiful, isn't it?"

It was.

I felt like I'd stepped into a luxury Mediterranean spa. A shallow pool ran the length of the room, elaborate mosaic tiles reflecting along its bottom in the blossoming patterns that reminded me of art from ancient Mesopotamia. White columns lined the pool and the wall. Each porcelain pillar had a lantern mounted to its center, all emitting the gentle glow of a tiny star. Lanterns dropped down from the ceiling above the center of the pool, continuing the evenly spaced pattern of starlight. Juliet roses, greenery, and aquamarine lounging settees, perfectly matching the blue of the pool, dotted the space between the columns.

"We'll have you relax here after the procedure," she said lightly.

I suppressed a gag, faking a smile through the repulsive thought of relaxing on a chair by the pool with a stranger's semen dripping down my leg. My hand flew to my mouth to conceal the nausea. She didn't seem to notice as she led the way. Moments later she helped me hang my things in what I wanted to call a locker room, but between the burning incense, the heated floors, the low lighting, and the luxurious wood, calling it a locker room felt like an insult.

She procured a fluffy white robe. "Please rinse off in preparation for the procedure. Do not redress, save for the robe. I'll wait for you outside. Take all the time you need."

A tremble overcame me the moment she left.

It was a perversion of my former profession. This was a day that belonged to Astarte. Our bodies were not ours.

I stood under the hot water for far too long. I wondered if Jessabelle would come and check on me if I didn't hurry up, but I couldn't force myself from the water. I had no plan. I was simply to move forward with the *procedure,* as she'd insisted on calling it. I wouldn't be lying on the crinkly paper of a hospital bed while fluorescent lights burned my retinas and cold speculums were inserted. This was gentle, plucking harps of spa music, hazy smoke, and the thrum of ancient magic.

I stepped from the shower and toweled off, trembling as if I stood in the Arctic rather than the balmy temperature fit for a cedar sauna. I stepped into the soft, fluffy robe and looked at myself in the mirror.

It had pockets.

I ran my fingers along the material and heard Jessabelle's voice from the far side of the door. "Are you almost ready, Merit?"

"Yes." I choked a quiet response. "Just one moment."

I hurried to the locker and yanked my purse from the hook. I had to have something—*anything.*

I may not have the knife, but I had a broach. I slipped the silver piece of jewelry into one pocket, then the golden poppet into the other. My hand went to my heart as if to catch a fluttering bird trying to escape its cage. I tried to tell myself that I'd been in these shoes hundreds of times before,

405

stepping out of the shower and preparing to meet someone unfamiliar.

But it wasn't the same. Not at all.

I emerged from the locker room, unable to keep the bubbling panic from my face.

"It's okay to be nervous," Jessabelle said smoothly. "I promise you'll only feel hesitancy for a moment longer. Astarte will ensure everything goes smoothly. The men will refer to her as Doctor Ayona, and I recommend you do the same for privacy, just as we will continue referring to you as Merit." She turned to me and let her olive-green eyes linger until they chilled my spine.

Everyone in the clinic knew my true name. Of course they did.

We stepped into a room so dark that it took my eyes a moment to adjust. My hands jerked toward Jessabelle as if to use her body as a shield, but my fingers froze before they made contact.

Jessabelle was not my friend.

My trembling intensified, though I did my best to conceal it. I straightened my shoulders as I looked at the nine well-dressed men in the room. Three standing tables dotted the room, each man holding what looked like a glass of cucumber water as they chatted with one another. The tables were counter high. They were not quite tall enough for them to rest their elbows, nor were they short enough for anyone to take a seat, had chairs been made available. Instead, many of them rested a hand on the table to support their weight while sipping on their drinks with the other. It looked like I'd interrupted a model casting party in a spa robe.

The walls of the room were black, adding to the sensation of shadows and depth. The lights were dim and buttery. I could see everyone, but I knew the flattering lighting would conceal anything that made us self-conscious. It was the perfect lighting for a 1920s speakeasy or for a Phoenician goddess's underground sex dungeon.

"Merit." Astarte breezed over to me from a shadow.

I nearly jumped out of my skin as she practically apparated, sliding a hand against the center of my back. Once again, she wore an expensive dress beneath a white lab coat. Unlike the black dress from the day before, her sparkling, sand-colored cocktail gown draped like glittering gems of the desert. She was ready to step out of her sterile lab coat and onto the stage.

"Please take the time to get to know our prospects," she practically purred. "Look at their build, listen to their voice, look into their eyes, and see whose genes call to yours. They've all been kept on a strict drink and drug-free diet upon entering our contracts, as well as submitted to regular bloodwork and endocrine panels, and they've followed my tailored exercise and meal plan. I can assure you, whoever you select will be of prime stock the world has to offer."

Stock.

I looked at the handsome men displayed like creatures in a terrarium. Presumably, they'd been left to stand so I could see their height, their build, their attributes. They smiled back somewhat apprehensively. I wonder what these men were told about the agreement or what had led them to consent to a doctor's insane procedure. Would the one I selected get an extra perk for his victory?

A few of my friends in the escort community worked model parties, paid for their ambience and availability. They were compensated for their time whether or not a guest led them away to a room. Most of those friends now owned multi-million-dollar sunset homes overlooking the cliffs of southern California. Perhaps the same was true for the donors.

"Do I just—"

"Talk to them!" Astarte gestured. She pushed a glass of sparkling cucumber water into my hand. She encouraged me with the press of her hand on my lower back.

The musical jingle of a small bell went off. She shot me an apologetic look, failing to conceal her annoyance as she left me to approach the wall.

"Doctor" came Anath's voice from the small box. "Someone is here to see you."

"They'll have to wait," she replied, voice sharp with irritation.

The black box blinked on in full color as I realized an entire glossy tablet had been embedded into the walls. Anath's black hair was in a slicked-back ponytail today, but her clothes were as dark and tight as they'd been the day before. "I wouldn't call unless it were important," she said. "Look at my eyes and tell me if I'm wasting your time. Don't send Jessabelle. This needs to be your call."

It had to be Caliban. I called on my years as Maribelle to keep my shoulders relaxed and summoned a soft smile, despite my urge to stiffen at the news. If their plan was in motion, then the best I could do was play my role and keep Astarte's guard down.

Astarte made a small, frustrated motion as she hit a button for Anath to disappear.

"Jess, take care of things for me?"

"Of course," answered the Soul Eater as the doctor disappeared from the room. Jessabelle tugged me gently toward the first table. "What features do you picture on your child? Picture his red curls and bright, emerald eyes with your cute nose," she said, running a hand over the first tall, muscled man with hair as red as flame. "Or your hazel eyes on his gold-brown skin," she said as she slipped to the next man. "Mixed babies are all the rage."

I struggled to swallow my horrified laugh. I nearly drew blood from my struggle to clap back at her, but I was practically naked, defenseless, and in a goddess's den. Perhaps this was not the moment to point out that comparing children and their genetic qualities to trends was outrageously offensive.

Jessabelle wandered between the men, sliding her hands over their arms, running her fingers through their hair, refilling my drink time after time as my nerves made my mouth feel progressively drier between every man. My heart thundered in my ears. I knew Caliban had asked me to trust him, but what did that trust entail? Was I to trust that he'd fund my pregnancy termination when I had a ginger child growing inside me? How far was I expected to go?

"Let me get you another. Stay here," she said as she plucked the third empty glass of sparkling water from my hand.

I looked up at the tall, Swedish-looking gentleman who offered me an apologetic smile. I thought he smelled like expensive cologne, but there was something indefinably masculine about his scent that I couldn't quite place. I couldn't help as I leaned forward, inhaling him with deep breaths.

"Is it a little uncomfortable to be put on the spot?" he asked. From the lilting accent of his voice, I was surprised to hear that he was, in fact, Scandinavian. Given the short notice, I'd expected all the men to be local. His shirt was well tailored, which I imagined was quite the feat to keep his pectorals from ripping a button-up in half.

I realized I'd been smelling a stranger and shook my head clear, embarrassed. I didn't know what had come over me, but I hoped he hadn't noticed. I did my best to gather my wits as I nodded. "I had no idea it would work like this. Do you live nearby?"

I recognized the man beside him from the binder as the architect called Ji-Hoon. He was dressed as if he'd stepped out of a magazine. He laughed lightly as he said, "He does. Johan plays in the NHL, so he's only two states away. For most of us, no, the doctor sends a plane." His English was as excellent as the Swede's, but once again it told me that he was far from local. "We have to be ready at a moment's notice. It's a ten-hour flight between here and Seoul."

"You came from Seoul?" I repeated incredulously. "I had no idea..."

The Swedish man shrugged easily. "Things will get easier once the meds kick in."

"Meds?" I asked as Jessabelle returned with another glass of water.

"I'm glad you're getting to know the men." She flashed a glistening smile. "If you're comfortable, Merit, I'll leave you to it. I'll be right here if you need me. Please just...listen to your body. Let it make the choice."

Jessabelle disappeared into a shadowed corner of the room, but I wasn't foolish enough to think she didn't see and hear everything that went on. I knew enough of the world—mortal or fae—to know every wall had ears. I gulped down the water, draining it halfway before she'd even escaped to the far side of the room.

The Swede nodded toward my water. "It helps with inhibitions."

"I..." I looked at him with confusion. "My water?"

The three men at the table exchanged laughs, but not at me. Almost in answer to my question, I felt a warming sensation course through my blood. I became aware of my heartbeat, but not in my chest. My pulse throbbed somewhere far more...intimate. I lifted my eyes in confusion as I felt the slick rush between my thighs. My sharp, sudden intake of air must have given me away.

"What did I tell you?" he said.

Ji-Hoon tilted his glass. "It's just as fun for us as it is for you. Everyone has a good time."

"And"—I swallowed, looking between the men at the table—"I get a baby and you get..."

"You're beautiful. More than beautiful," the third said, a man I hadn't yet spoken to. He spoke with flat, North American English and looked like he was on an Ivy League rowing team. "So, we get laid, which is a perk of its own. Especially with someone like you... But none of us will worry about money for the rest of our lives. Plus, you get a baby, which is what brought you here in the first place, right? The doctor gets to maintain the reputation as the most successful fertility clinic in the world. Everyone wins."

I took a step away from the table and nearly bumped into the man behind me. He put out a hand to catch my back

410

before it collided against the rim of his table and a pleasurable chill shot through me. I leaned into his touch before even seeing his face. If I'd been wearing panties, they would have been destroyed by a single, charged touch. I turned to look up at a gorgeous man with unnaturally blue eyes contrasting against his brown skin. Without meaning to, I bit my lip. He smiled in return as a current passed through us.

I turned toward him, my hands moving before my conscious mind as I rested both hands on his chest. A distant part of my brain heard him introduce himself as Yasin, from Pakistan. He rattled off the same statistics that I knew were meant to be common knowledge in the binder. His good job, his high IQ, his height, his weight, his family health were all said with performative necessity, but I knew he felt the same electricity I felt.

I swallowed but found my mouth was no longer dry. The throbbing within me grew into a craving. I took a step closer to him, and he slipped another hand around me as he peered down at me.

Jessabelle appeared at my side, but I was hardly conscious of her arrival. "You two get acquainted," she said, voice a sultry purr. "I'll dismiss the others."

Was music still playing? I wasn't sure. I could only hear the low rumble of his voice and the demanding throb of a heart-beat somewhere I couldn't control. My bare feet scrunched, toes curling against the heated marble.

Shapes moved as Jessabelle worked with the others. I was loosely aware that she was escorting the men from the room. The music in the room had changed, though I hadn't been conscious of its transition from the calming music known to bathhouses and spas to something with bass, something more primal, something that matched the pulse aching through me. My back arched as the warmth continued to fill me. Yasin spoke, and I knew I was supposed to be listening, but I couldn't stop picturing his mouth on me. I tilted my hair back slightly as I breathed in his masculine scent, exposing my neck to him. I pressed myself into him and parted my lips, hoping he'd kiss me. Maybe this was why I was in a robe. If he would just give the white, fluffy belt around my waist a tug… my breasts peaked at the thought as my body rolled again.

He'd left his hand on my arm. I wanted him to move it. To touch me. To stop talking. He was so goddamn pretty. He smelled indescribably good. Maybe if I moved closer…

The bell chimed again from the wall on the far side of the room. Jessabelle had one foot out the door as she ushered the suitors into the hall when she dismissed them to swiftly answer the persistent bell.

Rather than put the image on the glossy tablet as Astarte had done with Anath, Jessabelle picked up a slick black receiver. My eyes glazed over as I watched her, allowing her to disappear into the shadow like ink blotting over paper. I'd hardly been aware of the way my body continued to arch until my upper back rested on the table. My robe slipped off a single shoulder, exposing it to the world. Operating with a mind of its own, one of my legs wrapped around Yasin's and slid it gradually upward.

For no reason other than hazy amusement, half of my attention remained on Jessabelle while my body coursed with desire. She was in the room, and I didn't care. It would have been no more important to me than the episode of a sitcom that had played in the background the first time I'd met a client. Except I wanted this client. I thirsted for him. I needed him.

I caught Jessabelle's hiss as she repeated the word. "A cambion? That's not possible—"

Gibberish words. Nonsense. Not quite English. Not quite anything else, either.

Jessabelle paused while the person on the other end continued to speak. The word she'd said into the receiver was one I knew from somewhere. The distant, unimportant memory of a university glass, of mythology, of a historical figure, magic, a something or other…it dissolved into me,

412

wanting to sense lips around my nipple, to feel gentle suction on my breast. I grazed my fingers along my collar and moved my hips again as I felt how soft the fabric was, how the dim lighting was as perfect as an orange-red glow.

"I understand the implications," she said. "Yes, I fully comprehend the opportunity. I don't understand how he—"

More silence from Jessabelle as I admired her curves, watching her berry-dark mouth, the curve of her hips, her ass, her breasts. I wondered if she'd join us and extended a hand idly toward her, hoping she'd accept my bid. I wanted to touch her soft skin, to taste her, to feel her. I wanted mouths and hands; I wanted every nerve ending to dance with desire and satisfaction. The need heightened with each new throb of the bass as the music continued to fill the room. It was louder with every passing second until I could barely hear anything else.

Thump, thump, thump.

Jessabelle's voice was light, barely carrying above the music's pleasurable, pounding vibrations. She continued to argue into the receiver as she said, "The power is unparalleled, I know that. But what if she doesn't want—"

I wanted her to get off the phone and join us. It would be incredible, and I would be at the center. I wanted him inside me. I wanted her against me. I wanted the silk and velvet and slick, wet pleasure of cock and cunt side by side as I indulged. My toes curled against my need as the music continued to swell. It was so loud now I couldn't hear anything. I couldn't hear Yasin, or Jessabelle, or the world. Even the thoughts in my head were stifled and silenced against the thumping music that resonated through my body, my skin, my heart, my mind. It kept time with the throb between my legs.

It was like MDMA. It was like being a teenager. It was a craving in a world with no shame, no consequences, no judgment.

I closed my eyes as Yasin's lips pressed against my bare shoulder. They dragged slowly against my collarbone. I reached both hands above my head to tilt my head backward over the standing table. I felt like an erotic ballerina as I spun through the galaxy of want and pleasure and lust.

"Understood," Jessabelle said quickly. She was at my side in a second. She'd barely peeled Yasin off me and asked him to return to his room before I pressed into her. Her soft body, her curves, her cascading hair, her extravagant scent...one of my hands slipped up the back of her neck into her hair. "Merit." She said my name as a correction, but I barely heard her.

She didn't fight me as I used my free hand to pull her against me. I wanted to taste her throat. I wanted her skin beneath my lips, her salt under my tongue, her flavors inside me. Even her light chuckle felt good against my mouth as my tongue worked kiss over kiss, creeping up her neck onto her jaw.

Over my shoulder I heard a male voice. "She's been drugged?"

"The client's been thoroughly primed" came Astarte's reply. I didn't remember doors opening, had no recollection of others entering the room. I hummed with the need for connection, struggling to discern words above the noise. I could hear it, but I didn't care enough to make sense of it as she said, "This is what she wants. It's a gift greater than she could have ever anticipated if you're the sire. Trust me, it's a mutually beneficial deal for all parties. She's ready, if you are."

A tiny gasp escaped me as a distant part of me tried to pry myself off Jessabelle toward the voice. I felt a cool hand on my bare shoulder and my eyes opened, filling with diamonds and stars and bright, white light. I practically moaned his name, but he put his hand against my face, stopping my lips with his thumb. I popped his thumb into my mouth and sucked on the succulent flavors of fern and gin. I released Jessabelle entirely, her existence dissipating like vapor in the wind as I turned toward Caliban.

Chapter Thirty-Eight

I GRABBED HIS FREE HAND AND SLID IT OVER ME. HIS FINGERS flexed against me, and the sound that came out of me was truly primal.

"I assume this fit is suitable?" asked Astarte. I knew she was asking me, but I didn't care. Of course this fit was suitable. This was the one thing I wanted more than anything in the world. I wanted to feel his teeth through my skin, his fingers in my flesh, the throbbing pulse of his cock as he filled me. I grabbed for him and whimpered in disappointment that he was still clothed. His black shirt was an unwelcome barrier. His pants stood between me and the thing I wanted more than anything.

"Merit, I need to hear it from you," Astarte said firmly.

"Everything is perfect," I purred, and I meant it.

"Please." She remained cool. "Can you give me a—"

"Yes." I practically begged the word.

She could stay here and enjoy the show of her life as we made true, deep, perfect love. Jessabelle would be so lucky to stay against the wall and watch from the corner. I could be in front of kings and queens and emperors and gods and bishops and pastors and coliseums of pious women clutching their pearls; they'd be little more than noise. The electric, earth-changing, palpable chemistry that was about to pound through me was all I cared about.

Caliban was here. He'd come for me. Nothing else had ever mattered.

I glided through time and space as I moved off my tiptoes. I knew logically it was a small distance between standing and resting my ass firmly on the table, but I jumped backward onto the nearest surface. Caliban seemed to realize my intention before I was halfway off the ground and helped me onto the waist-high table, both of his hands on my hips. I groaned against the sensation and ran my fingers through his hair, balling my fists in the arctic fox strands. I was barely aware of how the table teetered against my disregard for the laws of physics, hardly noticing how Caliban had steadied both me and the table. The bass of the music piping into the room buzzed through me, filling every cell, every heartbeat, every breath. I arched again as I used my legs to draw him to me. I tore at the robe until it opened in the front, draping over my shoulders while exposing me to him.

I tried to say his name again, but the first hard *c* of his name barely escaped my throat before he grabbed my hair and pulled, hard. I yelped in a sound mixed between pleasure and pain as his name was lost to the smoky air around me.

I wanted all of it and more.

I wanted him to pull my hair. To slap me. To bend me over. To grab and grope and bite. I wanted leather and whips and straps. I wanted pain to heighten the pleasure. I wanted his mouth on my throat, his fingers clawing at me, his dick to throb inside of me as he kept time to the loud music—so loud, so wholly filling, so incredible, so sensational.

Astarte offered him a glass of water, but he said, "Trust me, I don't need it."

She seemed satisfied with the answer as he lowered his mouth to make contact with my throat. I wanted to cry out for him, ready to beg, to plead, to pray. I tried again to gasp his name, but he slipped two fingers into the back of my throat until I gagged on them. My eyes rolled into the back of my head as I slipped my tongue between each of the fingers, sliding off the counter. I grabbed his hand to keep it secured to my mouth as I continued sucking, drinking in the flavor of ferns and red tree trunks and moss-soft earth after the rain. I rotated until I was bent over the table, holding his fingers against my mouth with a vice-like grip.

If I hadn't been bent over the table, I wouldn't have seen the screen blink to life.

Anath had hit the intercom to showcase the anarchy occurring in the lobby. I released Caliban's fingers and abandoned the table to lean backward into him. I looped both hands behind me, one running through his silvery locks, the other grabbing at his hips while the disruptive color of the lobby cut through my haze.

I recognized...something.

I struggled to discern the life happening beyond the present bubble.

Anath was yelling. She said she'd tried to kill him. Kill him? That couldn't be right. It didn't matter. It was so far away, so unimportant.

My head spun as if I were twenty-one and had thrown back seventeen drinks on the same night. It was a rowdy frat bar where I tried to forget my life and my pain against the music that shook the walls. It was shot after shot after without the nausea, without the pain, without the regret. I didn't care as I watched the familiar face of the clerk from the Bellfield Inn appear on the screen, knowing his presence was impossible; it was a nonsensical vision. I wasn't interested in Anath's angered demand for backup, in her words, in her aggression. I barely saw Astarte cross to the tablet embedded in the wall and stand in front of it to block its light, as if she were more invested in blocking me from the spell it might break than anything going on in the Venus Clinic.

Caliban's hands continued to move over my front, exploring my stomach, my breasts, my throat, my thighs. My sighs of pleasure filled the gaps created by any concern from the others, uncaring, focused only on the one who held my heart, my body, my soul as I pressed my ass against him, feeling the member still trapped in his pants.

I reached around for him, aching for him.

Astarte covered the screen with her back as she hissed to Jessabelle, "Get up there and take care of this."

Jessabelle disappeared in a blink.

Good. The only two I needed in the room were Caliban and me. We were owed this pleasure. We didn't need their company.

Astarte had barely stepped away, back still to the screen in its final moments of electronic glow as I saw the silvery glint of a lasso spin above the clerk's head. Somewhere in the distant caves of my mind—somewhere more buried than the memories of past lives—I remembered Azrames and his meteor hammer. The screen went dark as the metallic shape escaped the clerk's hands and it launched for Anath. It blinked into shiny black nothingness just as Astarte reached us.

"Possession?" was the word I managed to speak, hips still rolling against Caliban's.

He knew what I was asking, even if I was barely present enough to form the question.

"Yes," he said, lips reaching the exposed line of demarcation that ran from my belly button to my sternum, separating my breasts, tracing it up my throat. "Possession," he repeated. The word was so fucking sexy on his lips. His hands ran over me, pressing into me. He explored my body with his fingertips as Astarte joined us at the table, as if Caliban were reiterating that he possessed me, which he did. I belonged to him and succumbed fully as his hands roamed me from the fluffy exterior of robe until his hands pressed against two hard shapes in my pocket. He pressed the metallic shapes in my robe into my body with significance as he pressed his mouth over mine. The metal hurt in a wonderful bite as he pushed them into my hips. "Such a good girl," he rumbled, lips over mine, scarcely louder than a whisper.

I drank in the praise. My hands flew to his face as I pulled him close to me. They drifted south to his clothes as I tried to tear him free of the fabric that separated us.

"I love—"

I couldn't finish my declaration. He bit my lip so hard I was sure I tasted blood. The words were stolen from my mouth as I drank him in, his tongue working against mine, his lips over mine, his mouth absorbing the droplets of blood stolen from my mouth.

"She's ready," said Astarte. "This is a greater deal that we could have hoped for."

Maybe her words were important. Maybe they weren't. I didn't care.

"I know," he said, not taking his mouth from my neck.

"She's ready," Astarte repeated. "We both are. Are you?"

"Do you want a third, Love?" Caliban asked.

He shouldn't have asked. I didn't. I didn't want anyone but him. I said nothing as I tried to tear at his shirt again, but he snatched both of my wrists into one hand.

He pushed me down into the table until my chest, my head, my upper body twisted as it slammed against its surface, leaving him behind me. With my hands in his grip like cuffs, I was practically immobilized. I wriggled unsuccessfully, staring at the glossy surface that remained black and lifeless on the wall.

Astarte took the gasp of my impact against the table as confirmation as she came closer, shedding her white lab coat like it was a snakeskin. She turned her back to Caliban and pulled her hair to the side as she offered him the zipper. Something permeated my pleasure in a distant, foreboding way as his hands went to her zipper and began to tug.

I struggled against the table, but Caliban pushed the twist of my wrists harder until I knew if I fought against his hold, my arms would break. No, I didn't want to share Caliban with Astarte. No, I didn't want anyone else to experience him, to taste him. No, I didn't want him to get pleasure from anyone else. Jealousy was stronger than the drug as I struggled to emerge from the sensual fog that smothered me. I flipped my face against the table with the tiny freedom allowed from my space.

Her dress dropped around her ankles.

No, I didn't want to share Caliban. I didn't want her here for this. I didn't want—

She slipped her hands through my hair, and my thoughts melted away against the touch of a goddess. I relaxed my face into the cool table. I made an approving noise, a desperate noise for more as she ran her fingers against my scalp. I fought against the *yes* and the *no* warring within me.

I knew she was naked between us, but as long as she continued the sensual scrape of her nails...they rained from my scalp down my back as she turned toward Caliban. I did love the sensation of her fingers... I relaxed again, wanting the tantalizing stroke of my scalp to continue. I didn't want a break in the pleasure as each nerve was stimulated with the pleasurable chill of fingernails.

"Do it," Astarte said, and I knew she was talking to Caliban.

Through the haze, I heard him ask me for confirmation once more. His voice was hitched with a sincerity I barely understood. I always wanted him. I wanted him day in and day out. My love life had been destroyed by my need for him even before I'd believed he was real. He was all I'd ever wanted. Yet something in his voice...

"I need you," I said.

"Love—"

"*Please*," I begged, needing him inside me more than the sun in the winter, more than water in the desert, more than air. I pressed myself into him, knowing my robe was hiked up over my hips. The only thing separating us was his pants, and I pushed into him as if hoping it would burst through its cage and into me. I wriggled against him until I heard the sound of something—a button? a zip?—then the only noise accompanying the deep pulsing bass of the music was my gasp.

My head kicked backward. I cried out in pleasure, in agony, in surprise, in desperation, in need as he slid into me. I was so wet that I accepted him fully in a second. I cried out in fullness, in victory as he stretched me, filled me, completed me.

His reciprocal groan was music to my ears—sweeter and more vital than the thundering songs that shook the walls. I still felt the cool press against my face and bared breasts. I was still aware of the dark, dimly lit room. I knew Astarte was here with us. But all I could feel was the heartbeat of the cock inside me. I gave myself over to it, wanting fingers to dig into my hips, wanting the slap of skin as he drove into me, wanting the claiming demand of thrust after thrust.

I waited. And waited.

It took a second for me to recognize the wet sounds of a kiss behind me.

Breaking free from the haze again, I tried to jerk free to see what was happening, but the painful twist of my wrists kept my arms rod-straight. I grunted as I resisted it all, resisted the drug, the threesome, the world as I heard their mouths meet. I was his, and he was mine. He pushed into me more deeply and I gasped, feeling the fabric of his pants against my ass cheeks as if he'd barely popped himself out of his zipper to take me. I wanted to enjoy it, but I couldn't. The lust slipped away as I heard the sounds of tongues and lips behind me again. I craned my neck just enough to see Astarte slip her hands into his hair. I tried to cry out, to stop their embrace as my eyes homed in on his free hand.

It didn't go to her, or to me.

His free hand slipped to the back of his pants. I was barely conscious enough to see the moment he released my wrists. My hands flew forward to grip the edge of the table, groaning against the release of my bone-breaking grip. Time slowed as I watched Astarte's hand in Caliban's hair. His free hand went to hers, balling in her dark locks the way they had in mine so many times. His wrist yanked her head back, and her lips parted in a smile. Her eyes closed in pleasure. I arched up to protest the moment I saw his hand break free from its hidden place as his face changed completely from pleasure to concentration. His arm arced as his hand pointed down, the ornately engraved dagger angled for her heart. Her eyes flashed open in the last second before the knife plunged into her chest, buried up to its hilt as it found the tender spot between her ribs. She'd barely begun to scream out in rage as his other hand yanked her head back farther. Blood spurted from her center as he freed the dagger from her heart and slashed her across the tender flesh of her throat.

I watched and felt...nothing. Was I supposed to?

Her cry cut into gurgles.

On the far wall, Jessabelle's face blinked onto the screen as she screamed for backup. I caught Azrames's gray-and-black form. The clerk had crumbled in the corner of the lobby, pool of blood so red it looked black collecting below his head. Jessabelle scarcely had time to scream as the lasso whipped above Az's head before the spiked hammer released. It shot across the room and embedded into the back of her skull. The screen went black.

Caliban pulled free from me, tying my robe as my head spun. I grabbed the table for stability. I heard the bizarre, squishing, crunching noise of sawing before I dared to look down at his blood-covered hands. I refused to let my eyes see the sight before me as he decapitated Astarte with the dagger. I blinked against it, struggling between arousal and horror, need and confusion, shock and terror.

"Caliban." I finally managed his name.

"Trust me," he said through gritted teeth, a muscle ticking in his jaw as he scooped me up. I looked to the slowly growing lake of vermillion that gushed from Astarte's prone shape. A woman...her eyes open in unblinking surprise... mouth ajar in a silent scream...she'd been so pretty...

I bounced in his arms as I looked over his shoulder, scarcely aware as we passed the locker rooms, the shallow pool, the pillars. He hit the bank for the elevators again and again as he impatiently summoned the machine.

As if speaking through dozens of shots, I slurred, "Is it broken?"

"The elevator?" he asked, still pressing the button.

As if speaking through molasses, I tried again. "The seal."

"Yes, Love," he growled, face set in a hard shape against the tremor of fury that he struggled to contain.

"Jump," I said. I could scarcely speak, nor did I want to. It was with the low purr of a bedroom voice that I slipped my hand toward his pants as I said, "Jump realms."

He shook his head, snatching my hand to stop me in my pursuit. "We can't leave Azrames with Anath. Stay in the elevator."

Azrames. I knew that name.

The moment the doors parted, he shot into the rectangular box and pressed the button for the lobby over and over again. I knew this was important. I knew I needed to focus, to fight, to be an asset. Instead, I buried my face against his neck and pressed my lips against the pulse in his jugular. I felt like a storybook vampire as I could sense the blood beneath his throat. I wanted it. I wanted every part of him.

I wasn't sure how much time had or hadn't passed when the elevator doors parted for the lobby.

"Stay put!"

Caliban set me on the ground, and I felt the slapping offense of a cold fish across the face as he abandoned me. He dashed into the sounds, the whir of metal, the scream, the chaos and noise of the lobby. I heard more than three voices. Whoever was in there, it wasn't just my demons and Anath. I'd witnessed Jessabelle's death on screen in the moments before...

I struggled to my knees as I hit the button for the door to open. It did in a second as I crawled from the elevator. I got to my feet on unsteady legs. Wine and whiskey and molly and coke and music and lust and passion and tension and craving

423

tore me into a thousand pieces, each vice grabbing me with greedy hands as it pulled me in every direction. I struggled to move forward, eyes nearly unseeing, head swimming, ears hearing little above the ancient throb of bass-heavy music. Their drums filled me, demanded of me, called to me.

There was another scream—but not one of terror. A feminine rallying cry sharpened my attention, affording me another small moment of lucidity. I tried to understand the shapes between the cream-colored couches, the Juliet roses, the mosaic tiles of the marble flooring, but I couldn't discern the shapes.

I barely made into the lobby when I fell to my knees, joints hitting the lobby floor with the purple, bruising pain of the cobblestones of Hell.

Anath broke her battle with the demons as she spun for me. She sprinted toward my prone form. Something shiny cut through the haze, if only for a moment. Azrames swung his lasso with the spiked, silvery ball at the end as he knocked her out of the way. He succeeded in stopping her advance, but I caught movement from everywhere as if I were a spider seeing out of the refraction of twelve arachnid eyes rather than two, useless human ones. The enemy was everywhere. And Caliban and Azrames were only two.

"Call him!" Caliban shouted across the lobby while he pummeled an entity. His brilliant eyes lifted to me again in a demand before another parasite scrambled toward him.

I struggled to understand the shapes that rallied to defend Anath. Parasitic entities. Cheshire cats. Evil. So many. Too many. She cried to them to continue her battles against Caliban and Azrames as she turned her attention to me once more.

My panicked gaze went between Caliban and Azrames to Jessabelle's still, bloodied form. The creatures continued to flood the lobby with incomprehensible speed. Blood filled the space in different colors—red coursed out of both the clerk and from the corporeal Jessabelle. Blue pulp oozed from the creatures as they fell. Oil-slick black seeped from Anath's brow as she rallied again for me.

Azrames lunged for her, tackling her to the ground as Caliban shouted to me again.

"Call him! Call Silas!"

I blinked at him in confusion. A child-like parasite began to crawl toward me with the forward motion of a crab. It cocked its too-human head as it eyed me. I tried to scramble backward as its smile widened. I recognized the scabs at the corner of its eerily wide smile, its brilliant, sapphire eyes too blue to be anything other than terrible. Its mouth split into tiny, blooded edges as its sharpened teeth continued to grin at me.

I crawled backward farther until my back hit the far wall of the elevator banks.

Once again, Caliban begged above the overwhelming noise of Anath and her parasitic army. "Call Silas!"

The angel? But that meant...

Caliban knew something I didn't. I trusted him. I should listen to him, right?

Fuck, I needed to be sober. I didn't know how to blink free from the haze stronger than drugs, than drink, than everything that suffocated me. I barely had the wherewithal to slip my hand into my pocket and grab the golden poppet. I wrapped my fingers around the shape and brought it to my mouth. I squinted against the approaching Cheshire cat as its head exploded in a blue spray the moment Azrames's meteor hammer made contact with its skull. Its goo rained around me like the thick, horrid memory I'd buried from Richard's basement. I would have died had it not been for...

Azrames turned for Anath as she advanced on him again. She lofted a weapon in the time it took me to bring the gilded poppet to my mouth and speak his name.

I didn't know how much time had passed.

I heard the unreal cries of parasites and the feminine scream of Anath. I heard the metallic clang of the meteor

425

hammer and the high, shrill ring of the dagger as Caliban slashed. It could have been one second or ten minutes. I had no concept of war or battle or fights. I could only perceive the enormous crystal chandelier, the blur of colors, the high-pitched noises, and the continuous throb between my thighs.

The glitter had barely appeared in a flash of white light before I heard three sentences in Caliban's powerful, authoritative voice over the sounds of battle.

"We've got this! She's still mortal! Save her!"

I barely had time to gasp at Silas's presence. The gold-dust shimmer of wings dissipated as I struggled to see him. I was loosely aware that my robe had fallen to pieces, breasts, belly-button, and everything in between exposed in my scramble. Perhaps spa robes were not the most qualified garb for war, but despite knowing I should care, I didn't. I looked up into his golden eyes, seeing those tiny halos burning around his pupils.

I extended a hand toward him.

Silas spun away from me. He locked eyes with Caliban as he said, "You want me to—"

"Take her!" Caliban shouted back.

My hand found his chest, then glided over his shoulder. I didn't want to be alone. I wanted to be held. I wanted to be close. I wanted…

The high-pitched scream of a Cheshire-cat smile advanced on us as another parasite rushed the bank of elevators. Silas scooped a hand around me. "Do you have your broach?"

One hand already gripped his golden poppet. My free hand slipped into the opposite pocket as I blearily procured the dangly, silver sølje. I nodded through glazed eyes. I was loosely aware of the flare of his nostrils as he flinched against my naked body, as if struggling for decency. He pressed me against him as the paint globes of cream and blue pulp and the diamond white of Caliban's skin ran down the canvas of my inner eyes until I saw only black.

426

Chapter Thirty-Nine

M Y HANDS AND KNEES HIT FAMILIAR GLITTERING, BLACK marble, the brunt only half-absorbed by a male body. I gasped for air as if resurfacing from a deep lake. I barely had time to take in my surroundings before a high, angry feminine voice filled the air. I fought against it for a fraction of a second, terrified it was Astarte or Anath or Jessabelle.

I scarcely registered the constellation of white and ginger freckles that dotted her arms and the free space above her soft breasts before I buried my face in her hair. I recognized the smell. The salt and conifers and sea spray of trust, of love, of friendship, of beauty. My hand ran over her neck and into her long, beautiful curls.

"What's wrong with her?" Fauna's voice demanded in high, startled horror.

I felt the words more than I heard them. Each word vibrated against my lips as I kissed her throat.

"I have no idea," Silas insisted. "I think I have to go back. She was with the Prince and Azrames—"

"Az was there?" She tried—and failed—to get me to stop kissing her neck.

She smelled too good. I missed her. I nuzzled into her.

She gave up and held me against her so tightly that I scarcely had room to move. My mouth couldn't find her.

My hands ran over her hair, her back. "You have to go back," she said.

"I'm already on it. You have this under control?"

"I have it," she barked. "Go!"

"Fauna, it wasn't—" Silas could barely gasp as his eyes widened.

"Go!"

✦

Fauna got me into the shower that night, though not for the reasons I'd wanted. She claimed the Phoenician reek and scent of my drug was unbearable. She stuck her fingers down my throat over and over again as I vomited up the cucumber waters I'd guzzled in the basement. I had tried to suck on her fingers the first time she'd shoved them in my mouth, which had caused her to laugh a coarse, humorless laugh as she yanked my hair back and shoved her fingers in deeper.

"You are in so much trouble, you goddamn shithead," she'd growled.

I was still pretty sure I wanted to fuck her.

I puked my guts out for three hours. Any time I thought I was done, I'd accept a glass of water from her, then slide my hand up her thigh. She'd pull the entirety of my hair into a tight fist and bend me over the toilet's edge as she continued forcing me to purge the drug from my system. I wasn't sure how many glasses of water, how many fingers to the back of my tongue, how many pats on the back, how many worried words rushed over me.

She waited until I stopped coming on to her before she struggled to get me into the shower. The hot water ran over us. Instead of searching for her legs, I bundle my face into my knees as the cleansing rain of the hot water drenched me.

She crawled into the shower with me.

"Where are they?" she insisted.

"I left them," I choked. "Why...why did Astarte let Caliban in? What happened?"

428

"I need you to get your shit together, Marlow. Tell me what happened."

I shook my head, feeling the hot water plaster my hair to my back as it covered my naked body. I tried to look up at Fauna, but it was too dark to see her. She hadn't turned on the lights as we'd spent hours in the bathroom while I'd dispelled the last of the drug from my system. I was trembling against its residual effects as I clutched myself more tightly.

"You and Azrames got to Bellfield. You found Caliban. You were looking for the Phoenicians. Then what? What happened?" Fauna begged, shaking me.

"Astarte," I said. "Fertility."

"Tell me!"

How could I explain to her that I would have fucked anything on two legs? I would have let the Soul Eater impregnate me if she'd had the equipment to do so. Once Caliban had arrived, my love and need for him had barely been enough to cut through my haze. I knew beyond a shadow of a doubt that even if Fauna's beloved had been the one to arrive in that room, I would have slipped my hand into his pants. I'd had no control.

"She drugged us." I shook my head. "I don't know how to explain it. I was supposed to get pregnant. She was there. It was...sex. Why did she let Caliban in? She knew who he was. How did she know? Why would she..."

She shouted over the pounding of the shower water. I yelped as she turned the knob to drench me in sobering ice-cold water. "Why was Silas there? Why did he take you?"

I looked at her through the cutting darkness. There was no light in my apartment. I knew she asked not just for me but with the knowledge Azrames was left behind, and it was my fault. I struggled for my eyes to adjust to the shadowed bathroom as I looked into her enormous eyes. I could scarcely make out her outline against the distant amber gloom of the lights that drifted up from the streets of the warehouse district. She crawled deeper into the shower until the water pummeled against her shoulders, face inches from mine.

"I'm sorry," I choked. "Caliban told me to call him. I don't know why he trusted him. I don't know what he knows. I'm so confused. I'm so…"

"I don't need your apologies." Fauna shook me again. "What happened to Az?"

I sobbed again as I clutched my knees, burying my face against my bruised, purple knees.

"Marlow!" she cried, grabbing my wet hair with anger rather than pleasure as she yanked my face from my knees. "You fucking dumbass, tell me what the hell you did! Where are our men! Where is Azrames! Tell me before I shove gummy worms down your throat until you asphyxiate!"

Her words were light, but her tone was not. She was worried.

"They were fighting," I said loudly through the water.

"Fighting where?"

I shook my head. My teeth began to chatter as the water leached through my skin and froze my muscles, my tendons, my blood.

"Where?!" she practically screamed, voice echoing between the glass and tile of the shower as steam filled the room.

"The heat, please," I begged.

"Spit out a single coherent thought and I will turn on the hot water and wrap you in a blanket and make you tea and rub your feet," she said, voice hitched with desperation.

"Caliban killed Astarte," I said. "He killed her. There was so much blood. She let him in and he knew she would, but I don't know how or why. He didn't tell me why, but *he* knew. She drugged me and—" I flinched away from the memory.

"Azrames!" She gave my wet hair another yank.

"Parasites!" I struggled to free myself from her hold as I flailed like a fish in the shower. My legs hit the ground with a wet splash as the hot water continued to burn us. I shook

430

my head free from her fist and grabbed her shoulders. "Anath was calling them. There were so many in the lobby. It was just Caliban and Azrames against so many. He made me call Silas to get me out of there. I didn't want to leave him."

I released her as I crumbled into myself. I no longer had my knees as support, face collapsing into the puddle of frigid water, lips barely above the tiny pool before it raced toward the drain. The water's temperature changed ever so slightly, inching from arctic to lukewarm to hot once more. Each drop ran from my back, my hair, from Fauna, over my collapsed form and into the tiny drilled holes in the corner of the shower.

She helped me up from the floor. The shrillness left her voice as she wrapped her arms around me, cradling me while heat rained down over us both. There was a gentleness to her questions as she asked, "Parasites and Anath? That's all who was left?"

I started to cry, but she squeezed me until my sobs abated.

"You're sure Astarte was dead? What of other Phoenician presences? Gods? Goddesses? Was Baal there?"

I shook my hair, sputtering as the water attempted to drown me. Her scent filled the shower as if I were scrubbing with forest-scented bath soaps and oils. I spoke through sludge and fog and steam, but my words came with slightly more ease as I said, "No. Caliban took Astarte down in the room with me in the middle of some…mating ritual. I don't know. I still have no idea why she let him in or what the fuck they were talking about. None of it made sense. But we were there, and then Azrames killed Jessabelle in the lobby—I didn't see it happen, but almost. She was dead. Baal wasn't there. Dagon didn't come for them. It was just Anath and the parasites."

She relaxed almost imperceptibly as I my sobs grew too loud to control. The sounds coming from me were louder than the pounding of the shower. My grief burned hotter than the water. My pain was more poignant than the absence

431

of our partners. She pulled my utterly naked body into her arms, still dressed in a soaked tee and drenched pants. She held me as she began to shush me.

"They'll be fine," she said.

"There were so many—"

Whatever remained of her fury and angst was gone. Her tone shifted, becoming the comforting, strange entity I'd known.

"It's okay," she promised.

"It's not," I said, struggling to breathe as my shoulders shook with tears.

She tucked me against herself as she said, "I know it doesn't seem like it right now, but it's going to be okay."

"You weren't there!" I sobbed, voice hitching into a hiccup. I choked into the water between the shower's steam and the puddle of her hair.

"Hell's Prince, its greatest assassin, and an angel of justice all stacked against a single goddess and her nothing army?"

"A goddess of war!" I cried. "Caliban begged Silas to get me out because it was so dangerous! Because it—"

"Hush," she said, stroking my hair. I knew she was still worried, but her tone, her body, her aura calmed as she said, "Because the stakes were so much higher for you, Marlow. You're mortal. Your safety is so delicate. And I get it. This cycle means infinitely more than the others. Your eyes are open, and the stakes are higher than they've ever been for all of us. That doesn't mean they aren't okay. The three of them can take any shitty, forgotten war goddess and the parasites she convinced to follow her. So few still worship the Phoenicians. Without the energy from an army of faithful, they're weak. They don't have temples. They aren't given mass sacrifices or godspouses or energy—"

"Fauna…"

Her hand continued to move against my hair, my back. I tried to focus on her through the pain that coursed through me like a lightning rod. I'd spent my life rejecting love, and

432

the moment I accepted its reality, it was to be snatched from me.

"Hush, Marlow," she repeated through the blackness as night gripped us wholly. I saw nothing. I felt only the outline of her body against the hot water. "I've got you," she said while I shook. Her voice cut through the choking shadows as she whispered, "I know it's dark. I know. But we're going to be sunflowers."

"What?" I almost gagged on the absurdity of the statement as I trembled in darkness, free-falling through the emptiness of oblivion. There was no hope, no warmth, no light as I shattered.

She tightened herself around me, arms on my body, a hand in my hair, like a mother, like a friend, like a sister as she said, "Have you heard that sunflowers turn to face each other when there's no sun in the sky?" She didn't wait for my response, allowing me to crumble into myself as if I were a black hole. "It's not true," she said quietly. "It's something cute, something made up, something people tell themselves about flowers to feel nice…but Marlow, right now there's no sun. And everything about your life has felt like make-believe up until the moment it's come true. So what if it's a myth that sunflowers look to each other when there's no sun in the sky? When has something being a myth ever stopped it from being real? Things feel hopeless right now, but they aren't. I promise you. You and me." She lifted my face, wiping the tears from my cheeks, her doe eyes burning into mine as she said, "Let's be sunflowers."

CHARACTER DRINK ORDERS

MARLOW

COFFEE   BLACK COFFEE WITH HONEY

ALCOHOL   AMARETTO ON THE ROCKS

CALIBAN

COFFEE   NITRO COLD BREW

ALCOHOL   ROSEMARY TOM COLLINS

FAUNA

COFFEE   WHOLE MILK LATTE
                6 PUMPS SWEETENER
                2 PUMPS VANILLA
                2 PUMPS CARAMEL
                + LIQUID COCAINE
                (IF AVAILABLE)

ALCOHOL   CANDY APPLE FIREBALL

AZRAMES

COFFEE   RED EYE

ALCOHOL   OAXACA OLD FASHIONED

SILAS

COFFEE   DECAF CINNAMON LATTE

ALCOHOL   WHISKEY NEAT

Acknowledgments

Before I thank anyone else, I want to raise a glass to my special place in Hell, with its Bugattis and booze, to arctic foxes, and to the world unseen. I'm sitting in a pub in Seattle (in a booth that just so happens to have a vintage poster of a Goetic demon hanging for decoration, which feels serendipitous) finishing my edits and toasting my third glass of white wine to every religious trauma bestie who deconstructed their faith and ended up looking at the world with an entirely different lens.

Thank you to Christa for seeing the spark in No Other Gods in its roughest first draft, to Letty for taking it on and building it with me, for Helena for bringing the cover and characters to life, my agents, Alex and Carolyn, for being my mental health champions and holding my hands through this terrifying world, and to Madison for believing in the universe and helping guide the vision into the world.

Thank you to Kelley, Grace, Haley, Allison, Lindsey, Cera, and the chaos goblins who dove headfirst into Team Demon. Thank you to Abella, Aziel, Sarah, and my little coven for standing with me on both sides of the veil. Thank you to Mr. Piper for snacks in bed and endless support.

Thank you to the Other Gods.

About the Author

Piper CJ, author of the bisexual fantasy series *The Night and Its Moon*, is a photographer, hobby linguist, and french fry enthusiast. She has an M.A. in folklore and a B.A. in broadcasting, which she used in her former life as a morning-show weather girl and hockey podcaster and in audio documentary work. Now when she isn't playing with her dogs, Arrow and Applesauce, she's making TikToks, binging cartoons, writing fantasy, or disappointing her parents.

Website: pipercj.com
Instagram: @piper_cj
TikTok: @pipercj